ellen
m_ccarthy
Guilt Ridden

ellen
mccarthy

Guilt Ridden

POOLBEG
Crimson

Published 2008
by Poolbeg Press Ltd
123 Grange Hill, Baldoyle
Dublin 13, Ireland
E-mail: poolbeg@poolbeg.com
www.poolbeg.com

© Ellen McCarthy 2008

Copyright for typesetting, layout, design
© Poolbeg Press Ltd

13 5 7 9 10 8 6 4 2

A catalogue record for this book is available from the British Library.

ISBN 978-1-84223 -339-9

Typeset by Patricia Hope in Sabon 10.5/14

Printed by
Litografia Rosés, S.A. Barcelona, Spain

Note on the author

Ellen McCarthy lives in Waterford city with her husband. She is the author of *Guarding Maggie* which is also published by Poolbeg Press.

More information on this author is available at
www.ellenmccarthy.ie

Acknowledgements

As always, I couldn't do anything without my husband, family and friends who put up with my long absences and funny moods, and who always support everything I do.

To Paula, Niamh, Sarah and Kieran at Poolbeg for providing me with support and encouragement whenever needed, and especially to Gaye Shortland for helping me to shape *Guilt Ridden*.

There are some people who deserve special thanks and they include Vanessa O'Loughlin at Inkwell Writers, Paul O'Brien, Kevin O'Connell and co. and Rachel O'Dowd.

And to everyone who helped produce my book, the people in production, publicity, the booksellers and of course the readers. Without you it would never happen.

To My Parents
Michael and Mary A McCarthy
For passing on their love of the written word

Time Passes and Just the Memories Are Left

PART ONE

Chapter 1

Amy watched her polished reflection divide into two as the elevator doors opened. Smiling widely and allowing her eyes to flick casually across the expectant faces lined up inside, she stood at the front of the car with her briefcase casually hanging by her side. Amy continued to smile to herself, knowing everyone in there had their eyes glued to the back of her shiny blonde head, delighted to have been in her line of vision first thing in the morning. They were obviously a bunch of new hirelings.

This was Amy's good deed first thing in the morning. Play the game and let the people feel important. In a blue-chip corporation like Helfers the illusion of opportunity was very important. By using the elevator, at least once a week it was possible to ask Amy Devine, the vice-president herself, how her weekend had gone or if she had any plans for next weekend or just simply to moan about the traffic. The play at camaraderie was good for morale and made everyone feel as though they were on the same level, even though the elevator went one floor above all of them. And if Amy herself were ever to step through the glass ceiling and into the shiny Helfers building in New York there would be a whole new elevator to ride.

When the doors closed behind her on the top floor, she walked down the hall to her corner office with both the Irish and United States flags waving cheerfully in the breeze outside her window. The illusionists just kept on performing for the company crowd. Amy had heard through the corporate grapevine that there might be some rerouting of operations through south-east Asia, but still those flags danced in the breeze announcing Helfers' special relationship to the people of Dublin, providing a sense that if they only had a parking space where they didn't have to keep moving and outwitting the parking attendant, life would be perfect.

Just exiting her office as Amy approached the door was a man she had never seen before, carrying a basket of mail. Amy flashed her bright smile on him, causing him to take the corner a bit too sharply and bang his elbow. A word pushed itself to the surface automatically but she barely caught the initial F sound before he swallowed it. His bumbling attempt at regaining his composure could take a while so Amy broke the ice.

"Anything interesting in there for me?"

"In here?" The poor man looked into his basket.

"I presume you left whatever it was in my office when you were in there."

"Of course."

By now he was an etching in mortification and Amy genuinely felt sorry for him. "Miss Devine," he added hastily.

"Oh, please! Call me Amy." She held out one of her long white hands.

He tried to form the word but he couldn't – he just held out his hand and limply gripped hers.

"Thank you, Kevin. How are things in the mail office?"

"How do you know who I am?"

"Your name tag – and you're carrying the mail."

By now poor Kevin looked close to death.

"Very good! Well spotted!" He gave a short laugh, a last attempt at confidence.

"That's how I got the corner office, Kevin. See you tomorrow."

Amy entered her office and Kevin gratefully took his leave.

The outer office was empty. Amy walked past her assistant's desk and opened the door to her own office.

You could set your clock by her assistant's routine. Two minutes later, after Amy had turned her swivel-chair and sat with her face towards the bright blue sky, he came in with a steaming mug of coffee and the opened mail. A coffee pot and a silver letter-opener were just another opportunity to perform in this equal opportunities company. Greg Bannon stood a moment and, in his slightly camp way, discussed his latest crisis and the traffic jam he found himself in on the way home yesterday and then left Amy to her reading.

Weary and bored after five minutes, Amy gratefully reached the last envelope. It was a large brown manila stuffed full of paper. There was no sender's name and address on the back. She turned it over and looked at the front. It was marked personal. Amy pulled out the sheaf of papers and laid it on her desk.

Written in bold black lettering across the front of the top page was a single word: RUTH

Amy's heart gave a jump.

A typed single sheet of paper fluttered out when she shook the envelope. No stamped addressed envelope enclosed.

She picked up the paper and read it and suddenly her carefully groomed and manicured life came tumbling down around her.

Dear Miss Devine,

I know this manuscript will come as a surprise. I'd meant to send it to you a long time ago after Ruth's death but it took longer than expected to compile. You were working in Marlow Publishing at the time. I was disappointed to hear of your move but I'm sure you still have plenty of contacts in that area.

I know Ruth's story has appeared many times in various collections over the years but this one is different. This is the definitive account of what happened. I have collated most of the data I gathered on Ruth and am presenting it to you in rough book format. I've used newspaper articles, her own diaries and my personal knowledge of her in my writing. Ruth was a compulsive chronicler of her life and the world around her. Her diaries were like vast essays detailing the most minute details of her daily activities and were indispensable in my writing of this manuscript. Coming to know her as I did, I suspect a certain level of graphorrhoea: her need to write was compulsive and abnormal and she consumed vast amounts of paper, spewing her thoughts and feelings on to the page.

Occasionally I have used some creative licence in order to protect some things that perhaps should remain a secret even from you. Also I must insist that you don't contact any outside groups until I've finished my story, otherwise I won't be able to tell you what really happened to Ruth. I need to know I can trust you so I haven't revealed the whole story here.

I hope you enjoy reading our story.

It was unsigned.

Amy pressed the button on her desk and called for more coffee. Marlow was a publishing house in the UK and New York. After college Amy had worked for them but only from the business side of marketing and advertising. She had never been close to the area of publishing and editing. Still, she was sure this was just somebody's crude attempt at getting a publishing deal.

Someone who thought her personal connection to Ruth Devine might help them. It was distasteful and already she disliked this writer.

She turned to the back page of the manuscript and saw the words *To be continued.* Whatever he had to say was coming in instalments.

Once her assistant had brought the coffee and left the room, she turned her chair away from the sun and placed the manuscript on her desk.

Feeling sick at the prospect of re-entering this area of her life she started reading.

Ruth was back in her life after fifteen years.

I watched the involuntary swallow and the barely visible arching of her stiff back as Ruth took a sip from her coffee, her eyes riveted on the newspaper before her. "YOUNG WOMAN FOUND DEAD IN DUBLIN." The headline stood out in bold on the front page. I had my own copy open on the canteen table in front of me as I followed the progress of her eyes down the page.

An eighteen-year-old girl had been killed in Bushy Park near her home in the Rathfarnham area of Dublin. The middle-class suburban neighbourhood was *"reeling from the shock of the murder"*.

Newspapers always make these generic statements, don't they?

The dead girl was a student at Waterford Regional Technical College, now known as the Waterford

Institute of Technology. Her name was Sinéad Daly. She and Ruth were in the same class in college. There were thirty-three students in that class and Sinéad was one of the younger ones. Her group hung around in a gang of about ten. I would see them in the canteen or outside the college. They talked the most and wore the most make-up. The extended group contained about eight boys – the groupies, I always called them.

Sinéad had been out of college all that week and had missed her exams because she was sick. Sinéad was always sick when something important was happening in class.

I watched Ruth's face as she scanned quickly through the main details of the article. Her intensity was visible from across the room.

Sinéad left her home Monday afternoon to pay a visit to a friend. The gardaí were appealing for witnesses who might help shed some light on her whereabouts between then and early Tuesday morning when they found the body. The friend, not named in the article, told the gardaí she never arrived as they had planned, though she did call. Sinéad said she had something else on and would see her later. She received the call at six o'clock on Monday morning.

Ruth saw the story on Wednesday.

The body was found on Tuesday morning by a passer-by on the way to work. The coroner's report wouldn't be published yet but a source said she had been dead some hours when she was discovered.

The newspaper showed a photo of the path where they found her. It was next to an oval depression at the base of a small waterfall. At the angle the photograph was taken you could see the waterfall as it fell down over a collection of rocks into the basin. From there the water ran into a gully and onwards to where the picture didn't show. It was odd for me seeing it isolated like this in a grainy black and white image. It made it sort of surreal.

I could see that Ruth was hooked on the story. She was fascinated by murder and here was one in her world. Someone she knew. Something she could really let her imagination work on.

Steam rose from her coffee in a steady stream and her eyes wandered up after each wisp until it faded. It was too hot to drink so she just dropped two sugar lumps into the cup and played with the plastic spoon. Her eyes wandered around the room, unable to focus. There were few students in that morning, just a small spattering through the tables, but the place could have been empty for all the notice Ruth took. I felt my breath quicken as she glanced in my direction but we never made eye contact. Ruth was too preoccupied. One of her classmates was dead. Murdered. This crime was so real for her.

As I watched her finish reading the article and saw the drooping angle of her shoulders, my face broke into a smile. Over the months since she'd started in the college I'd watched her read her newspapers and crime novels, always alone, and though it hadn't been my original intention, here she was now, reading my story. My murder was in there on the printed page, staring up at her, teasing her into its depths.

We'd arrived two minutes apart that morning and I saw her buy *The Times*. It seems like an odd paper for a student to buy but she bought it for the crosswords. I passed by her chair many times and saw her engrossed in them and oblivious to her surroundings. Ruth was never a conventional student. I'd already seen the headlines so I was really excited about seeing her response. You know yourself in your line of work how satisfying it is when you get the validation you deserve for a job well done. She hadn't noticed the story on the cover then. I watched her with anticipation walking down from the counter to her usual table. The story took up three-quarters of the page. I suppose nothing more exciting had happened that day.

To be truthful I hadn't really expected her to be in college. It was the last day before the Christmas holidays. Most students wouldn't bother turning up.

But then Ruth was different. Wasn't she?

She was beautiful in a delicate way. She always wore jeans and bright jumpers, never skimpy or revealing clothes. For some reason her clothes were always a size too big like she needed to grow into them. I knew she had a beautiful body. Don't get me wrong, I'm not a pervert, but I'd seen it through a window at her house once. She hadn't bothered to close the curtains because you would have to be standing in her garden to see her. Isn't it funny how people get so complacent about the security of their own patch?

I loved her from the first moment I saw her. That was such a long time ago. Our lives had gone through many changes since. Ruth always had so much grace and energy. But you wouldn't have known her then. It was after you left. For many years our paths had taken different directions but when she went back to college they merged once again.

I really wanted to introduce myself in September but I couldn't. She didn't recognise me even though I followed her every move. I discovered the time she came to college and soon had most of her timetable figured out. I knew when she had lunch and when she went home.

Often she would sit gazing over the sea of canteen faces but her gaze would never alight on any individual for long. Many times I wanted to catch her eye but I never had the courage. Not then anyway! In my heart I was afraid of what she might see. It was too soon to share any of that.

After a few weeks I found out where she lived. That was easy. The bus left every day from outside the college and stopped almost outside her door. I would step off behind her and casually follow her up the road. At every step I'd watch the little curls at the back of her neck bounce and convince myself that any second now she'd turn around, but she never did.

I yearned for her but I feared rejection so I was

content, for then at least, to watch and wait. She would see me when the time was right.

Shortly after that I had the perfect opportunity to meet her again and tell her who I was but in the end I was just too frightened of rejection. It was one afternoon as she returned from college. She got off the bus and dropped her wallet. I picked it up and ran my hands over it and held it to my nose, smelling the brocade cover. It was like a trace of her still clung to it.

I stood in the phone box across the road from her house, holding the wallet in my hand, and watched her front door. You, of course, must remember her house, a small mid-terrace lacking in pretension. The door was painted in red gloss. The windows flowed with wooden flower boxes turning a bit wild. It looked like a little house all dressed up but just not quite getting it right.

When she was a little girl she was just like that house, all dressed up with her toes turned in and a shy smile on her face. Ruth looked like she raided the rag-box for clothes when I knew her. But she was such an individual. Her brown hair was always a mess and badly needed combing. I used to feel myself getting hot fantasising about combing it for her. In those fantasies she would sit on my knee facing away from me and when I finished she would lean back against my chest. I would wrap my arms tightly around her tummy and feel my strong muscles protecting her small body. I imagined her whole abdomen would fit in the palm of my hand. My hands are large but how would you know that without me telling you?

13

I realised she lived alone – at least I never saw anyone else there. The only visitors were her family. Her mum came once a week and sometimes her dad. Sometimes friends would visit, but not so often.

I stood there in the phone box that afternoon for half an hour, though I knew it was dangerous for me to hang about during daylight, until I saw the red door opening. Ruth came out and hurried around the corner to the shop. Two minutes later she came running back and crossed the street towards the phone box, directly towards me. I put the telephone receiver down and, pulling up my hood, exited the phone box. I held the door for her but she went into the box without looking up, just muttering "Thanks."

In the phone box she spoke while looking up the road towards the school. That road was so quiet and sometimes very lonely. Maybe she turned towards life. This thought made me love her even more. I hesitated for a second, watching her dial as young people played basketball in the schoolyard.

When I was sure she'd started her conversation I crossed the street and dropped the wallet in the letterbox. I didn't have the courage to leave a note. I just didn't know what to say.

As I'd waited in the phone booth I'd looked through the wallet. Inside was a photograph of two little girls. I recognised Ruth and the little blonde girl was you. I took the photo and put it in the pocket of my shirt. I could feel it next to my heart as I walked away from her door that day. It crinkled against my skin like it was whispering to me that I had a little piece of her now. I still carry that picture with me. Ruth is a shadow now but you are as vibrant as ever.

That was a good day. Somehow touching her stuff and looking into her inner world like that brought me closer to her.

Ruth! Often I found myself just saying her name over and over. I would repeat it to myself as I went to sleep.

I apologise. I've gone way back in my story. That morning, the morning the story appeared in the paper, I picked up my bag and followed her into the corridor when she went for her class. I was in a different class, different course in fact, but we shared the same corridor on Wednesday. She was already out of sight when I exited the canteen. I wound my way through the hall and could almost smell her as I approached her classroom door. The lecturer was late that day so the door was still open as I went by. I turned my head slightly and there she was at her desk, her head down, rereading the article. Around her the class was in an uproar. They were all talking about Sinéad. Many students had only found out that morning in class. She made her last public performance on the front page of the national newspapers. I smiled again, continuing on to my own class, nodding to people as I passed them. Of course all classes were subsequently cancelled that day. It was all thanks to me! Life was good and I knew then that it would only get better.

Chapter 2

Amy dragged herself away from the pages and jumped from her chair. The initial shock was wearing off and the enormity of what she held in her hands was starting to sink in. The entire island of Ireland had been trying for fifteen years to find out what had become of her first cousin Ruth Devine. Amy looked at the bundle in her hands: a manuscript that possibly was the key to Ruth's disappearance. Could it be authentic or was it just some crazy author using her family's tragedy as a hook to get his book noticed?

He could have sent it to Marlow's or any publisher himself but maybe he thought that Amy's personal relationship with Ruth could gain him an editor's ear. Why was she assuming it was a "he", she wondered to herself. She conceded that it was difficult to get someone to look at your work.

For a moment she considered sending it back with a note attached, rejecting him on the grounds of poor taste but then she remembered he hadn't enclosed his name and address.

Of course he wouldn't, would he, if he was in fact a murderer?

The only way to truly evaluate what she had was to read on and see if it was something she should hand over to the police. Like any true reader it never even entered her head to read the end and just see what happened.

*A*s *explained earlier,* some of this is taken from Ruth's diaries as well as conversations we shared later so don't imagine that I'm omniscient. I don't have any such skills.

The wind howled outside the window later that night and storms were expected to continue over Christmas. Ruth sat in front of the open fire, wiggling her toes towards the flames. Fire warmed her heart, giving her comfort and inspiration. In its flames she saw a tamed enemy. The potential danger of fire held a strange attraction for her. She wrote about this often and was quite eloquent in her descriptions. Its crackling was like company to her. Lighting it was a ritual. The fireplace was the heart of her room and in its circle she felt safe. Ruth liked to imagine the glow of the fire as her only protection from enemies. She imagined barks and soft footfalls surrounding and encircling her camp. Adrenaline would course through her veins as a howl sounded in the night air:

a throwback to some prehistoric ancestor maybe. Sometimes she would just poke the fire to awaken it and watch the flurry of sparks fly up the chimney: onwards and upwards. As in life, she thought – eventually everything moved out of the picture.

Most of her class knew Sinéad well and those who turned up for the last day of college were too wound up to concentrate. Under the circumstances the lecturers had decided it was better if they all went home. Ruth now had a nice long evening stretching ahead to enjoy. Though long seemed an ominous word sometimes with her life being so isolated.

Her living-room was small. Its sparse decoration suited her mindset. She loved that room. It represented peace and tranquillity for her. It was like a womb. A place she could curl into and be safe.

Ruth didn't have many possessions. Just a computer, some books and those four walls which she felt nurtured her and kept her sane enough to face the world. Her family spent years telling her she'd become a recluse living alone like that. They told her it would drain her spirit. But then you probably know that already.

Ruth had put up a Christmas tree a few days prior to that. She always felt the house was naked without one. Ruth and her dad used to make trips into the local forestry to find a suitable tree for Christmas when she lived at home. Did you ever go on those trips? The helpless little Devine nobody wanted. Did you tag along behind, trying to catch up, trying to find a place in their world?

At home the base of the tree would be loaded with presents but this tree was a bit bare. The few presents underneath were for her family. She would take them home in a few days. I wonder what she bought you that year?

Ruth always had a fixation on crime. Ever since primary school she watched crime shows on television. It became an addiction. The first thing she did every morning was read the crime stories in the paper. But crime was for newspapers and books and television. This one was in her world. The puzzle of the murder buzzed about in her head as she sat there feeling Neanderthal by the fireside.

The window of her sitting-room looked into the garden. The black hole of the window didn't normally bother her. She would sit there with her legs stretched in front of her, stockinged toes twitching in the glow of the fire. Streaks of rain ran down the window in little rivulets. Each one ran a distance and then veered off, connecting with another, forming a pool at the bottom. The drops reflected the lights of the tree, producing little rainbows.

One night I sat on that couch when she wasn't there and noticed the shape of the window. Surrounded by the curtains it looked like an eye with the black pupil looking back at you. She thought that too and sometimes this rattled her a bit and she would close them to stop the imaginary eye from looking at her.

Ruth wrote in detail about that stormy night in her diary. Her mind was full of the images she'd conjured up of Sinéad's death. Because she knew her, it was easy for her subconscious to conjure up such graphic images that they made her flinch. Sinéad had been stabbed. Ruth was plagued with the image of the knife entering her body. She was trying to face the fear head on and eliminate it but it pierced her sense of security as surely as it had pierced the body of Sinéad.

The knife: a phallic object of penetration. She'd read that description somewhere. Did its use indicate sexual motive, she wondered.

It certainly didn't, I can assure you of that, but how was she to know?

Was it just opportunistic? *The body was left uncovered in cold-blooded disregard for post-mortem dignity.j* Could the murderer just walk away knowing she was lying there dead or dying, knowing the next day some person would just walk along and happen upon the body?

Amy, you can do anything in this life when you have to but I'll explain all that in time.

Ruth tried to get her mind around what she saw as such a senseless act. The questions just kept circulating in her brain.

The clock on the mantel chimed: news time. She grabbed the remote control and switched on the television. Sinéad's face filled the screen. They gave the usual information: age, description, the clothes she was last seen wearing and the victim's last known whereabouts. Then they discussed the method of murder. She watched crime-scene tape and luminous Garda jackets surrounding the small man-made waterfall. In the background the reporter went over the same facts she'd read earlier.

They showed Sinéad's face again, her small face framed by long hair and crinkled up in a happy smile. An arm could be seen draped around her shoulder. She wondered who owned that arm. Was he watching now? Did he kill her? The scene switched to the family home. Now her parents were giving a passionate plea for information at a police press conference. She noticed Sinéad looked like her dad.

Ruth sat inside all evening listening to the wind blowing against the panes and eventually fell asleep, awaking stiff and cold hours later. The fire had gone out and the room was in total darkness except for the tree. She sat up and pulled the blankets, which she always had folded on the arm of the couch, around her.

In the kitchen she opened the extraction-fan hood over the cooker. It had a built-in light and was bright enough for her to see what she was doing. She plugged the kettle in and put a sachet of drinking chocolate into a mug. As she drank she watched the trees swaying in the storm outside the window. She loved the power and energy of a storm. Despite the angry weather the night was bright. Her heart jumped and power surged in her veins. It was cool knowing everyone else was asleep, in their beds. She stirred her drink and blew her breath into the steam and noticed a sudden movement outside to the right. Next door's white cat came running from the bushes. Poor cat! Ruth opened the door beside her and called him.

He came in, a wretched little ragged ball of fluff. He was usually more grey than white, because he slept in a coal-shed next door. She locked the door again behind him and he wound his way lovingly around her legs. He belonged to her neighbour but he preferred to spend his time with Ruth. She got some kitchen paper and dried him off, cleaning his feet.

Together they climbed the stairs to her room where they lay as the wind and rain lulled them to sleep.

A road ran parallel to Ruth's road and I'd found an alley on a previous trip which ran from this road to the back of Ruth's garden. There was a student house on the corner so a student turning into this alley at any time raised no eyebrows. There was a break in the wooden fence at the base of Ruth's garden, which I assume must have been an old garden gate opening off the alley at one time. It was now closed up by planks of wood so all I had to do was remove some nails, lift a few of the planks, sneak in and then replace them behind me.

I wanted to go there that night, the night of the storm, but then wondered if I should, the rain being so heavy. I didn't want to arouse suspicion. I knew I would leave footprints in the wet soil. If I went, I'd have to stay well back from the house. The previous time it rained I'd stayed near the entrance and obliterated my marks with a piece of wood before I left, but that left tracks too if she looked. Maybe she thought that the cat did a lot of digging.

Earlier that evening on my way home, I had found a black anorak with a hood on the bus. It was draped on the seat in front of me. I wondered if anyone would notice if I took it. Obviously not, I realised two minutes later as I walked up the road with the jacket snugly wrapped around me. That was an omen.

Later I stood in front of my long mirror dressed in the black anorak, with a pair of black jeans and polo neck. I posed and fantasised about her, twisting my body provocatively and thrusting my hips towards my reflection, picturing her there too, my breath laboured as I savoured the thought of the sweep of her hair and the curve of her cheek. I looked deeply into her eyes as she bent down and I could see her stoop to her hands and knees in front of me. She reached her hands up and unzipped my trousers. Ruth didn't stare in my fantasies; she would demurely lower her eyes. I gasped as a huge orgasm shattered the image.

We never got very far in my fantasies; all too soon I was alone again and the tomb that was my room started to close in around me. For a moment I would stand chastising myself for degrading her like this.

Ruth was different. That's what made her so special to me and there I stood, turning her into a whore for my pleasure. I don't want pity for this. My life was lonely but I had her in my heart. I wanted to cherish her but it would take time for me to get that close.

My lack of self-control left me feeling compelled to go and make sure she was okay; these urges made me afraid for her. I had to check that she was safe.

In the bitter cold damp air I sat under an overhanging bush at the base of Ruth's garden. That tension could still be felt in my loins as I watched her house. Even her house had the countenance of innocence. My position in her life was clear now. I was her protector and I would make sure nothing bad happened to her.

At that moment the window drew my eyes to it. Ruth was looking out and just then it seemed as though she was looking directly into my eyes. My heart pounded in my chest and the echo deafened my ears. She was wrapped in her blanket as she stirred her drink. Always that cute little gesture of blowing across her cup. Watching her drink, I felt like I knew her every movement but inadvertently I leaned too far forward. The spell was broken when suddenly that damned cat heard me and raced out into the garden.

I held my breath, too afraid to move, as Ruth opened the back door. Would she see me? It was too soon. I wasn't ready for that yet. My heart hammered in my chest.

But I exhaled in relief and watched transfixed from my vantage point as the cat streaked inside and she turned back into her house. Moments later the Christmas tree lights went off and the house sank into total darkness. I sat there a while longer until I knew she was sleeping and safe and then turned and went home.

After that night I felt attached to that jacket and the wall of darkness it afforded me. I decided I'd wear it every day. Nothing could touch me in it and it made me feel closer to her. I felt cocooned in a pool of darkness as I crossed the town.

That night I slept as the wind blew, a smile of fulfilment softening my face. My sleep was deep and relaxed. The jacket hung on the back of a chair by my bed and a photo of Ruth sat on my locker. I'd snapped it weeks before. She didn't know. She was sitting in the park watching something in the distance. I loved the intense concentration on her face. Her photo was like the gatekeeper guarding my bedside. Around the room the eyes of my playmates helped her keep her vigil, their luscious bodies writhing through my dreams.

Chapter 3

Amy was shaking. *"The little Devine nobody wanted."* Tears welled up and she couldn't stop them. This creep not only seemed to know Ruth but he had her pegged too. The vice-president suddenly felt like the eight-year-old girl banished from home. She didn't know what to do. Should she go to the police? By now she was convinced that this guy wasn't normal though the extent of his madness couldn't be quantified by two chapters of a book. It could still be someone who'd done his research. But something about his words held the ring of truth.

Amy's eyes were drawn to the calendar on her desk and the bold black numbers indicating the date: **January 10th** They were just two weeks away from the fifteenth anniversary of the day Ruth disappeared. For many years that date had loomed darkly months in advance and for the few days before and after the anniversary she didn't read the papers or watch the news to avoid the inevitable anniversary media onslaught. The girl in the news reports and in the crime collections she saw in the bookshops was a media invention and not the Ruth Devine she'd known. But recently the disappearance of Ruth Devine had lost some of its significance, both for Amy and the country in general.

She needed to do some work but she wanted to read a bit more before she decided what to do with this book. Pushing all thoughts of work out of her brain she slipped back into the manuscript.

*N*ext morning Ruth stretched and accidentally knocked the cat off the bed. He sat where he fell, his yellow eyes fixed on her face, his long tail swishing in temper. She patted his blanket, urging him back onto the bed, but he haughtily lifted his head and walked out of the room, making his way to the kitchen. It was time for breakfast.

"OK, huffy!"

Ruth stood up, stretching. She rubbed the sleep out of her eyes and dragged herself to the bathroom. It was an attic conversion with a dormer window and a slanted ceiling. The walls and ceiling had the same pink wallpaper with tiny flowers embossed on it. Her shower was tiled in white splashed with pale blue clouds tinged with pink on the edges.

Ruth had gone back to college as a mature student, having worked for a few years first. She'd been a careful saver and with the help of her parents became a homeowner at twenty. When Ruth bought that house her finances wouldn't stretch to patterned tiles so she home-customised instead. She made her own stencils using blue enamel paint and a splash of pink. The sun usually poured through the window, reflecting off the tiles and banishing the gloom, but not that day as it was raining. A grey sky cast long shadows across the room so she had to turn on the light. She looked at herself in the mirror and wished she'd kept her eyes closed. Two dark-rimmed eyes stared back at her, framed by a shock of dark hair.

She put her hand back and turned on the shower to thaw out her bones. Waiting for it to heat up, she sat daydreaming on the toilet. The day would be long without college to keep her occupied. It stretched ahead of her empty; the image was already draining her spirit.

Ruth had been at the college for three months at that stage and she hadn't missed one day. One day wouldn't make a difference but she was the diligent new student turning up every day and on time. She was the oldest class nerd but she'd started that way and by then she was afraid to change.

After her shower she still couldn't muster up any enthusiasm for the day. She dressed and went downstairs and found Cat sitting patiently in front of the cupboard door.

"You're not even my cat, you dope!"

He blinked and turned his face back to the door.

She poured out some dried food for him and placed the dish outside. Then she flicked the switch on the kettle and waited for it to boil. Pouring hot water into the teapot, she sat at the table. A plan was starting to form in her brain.

She wanted to go to Dublin and visit the scene of Sinéad's murder. She had no idea why. It was a compulsion. Curiosity, she supposed. The mechanics of the crime scene had always interested her. She wanted to find a reason for the murder; the scene might give her one.

Besides, she had dreamt of the scene last night in startling detail.

She looked at her clock. It was still only nine; she had over an hour to catch the train. Before she had a chance to change her mind she reached for her phone and dialled a taxi. The dispatcher told her one would be there by nine thirty.

Ruth wondered if she was becoming ghoulish as she scrambled around, grabbing her bag, purse, and keys. She frowned picking up her wallet, suddenly remembering its strange return.

She'd missed it one afternoon when she went to the shop for bread. On her way back she ran across the road to phone the bus company and see if anyone had handed it in but when she got back, to her surprise, it was on the mat in her hall. On opening it, she found that all her money was still inside. The only thing missing was the photo of her and Amy. The photo wasn't very important. She carried it more out of habit than anything else but it made her feel weird to know someone had stolen it. She knew it couldn't have fallen out because it was in a buttoned compartment. She didn't have her address in the wallet or any picture ID so the finder must have been someone who knew where she lived.

Ruth bounced back to reality as a sharp knock sounded on the door. The taxi driver had got fed up hooting for her and had come to the door. She followed him out to the car.

Ruth's train approached its last stop, Heuston Station. She gathered her stuff and headed towards the front of the train so that she could make a quick exit. The station was milling with people. She hurried out the side entrance to the taxi rank and managed to grab one of the first taxis in the line. In another five minutes they would all have been snapped up. She directed the driver to drop her in Westmoreland Street. Coffee in Bewley's was always her first stop on a trip to Dublin.

Though she didn't smoke she usually sat near the smoker's section, a nest of seats at the back of the café. Despite herself, she had to admit that from a voyeur's point of view smokers were more interesting. Ruth sat with her diary and pen by her coffee cup. She was never separated from this book.

There was of course the usual mixture of coffee drinkers. An old lady with a small trolley full of belongings stuffed in plastic shopping bags sat by the door. The bags were worn; embroidered slippers and books protruded from the top. She was in mid-conversation with an invisible friend. She pointed at Ruth and then laughed. Ruth smiled back, wondering what the friend thought of the joke.

Next to her was a man approaching fifty with greying hair going a little wild, tied in a ponytail. He sported a goatee beard with some overgrowth and a pair of Yeats-style glasses. He was smoking copiously and watching the people surrounding him, including Ruth. In fact at one point they were looking at each other with pens poised for writing. On the table by his coffee, in a mirror image of Ruth's position, he had placed his notebook. He would glance conspicuously around him from time to time and then go back to his writing. She'd love to have been able to peek at his notebook. She suspected he was doing doodles on the page. She felt guilty as she reached for her own diary. Here she was, sitting sniggering at another potential author. For all she knew he could be this generation's Joyce.

All around her she could see the evidence of the immigration which was just beginning in Ireland. Some of the waiting staff appeared to be non-Irish as were many of the coffee drinkers. A coffee in a historic Dublin coffee house to go with their English language classes: required reading *Dubliners*. Conveniently The Dublin School of English was upstairs over the café.

The back wall of the coffee house boasted a

stained-glass window: an oasis of glass in a wall of Chinese-print wallpaper. The dark wood furnishings brooded. Bright china dishes relieved the shelves with splashes of colour. In the centre of the side wall a large open fireplace housed a real coal fire. Surrounding the glow was a heavy wooden fireplace inlaid with copper. The pendulum of a clock swayed overhead while urns and potted plants dotted the floor throughout the room.

Ruth tuned in on the Bewley's sounds. The wooden legs of tables scraped the tiles and the clink and clatter of cutlery and dishes permeated the background. The cappuccino was by then a central feature in Ireland's café culture and the sound of steaming milk drifted from the counter. The days of the Soy Latte hadn't arrived yet and cappuccinos were still exotic.

As she collected the last of the muffin crumbs from her plate, she looked at her watch. It was two thirty. Time to resume her morbid little trip to Rathfarnham. She got up and left by the front door. The rain had started up again and the sea of umbrellas slowed the foot traffic as she turned right up Westmoreland Street towards Trinity College for the bus to Terenure. She could walk from there.

Just a few doors up from the café a flower vendor stood on the side of the footpath, her blooms protected from the rain by sheets of clear plastic. Ruth gave her some money and took a bunch of white flowers, feeling the gesture might justify her trip. She crossed at the traffic lights to College Street and stood in line for the bus, lost in a whirl of humanity. After a few minutes number 15A came along and the crowd pushed forward, almost dragging her onto the bus.

The crowd was dense so Ruth tried upstairs for a seat. Her legs were wet from the rain-soaked umbrellas hanging from the arms of the other passengers. There was one seat upstairs right at the front of the bus but a very large man was sitting in it, which would leave her stuck on the edge. The journey at this time of day should take at least forty minutes and she was uncomfortable with people sitting too close to her – they made her nervous. So she pushed her way back down the damp steps and stood instead.

Halfway down Rathmines Road two men got on the bus and stood beside her. They'd been drinking and the smell of alcohol was overpowering. They were absorbed in a dispute and it quickly intensified. Middle-aged or victims of neglect, Ruth wasn't sure. She stood as far back from them as she could, tenderly protecting her flowers from their waving hands.

As Ruth nervously longed for the bus to reach her stop, one of the men grabbed the other by the collar and shouted: "I know, you bastard!" Ruth could smell the grimy hair of the man when his head was pushed into her face.

Ruth jumped off at the stop before hers. She was shaking. So much for bravely investigating a crime scene, she thought, as she walked through Terenure Village.

She'd checked the park on the map before she left Bewley's and, though on the edge of Rathfarnham, she'd thought it was closer to Terenure. At Vaughan's Corner she turned left.

She hurried along down Rathfarnham Road. The rain had slowed to an icy drizzle.

Where the road crossed Dodder Park Road, she saw at a distance the high stone wall that surrounded Bushy Park with the Dodder River running alongside it and an expanse of green stretching down to the river from the Dodder Park Road. But she couldn't see any entrance to the park. She must have made a mistake. This looked like the back of the park. Perhaps she took a wrong turn in Terenure Village.

She wondered nervously how isolated this park was going to be. It had looked big on the map but it was impossible to see how big it was from where she stood.

Perhaps there was an entrance down there that she couldn't see? She decided to try. She turned down a small path which cut through the grass to the riverbank, leaving the traffic behind her, the question of isolation again playing on her mind.

By coincidence she was going in the right direction for the crime scene she'd come to see.

As she reached the riverbank crime-scene tape impeded her progress. This surprised her as she knew Sinéad had been murdered inside the park. Perhaps they thought the killer made his escape in this direction or disposed of evidence in the river or the bushes along its bank. She'd never approached a real crime scene before and had forgotten about the forensic examination.

Maybe they'd finished investigating and left the tape, she thought, justifying herself as she stepped over the barrier.

She walked on along the river. In the distance she could make out some movement as fluorescent shapes came into view. It looked as though they were beating the bushes by the river. At various points in the river chunks of rubbish were suspended from trees and melted into the water from the riverbank. This gave it a seedy air. A family of ducks swam towards her, oblivious to the cold of the day and the grime of their surroundings. The resemblance between the actual place and her dreams last night astounded her.

She hadn't gone too far when she noticed stepping stones crossing over the river. On the other side a set of steps went up and through the wall.

Her heart was starting to beat faster. The murder took place some time in the afternoon, not much later than this. Were people walking their dogs then? She could hear a dog barking now. She turned to look. A dog came into view; it was a German Shepherd on a lead, walking beside a brightly jacketed garda.

Ruth was good at playing dumb. She crossed the steps with care. After the rain they'd been having, some stones were slippery and she didn't want a broken ankle and to have to call out for help. Safely on the other side, she avoided looking around at the approaching garda and walked up the steps into the park, ignoring a call for her to stop.

The sight she saw at the top was lovely – not the sinister spectacle she was expecting. There was no sense of foreboding or horror as she looked around, the feelings she expected from the scene of a violent crime. The park spread in front of her, sheltered by a belt of trees. There was a large oval pond as clear as a piece of glass. Weeping willows drooped their branches sadly over the water. Mallard ducks and moorhens swam to and fro, leaving tiny trails as they looked for scraps. A large dangly-legged crane made an embarrassing spectacle of himself as he crash-landed on to the clear surface of the water.

Ruth turned her head to the right. There it was – the sight she came to see, a waterfall flowing down into the pond. It had rained heavily during the night so unlike in the picture in the paper there was now quite a lot of water. By the base was where they found the body. She could see the crime-scene tape surrounding the area which was dotted with men in white suits and masks, while fluorescent-clad gardaí were outside protecting the barrier. Others were walking in a straight line, eyes focused on the ground at their feet. More dogs barked.

The white space-suits were examining the immediate crime scene. She could see one leaning over a briefcase, putting jars inside. This must be the technical team:

photographers, entomologists, ballistics or fingerprint experts. The State Pathologist Marian Byrne was carrying out the autopsy, probably at the city morgue. These people were just trying to find forensic evidence to link the killer to the scene.

Ruth had read many times that a murderer could return to the scene of his crime and watch the recovery of the body as a sort of black pilgrimage.

I didn't do that because I didn't want to get caught but, thanks to Ruth's impulsive nature, I got to do it anyway through her eyes.

The thought of Sinéad's killer being in the area was making her nervous. She looked around cautiously. There was no one suspicious there. Unless he was a garda? A shiver swept up her back. She stole another glance at the gardaí; no one seemed to notice the woman peeping at them from around a tree. She started giggling to herself. She was starting to feel very silly. What was she doing, she thought for the hundredth time. Her mind started to meander again. She wondered how long the spirit would linger in an area of violent crime. Trees surrounded where she stood. It was perhaps four acres in area. The temperature was very low; close to the minuses. The overcast sky bathed the lake in a grey glow. Ruth had always considered herself to have some form of extrasensory perception. She was very sensitive to the moods of those around her but here she felt nothing. She was just very cold.

Dark clouds rolled in. Ruth was too nervous to

venture further into the open park. She turned to head back out but standing in her path was the guard she had seen earlier, with the dog straining on his leash.

My mind had been buzzing all that morning. I knew I wouldn't be seeing Ruth at college that day. After watching her since the first day she'd arrived in the college everything felt empty without her. Everything she did was like clockwork. She arrived at the same time every day. Did all the same things. I didn't realise what a gap it would make if for some reason she weren't there. That day I was full of nervous energy with no outlet.

When I got up I'd intended on going to see her but I just couldn't figure out how to do this discreetly. What if she stayed in her house all day and never went out? She might even go home early for Christmas. Then I wouldn't see her for weeks. Ballyreid certainly wasn't a place where you could do much unnoticed. As I'm sure you remember.

At five twenty I couldn't handle it any more so I got the bus to her door. I got off and sat on a wall down the road. I sat there for an hour but there was no sign of movement. In desperation to find out what was going on, I went around the block and entered her property from the back. Her house was in total darkness and I could feel its oppressive emptiness.

There was a window open upstairs at the back. I knew it was her bedroom which ran from the front to the back of the house. Double-checking that I was still alone, I climbed onto the garden shed. There was a concrete moulding along the wall running under the window, just wide enough to stand your toes on. I stepped off the shed onto the moulding and gingerly edged my way across on tiptoes until I reached the window. I put my hand in through the small open part on top and opened the large section underneath, then climbed into her bedroom. Being nervous, my sweaty hands could barely grip the window. I was as scared as she would be if she found me there.

I was afraid to turn on any lights in case it would give my presence away. Slowly my eyes were adjusting to the light. I didn't touch anything, just wandered around the room, sensing her presence and smelling her perfume. Her pyjamas were folded on her pillow. I lay on her bed and placed my cheek against them, watching what she could see when she opened her eyes every morning. The soft mattress moulded itself to my body and the sweet smell of her sheets drifted into my nostrils as the soft touch of her flannel pyjamas cooled my burning cheek. For a few moments I closed my eyes and drifted through the thick silence all around me. Ruth's street was quiet. I was so peaceful lying there and so untouched by the usual sadness of my life. I could almost feel her arms reach out from the other side of the bed to hold me.

I opened my eyes at last, afraid I might fall asleep in this oasis I'd found myself in. As you can imagine, it would be a disaster if she walked into her room, switched on her light and saw me lying there in her bed.

My eyes focused on her locker. On it sat a worn book of fairy tales of an old-fashioned type. I picked it up and tenderly touched the cover, feeling the rough edges and frayed threads under my fingertips. It was obviously a much-read book. Holding it under the glowing face of her clock, I could see it was a collection of stories by Sinéad DeValera. I opened the front cover. Written inside in a child's handwriting was: *Miss Ruth Devine, Ballyreid. Waterford. 25th of July 1985.* She was fourteen years old then. I could picture her so clearly at that age because that was the summer when I first met her. I was ten. We'll return to this later. I looked again at the cover like a lined face looking up at me and thought this book had probably lain beside her bed ever since that summer. Maybe that time was precious to her too. She'd obviously dated it for a reason. I picked up the book and looked underneath. There was a leather-bound diary there. It was thick and stuffed with information chronicled in her tiny handwriting. Ruth covered more detail than you could imagine in such a small space. Picking it up, I saw her words spread across the pages like an endless stream of consciousness. I tried to speed-read and glean as much information as I could but her thoughts had poured out onto the page in such a way that would require careful study to interpret them.

The downstairs door opened suddenly and a strip of light appeared under the bedroom door. I stood and listened: she was back. And she was climbing the stairs. I moved quickly, squeezing back out the window. Standing balanced on my toes on the ledge outside, I closed the window but didn't have time to fasten the catch. Then I made my way slowly back to the safety of the shed roof.

Back on the ground, I slipped out through the fence at the back of her garden and strode down the alley to the road. A new feeling of exhilaration coursed through my veins. I'd never felt so alive, so much in love. The feeling was strong as I ran all the way home, feeling the blood pulse in my temples and seeing the words from her diary, her words running through my head.

Chapter 4

Amy couldn't stay inside any longer. Thoughts whirled in her head. Ruth carried a photo of the two of them in her wallet. That was the most absurd thing she had ever heard. Ruth tortured her all the time she spent with her, so why on earth would she keep her picture? Ruth had known this guy. During the summer of 1985 they had somehow spent time together. She looked out the window onto the street outside. The weather was still bright. It was cold but right now she didn't care. The walls of the office were closing in around her, making it difficult to breathe. She had to get outside for a while.

She grabbed her coat, bundled the pages into a folder and left the office, muttering about a migraine to her assistant who tried to efficiently suggest moving a meeting she was due to attend. Amy didn't care what he did with it. For once she avoided the elevator and raced down the plush-carpeted stairs. There was nobody on the way up as they were all at the bottom waiting to get on the elevator. They turned en masse, amazed to see a frazzled Amy Devine running down the stairs two steps at a time.

Outside, the footpaths surrounding Stephen's Green teemed with tramping feet like ants making their way back to the nest. Amy cut her way through the crowds and, crossing the street with the green light, entered the park. Right in the heart of the green, by the rose garden, stood her favourite bench. It was just down from a monument to the Countess Markievicz. Amy wasn't exactly a major in the Irish Citizen Army and this wasn't 1916, but she too felt very much under siege. The bench she was heading towards sat in the sun for most of the day and it would be warm there despite the time of year. Luckily it was free. She sat down and turned her face up to the sun. Gradually she relaxed under its rays and, when her breathing normalised, she opened the folder and began to read the rest of the pages.

Ruth jumped when she turned and saw the guard watching her.

"Excuse me, Miss. Did you not hear me call you back there?"

"Sorry, no," Ruth said.

She could feel her cheeks burning. No matter how hard she tried, she couldn't meet his stare. There was a hard direct look in his eyes. It made her want to squirm. Her eyes were examining a piece of glass embedded in the ground. She had guilt oozing out of her pores.

"What are you doing here?" he asked.

She held up her flowers. "I brought these. I knew Sinéad."

He started asking her a litany of questions, recording her answers in a notebook.

"We need your address, Miss Devine, in case we need to talk to you again."

She gave him both of her Waterford addresses.

"So this is the first time you've ever been to this park?"

"Yes." She tried to concentrate her gaze on his face. She was so cold.

"Is everything all right?" came a voice from behind Ruth.

She jumped again. She turned to see an older man there, his eyes flicking thoughtfully from one face to another, waiting for a response.

"Miss Devine, this is Inspector Sheedy," said the garda. "He's heading this investigation."

Ruth extended her hand. He didn't take it. The blush in her cheeks deepened.

"Ruth is a student in WRTC," said the garda. "She's here on a day trip to bring flowers for the victim."

Ruth detected mockery.

He repeated the bones of their conversation, fixing his gaze on the senior officer's face as if they were speaking in a secret code.

"Miss Devine," said Inspector Sheedy then, "we have all your details if we need to contact you again."

He held out his hand. Ruth extended hers. His eyes twinkled as he shook it.

"The flowers, Miss Devine? I'll take them to the scene for you."

Ruth pushed them towards him and as quickly as her rubbery legs could carry her, she left the park and began to retrace her steps back to her bus stop. She couldn't believe her stupidity. Of course there would be an investigation going on for days. She should have known that. She walked in a daze with her arms clasped around her middle, her head bent against the wind. Fears that had been creeping into her mind over the last few months were taking root. She climbed on to the bus, her thoughts plagued by them.

She arrived back in Waterford late that evening. She'd slept most of the way. Her legs were asleep and she felt groggy, starving too. Her stomach growling, she walked to the Chinese takeaway where she ordered vegetables in black bean sauce and huddled shivering in her coat as she waited for her food. She retraced her steps to the taxi rank, hugging the food tightly for warmth. It was too cold to walk. There was one taxi sitting there and she jumped in.

When she got into her house the sitting-room was still warm. Her heater was on a timer. She took a plate and some juice to the couch and cuddled into her blankets. Then a glance at the clock showed it was nine. Nearly spilling her food, she switched on the TV.

The RTÉ news was just starting. Ruth felt queasy and could eat only a little of her food. The room was cold now and even the blanket wasn't keeping her warm. A depression had crept in. Her self-imposed isolation was closing in around her. She felt the emptiness of the house so she closed the curtains. It was one of those nights: a night to put the light on and pull the blanket closer around her. She flicked through the channels and watched a few programmes without really seeing anything.

She went to the kitchen, made herself a cup of tea and stood at the back door calling for the cat. There was no sign of him tonight. She craved something warm to hold. She pushed her hair back from her face, tidied up the remains of her food and piled the dishes in the sink before filling herself a hot water bottle.

The stirrings of a panic attack started when she entered the bedroom and she found it difficult to catch her breath. Why? She stripped her clothes off, throwing them on the chair, and then turned to get her nightclothes off the pillow.

Ruth was meticulous about everything she did. She always folded her clothes, smoothing them and putting them in their proper place. She stared at her folded pyjamas. There was a depression in the centre of them. She paused, looking at their folded shape. It must have been the cat. Sometimes he came in through the bathroom window off the flat roof. The pyjamas were flannel and very warm so he liked to snuggle in there.

She got into her pyjamas and sat on the end of the bed cleansing her face. She glanced around the room. Something still didn't feel right. Her eyes stopped at the bedside table. Her diary. The cat wouldn't be reading that. Her diary was sideways on the locker under her book. She walked over and pushed it back in a straight line under the book. Perhaps she'd brushed against it getting up. A strong sense of something wrong niggled in the back of her mind. Something else in the room was out of place. She looked around her, then paused and pulled up the front of her pyjamas to her nose. There was a strong smell off them. It filled her nose and was too strong to be perfume. It was some type of aftershave.

Ruth's frightened eyes took in the rest of her room. Her mother had a key to her home, but no one else. She ran downstairs where she slipped on the bottom two steps and felt her rump bone crack off the timber. Wincing with pain, she grabbed the phone and dialled her mother's number. She felt the seconds ticking as the phone rang. Then she heard her mother's drowsy voice.

"Yes – Devines!"

"Hi, Mam!"

"Ruth! What are you doing calling this time of the night?"

"It's only one o'clock. Did you call here today? Did you say you would? I went to Dublin. Christmas shopping."

"No, darling – slow down – I never said I was coming down today – you must have dreamt it."

"Perhaps! I was nodding off when I thought about it. So – you weren't here in the house today?"

"No. Why do you ask? Is there something wrong?" Her mother's voice was beginning to sound alarmed.

"Oh, no, no – I just thought you said you would."

"Go back to bed, pet, and have a good sleep. You're coming up to us tomorrow, aren't you?"

"Yes. I'll be there by six thirty."

"Love you, darling. See you then."

Ruth was trembling. She did a quick scout around the house and checked on everything. Nothing else seemed out of place. She thought about the wallet again.

She went back upstairs and stripped off her pyjamas before jumping into the shower. She scrubbed her body clean of the intruder and got a new pair of pyjamas. She grabbed all the bedclothes off the bed and threw them into the washing-machine.

When everything was changed, she got into bed. With a glass of whiskey in her hand, her hot water bottle at her feet and a warm cardigan around her shoulders, she started to relax.

Despite knowing I'd been there, she wrote in her diary that night. When I read the entries I was surprised. Ruth knew someone had touched her things and read her words. Why would you continue to write in a diary after something like that? I could only assume that she didn't care if I read her words. Though she was frightened, I think perhaps it awakened something in her to think someone had read them. From that moment on she altered her writing style. She still churned out her rambling thoughts but for some reason she finished with footnotes. From that night onwards her day's writing ended with three or four bullet points highlighting the important issues of her day. I feared when I noticed this that perhaps I was no longer reading the real Ruth but that since now she knew she had readers she was creating a writing persona. I didn't want her to obscure my view of her behind a carefully crafted partition.

After she finished her whiskey that night, she sat up in bed so she wouldn't sleep and listened to every sound, with the darkness softened by the glow from her plug-in nightlight. Eventually she slept sitting up. She had a stone paperweight in her hand under the covers.

Chapter 5

Amy had never known Ruth in her adult life and she had never expected to be reading her final experiences like this. But was she seeing the real Ruth now? She remembered her version of Ruth. When Ruth knew she was being watched, did she in fact begin to craft her words with care to present them as she hoped they would be read? Now, Amy was here fifteen years later reading Ruth's experiences – as a stalker had edited them. Was the truth in there somewhere? If so, whose truth?

Amy knew now she should take the manuscript to the police straight away and get them to start an immediate investigation into who might have sent it. But the writer had said nothing yet to suggest he was involved in Ruth's disappearance and with this thought she justified her continued reading of the manuscript.

She wanted to know more. Ruth was a woman who had been a mystery to her all her life. Because of Ruth, Amy had grown up in Dublin away from the countryside of her early childhood. Ruth's jealousy and vindictiveness had escalated to such an extent that the young Amy had to move to Ranelagh and live with her grandaunt. Amy had never forgotten the first day she walked through Aunt Irene's door. The first thing that hit her was the smell, a deep-rooted smell of age and death that seeped out of the walls and escaped from the floor. Irene was the younger sister of Amy's paternal grandmother and was in her seventies when Amy came to stay. It wasn't an ideal situation but, things being the way they were with Ruth, there was nothing else they could do.

Every flat surface in Irene's house was covered in framed photos of family members, covering generations of Amy's bloodline. Their eyes followed the little girl as her small footsteps picked their way through the silence that had been their lot for the past twenty years. Amy felt like apologising for the noise. At some time Irene had a penchant for houseplants but they had grown up and around the walls, winding their way as far as possible from the roots that were wildly trying to break their way out of their suffocating pots. Amy understood how they felt. She inherited the house when Irene died and the first thing she did was gut it. One night she sat with a glass of wine, looking at the skip parked outside the front door with the broken remains of the house crammed inside. Sheets of dry wall plastered with outdated layers of flowered wallpaper provided a grotesque backdrop to the skeletal remains of the house's furniture.

Amy's aim had been to redecorate the house and find a buyer but the whole thing took longer than expected and by the time she got to the end of the project the Celtic Tiger had taken hold and now her aunt's former home was a million-euro property in the heart of one of the most sought-after areas of Dublin. Now she wouldn't dream of leaving it. She loved every stone of it and Irene for giving it to her. Amy had the resources that Irene never had and the house badly needed. It glowed with life now and every other week she had an estate agent knocking on her door wondering if she wanted to sell. Ruth seemed to have loved her house too. Already parallels were forming between herself and Ruth. She lowered her head and went back to her reading.

Ruth opened her eyes. A bright winter sun smiled at her but the blackness of the night before still clung.

Now she knew where her recent anxiety attacks had come from. It had nothing to do with the murder in Dublin. She'd been looking for something to blame. There'd been a presence in her life for God knows how long. She'd sensed it. Last night when she returned from Dublin and entered her room it had settled on her shoulders. However, until the moment she saw the disturbed space on her bedside table the pieces hadn't fallen into place.

She tried to cheat sleep but she must have snuggled down in the bed at some stage. In her first two years in this house her sleep had been peaceful. But now this shadow was weighing her down and her mind was heavy. It was worse during the hours of darkness. The winter sun was strong enough to chase away most of the blues.

She lay there thinking. At that moment the curtains blew into the room.

Ruth went to the window and held back the curtain to close the small pane on top which was open. Then she noticed the catch on the large section underneath was unfastened. Ruth was obsessive about everything she did and she immediately knew with certainty that there was no way that she would ever have left the bigger window open. Oh God, she moaned. Someone came in my window. Was I home? She felt ill. She rushed around checking every door and corner for any other signs of disturbance. She didn't notice anything. Everything was secure. All the windows had security locks on them. She'd never used them before but they were all going on now.

She took a long shower. Her tiny bathroom couldn't fit in a bathtub. A bath would have been just what she needed then. Incense, bubbles and essential oils wafted through her imagination as she soaped herself for the third time.

After she dried off Ruth looked longingly at her bed. She decided to slip between the covers for two minutes. Two hours later she opened her eyes to a heavy body and a throbbing head. This was normal for Ruth if she overslept. She stretched and turned, crying softly into her pillow.

She dressed and went downstairs. There was really no rush to go into town and finish her Christmas shopping. On Sundays the shops didn't open until twelve. She'd have lunch at home and go in the afternoon.

She opened the freezer, took out a salmon cutlet and placed it under the grill. She washed some green salad and went to the bread bin for bread. Nothing, she was all out.

She ran around the corner to the shop, grabbed a loaf and a copy of the *Independent* and was about to run from the shop when Mrs Dee spoke.

"Good morning, Ruth."

Ruth blushed. "Sorry! My mind's miles away."

She returned Mrs Dee's smile and paid for the items. She was itching to go but Mrs Dee was in the mood for chatting.

"Terrible tragedy in Dublin, Ruth, wasn't it? That poor girl! It's not safe anywhere! Not even in your own home. She was a student here. Did you know her?" Mrs Dee loved a good gossip.

"Yes. She was in my class. Mrs Dee, I have to go – I have something under the grill."

When she got in she turned her cutlet and sat at the table. She spread the paper out in front of her and scanned the headlines.

The house was starting to feel claustrophobic. The walls were closing in around her. She couldn't face eating here. She took her salmon, placed it on a plate and put it in the fridge. She double-checked all her locks. Then she got her things together and left, taking the paper with her because she wanted to read it again.

The bus was there when she crossed the street. Ruth hated shopping but she thought that being surrounded by people might help her feel better.

As the bus pulled out I ran up and knocked on the door. The driver stopped and let me on. Ruth didn't look up; she was rereading the article on the murder. She didn't notice as I gently brushed the back of my fingers along the edges of her hair or feel the penetrating gaze of my eyes watching her from the back of the bus.

In town Ruth had half an hour before the shops opened. She wanted to relax a bit. She sat in a coffee shop and thoughts invaded her mind. The feeling of gloom increased gradually. Someone had invaded her privacy and been in her space. For how long, Ruth couldn't tell. She wondered if this was what Sinéad felt prior to death? Had she ignored her instincts and warnings?

Ruth hated the thought of being fragile. She didn't want to think of her own mortality. Independence didn't come easy to her. As she got older solitude became her refuge and now it made her an easy target. Ruth had been an outgoing child but had started to retreat into herself when she was eighteen. The adult world hadn't worked out as she expected. She spent hours at a time in her teens in front of the mirror coming to terms with the new person that was looking back at her. She couldn't bear to look away. She was pretty. Not gorgeous, but definitely pretty. She was evolving into a creature that she didn't understand with a potential that she didn't know how to exploit. She started to drink at that time because despite her confidence as a child it hadn't yet translated into adulthood. After each drink she would feel her confidence increasing steadily. With the few girls she was close to she went out every Saturday night. Every place she looked she was catching men watching her. After a few drinks she would return the looks with bright playful smiles, this new being inside her calling the shots. One night towards the end of the evening, intoxicated with drink and attention, someone asked her to dance.

It was one of the last nights towards the end of the summer holidays as she was leaving the dance floor. A strong hand grabbed hers and led her back out for the slow set. He was a neighbour, at least thirty and very touchy. Ruth had known him all her life but that night she saw something in him she'd never seen before. She could feel a hot blush covering her neck. He led with authority. As they moved she felt her inhibitions and any vestige of thoughts of his wife slipping away. He moulded his body to hers. His hands moved up and down her body but she tensed as his hands eased down towards the base of her back while he smiled and kissed her gently on the mouth. She was scared but kissed him back. The dance ended so he grabbed her hand again, guiding her off the dance floor and out the back door of the club. She had never left the club with someone before but all her friends did regularly. Because it was so close to the end of the summer, and knowing that she wouldn't be out again until the Christmas holidays, she decided to take a chance. Besides, he was a family friend.

Outside he continued exploring her body. Ruth felt like she was floating in heaven and relaxed totally. Then things changed. His kisses and hands started to get rougher and more insistent. He shoved her back onto a windowsill and she could feel his hands roughly moving up her thighs under her skirt.

She tried to push him away but his weight was pinning her down. He grabbed her underwear and pulled at it roughly. She could hear it ripping. He held her with one hand and opened his trousers with the other. He prised her legs apart and pressed himself against her, almost inside her. She mustered up every ounce of strength she had and head-butted him. He loosened his grip as blood started running down his upper lip. For a moment he grabbed her throat and his black eyes flashed in the light of the window. A door opened to their left and a shaft of light held them in its grip. Ruth used the opportunity to pull away and ran inside. She could feel the same eyes as before watching her as she ran to the bathroom. She felt tarnished and stained. She had a bump on her forehead and her underwear was outside in the grass. She felt everyone must know what happened.

The next week was the last night of the holidays and Ruth went again to the same club. He was standing at the bar with his arm around a young girl who went to Ruth's school, perhaps a little older than Ruth but considerably younger than his wife. She was standing right in front of him by the time she saw him.

"Hi, Ruth!" He tried to catch her eye as a sneer spread across his face.

Ruth brushed past him and didn't look back. Ballyreid was too small to avoid anyone but in time he gave up taunting her and she stopped caring. The only people she'd ever tried to tell were her parents but that was another memory she couldn't open her mind to then.

That experience showed Ruth her first glimpse of the predator and taught her who to be wary of. But Ruth took everything to the extreme, including wariness.

She'd been sitting in the coffee shop with her head in her hands as those unbidden memories flooded in. The waitress put a hand on her shoulder. I was sitting three tables away and I longed to reach out and wipe

the demons from her brain. Later as I explored her
diaries I found that entry and remembered the date.
My hatred of that man matched my love for Ruth.

"Are you all right?" The waitress's concerned eyes
looked into Ruth's.

She smiled back. "Yes. It's just a headache. I've taken
two Paracetamols. I'm waiting for them to work."

Lying was so easy sometimes. She picked up her
bag and walked into the winter sunshine. She'd
better do some shopping. A few more hours and she
could go back to bed. She was supposed to be going
home tonight – she'd promised her mother. She'd just
have to go tomorrow instead.

She sat in the front of the bus on the way home, so
lost in her own world she went right by her house. She
came back to reality when she saw the Maxol Service
Station which was about half a mile further than her
house. She pushed the button and hopped off. No
wonder she never learned to drive, she thought – she'd
aim for Dublin and end up in Limerick.

I stayed on the bus to make sure she got home safely.
I could see the confusion on her face at the way her
mind was slipping away from her. I couldn't get off
the bus with her because she would see me – she was
the only one getting off at that stop. So I had to
watch her as she made her way down the street with
my heart by her side every step of the way.

It was dark when she reached her street. She watched her front door as she walked towards it. She usually didn't see it from this angle. Her resolve was eroding and palpitations started when she reached it.

She slipped her key into the lock and walked into the hall, dropping her keys on the hall table as she passed. She hung her coat over the back of her couch. The house was in total darkness. Any vestige of daylight left was not getting through these windows. She went upstairs and sat on her bed, staring into space, listening to the sounds of the house.

This was Ruth's life then, walls of silence surrounding rooms of emptiness.

Chapter 6

Amy felt an unexpected pang of empathy for Ruth. She had never known this side of her before. Whenever she thought about her, she remembered the anger and the sneaky taunts when Ruth had thought nobody was looking. Ruth was arrogant and confident then, a child with her world wrapped firmly around her little finger. Her life hadn't taken the path Amy had expected.

The sun had gone behind a bank of grey clouds and rain was imminent. Amy knew she couldn't go back to work today. There was no way she could concentrate and the staff would certainly notice the faraway look in her eyes. She decided to go home. Normally she walked if she left work early but not today – she decided to get the LUAS and avoid getting a soaking. Once more she gathered her papers into the folder, walked from the park, crossed the street and went up Harcourt Street. Beside her the LUAS trundled along, making its way on to Stephen's Green. A stab pierced her heart as she realised Ruth had never seen this Dublin – the Light Rail System was just a long-distance plan in those days. As she walked she found her eyes sneaking a peek into the basement offices nestled under the street, where boys in white shirts and ties looked longingly out at ground level and the outside world moving along without them. At the top of the street the discreet blue globe with the familiar *Garda* written across it announced the presence of the Harcourt Street Police Station.

The folder burned in her hands. She should take it inside and show them what she had. But she could only imagine how many man-hours these guys had already spent chasing down every lead pertaining to her cousin's disappearance. Would they even believe her if she produced this book?

She looked at the times of the next trains. Two minutes, seven minutes and twelve minutes. She bought her ticket and shifted from one foot to another, thinking about her options. She still couldn't decide between home and the police so she decided to give herself some time and stepped into Starbucks. A long line snaked from the counter but she knew from experience that most of them would be heading back out into the cold to climb onto the next train. She ordered a Venti Soy Latte and sat at the counter looking out onto the street. Even the coffee shops had changed over the past fifteen years. Amy cast her mind back to Ruth's visit to Bewley's. Bewley's was gone now and the building stood deserted and empty. Starbucks was something in those days whose reputation seeped out of America through books and movies. Little bits of Ireland eroded and fell away each day to be replaced by bricks imported from corporate America.

Suddenly Amy wanted to get close to this new Ruth who had come into her life so unexpectedly. With a knot in her stomach she took a long drink from her coffee and dropped her eyes back to the manuscript.

That night was so cold I nearly gave up my vigil. I had got off the bus at the next stop after Ruth's and run back to her house. I couldn't leave her alone after seeing her distress. I sheltered in the dark phone box, having taken the precaution of smashing the light bulb. My hands were tucked into my jacket and I kept the hood up to protect my ears. I was wearing two pairs of socks but my feet were still numb. I had to stomp constantly to keep them warm.

I was watching the front of her house. She had entered the house at eight o'clock and gone upstairs straight away and put the light on.

It was fascinating to watch her. The roads were quiet and few cars passed. At one point a car stopped next door to her house. She turned her lights off and peered out through the curtains. Satisfied it was at the next door down, she turned back inside and put on the light.

I didn't realise it yet but she had already spotted me in the phone box.

Fifteen minutes later a car pulled up about two doors away from hers. Again her face appeared between the curtains. I was only able to see her because I was watching from an angle. She barely parted the curtains. I could see the white of her shirt between them. Who was she expecting?

Almost as I thought this yet another car turned the corner. This time it was a taxi and it pulled up outside her door. The curtains parted and a shadow stood between them. A young woman about Ruth's age got out with a large holdall and knocked loudly on the door, while the taxi waited.

That was you, Amy, I was later to discover.

While you knocked, above you the curtains remained slightly open. You knocked again and stood back to look up at the window. Instantly the shadow stepped back. You repeated your knocking more loudly but the house remained still and quiet in the cold wind.

I watched each move you made as you tried vainly to gain entry to the house. I saw your sagging shoulders and downcast face as you got back into your taxi and drove away. Always trying to climb the family tree, weren't you, Amy?

I watched the rear lights of your taxi like two tiny red dots as you travelled down the road and took a sharp left, back towards the city centre. Then I looked back up at Ruth's window. Like a ghost she stood between the curtains, looking out onto the road. Her white face was drawn and incredibly sad.

I was elated. As you can imagine it's wonderful to secretly watch an unfolding drama like that. I was a born voyeur. Probing for information wasn't my thing. In my experience information people imparted willingly was usually tainted by self-interest and deeply biased. But if you had the opportunity to observe and the tenacity to follow the trails of people's lives, you usually found the deep dark truths hidden behind smiles and gestures. The secret places they would normally protect.

But I knew that night I'd stumbled upon your innermost places, your secret lives – hers and yours, Amy. Inside I knew this must be the other little girl in the photo from the wallet and I could see the depth of distress you caused each other. It was something I'd never have seen at college.

So why carry your picture if she hated you so much? Time would tell.

Amy sipped her coffee with her eyes watching the bustling figures passing outside the window, their arms stretched to a new length while they struggled with the bagged remains of the January sales. She vividly remembered that night when she arrived at Ruth's house.

The visit to Ballyreid had been one of Nuala's bright ideas. Nuala was Ruth's mother and had suffered so much guilt at banishing the little orphan from the family fold that every so often she would initiate these family gatherings out of the blue. Amy always wanted so badly to refuse but what could she do? Nobody had meant to hurt her, apart from Ruth, and certainly not Nuala. Between them all, they had set her up in the best place they could think of at that time and eventually they were proven right. It had been the best place.

Nuala's plan for that weekend had been for Amy to go to Ballyreid and spend some time there with the family, but Amy had stupidly thought that maybe she should try and see Ruth privately first. The girls were now in their twenties so it just seemed silly to hang onto the bitterness.

When she arrived in Waterford she decided to get a taxi to Ruth's and see if she was home. Or more importantly see if she was home to her. If she wasn't, Amy would leave it until the next day to go to Ballyreid and stay that night in a bed and breakfast. Amy had sent Ruth a letter explaining the plan. There hadn't been any negative response so she hoped that was a positive sign.

Amy's train arrived in Plunkett station thirty minutes late. She went out the front door of the station and jumped straight into a taxi. In her heart she knew this was a futile journey. She gave Ruth's address to the taxi driver and then she leaned her throbbing head against the window-pane.

The town was cold and wet that night and the

streets were pretty much deserted. As they crossed the river the cold silvery lights of the quay shone on the water. It looked like a long strip of Kilkenny marble cutting a channel between Ferrybank and Waterford city. The sky was clear in places but mostly it was choked with thick purple and black wads of cloud. It was as overcast as her heart.

In ten minutes she was at Ruth's. She hesitated before getting out, looking at its façade through the misty window. She thought it looked quite pretty, though a little neglected. It needed painting and the window boxes were overgrown. This was her first visit so her eyes took in every detail.

Amy's intuition warned her to hold the taxi while she knocked at the door. She knocked loudly a few times and stood back to look up at the upstairs window. There wasn't even a twitch from the lonely little house. But it felt as if others, as well as the house itself, were standing there silently watching. The feeling was making the hairs on the back of Amy's head stand on end. Now she knew why. Not only was Ruth watching her but an unknown individual had been close by taking in every detail as well.

Up until this moment Amy had been unsure if the writer's recounting of her cousin's life had been reliable. Now she knew at least some of it was. The details of that night were still clear in her mind and his account was so accurate that he had to have been there.

After a few minutes the taxi driver had impatiently called out, "Are you ready?"

Amy turned and got back into the car. She sat back rigidly in her seat, embarrassed at her stupidity in thinking this could possibly have worked. How could she have been so naive?

The driver's tone changed when he saw her solemn face. "Where to now, Miss?"

"The Dell House." She gave the name of a bed and breakfast they'd passed on the way. It had a vacancy sign up outside.

In a few minutes the taxi pulled up outside the door and Amy jumped out to ring the bell and check availability, leaving her bag in the taxi.

The street was dark and cold, the moon hidden behind a dark bank of clouds. A cold wind was sweeping down the streets whipping Amy's blonde hair across her face. Her cheeks were numb from the touch of its icy fingers. The night seemed to be trying to match the coldness of her heart, beat for beat.

After what seemed like ages the door opened into a large well-lit entrance hall warmly decorated. A staircase swept upwards from the centre of the hall to a landing above. Curved banisters went to the left and the right. Her eyes were drawn up to the first floor. The outside of the building gave no indication that the entrance hall would be that impressive.

The middle-aged landlady greeted her with an outstretched hand and a warm smile that glowed through red lips which bled into her lined face. She was dressed in a cream skirt and a yellow twin set with a string of tiny seed pearls at her throat. Amy was sure she had seen a movie with this exact scene in its opening sequence.

There was one room available. A feeling of relief had washed over her and she felt the first smile of the evening soften her face. She popped back outside, grabbed her bag and paid the taxi driver.

The room she'd been directed to was huge and her bed was big even compared to the size of the room. A newly painted white ceiling stretched high above her head. The furniture was heavy and dark but all the accessories were delicate and feminine.

Exhaustion hit Amy. She dropped all her belongings on the floor and stripped to her underwear, then crawled into bed. Cool sheets greeted her skin and her head sank into soft scented pillows.

She drifted into a fitful sleep punctuated by visions of twitching curtains and Ruth slamming doors in her face. Amy had been completely aware even that night that her cousin had been inside refusing to open the door.

That night the road outside Ruth's house had been crowded indeed.

Chapter 7

Around Amy the click of laptop keyboards and
murmured tones seeped into her consciousness as she
sat in Starbucks. One particular voice drifted through
the bank of noise, audible above everything else. A
quieter voice was responding. She didn't need to turn
around – she knew it was a department head from
Helfers and a junior. Amy wondered if they had seen
her. Minutes passed, then the voices were gone. Slowly
she turned towards the door but the owners of the
voices were nowhere to be seen.

That was her cue. She really didn't want to speak
to anyone.

To avoid meeting anyone else she might know she
decided to go home and think. She'd written off the
whole idea of going to the gardaí now. She would
think again when she had more information. At the
moment the stalker was just wandering down memory
lane and bringing Amy Devine with him.

The LUAS platform was more crowded now and Amy needed to push herself forward to get on. As the train trundled down Adelaide Road and across to Peter's Place she had to struggle to stop herself from being pushed over. At the Charlemont stop she looked up at a building studded with brightly lit offices facing out onto the road far below, under the LUAS bridge. Each block of light encased the bustling bodies above like worker bees in a hive, a wall of brightly lit boxes like a corporate honeycomb of activity. Amy felt herself struggling for breath. The train and the city felt crowded and all around her she felt discontent and longing as people tried desperately to break free. Remembering her yoga classes, she concentrated on each breath and tried to calm her racing heart.

By the time she reached her Beechwood stop it was gone lunchtime and she was starving. She stopped at the shop, picked up some essentials and started walking towards her house. As she walked she was once more struck by the similarity of the routine of her life and Ruth's. Even with her MBA, her position as vice-president in Helfers and a million-euro house, when it came down to the little things their lives were just the same.

Some of the streets around here were lined with identical houses, row after row of Georgian splendour, red-bricked ribbons of architecture tying together the progeny of the Celtic Tiger. Though beautiful in their way they held no charm for Amy. Her street stretched before her with houses a mixture of styles and stages of regeneration, peacefully co-existing under the shadow of their imposing neighbours.

Amy hadn't touched the outside of her house. This was part of its charm. You entered the property through a rickety iron gate, which opened onto a small gravel path with a postage-stamp lawn and a flowerbed on either side. Amy only planted traditional flowers that went with the façade. Hydrangeas, laurels and lavender lined the side walls, always kept in neat trim by her once-a-month gardener. A small flight of eight stone steps led up to her red-gloss door topped by an original fanlight window. For a moment she looked at the door. Why had she painted it the same colour as Ruth's? In Irene's day it had been green.

Amy dropped her keys on the consul table in the hall. A large antique mirror hung over it and she caught a glimpse of her pale face. Normally she was groomed and immaculate, a woman hyperaware of the necessity for keeping up appearances. After only one morning with this manuscript in her hands it had chipped away at her carefully laid foundations. She couldn't let a writer steal her sense of security. Until she knew otherwise they were just words. She climbed the stairs and changed into a robe. Unlike Ruth, Amy did have a large ornate bath and she needed it right now. She ran a deeply scented bubble bath and soaked the memories back into perspective. Donning a pair of tracksuit bottoms and a sweatshirt she went back downstairs to make something to eat.

An hour later Amy sat in her kitchen with the

manuscript propped against the milk on the table while beside her a sandwich lay forgotten on the plate as her eyes scanned the pages.

Later I learned that by then Ruth was convinced she was being watched all the time. She regularly checked her house to see any signs of me but nothing had been moved and she knew that. She'd left little traps around to show if someone had been there but they were undisturbed. Traps such as books arranged a certain way, her drawers arranged in a particular order or pieces of thread taped across the bottom of doors between the frame and the actual door. Obviously at that time I knew nothing about this but I did suspect I needed to be more careful.

That night you knocked on her door, despite the lack of further evidence of an intruder, she felt very uneasy. Consequently she alternated between her windows front and back to keep watch on the outside of her property. Not a thing moved in the back that she could see, though it was dark. But after a short time she realised there was something unusual out front. She became aware of me standing in the phone box. The diary entry read: *"It was a man and he must have been freezing."*

Ruth couldn't see whether or not I was actually using the phone because the light was out. She had never seen the light out before but that night it was and she immediately noted that as unusual. No! She knew straight away something was wrong. She knew when she came back at eight o'clock it had been on but when she looked out sometime later it was off. In her diary she said: *"I thought to myself, he'll have trouble dialling his number in the dark."*

I'm sure you're wondering why she didn't call the police but she had no proof and she didn't want to look stupid.

Ruth had other things on her mind that night too. You! Your letter had thrown her. She resisted change and she'd made her peace with what she did to you over the years. She was a child and of course you can't hold a child responsible for her actions. Your letter requesting a cousinly conference seemed unnecessary and actually quite needy and I have to agree. You were adults then so why not just let it go?

Anyway, Ruth stepped close to the window as you left and stared after your taxi as I also was doing. Then for one moment she saw me move as I turned my head back to look at her. She knew then that I was watching her. She felt spine-tingles for that split second and then stepped right back, leaving the light off. She put on a dark jumper in case I'd see her light blouse in the moonlight.

But I could still sense her there and see the glimmer of her white face. After about ten minutes I knew there was no use in waiting, that she would keep watching. There is only one way in and out of a phone booth so I came out with my head concealed by the hood of my jacket. I turned my back on her and walked up the street away from her house. At this distance she could see I was a man. She could see I was tall and fit. I was so aware of her eyes taking in my every move. She wrote: *"He had an arrogant walk."* Apart from that and my dark clothes no other detail stood out.

As I walked away she ran down the stairs as fast as she could and went into the street to see which direction I took. She couldn't see all the way down the street from her window. As she stood in the centre of the road she was terrified – and I suspect more than a little intrigued – in case I would turn around and see her, but I didn't. At this point my retreating body was all she needed to see. I would reveal more in time. In this moment I just wanted her to know I was there, know I was part of her life. I made a right turn away from the town towards a number of large housing estates. She didn't need to know how to find me. When it was necessary I would come to her. She really had no idea yet what she was looking for. But her hammering heart was certain this was important.

Amy was finding it hard to keep reading. What was she meant to do? Was she meant to pity Ruth? Over the past fifteen years she didn't know what she felt about Ruth and her disappearance. The country was shocked and outraged. Her aunt and uncle fell apart and it took many years before they got any semblance of their old lives back. Should she be ashamed that she just heaved a sigh of relief that she would never have to put up with Ruth again? Of course there had been curiosity as to what might have happened and yes, every so often a violent murder would be shown on television and, despite how she felt about Ruth, she hoped in her heart that if she was dead she hadn't suffered. She hoped that whatever happened, it had been quick. There was always the thought in the back of her mind that, though she hoped she'd never have to meet Ruth again, maybe somewhere in the world she was sipping a cocktail after morphing into a wonderfully happy person. Then she thought that if Ruth had found herself she had done it at the expense of the peace of mind of her parents and anybody else who might have loved her.

Throughout their childhood Ruth had pushed Amy into ever-decreasing corners. If Amy was in her line of vision at all Ruth was upset. Sometimes Amy just stayed in her room lost in a book and out of Ruth's way completely. She soon realised that to keep Ruth happy she would have to evaporate and float away on the breeze.

At that time Amy took wholeheartedly to running. The training regime suited her competitive nature. The dedication and concentration got her mind off her family. Running got her out of the house and into the world. It saved her too when she went to Dublin. Through every stressful time of her life, running had been her friend.

Back then in Ballyreid, Maurice had seemed oblivious to Ruth's feelings towards Amy. He obviously thought they were at "that awkward stage" and would grow out of it. It was clear that Nuala was only too aware of the pain the little Amy was going through every day. Maybe she was afraid that her interference would make things worse. She must have seen the black looks that crossed Ruth's face whenever the two were together and saw the hostile gestures when she thought her mother's back was turned. Things went unchecked until permanent damage had been done.

Chapter 8

Amy was sipping a coffee, sitting in the front room of her home. Her armchair stood on a polished parquet floor in front of an open wood fire. In reading the manuscript she was getting a much clearer picture of the adult Ruth, whom she had never had an opportunity to know. She didn't recognise her from the girl she knew in childhood. The woman she'd become was frightened and isolated, a woman who was trying to become somebody and take control of her life while in the background unknown to her someone was watching and manipulating her every move. Amy's eyes wandered to the envelope that had contained the manuscript. It was not stamped. It was hand-delivered. Was he in Dublin now and if so was he watching her? Was that the purpose of this manuscript? Had he transferred his attentions from Ruth Devine to Amy Devine? A log loosened in the grate and a spray of sparks flew onto the mat. Amy jumped violently. Her nerves were frayed tonight. Should she forget the fact that she wasn't going to find out about Ruth's fate in this instalment and take her chances and go to the police? Ruth never did much for her when she was alive, so why shouldn't she just protect herself? This guy could be watching her right now. Her house was a lot bigger than Ruth's. He could be living in here with her and it might be a week before she'd find him. Her kitchen, study and laundry room were all at basement level downstairs, her living rooms on the ground floor, her bedroom suite on the first floor and her gym in the attic; she was acutely aware of all those stairs and corners between the attic and the garden level. Trying to minimise her panic she walked slowly to the alarm panel in the hall and checked everything was set correctly. She set the internal alarm for the attic. Any movement inside its walls would immediately set it off. When she walked down the hall and opened the door leading to the kitchen stairs, a funnel of darkness greeted her. Quickly she snapped on the light, illuminating the steps before descending to the lower level of the house. Despite living alone in the city Amy had never felt fear before and she hated doing so now. When she entered the kitchen she'd popped two pieces of wholemeal bread in the toaster. She jumped violently now as they popped, with one landing on the floor at her feet. Chastising herself for her suggestibility, she made herself a snack and a hot drink. Then she checked the kitchen door, which led out into the back garden, and the study door which led to the front steps going up to street level.

Satisfied that these were tightly locked she went back upstairs to the alarm panel and set the internal alarm for the lower level. Then she settled down in front of the fire and continued with her reading.

The coincidences of this world never stop amazing me. I would often sit afterwards, thinking back over everything, and it was like a scavenger hunt. The whole thing was really a matter of following the clues someone had placed on the map of my life.

Leaving the phone box that night I felt her eyes following me and I knew then that in that moment our worlds had become one for the first time since childhood. I strode away purposefully from the phone booth, displaying my height and gait for her to see. The exhilaration of knowing she was watching my body move – I can hardly describe it. She'd known it was my scent on her pillow. You know yourself how important scent is to memory. When you smell something it's forever associated with that memory and once you smell it again you are immediately transported to another time or place.

My hands had touched her things. Ruth didn't know for certain what, so everything in her house could have been touched. I knew she would feel that every day. My eyes read her diary so she knew in her heart that I had her thoughts in my head. She didn't know I had her photo by my bed but I did. I could look into those eyes whenever I wanted. But my point is, Ruth knew now she was in my head and in my heart and when the time was right she would see my face. Everything happened according to the master plan. The pieces fell into place when the time was right. I was totally confident of that since the first day I saw Ruth in the college. What are the odds that my first love, who I hadn't seen in eight years, would cross my path as I walked to my first class? It was our destiny.

Then there was you. I often wondered about you because you figured strongly in her story. I was curious to know more about you. But I had other things in my life. Then one day last year I saw you on the television talking about your company's expansion into Mayo. Was the rent getting too high in Dublin? I remembered how you had tried to reach Ruth that night at her house. I watched you speaking with such passion and found myself wanting you to know what happened. I thought you should know where she went.

We're reaching the end of this part of the story, Amy. I need you to do something for me now before I can let you have the rest of it. I worry about you, an orphan isolated from the rest of your family and I would like to help you to go back. I want you to return to Ballyreid. Once you do I will contact you with the next instalment of the manuscript.

Amy knew now the stalker's attentions were transferred from Ruth to her. This was no writer trying to get his book published.

Should she go back to Ballyreid? Could she go back? She hadn't spoken to Nuala and Maurice in a long time. They sent Christmas cards and Nuala still sent her a couple of letters every year but beyond that they had lost contact. Maybe she should go back. But was she crazy letting a possible psychopath dictate her actions?

Amy felt very tired. The stress of the day had caught up with her. Feeling groggy, she set the house alarms and went up to bed.

Her room was two rooms knocked into one. A pair of floor-to-ceiling sliding doors stood to one side of her room. One opened into a large walk-in wardrobe and the other into her en-suite bathroom. Her heart hammered as she approached these and she found herself taking deep breaths to control her panic. But it was unnecessary: everything was just as she'd left it earlier in the day. When she'd finished her nightly routine she turned the lock on her bedroom door and crawled into her bed exhausted.

Nothing happened during the night and Amy slept soundly. Next morning, after dragging herself into her shower and finding something to wear from her dressing-room, she descended the stairs, turning the alarms from internal to perimeter as she went. She made herself a pot of strong coffee and toasted a bagel. With her mind consumed by a cousin she had long ago learned to forget, she munched on her breakfast. The thought of going home was starting to appeal to her. Amy piled her dishes into the sink to wash later and stood looking into her garden. It was always a peaceful oasis in a bustling city but now Amy saw it from another point of view. The ornamental bushes sitting on her deck in large wooden tubs would form substantial hiding places at night as they blended into pools of darkness. Her garden was surrounded by a high stone wall and wasn't overlooked on any side. It was a perfect place for a practised stalker to set up camp.

Shaking off this feeling of gloom Amy got ready for work. Like Ruth had done fifteen years ago, she checked her house, top to bottom, ensuring windows and doors were all tightly shut. Then she set her alarm. A shaft of bright sunlight warmed her front steps this morning and hit her as soon as she opened the door. She put her sunglasses on as she descended the steps and immediately saw a note pinned to her gate. It was a plain sheet of white paper with the words "*Good Morning*" computer-printed in bold letters with a smiley face. Amy took a tissue from her bag, plucked the paper from the gate and went back inside. She got a Ziploc bag from the kitchen and folded the paper inside. At some stage in the future she suspected this paper might be needed as evidence. She walked into her study and locked it into the safe.

The LUAS was on time and despite her delay she was still early for work.

There was more than one whispered conversation that morning about Amy Devine. Everyone in the elevator had noticed the faraway look in her eyes.

Greg had to repeat himself twice when he dropped her coffee and mail on the desk. Amy just nodded at him as she stood at the window looking down onto the street. Then she had a thought.

"Greg."

"Yes?" He turned with his hand on the door.

"That large envelope you dropped in yesterday, who delivered that?"

"Kevin brought it up with the rest of the stuff. Why? Was there a problem?"

"No. It's fine. I just wondered because it was hand-delivered."

"That's not that unusual, is it? Would you prefer Kevin not to drop up hand-delivered things in future?"

"Of course not. No! It just reminded me of that anthrax scare a few years ago. We should just be careful, that's all."

"Of course."

She knew she'd offended him – he prided himself on his efficiency. But she had to ask that question. Now she'd have to ask downstairs. She was hoping to avoid that. Greg was very discreet but she couldn't be so sure about the others.

Amy drank her coffee while she checked out the train timetable. Normally she'd ask Greg to do that for her but she didn't want to answer any questions about why she needed to book a ticket to Waterford. She looked at the clock. Ten o'clock – she had a while yet before the train. She looked over her appointment book and saw that there was nothing too urgent for the next few days.

She picked up the phone and dialled some numbers. Numbers she knew by heart but never used.

"Hi," she said.

"This is Devines'."

"Nuala, it's me, Amy."

There was a long pause at the other end and Amy was afraid she'd hung up.

"Nuala?"

"I'm still here. I'm just surprised to hear from you."

"I know. Nuala, I was thinking about taking a few days off and coming to Ballyreid. If that's all right with you."

"Of course, Amy, we'd love to see you. We'd be thrilled. Will you be driving?" Nuala was babbling in her confusion at this unexpected call.

"No. I don't have a car. I always think it's a waste since I live in the city and on the LUAS more or less. So I'd get the train to Waterford and then the bus to Dungarvan. I could be there this evening at six thirty."

"I'll pick you up off the bus."

"All right. I'll see you later."

Amy put down the phone, her heart still pounding. She couldn't believe he was making her do this.

Chapter 9

Amy stopped on her way out and asked Kevin about the package he'd brought up to her office.

He looked at her blankly. "It was dropped into the post room. Before I got to work."

Then she stopped at the security desk and asked Paul the security guard if he remembered it.

"Absolutely. It was in the mail box when I came on duty."

The security staff doubled as mailroom staff but if it were left in last night Paul wouldn't know anything more about it – his shift hadn't begun until seven thirty that morning.

Amy thought for a moment before speaking.

"Paul, can I see the security tapes from the door for last night?"

He looked puzzled. "Sure. It will take a few minutes."

"Okay. I'll be back in ten minutes. I'll go get a coffee in West Coast. Do you want one?"

"I'd love one. A Tall Skinny Cappuccino, please."

"Right." Amy was a little surprised at the order. Skinny wasn't a word she'd associate with Paul.

She stood in line at the register, her mind in another county as she waited for the drinks and a fresh croissant.

But Paul's tapes didn't make her any the wiser. A teenager in white tracksuit bottoms and a grey top with the hood pulled right up had dropped in the manuscript at about six forty-five. He was small and slightly bow-legged and certainly didn't match Ruth's stalker either in expected age or according to his own description.

Amy was annoyed. "Wouldn't you check an unusual delivery like that immediately? I mean, it could have been anything."

"I'm sorry," said Paul. "Of course we normally would. There was a new security guard on last night. It was his first night here alone. We'll sort it." His face was grim.

"Do that." Amy wasn't normally heavy handed but she wasn't used to feeling so out of control.

"Yes. I will." Paul was not happy at being told off like this.

Amy raised her eyebrows dismissively and walked off. She had some things to take care of upstairs before her taxi arrived, including picking up the overnight bag she always kept in her office.

Amy's taxi was late and got to the station just a few minutes before the train was due to depart. She had to rush inside, grab her ticket from the vending machine, a bottle of water from the kiosk, and run down the platform. The train left on the dot and Amy was expecting to be in Waterford in plenty of time for the early bus to Dungarvan where Nuala was going to pick her up.

However, less than an hour into the journey, the train broke down in the middle of nowhere. Amy woke up from a nap and craned her neck to see what the problem was but all she could see were green fields and high hedgerows stretching into the distance on all sides. The sky continued to darken outside as huge clouds blocked the sun and large full drops of rain landed on the glass in front of her eyes. They were stuck somewhere between towns. She looked around the carriage. The other passengers were restless too.

Across the aisle an old lady was watching her.

"Where are we?" asked Amy.

"The train's been stopped this last twenty minutes. There's some sort of engine trouble. These people are always on strike." She sniffed loudly. "Maybe we'd care about their problems if they offered a better service while they were working."

Amy smiled. The conductor was coming towards her.

"Excuse me, how long will it be before we get to Waterford?" she asked him.

The conductor grinned through gapped teeth and chapped lips. "Well, my dear, not for a while yet – we still haven't reached Kilkenny. We have a mechanic outside working on the engine. You've had a relaxing journey so far?" He laughed at his own amusing observation.

Amy was tempted to be rude but the carriage gave a shudder and the train lurched forward.

"Ah, here we go. On our way now, we'll have you home in no time."

Amy sank back into her seat. The train gathered speed. She gazed at herself in the window-pane as the train whizzed through a tunnel. Home. The concept of *home* was a bit confusing for Amy. Could she call Ballyreid home, having been born there and lived there for the first eight years of her life? Irene's house was where she'd spent most of her life. It was home to her now. What could she call Ballyreid?

Amy's parents were killed in a car crash when she was four years old. Memories came flooding back with little encouragement. She was with her grandmother while her parents went on a break to Clare to celebrate their sixth wedding anniversary.

To her childlike eyes they were beautiful people and time had never tarnished that image. Her mother was tall like she herself was now: athletic but very feminine. She was about five eight, she supposed. Her hair was blonde like Amy's and always hung loose, complementing her pale skin and blue eyes.

Her father had a chunky build and was about three inches taller than her mother. His features were rugged. He had fair hair and Nuala had told her his eyes were hazel. It was the look in those eyes that Amy never forgot. They were always twinkling. She had a photo of him sitting on her window at home. In her eyes that smile could eclipse the sun.

Most people got to see their parents grow old, saw their lives go through many stages. Amy had never seen any of that. In her mind her parents were still young and beautiful, and they always would be.

In her memory she could hear the sounds of her grandmother's farmyard. The calf had gone to the mart that morning. Her father had seen to it before he got dressed to go to Clare. The poor cow was screaming all day searching for her calf. Her mother said the sound made her feel very sad. Daddy put his arms around her and laughed, calling her a big softy. Amy stood with her hands on her hips asking why the cow couldn't keep her baby. They all laughed at her and mimicked her stance. She was deeply offended.

Amy's mother was upset leaving her daughter. Amy could see the torn look in her eyes when she looked up into her husband's face but you could tell she was dreaming about the weekend to come.

Amy was already being left behind. She sat on Granny's front step as they prepared to leave, rested her chin sideways on her entwined hands and watched them out of the corner of her eye.

Her mother crouched down and kissed her forehead, stroking her hair.

"I'm sorry, baby, it won't be forever. It's only for a weekend. We'll be there to meet you after school on Monday."

Then in a rush of affection Daddy lifted her up in

his arms and hugged her close. Her mother came over and squeezed into his arms as well. Amy's tiny frame was crushed between their bodies. She could feel the softness of her mother's breasts pressed against her back and the hardness of her father's chest against her. Their three faces were combined as one, enveloped in the smell of apple shampoo. Both her parents must have washed their hair in it that morning. Even now when Amy needed consolation she would wash her hair in it.

They gave her a final kiss, put her down on the ground and jumped into the car. Her mother blew kisses at her from the front seat and then they were gone, out of her life forever. She remembered crying and Granny and Nuala had made a big fuss of her. As far as she could remember Ruth was there too. Ruth was very close to her Aunty Kitty, Amy's mother.

Amy was sure some of this was memory and some was wistful fantasy but she didn't care. To her it was a solid and treasured fact.

At six thirty the next evening her grandmother sat her down and told her that those beautiful apple-scented people were never coming back. There had been a terrible crash.

Granny was a kind and gentle person but, like many people living in the countryside, she felt that death was a fact of life and shouldn't be skirted around. Amy was spared any graphic detail but she was never kept in ignorance of the truth.

She remembered standing like a little soldier as

they waked her parents side by side in the parlour. Family and neighbours recited the rosary around the single beds put in there for the occasion with plain white bedspreads on them. Her parents lay, dressed in their Sunday finery as Granny used to call it. All the other furniture had been moved out and put in the barn.

All Amy could remember was the coldness of their skin as she touched their cheeks. The mourners stiffened when they saw her approach, wondering if they should lead her away. They were immobilised by their inadequacy as they watched the tiny fingers stroke her mother's face. Her mother's soft white skin was like alabaster and her father's sparkling eyes were closed. Amy stood in the room and demanded they put the heating on and warm them up. Some female relatives started to cry while the men hung their heads and looked at the floor. This was over thirty years ago and sensibilities were different then. It's unlikely anyone now would let a four-year-old stand alone at her parents' wake.

When Amy was older she found out more of the details of the crash. At the time her grandmother, in her usual fatalistic style, told her they were gone to God. She said He needed them more. This seemed selfish to Amy. Why would God, who had access to so many people, need to take the only two she had? When she mentioned this to Granny the response she got was: "It's not for us to question God's motives." This never satisfied Amy.

She started prying into the events surrounding the crash years later when she was in her mid-teens. She discovered her parents had been taking a sharp bend in the road when the car went over the edge down into a field. When they were discovered the next day they were both dead.

It was assumed her mother had died first. She probably died instantly on hitting her head on the roof of the car and breaking her neck. Her father had two broken legs and was pinned under the crumpled dash area. His injuries were not life-threatening if he had been found in time. He bled to death over a period of hours according to the coroner's report. He was found holding his wife's hand.

For most of her early life Amy's dreams were haunted by the image of her parents' death. Relatives tried to do their best for her, but she lost the security of her childhood in the most violent way and the black gulf left in its wake could never be breached by duty and Irene's sparse home life certainly hadn't the resources she needed.

Amy worked every day towards the moment she could leave the remnants of her old world behind. She studied hard and trained hard. Her dream was to one day win an athletics scholarship as far away from her memories as possible. She knew she had no hope of getting to college by conventional means. The funds just didn't exist. Her parents weren't well off and any insurance covered expenses for the funeral and gave Irene an allowance to help take care of her.

The train lurched again and Amy watched the lights of Kilkenny fade into the distance. Her coach was now rolling into the Irish countryside.

Her heart was heavy.

When she left school Amy won a scholarship to a college in California. That was her way out. She left for better things with her head held high. She studied business for four years and with a degree she came back to Dublin to prove to everyone she was a success. Almost straight away she got a job with Marlow Publishing in London who regularly sent her back to the States for training programmes. They paid for her MBA. It was during one of these trips that Irene died. Irene had left her the house, so she had to get another job which would allow her to stay closer to home so she could oversee the building work she'd started on it. At this point she'd intended selling it. She wanted to get rid of her past in one go. She didn't know when it happened but somewhere along the way she became happy. She loved her new job and had risen steadily through the ranks and then she totally fell in love with her house and after that there was no question of selling it.

There was no man in Amy's life at the moment. But being with men had never been a problem for her. Easy come, easy go, she supposed. Men liked her and she liked them, but there was never anything permanent in any of her relationships. Initially they had to inspire her to pique her interest but that usually fizzled out once the initial getting-to-know-you was over. In her heart she held them up to her parents' amazing love story and they were like glass to diamonds. Amy was looking for diamonds.

She was still a quiet person and not very socially driven. She had some friends but she usually kept herself to herself. It would appear that was also the way Ruth turned out. Was that what attracted *him* to them?

Chapter 10

Once she arrived in Waterford, Amy ran out the front door of the station and across the bridge. She turned left down the quay, her quick eyes taking in all the changes since last time she was there. The Árd Rí hotel looked a bit worse for wear and the Bell ships were moved from Ferrybank to further down the river towards New Ross. Blocks of brand-new apartments had mushroomed on every available site in the city. Box-like apartments were rapidly replacing the old architecture of Waterford.

Amy got to the bus station on the quay with only minutes to spare. She paid for her ticket inside the small terminal and got on the bus, still breathless from her run. She scanned the faces turned towards her as she walked down the aisle, wondering now if he was one of them. Amy sat into a window seat, a frown etched into her face. At least half the people on the bus were males in their early thirties. He could really be any one of them. Amy knew that at some stage, once he was sure she was in fact going home, he would probably give her the next instalment of Ruth's story.

The driver got on and announced the bus would be ten minutes late because of mechanical problems. Amy smiled wryly at this, then whiled away the minutes gazing out through the frosty glass at the traffic on the quay.

Ballyreid was a moderately sized village beyond Dungarvan. There was a church, a school, a couple of pubs, a coffee shop, a garda station and one mini-market stretching along the main street. At the junction by the mini-market a road veered off to the right passing a small housing estate, the Church of Ireland, the fruit and vegetable shop, then on for about a quarter of a mile past Ballyreid's last pub and finally to the Devines' house. Devines' was always known as "the last house in the village". Though plenty more had since been built past it, locals still called it that.

The bus didn't go that way so Nuala would need to come into Dungarvan and pick her up from the bus stop on Davitt's Quay.

She found to her surprise that her eyes were filled with tears and she had to wipe them away as the bus moved away from the pavement and drove out into the country. The fields and houses flashed by as she ran her mind over walking the main street in Ballyreid with her grandmother or going to church with the extended Devine family. Back then she felt like part of a family. It all fell apart so suddenly. In her Dublin life she didn't care but today she was making a trip where she would stand out in her isolation.

As she got closer to home she tried to remember exactly when she'd last seen Nuala and Maurice and found she couldn't remember the exact date. It was definitely since Ruth's disappearance. She'd had lunch with them a few times in Dublin when Maurice came up to have a check-up in St James' hospital.

The bus came to a halt in the town. Amy got off and stood at the bus stop, holding the strap of her bag. She felt like a kid on her way home from school. She scanned the crowd until she saw Nuala's familiar shape walking down the footpath towards her. She had a tentative smile spread across her tiny face. Though almost sixty, she walked with a light step full of energy. Today she looked a bit nervous.

Nuala held out her arms and hugged Amy tightly to her. She had to rise up on her tippy-toes to kiss her rangy niece on the cheek.

"Darling, I am so glad to see you! You have no idea how happy you've made us coming to visit like this." Her eyes were swimming in tears.

Nuala was so like Ruth in every detail it was disturbing. They were roughly the same height, weight and colouring – five foot two, seven and a half stone – and had the same creamy skin and blue eyes. Nuala's face was the slightly lined original and Ruth's had been a shiny new copy. The only real difference between the two was personality.

Nuala had always been cheerful, homely and very

affectionate. She always tried to see the goodness in everyone. Her daughter was her spiteful and selfish opposite. Amy didn't know what Nuala was like now, after the tragedy of losing her daughter.

Lithe and quick on her feet, Nuala bounced along beside her niece, anxious to get back to the car out of the damp day. Her little arm was wrapped protectively around Amy's waist and gradually she was melting the fear in Amy's heart. Amy was actually able to look down on the top of Nuala's head. She laughed suddenly, for the first time in days, and planted an affectionate kiss on the top of her aunt's head.

"You haven't grown an inch!"

"Cheek!" Nuala gave her waist a quick pinch.

Together they stepped into Nuala's little Ford Fiesta and started the ten-mile journey to Ballyreid.

PART TWO

Chapter 11

Her grandmother's death left a deep void in little Amy's life. The odd time she did come back to Ballyreid she braced herself for when she would see the old house. There was a new family living there now. Her grandmother's house was at the end of the first turn left past Nuala's house. This road was known locally as Devine Road. It ran for half a mile through Devine land on both sides, to end in her grandmother's old yard. The new family living there were like inhabitants of an oasis in Devine country.

The Devines' land would be considered arable pastureland and was always well cared for. Herds of pedigree cattle, mostly for beef these days, dotted the fields. As farmers they were probably quite wealthy but when it came to disposable income they kept their fists tightly closed. Any profit was ploughed straight back into the land as money sitting in a bank account was considered a sinful waste, not to mention a temptation to the taxman. Nuala and Maurice had never been tempted to sell any roadside sites. Neither of them wanted strangers moving onto their land. Due to its proximity to the village the value of that land increased almost daily.

The road up to her grandmother's house was picture perfect. It was a typical rural Irish road, narrow and twisted with a crease of grass growing down the centre. The hedges were high on either side and at times of the year threatened to engulf the whole road until the clippers had to come and free the residents from their encroaching branches.

When you were travelling along that road your first view of the entrance to the house came as a surprise. As you rounded the last bend a pair of imposing stone pillars with pointed tops and wrought-iron gates appeared out of the banks of green hedgerow. Amy's father had bought them many years ago at auction. They originally came from a minor manor house some place in Tipperary.

Nuala had driven straight to the old farmhouse. She knew the trip would mean a lot to Amy. It was now dark. Standing now with her nose pressed between the bars of the gate, Amy could just see the stone steps she'd sat on the day her parents left. In the summer those steps were trimmed with pots of chrysanthemums blooming richly, brightening the whole yard. Now they sat cold and damp drenched by a winter deluge.

Then there wasn't the time for proper gardening

yet the place was always awash with colour. Clumps of purple climbing flowers clung to the spaces by the side of the stone steps. The overgrown flowerbeds by the wall housed an infestation of weeds: yet they seemed to share their space quite happily with bluebells, pansies, marigolds and primroses. Roses travelled all over the wall, waving blooms over the path and dropping petals onto the steps like confetti.

It was a family tradition when the girls were little to spend Sunday afternoons going for drives in the car. These would usually include a trip to an old house at her grandmother's request. Her grandmother picked flowers up in every stately garden she visited. She snipped them off as little cuttings, which she then cleverly concealed and smuggled out in her scarf.

One day many years ago an American tourist looking for directions respectfully asked her what she rooted them in.

"Cow shit, sir," she'd replied with equal respect, and pointed with her arthritic fingers to an old metal bucket standing by the dairy door in which stood her latest collection.

He threw back his head, roaring with laughter. This delighted her grandmother and she invited him in for a pot of tea. After that meeting they corresponded regularly until he died suddenly of cancer, aged eighty-three. Granny lit a candle in the church every day for his soul until she died herself. Though they only met in person once, Mrs Devine considered him a cherished friend. Her grandmother made the world feel like a village and everyone she met was a possible friend.

For the last four years of her life her grandmother's mind was sharp but her body had deteriorated. Her heart was bad and she became virtually bedridden with arthritis. Amy was seven years old and too much of a handful for the old lady. Nuala took her to live with her and her grandmother moved permanently to a residential home.

This transition was a tough one for Amy. The coldness of her cousin and the confusion of her new circumstances were in such sharp contrast to the warm home she'd shared with her grandmother.

Nuala stood near Amy at the gate, unwilling to impose on her thoughts while she looked at the farmyard. Nuala's family, the Donnellys, came from a small terrace house in Ballyreid. Her father died when she was young. He'd worked all his life for the local County Council on the road crew.

Amy's mother Kitty was the younger of the two girls. Their mother died when she was sixteen. Nuala, being two years older, was already out of school and working as a clerk in the Council. Kitty was in her Leaving Cert year. Nuala looked after everything for that year to give her younger sister the opportunity to finish her education and get a good job. Two weeks after her final exam Kitty went to work for a local solicitor as a secretary.

In November that year the two girls went to a dance in Ballyreid. This was the night Nuala first met Maurice Devine. Maurice never left Nuala's side all night and when it was time to go home his brother James came to collect him. James offered Nuala a lift home but Nuala said she had to go and find her younger sister Kitty, so the boys said they'd wait and take them both home.

Nuala later told Amy that James's eyes nearly popped out of his head when he first saw Kitty. It was love at first sight for both of them. The two brothers and two sisters had a joint wedding the following summer. It was a well-kept secret that Ruth was already on the way.

Two years later Amy became the new baby of the family. The two families were close and in the beginning so were the two little girls. Ruth played with her little cousin as you would a doll. Kitty was her adored aunt and Amy their shared baby. But all that changed when Amy came to live with them. She was no longer her toy. Amy had lost her mother and then her grandmother and now she was attaching herself to Ruth's mother too. The young Ruth couldn't cope with the competition.

Amy never got the memory of her parents' death out of her mind. She could still see the coffins being lowered into the ground. She was four years old and nobody knew how to talk to her about it.

They all suffered the loss of Kitty. That crash had changed the course of all their lives. They were a tightly knit family, sparse in members, and Kitty was the glue that held them all together, the sun that shone in all their lives.

Amy jumped as Nuala spoke.

"Amy, are you all right?"

Nuala reached over and held Amy's hand and for a brief moment Amy felt the love of close family. The unexpectedness of it was like a punch in her ribs. She flinched from its sharpness.

Amy stood back and watched her aunt's face. Maurice told her once Nuala loved to see her coming back because she reminded her so much of Kitty. It broke her heart that she'd had to let her little sister's daughter go out of their lives. But she did let her go. Nuala succumbed to pressure from Ruth and sent her away and, though Amy didn't feel anger towards her, she found it hard to love her now. Then a strange feeling came over her as she felt Nuala's arms go around her.

She'd never expected to find home on this trip. She thought she was just going to go through the motions and pick up the second instalment of the manuscript.

Awkwardly she pulled out of Nuala's embrace.

Amy turned her eyes towards the window as the car descended the road again and the once familiar countryside slipped by. This was going to be more complicated than she'd thought.

Nuala brought the car to a crunching halt outside the door of the Devine house, a bungalow. For a moment Amy sat looking around her, taking in the bare trees dotting the lawn and the freshly trimmed hedges snaking their way around the perimeter of the property. A high-pitched sound caught her attention. A frail old dog came out to meet them. He was an old black and white border collie. Amy felt a flood of tears edge their way to the surface. Brandy. She turned to Nuala.

"Brandy is still alive?"

"No," she laughed. "This is her grandson, Peter."

"You called a dog Peter?"

"We did. He's fifteen. Gosh, Brandy would be well over thirty if she was still around."

Another pang pierced Amy. She hadn't even heard when her childhood pet died. Brandy had been Granny's dog and moved up here with Amy after Granny went into the home. Amy had just wanted to grab onto anything that seemed familiar.

She had the door of the car open and was sitting looking around her when Peter walked to her and placed his old grey snout on her knee.

"Well, hello to you too!" She ran her hand over his back as he looked up into her face. Their moment was broken by the arrival of her uncle.

Maurice came to the door in his old denim jeans and his brown jumper with the left elbow torn out of it. Amy could have sworn that man had had some variation of that same ensemble on since the first time she'd laid eyes on him. He hugged her tightly. Amy was at a loss as she entered the house with her aunt and uncle. None of this was what she'd expected when she'd decided to make this trip.

Inside the house the table was set for lunch. There was a roast chicken, mashed potatoes, vegetables and gravy. A bustling Nuala was heaping the food onto plates.

"Sit down, everyone. Sit down!"

As soon as they sat down both her aunt and uncle launched into a sea of questions about her life in Dublin.

"How is the house?" Maurice led the questions. "I suppose Irene wouldn't recognise it?"

"It's finished. It took longer than I thought but it was worth it."

"I'm sure it was. Do you get lonely living in it by yourself? It's a big house." Nuala had skilfully guided the conversation around to what she really wanted to know.

Amy smiled, knowing she was asking about a man. "I never get lonely. I love my own company."

"That's what Ruth used to say."

Amy felt a chill up her back. In that moment she wanted to get away from them. How could she tell them what she'd found out? How could she explain to them why she didn't go to the police immediately and help them to find out what had become of their beloved Ruth?

Lunch continued in an uncomfortable silence, then they washed up and Maurice went back outside to the farm. As soon as the last dish was dried, Amy turned around to face her aunt.

"Nuala. I'm tired after the trip. I think I'll lie down."

"Okay."

She felt Nuala watching her leave the room. She knew she was a living reminder of all the people missing from their table. Nuala's mother-in-law, her sister, her daughter, all the women that were once part of her family were gone and here *she* was, a woman who'd become a stranger to her, had known them all. She felt Nuala wanted to grab this opportunity to bring her back into the family but she didn't know how.

Amy needed to think. She lay on her old bed and in a short time she was asleep.

After a couple of hours she woke, stretched and lay back. She looked at the ceiling and counted the patterns on it. There were always loads of tiny patterns engraved into the paint: paint bubbles, brush hairs, cobwebs and dust and for some reason a footprint that had been there since the day she moved in. At seven years of age she'd agonised over what kind of creature might have been walking on her ceiling. She used to switch the lights on every so often to check that the creature wasn't there over her bed. One night she stayed up late when there was a baby-sitter looking after them. The baby-sitter was a girl barely in her teens and so she allowed them to watch *Salem's Lot*. Little Amy had nightmares for ages afterwards. In her sleep she could see vampires hanging from her ceiling and always one of them looked just like Ruth.

Her mind wandered back to what Ruth's thoughts might have been as she looked over her shoulder, expecting her stalker to find her. Who did she picture hanging from her ceiling?

Amy jumped off the bed and left her room, walking down the hall and into the empty kitchen. She walked out the front door. Peter saw her as soon as she entered the yard and walked slowly over to meet this softly spoken person that seemed so moved to meet him. He started hopping around her, as quickly as old dogs can hop.

She walked to the road and then in the direction of her grandmother's house.

Amy followed Ruth everywhere when they were children. Ruth would never notice, or not until the end – otherwise she would have told her to get lost. Today Amy trudged along with her head down against the winter wind, wondering why she had done that. What had she been expecting to get from her cousin? She walked on as far as her grandmother's gate. As before, the yard and house seemed deserted. Amy had a vague memory that the new owners only used it as a weekend house. Amy was drawn to this spot, the spot where her life had changed forever all those years ago. So much of her life had taken place within that yard. As she looked around her, the memory of Ruth's voice interrupted her thoughts.

"Well! Squirt!"

Amy turned in fear, trying to find somewhere to go to get out of her reach. The tone of Ruth's voice told her she'd made a mistake in allowing herself to be caught alone with her.

"I'm going home." The little Amy turned defiantly to walk away but the sharp pain of her long blonde hair being pulled rooted her to the spot.

"Ow! Ruth! Stop that!" she gasped through gapped teeth.

Ruth held her face inches from her cousin's and mimicked her words. "Ow. Ruth. Stop that." Her face was screwed up with hatred. "What are you going to do, squirt? Are you going to tell Mammy? Oh! But you don't have a mammy, do you, Amy?"

Then Amy felt a sharp pain in her knees as Ruth pushed her to the ground and walked away. Amy went back home, her tights torn and blood caked on her knees.

"Amy, are you all right?" Nuala ran to her niece's side.

Amy had stood there looking at Ruth, unable to speak for fear of the reprisal. Nuala looked from one to the other. She knew what must have happened but she didn't want to hear the words. Nuala needed to find a solution without ever having to really face the reality of her daughter's cruelty. So she'd decided that the best thing for all concerned would be for her to take care of her daughter and pass Amy on to someone else.

Irene lived alone, having never married. She was Maurice's maiden aunt. She had no responsibilities and a large house so she seemed the ideal candidate to take on the job. None of them had spent a lot of time with Irene and they certainly hadn't lived with her in her home, so they didn't know how sparse Amy's life would be there.

Chapter 12

During the evening the wind and rain got
progressively worse and it howled around the eaves.
Sometimes it seemed strong enough to whip the roof
off the house. When Amy came back, Maurice and
Nuala were laying the table for tea. The kitchen was
quiet with the only sounds coming from the timber
sparking in the stove and the clock ticking on the wall.

Amy had never been much of a voice in this family.
She usually observed from a distance. It was funny the
way such habits became ingrained. In her Dublin life
she was successful and confident but here she was still
a little girl floating like a spirit through the house.

Nuala and Maurice didn't seem in the mood for
any form of conversation amongst themselves.
Something must have been said since lunch. A definite
atmosphere had developed. This wasn't encouraging
Amy to get involved since she thought she might be
the problem. Nuala was stirring something on the

stove and Maurice was reading the newspaper by the window in his usual spot. As far back as Amy could remember that was his spot night or day. Even before she came to live here she always knew that was where he'd be if he wasn't working. All his life he'd been a fan of the tabloids and she could see a bundle of them in the newspaper rack by his chair.

Nuala loved her home. She kept a neat and ordered house and nothing was ever out of its place. There was never an item required that wasn't to hand. Each thing was in the same place as it was yesterday and the day before and in the same condition it was in twenty years ago. Nuala and Maurice received wedding presents that were still good enough for daily use.

Amy looked around at the tiling with the overflowing fruit bowls painted on them. The formica countertops were in pristine condition. Pottery bowls and pots added splashes of homely colour to the shelves and worktops. Pots of green plants lined the window ledge, drooping over the sink. The ceiling was low and kept the heat in the room, which sometimes caused the temperature to rise to a stifling high.

Every spring, regardless of what else might be going on in the world, certain things had to be done in the Devine household. The chimney was swept, the painting was done and all the carpets were cleaned from top to bottom of the house.

When every visible area in the house was shipshape, Nuala turned her attention elsewhere. First the garage got the works and then the attic. She turned these over, getting rid of rubbish and clutter and tenderly going over old memories and keepsakes. For two or three days in April Nuala sat with endless cups of tea going cold around her. She looked through old photograph albums and ran her fingers over old dresses herself and Kitty used to wear. Half the job of clearing the attic occurred within the confines of Nuala's mind. The ghosts of the people she loved were waiting there under the eaves for her to join them. Along with them she explored old memories and wandered down old avenues, keeping alive the past and clearing the way for a future yet to unfold.

As the years rolled on routine seemed to have completely taken over the running of the household. It operated in perfect military precision. The two elder Devines worked their days silently side by side. They pruned out the unnecessary small talk and operated within zones, so that each had full responsibility for a particular area. There was no overlapping; time wasn't frittered away and the future for them seemed to have been and gone.

Amy looked around sadly and wondered where they would use that banked time.

They hadn't had a holiday in over fifteen years. Each one had their night out every week. Nuala went out with her friend Moira on a Thursday. Maurice went out with the lads on Friday. The rest of the week they spent consumed by their everyday life in all its mundane colours.

Nuala and her friend Moira met every week for a

pizza and then on to the pub at the bottom of Main Street. Once there had been four in their group – Nuala, Moira, Kitty and Gemma Lynch – but it was just Nuala and Moira now. Nuala still had a framed photo of the girls on the mantelpiece in her sitting-room. In the photo Kitty was the centre of the group, a blonde angel in the midst of her dark sisters. A friend took it on a night out in the seventies. They were standing in the doorway of Molloys', all with long hair down over their shoulders, in long skirts and peasant shirts. Nuala had told Amy that they'd carefully arranged that look. Mark Molloy took the photo. They knew beforehand that he would have the camera so they'd all synchronised their outfits. A moment preserved for eternity. The girls all flicked their hair over the same shoulder and with a large smile on each face they flirted with the camera. It stood there now in memory of Kitty and Gemma.

In Ballyreid, Molloys' was a local landmark. The same people had drunk in that pub for the last forty years. It was a fact that everyone in the pub had known each other since childhood. The decor inside hadn't changed since 1980. Nuala remembered vividly when it happened. The pub closed for a week for refurbishment. For that week the gang met in Browns' across the street and the next week they were all excited as they headed back across the road to see what the new look would be. Nuala said it took a while to get the feel back.

All the regulars arrived at their own designated

times. Everyone knew that Nuala and her friends would arrive in between eight and eight fifteen.

Jim Bradley would arrive as usual at nine o'clock after having a quick one with his brother in Browns'. Eileen Owen would come in a few minutes afterwards and sit with him at the bar. They'd been doing this since leaving school in 1969. They'd both married in the interim and the two couples spent their time in the same spot until Eileen's husband died in a crash and Jim's wife left for England with a monk. Many a night's conversation in Molloys' had revolved around that topic. The two of them still sat side by side in the bar, deep in conversation, but you wouldn't see Jim sitting in church on Sunday.

In 1990 Barry Dunne had a car accident on the way into town on a Thursday night. Help came within an hour. Nobody doubted the reason why – they knew he survived because his friend Rob was his cards partner on a Thursday and he'd never miss a game without getting word to him first. For ten years the boys played forty-five at the low table in the corner by the cigarette machine. The night of the crash Rob got the car and drove the route Barry would normally take to get to the village. He saw where the car went off the road. He ran to a neighbour's house just down the road and called the local doctor and the ambulance. A lot could be said for routine, he'd often said afterwards at the bar. With froth on his moustache and a tear in his eye, he looked at the man beside him who'd been his closest friend since childhood. Nobody needed clarification; they all knew exactly what he meant.

Nuala had always been a Molloys' girl but Maurice went to Browns'. Marriage hadn't changed that. Friday morning and Saturday were the only times full of talk in the house as both recounted the local gossip they'd picked up in the pub.

Browns' changed regularly over the years, but Maurice always said with pleasure that "the old bandits" still stood in the same place on a Friday night. They stood in the little snug off to the right of the front door, watching the changing faces of the youth of Ballyreid as they congregated in the remainder of the pub. It was the combination of regularity and change that kept Maurice coming back. He had his cronies to drink and gossip with and the rest of the village to watch. Every Friday night someone had come back for the weekend or left for England or America. Maurice noticed the destinations were getting more exotic by the year. Last Friday he'd been talking to young Rory, Gary Brown's son, who had come back from Vietnam. No one ever went there until recently. Maurice found the young people fascinating.

Now Amy looked fondly at him as he sat there, his toes twitching in his wool socks and his lined face concentrating on his paper. Ballyreid was another world to her but one she suddenly realised she missed.

She turned her attention to helping Nuala get the food on the table. Nuala's head bowed low as she stirred a saucepan on the stove. She was daydreaming into the bubbles. Amy put a protective arm around her shoulder. Nuala turned her face towards her and there were tears in her eyes.

"Nuala, are you all right?"

"I was just thinking about your mother. I loved her: she was my sister. We always thought our daughters would grow up together."

Tears were sliding off her nose. Amy didn't like to mention they were splashing on the edge of the saucepan. She didn't know what to say.

"I lost my sister and my daughter and it hurts so much. Really hurts. Especially when I don't know what happened to Ruth. I had her for twenty-two years before she was taken from me. Sometimes it's like she was just a dream." Nuala sniffed and a few extra tears landed in the pot.

Amy felt low as she stood there beside her aunt knowing what she now knew. Nuala's first reaction would be to rush to the police and then they might never get the rest of the story. Maybe that was the way to go. There could be fingerprints and DNA on those pages and on the envelope, evidence that Amy was destroying as she read through them. Amy had never felt so guilty.

"Nuala, I'll finish up. You go get ready for tea."

Nuala gave her a watery smile and a pat on the arm. "You're a good girl, you know." Amy smiled back, feeling like a hypocrite, and continued with the stirring.

At dinner each person sitting at the table examined their plates with the intensity of a biological experiment. They cut the food and delicately loaded it on to their cutlery. Then they paused for a second, savouring the smell before placing it in their mouths. Then the whole experience began again.

The atmosphere was as loaded as their forks and silence hung above the table like a canopy. The sound of the clock permeated their thoughts, joined by the sparking of the stove and now by the clicking of knives and forks on crockery. In the background, if you paused long enough and concentrated, you could hear the breathing and chewing motions of the eaters as they diligently found an alternative to speech.

Amy was painfully aware that they had nothing to say to each other. She looked over at her aunt as she played with a piece of carrot on her plate. It was as if a wall had built up around her and none of them could get inside. She was in there with her thoughts of Ruth and Kitty. They were shut off from her.

Maurice seemed to have resigned himself to this silence. He just sat there quietly eating as though this was normal. Had it been like this since Ruth disappeared?

There was an intake of breath as one of them tried to think of something to say to bridge the gap. But the breath was released and with it came a resumption of silence.

The meal lasted about twenty minutes. The longest twenty minutes of their lives. It was as if they were paralysed. The ringing of the phone finally broke the silence. Nuala jumped and practically knocked over her chair in her desperation for some outside conversation. She walked to the phone and grabbed the receiver.

"Hello? Devines'." A look of surprise tinged with interest spread over her face.

"Amy, it's for you." She turned to Amy and held out the phone.

Amy looked even more surprised but, grateful for the interruption, she quickly got up, walked over to her aunt and took the phone.

"Hello?"

There was only silence.

"Hello?" she said again.

Amy trembled. She knew it was the writer. She didn't want to call out too loudly.

"Hello?" she said again.

Her eyes fell on the open curtains of the window over the sink. She stared at the black hole. A tingling down her spine told her that someone was out there watching her. She could tell by the silence and lack of a ring tone that someone was listening to her on the other end and she was sure that whoever it was, he was watching her also.

Amy decided to put down the phone.

"Goodbye, Amy," a muffled voice spoke to her.

Amy said nothing. She knew the shake in her voice would reveal her fear. Palpitations started in her chest.

The momentary pause continued and then a laugh erupted from the receiver.

"I have to go now." Amy heard her voice as if it were from someone else's throat.

"I'm having dinner. I'll talk to you later."

The line went dead in her hand.

Almost in a trance, Amy put down the phone.

She turned slowly and walked back over to the table. Nuala had stepped out of the room but Maurice was watching her with interest.

"Someone from work," she lied. "Checking to see if I've arrived safely."

She looked at him and saw the open honest expression on his face, unaware of the secret she was keeping from him.

Nuala came back and sat down at the table.

"Someone from work looking for Amy." Maurice relayed Amy's statement to her.

Nuala spoke directly to her for the first time since they had started dinner. "You've only just got here. They should give you some peace."

Amy flinched. "They don't make a habit of it." She had no idea why she was defending work when they hadn't even called in the first place but something about Nuala's accusing tone grated on her sometimes. Even in little things she seemed to have turned into this person with a need to express blame. "Don't be so defensive." Nuala frowned and went back to her dinner, clearly annoyed at this prickly girl who refused to let her into her life.

Maurice sat there, looking as if there were words sitting on the tip of his tongue but they had got stuck.

Amy knew now she was in way over her head. If

that was the writer he had their landline number and could have been out there looking into her face, listening to her voice as she looked at a blank window. Keeping this secret could be the biggest mistake she'd ever made.

Chapter 13

The next morning the rain was still drizzling but the heavy wind had stopped. Amy lay on her side watching the apple tree outside her window dripping water onto the waterlogged ground beneath. It was over an hour since she'd heard Nuala get up. She didn't want to get anyone's back up by lying too long in bed but she couldn't face them yet. Her mind was tortured by what she had allowed to happen to herself. The writer must be thrilled. The two cousins had walked right into his plans like flies onto sticky paper, without question.

Amy wasn't like Ruth had been. She wasn't a twenty-two-year-old student just out into the world. Amy helped run the Dublin division of an international corporation. She was the youngest person the company had ever placed in that position. Amy had always been a Type A personality. She won her scholarship to the States when she was seventeen and had her MBA by the time she was twenty-seven, finishing at the top of her class with a 4.0 GPA. Career-wise, the last eight years had been nothing short of meteoric. She didn't make mistakes.

She groaned out loud at her stupidity now. She knew why she'd done it, why she had come here. She wanted the manuscript, yes, but she also wanted to know more about this family. She had been thrown out and here was a chance to see what was going on without her. Maybe she needed to see a little bit of what she'd missed.

She wondered if the stalker was someone she knew? Could he have been in her circle over the last few weeks or months?

She thought back over the first part of the manuscript, the murder of Sinéad Daly. She ran her mind over the Irish murders she could remember over the last fifteen years. She couldn't recall that one. Maybe she should look up some information on it. It would at least give her something to do.

She threw back the bedclothes and swung her feet onto the mat. It was time to face her relatives.

After breakfast she helped her aunt to wash up and clean the kitchen, then she took another cup of tea to the stove and sat on the couch that always stood in front of it.

"Amy, you can't just sit around all day. Take my car and go to the village or go into Dungarvan."

"I'll walk to the village. I need to go to the library."

Nuala started to laugh. "Honey, you've been in the

city far too long. Ballyreid hasn't got a library. You'll have to go into Dungarvan."

"Okay." She raised an eyebrow. "I suppose there isn't an internet café either?"

Nuala laughed again. "None in Ballyreid. Dungarvan."

"I'll go to Dungarvan then." Amy had everything she needed on her doorstep in Dublin.

Nuala handed her the keys for her Ford Fiesta.

"What if you need the car?" asked Amy.

"I'll borrow Maurice's. Go."

Amy was delighted to get out of the house. She had to do something about the manuscript, even something useless, just to feel active.

The library was on the quay in the town. Amy parked the car in the Tesco car park and walked the short distance there. The tide was in fully and the boats moored in the bay bobbed gently with the lapping waves. The wind was strengthening as it blew in from the sea. Amy stood for a moment on the edge of the quay, watching the various boats as they danced together.

Inside the library she sat at an empty terminal and switched on the screen. Not knowing what on earth she was looking for, she searched through reams of information on Irish murders. Sinéad's case popped up again and again but as she read through the information Amy had a sick feeling in the pit of her stomach. She'd expected to find an unsolved crime but with enough information profiling the type of man who might have committed it to give her an inkling of who it might be. Considering he probably was already in her life somewhere, she felt that with even the smallest nugget of information she could pick him out. Instead she found a closed case. Sinéad Daly had also been from Dublin. She grew up in Terenure in quite a wealthy family. No wonder they met in Bushy Park. It was just up the road for her. A homeless man who frequently slept in the park had been charged with her murder and found guilty. Apparently he was in possession of the knife when they found him. Amy searched but she couldn't find any reference to him now. Did the writer just pretend to carry out this murder as a starting point for his manuscript? If that were the case it was quite possible that he'd made up the whole thing. But there was a lot of detail in there that couldn't be gleaned from the Internet. Maybe he really was just a writer who had interviewed a lot of people for his book. No! That night, the night she arrived at Ruth's house, couldn't have come from anyone else. Amy never talked about it because she was too embarrassed and she assumed Ruth wouldn't either, as it didn't show her in a very good light. No! He'd got away with two murders. Sinéad Daly and Ruth Devine. Amy felt ill and wanted to go back to the house and lie down. But Nuala wouldn't approve. Coffee might prop her up for a while.

She decided against Dungarvan and instead went back to Ballyreid to the local coffee shop. It had been a long time since she'd been there.

She stood outside, looking at the coffee shop door. Moira, Nuala and Kitty's friend, owned it. Would she recognise her?

"The coffee is good." A voice spoke from behind her.

Amy turned to see a man over six feet tall with brown hair and a bright smile standing there. For a moment she felt herself go pale. Was it the writer finally making himself known to her?

"Are you all right?"

"Yes. I'm fine. I just haven't been in there in a long time." Amy spoke with hesitation.

"Well, I've lived here for over ten years and I don't think it's changed since then. So I think you're safe."

"Thanks." Amy turned towards the door.

"Hey!"

Amy looked at him. Moira's was straight opposite the police station and Amy couldn't stop her eyes from darting in that direction.

"Can I buy you a coffee?"

She thought for a moment. "Okay," she cautiously agreed.

"Great!" He smiled back at her and held her gaze for a moment.

Amy actually felt a blush creeping up her neck. That was something that hadn't happened for a long time. His smile deepened and so did her blush.

"Come on!" He opened the door and stepped back to let her enter.

Amy felt a tingle up her spine. She felt like turning

and running back out again when Moira came hurtling across the shop at her, her arms stretched wide, and hugged her tightly. She was taller than Amy and built like a shot putter. Amy was afraid her ribs would crack as she squeezed her. Amy was still in shape but she was nothing on Moira.

"Amy! Oh my! I heard you were down. Nuala was on the phone this morning. She told me she'd sent you into Dungarvan and I thought I'd never get to see you. Sit down, pet! I haven't seen you since you were *that* big!"

How big is "that big", Amy wondered?

"How's Dublin? And you've done up Irene's house and you're living in it. I was there years ago. It's a beautiful house, isn't it? It's a bit big for one person. It was certainly too big for Irene. I hear she let it go to rack and ruin. Your grandmother was born there so I suppose it's nice to see it still in the family. How's your job going?"

It seemed to be quick-fire questions with Moira. She never waited for any answers, just bustled about letting you know she cared enough to ask.

She still had Amy's hand held as she talked.

"Here, pet, sit down."

It was the window seat. She cleared the table and talked at the same time. Amy still hadn't had a chance to say anything and her new friend was just trailing along behind.

"Anyway, my love," Moira said, finally stepping back, "what can I get you?" Then she looked at the man and laughed. "Sorry, Brian! I'm not ignoring you but I see you every day. This girlie I haven't seen for twelve years or more."

Brian looked at her and smiled as he sat down. He obviously knew there was no need to answer as Moira was on to the next topic before you gathered your thoughts. On she went, and then somewhere in the middle of it all she'd got their order and was bustling back behind the counter. Neither of them spoke as they watched her pour coffee. There was no point. An interruption was inevitable. When they were served their coffee and had started eating the chocolate biscuits they hadn't ordered but Moira insisted they have, she moved on. They knew she would leave them alone now and go on to the next customer.

"I love her," Amy said. "She's like a whirlwind. She's one of my aunt's oldest friends. They grew up next door to each other here in the town."

"I know." He laughed. "I know Maurice and Nuala well."

"How did you know who my aunt is?"

"She's the only Nuala I know who's close to Moira. Anyway, Miss Devine, tell me about yourself."

Amy laughed. "This is like a job interview. You know my name and my aunt and uncle so I think you know enough."

"Not nearly enough. How come we don't see you around here more often?"

Amy hesitated. He had such an easygoing friendly personality but there was a probing quality to his questions that was a bit disconcerting.

"I live in Dublin."

"I can tell by the Dublin 4 accent."

"I don't speak like that."

"Yes, Miss Devine, you do."

Amy laughed. She knew that she had a hint of a Dublin accent. She had lived there since she was eight so it was hardly a surprise. However, the posh tones of the south Dublin suburb with the Dublin 4 postcode was something she'd tried to avoid. She tried to pinpoint where her caller's accent came from but it was quite bland and not particularly strong. The muffled quality of the voice made it difficult to analyse.

Amy didn't want to tell Brian what she did for a living. If he already thought she had a fancy accent, then what would he think of her job title? Amy had never thought like this before. She'd always been proud of her achievements.

"Why are you so serious?" he asked.

"I'm usually not. I just have a lot on my mind. Tell me about you, Brian."

"Em . . . I work across the street."

Amy suddenly realised he was having the same problem. The building across the street was the police station.

"You're a guard."

"I am." He looked uncomfortable now.

Was this an omen? The first person she'd spoken to in Ballyreid turned out to be a guard. He should have been the first person she spoke to when she arrived. Then she had a thought.

"You said you've been here ten years."

"Yes."

She could tell by his face that he knew exactly what she was getting to. "So you investigated Ruth's disappearance."

"Well, it was earlier than that she disappeared and I wasn't in charge then. But I did work on part of the investigation. You know yourself, for a long time afterwards there would be the occasional appeal and we would follow with some new line of questioning but it never amounted to anything. It tore your aunt and uncle apart. They never got over it."

"Was there ever a clear suspect?" Amy hoped to gain some insight into this.

"At one point. Yes. But he disappeared shortly afterwards too." Brian looked very uncomfortable and immediately checked to see where Moira was.

"Who was he?"

He lowered his voice. "Moira's son Philip."

"Moira's *son*?" Amy was shocked.

"Nuala came to us and put him forward as a suspect but we really didn't think he was. He was an alcoholic and was too drunk most of the time to have taken the body and have it never found. Kill her on the street – yes! And walk off. That would be more his style. He was checked him out thoroughly and a buddy gave him an alibi."

Amy thought back to the manuscript. The man who killed Sinéad did that. According to the manuscript he killed her in a park and just walked away.

"He was just the town drunk. We don't think it was him."

"But where did he go afterwards?"

"Who knows?" Brian seemed bored now with the subject. "Were you and Ruth close?"

"When we were little but not as we grew up." Well, Brian, thanks for the coffee but I should go home and have my lunch."

"What did I tell you, you posh Dublin person? It's called dinner around here."

Amy laughed as she stood up. "It can't be dinner at midday. It's too early for wine and I need a bottle with my dinner."

"I'll remember that." He stood and his eyes twinkled down into hers.

She noted that fact carefully. Being five eight herself it was a nice fact that he was a little taller. Considering why she was here, she was nuts to even consider a date with someone in the force, especially one who actually worked on her cousin's case, yet she heard herself say "Yes."

As she left she looked into the watchful eyes of Moira who winked at her while she poured coffee for a couple across the room. Amy knew that by the time she got home her coffee with Brian would be common knowledge. She wondered if it was common knowledge that Nuala had got the police to check out Philip Lennon as her daughter's kidnapper.

Amy walked back to the car and climbed inside as a light rain was falling. This morning had taken an unexpected turn. With the back of her hand she wiped the fog off the window and put the car into first gear. As she turned on the wipers a blur streaked across her vision. A large brown envelope was pressed under the wipers on the passenger side. She jumped out of the car, looking around at the people walking on both sides of the street but nobody looked in any way unusual. Amy pulled the envelope from under the wiper. The ink was just starting to run with the rain and the envelope was torn where the wiper had dragged it across the windscreen. Amy immediately recognised the handwriting on the front.

Chapter 14

Amy raced through her lunch that afternoon but nobody seemed to notice. Nuala was going out and Maurice had a ton of work to do on the farm. Amy offered to do the washing-up to get rid of them faster. As soon as the last dish was on the draining rack she retired to her room.

Now she might get some information that she could finally take to the police. As she pulled the sheaf of paper from the envelope, a bunch of photographs tumbled out as well. There were three in all. She lined them up on the bedspread. They were dated on the back. The first one was taken four months ago. Amy immediately recognised it. In it she was having dinner with some work colleagues in a restaurant on Stephen's Green. So he was watching her four months ago. The second one was a month later. She was shopping in Marks and Spencer's on Grafton Street on her lunch break. She could date it even without him writing on the back because she remembered the suit she wore that day. It only ever came out of the wardrobe for very special occasions. That day she'd had an important meeting. The third one sent shock waves down her spine. It showed her in her own garden pruning a hedge. He really had been into every part of her world for at least four months.

And now he was in Ballyreid. Was he staying locally? Maybe in a guesthouse? Or did he live in the area? Putting the questions aside for a moment she opened the manuscript and started reading.

Thank you, Amy, for accepting my invitation to come back to Ballyreid. Standing in the howling wind and swirling rain last night, watching you all, I felt exhilarated beyond anything I thought I could ever be. I wore a warm jacket and a black knitted cap snugly pressed down on my head. The chill was severe and was threatening to freeze the blood supply in my face.

It was like watching TV. I could see the Devines sitting at the dinner table, engrossed in their food, examining each piece as if it held the cure for AIDS. The dialogue was minimal but the effect was staggering. It was like a ringside seat in the Novelty Family of the Week Show. For a brief second I thought I should check the controls. It was as though the screen had frozen on me. No, there they went again, heads bobbing towards their plate, arms rising in slow motion to meet them; first the old man, then the old woman and then you, Amy. So you could function together as a family, the Devines. The Devine Comedy! You should hear me laugh when I thought of that.

Amy, you were looking a bit pale and tired. I hope you are taking care of yourself. You're like Ruth. You spend too long on your own. That can't be good for anyone. It will erode and undermine everything in your life to have no one to share it with. I know that for a fact. I have nobody. I feel so alone sometimes. The pain had come back and was starting to burn inside before I met you, Amy.

That pain. It was physical but I knew it wasn't a physical disorder. It was a physical manifestation of a psychological yearning. I smile when I say that. I've become so self-aware. I've always floated in outer space since being a young boy. It felt as if gravity had released its grip on me a long time ago and left me hovering over the ground just before the wind took me away, watching other people from above and beyond. It really felt like an out-of-body experience.

That was until I met you, Amy. You grounded me with a bang that day I saw you on the television. If I hadn't been so scared, so out of practice in communicating, I would have walked right up to you in Dublin and introduced myself. Not as the man who took your cousin but as a man in my own right. But then what? A quick fling or maybe a slow one over a week or two and then we would have gone our separate ways, because nothing lasts for me.

This way I can lay a foundation and prepare the

ground. This way we can truly know each other, really form a connection. When we come together it will be like a spiritual union of souls.

Tonight, Amy, without even stopping to restrain myself and ask questions I pulled my mobile out of my pocket. I knew it was dangerous. Maybe I was taking too many steps at once. To preserve some level of privacy I switched off the ID on my phone. But it's not registered to me anyway. I dialled your number. Simple people unaware of the existence of danger, your relatives would never think of having their number unlisted of course.

I watched Aunty rise from the table and go to the counter. It was a bit strange watching her walk in my direction and pick up the phone.

"Hello? Devines'."

At first I was taken aback with the bright greeting from this quiet-looking woman. "Hi, Mrs Devine. Can I speak to Amy, please?"

I waited what seemed like an eternity as you rose from your place and walked straight towards me to pick up the phone.

By now I no longer felt the cold. My hands were warm and my face flushed. A trickle of sweat was running down my back.

"Hello."

Your voice flowed into my ear. Your voice is a bit huskier than I remembered it to be. The shock of this left me momentarily speechless. Perhaps the stress is getting to you.

"Hello," you said again.

The second hello brought me thumping back to reality.

"Hello?"

As we spoke it was as though the distance between us had halved. I stepped back in case you could see me. I was excited and fearful when you looked straight at the window. I was looking at you and you were looking right back. You will see my face in time and make journeys deep into my eyes, straight into the depths of my soul. I have so much there to show you.

When you placed the phone back on its base I watched you move as you walked back to the table. I could see the tension in your steps, your shoulders echoing the knowledge that my eyes were following the curves of your body.

You sat down and looked at your relatives. From the look on your face and the angle of their heads you were explaining me away as a work colleague.

I knew I was flirting a bit too openly with danger tonight. Anyone could have seen me.

Keeping to the shadow of the hedge I walked back out to the road so I could get home. It was way too wet anyway. As I walked away a noise disturbed me and I turned back.

The old man appeared at the back door, letting out the dog. I saw you standing anxiously by his side. Your voice carried across the garden telling your uncle it was too cold and wet for the dog, but that you would wait until the mutt finished and that he should go back inside. Were you afraid the big bad wolf would steal your uncle? How sweet of you to stand there and protect him.

"I'll wait with you, pet." I heard his dull voice and saw him place his arm around your shoulders.

You stood side by side as the dog squatted on the lawn. When he'd wiped his feet he did a little trot around and circled the bush where I'd been standing and started to follow my scent towards the road. I stood poised, ready to grab the thing if he came near me. I couldn't possibly be caught by a *dog*. But then you called him back and he came back with a stubborn backward glance at the path, trying to see the owner of that smell.

I watched transfixed as darkness once again enveloped your garden and marvelled at the narrowness of my escape from detection. The nearness of you all had heightened an instinct in me of which I was only starting to become aware. It was like I sensed you all about to get up from the table and had known I had to be just beyond the reaching fingers of the light when the door opened.

When I was younger I lit a bonfire in the back garden of my house in Dublin. It was Halloween. All the other kids in the area did the same but they had the big communal fire. I liked my own private fire away from the others. I stood and watched it and felt a sense of power stirring in me, seeing the dry wood catch fire and throw sparks up into the air. As the heat grew and the singing of the burning wood got louder the feelings inside me reached a crescendo.

I stood there in the glow, watching a cat circling the

blaze. It walked just on the rim of the fire, barely visible against mottled shadows on the lawn. I was transfixed by the glow in the cat's eyes and the stealth of its movements. Suddenly the cat pounced on a shadow. My untrained eye saw nothing except the shadow of the flame but the cat had a wiggling mouse in his jaws. He sat there on the edge of the glow with the mouse getting weaker in his mouth. His tail swished a powerful swish and his intense green eyes continued to stare with unwavering focus into the glow.

To this day I've never forgotten that moment. Never forgotten the thrill of seeing a real hunter at work. Seeing his prey brought down and weakened in his grasp while he stared with awe at the most beautiful, powerful thing he'd ever seen. He had the process of the kill worked to such precision he barely had to take his eyes off the fire. I felt like that cat tonight circling your fire, standing just out of your gaze. If you concentrated, if you really looked you might see me circling but I knew you wouldn't – that kind of skill was for the likes of me and the cat. The true skill of the hunt is ours alone. I smiled walking away from your property, a smile of joy. I walked to my car parked on the brow of the hill, sat into it and turned the key. The engine sparked to life and I drove away. I feel so connected to you now.

His words stung her as she worked her way painfully through them. His language was getting more intimate. With a new sense of fear and urgency Amy wanted to find something so she could contact the police with some definite information in order to get this guy. Inside, the fear that she may have let him too deeply into her world whispered in her gut and a growing sense of trepidation was consuming her. Yet she was still compelled to read on. Once more she picked up the pages.

You are now where Ruth was fifteen years ago. What better way to show you what happened than to put you in the exact same place where she was then? Do you feel the uncertainty of being at home when suddenly your life is in turmoil and you can't tell anyone why? Do you feel the oppressiveness of knowing everyone is watching you grow more uncertain every day?

Ruth too lay in bed in Ballyreid and tried to make sense of what was happening to her. Her body felt heavier than she could ever remember. She couldn't keep her eyes open. Being at home should have made her feel safe.

She knew it was unforgivable the way she left you standing out on the street. She felt so guilty about the way she was treating you. There was no basis for it. She certainly would never grow fond of you, but even to her the persecution was starting to grate. For an uncomfortable moment she started to wonder what it must have been like for you to lose everything so young and be forced into living with relatives who didn't want you. If that had been me, she thought, knocking at her door, there is no way she would have left me outside.

The tender way you worded the letter you'd sent and your hopes that maybe you could try to be friends for Nuala's sake was pressing on her conscience. She felt you didn't deserve that. When you stood on the footpath outside her door looking up at the window she almost sobbed out loud but that would have robbed her of the last shred of dignity she had left. The invasion of her home had given her an inkling of how you must have felt when you lost yours.

Ruth was in school the day she heard about her aunt and uncle's crash. They brought her home early in case the rumours spreading around the yard upset her. She couldn't get Aunty Kitty's face out of her head. Kitty was the most important person in her world next to her mum. She was tall like you and had the shiniest eyes she'd ever seen. Her hair was always like a halo of sunshine. At least it seemed like that in her memory.

Ruth remembered Kitty's laugh – it was the most infectious thing about her. She would get totally carried away laughing until there were tears in her eyes. After a few minutes everyone in the room would be laughing with her. Kitty was everyone's pride and joy. She was the family treasure.

Kitty doted on her little niece Ruth. Being the first baby in the family, she got everyone's undivided attention. Ruth still had a picture pasted on the inside of her wardrobe door, of Kitty holding her tightly in her arms and giving her chubby cheek a kiss. "A plaster!" she used to say and burst out laughing at the little girl pretending to rub it away. The ritual was always the same, Kitty would plant the big noisy plaster on her cheek and Ruth would wipe it away and go "Ugh! Spit!". Then they would all roar with laughter and Kitty would scoop her into her arms again.

Thinking about Kitty made her very sad. Ruth was almost as old then as Kitty had been when she died. She had seemed so grown up: a real woman. Now when Ruth looked back at the pictures Kitty was just a girl.

James, on the other hand, appeared sterner. He laughed a lot with the adults but he didn't have the same way with children as his wife did. He seemed to resent anybody who took Kitty's attention away from him. The most enduring memory Ruth had of the day they died was of her sneaking over first thing to kiss Kitty goodbye. Ruth walked into the yard and saw Granny at the dairy door holding your hand. You had a fixation at the time with the calves so she assumed Granny must have been bringing you in to say hello to them. In hindsight she thought that Granny knew there was a storm brewing and took you out so you wouldn't witness an argument.

Ruth walked into the house but there was no one in the kitchen. She walked through and into the hall and poked her head around the sitting-room door but there was no one there either. She could hear raised voices in the back bedroom, James and Kitty's room. Ruth was six years old and privacy wasn't an issue for her. She strode down the hall to the partially open bedroom door.

She placed her hand on the handle and was just about to enter when James raised his voice and Kitty started to cry. Ruth was scared by the angry voice so she halted at the door.

Kitty sobbed. "Darling! I don't want to go this weekend. It's Ruth's birthday and your mother wants a party for the children. Amy will be so excited."

"For pity's sake, woman, it's only a weekend. Ruth will have fifty more birthdays and Amy will be excited many more times in her life."

"I feel bad not being there for a family event."

"What event? She's six years old."

Kitty's voice was starting to rise. "You resent the children, don't you?"

"You're obsessed with them! One's not even yours. Amy is only four. She's got my mother pecking around her like a hen all the time. Surely you can spare me some time occasionally?"

"James!" Kitty was shocked. "She's my baby. She's so little and she needs me. What will you be like when we have a second one?"

James's voice lowered an octave and he spoke

calmly. "There won't be another. I've told you that. Sometimes I'm sorry we had any."

"You shit!" Kitty shouted.

Then suddenly Ruth heard a sharp yell of pain from Kitty and the room went silent except for Kitty's sobbing.

Ruth started to cry and crept away up the hall as the sound of Kitty's sobs drifted into the background.

She never ever repeated this conversation to anyone. She knew it would break your heart. Even at her most vicious she knew she'd be opening a door she could never come back through if she said anything. Apart from you, her mother would be devastated to know how sad her sister's married life had been.

Looking back at the conversation, it still upset Ruth. As she got older she started to read more into it – more than she'd been old enough to understand at the time. Kitty had a perfect place in her memory but James took on the appearance of evil. You adored your daddy even though Ruth knew he had barely spent any time with you. You were just too little to remember beyond the final goodbye on the steps. That was firm in your memory because people kept repeating it to you.

Ruth felt in her heart they'd been fighting when the car went off the road. That was the cause of the crash and their deaths. If Ruth hadn't demanded so much of Kitty's time, she would be alive today. She would be heading to Molloys' every week with

Nuala and Moira or going to Dublin to spend the day shopping with you.

The night before the trip to Clare, Ruth had begged Kitty to be there for her party. Kitty hugged her. "Maybe, baby!" she said with a giggle. "We'll see what we can do about switching weekends and going to Clare next week."

Ruth wondered if guilt played a part in the despicable way she treated you over the years. Of course there was also anger and jealousy that Kitty loved her little daughter more than she'd loved Ruth. Ruth just couldn't let that happen with her own mother. You were so lovable, you see, as a little girl. She could see that, when she looked at old photos. Ruth had to get you out of her space so she wouldn't have to compete *with Kitty's daughter.*

Ruth curled into the foetal position and bunched her pillow up into a ball in her arms, then buried her face deep into it. You could always tell immediately, even with your eyes closed, that you were home. The smell of fresh air, sunshine and drizzle wafted up into her nostrils from the pillowcase. In Nuala's house you got clean sheets once a week and clean pillowcases twice a week. The smell was like balm for Ruth's shattered soul. Breathing it in, she could feel all the little pieces of her life moving around trying to get back together.

Chapter 15

Amy sat on the floor with her head in her hands as huge sobs shook her body. Everything she'd ever believed in had come tumbling down around her. The man that Ruth spoke of in her diary was nothing like the man she remembered as Daddy. In her mind James was strong and dependable and her life was always the worse for not having those qualities in it. Her mother was vivacious, fun-loving and beautiful and every day she kept this image in her brain as the role model she craved. Their love story was the example of everything she wished her life would bring. She had compared every relationship she'd ever had to theirs and they were always lacking the luminosity she saw in her parents' love story. Amy had always believed they were two young people deeply in love and just starting off in life. Two people who had that journey shortened. Now it might all have been lies, a fairy tale spun to comfort a grieving little girl. Her world was rocked today. She was too shaken to question the source of the information but, though she knew he was probably wording his writing for maximum pain and effect, there must be a grain of truth in it. The fact that it was possible that any part of her memories might be fiction tainted everything.

Finally, too exhausted to cry any more she lay on the bed and dozed.

When she awoke thirty minutes later the worried face of Nuala was looking down on her.

"Are you all right, Amy? Is something the matter?"

"No. I'm just tired." Amy pushed her pillow off the bed, covering the sheaf of papers lying on the mat beside it.

"Well, your dinner is ready."

Amy noticed that immediately after she said she was just tired Nuala's expression had changed from concern to disapproval.

"Thanks, Nuala. I'll be up in a minute."

Amy tried hard to pull herself together before going to join Nuala and Maurice. Thinking back over the writer's words, she also remembered her feelings as she stood out there in the yard. It all came back to her, the tone of his voice, the fear watching Peter sniffing down the path. Standing there with Maurice by her side, knowing he was in the yard watching them, was unbearable. She felt scared for this family. In Dublin she hadn't taken this seriously. Amy was so used to taking control and fixing everything herself that she'd assumed she'd just read a few pages, come up with a solution and a fifteen-year-old mystery might be solved. Back then it seemed like her problem. Nuala would be livid if she knew that her niece had information which might possibly help them to find out what happened to her only daughter. Then she thought of her new friend Brian who had more or less started his career on her cousin's disappearance. What would he think of a grown woman who was more interested in finding out what other people thought of her, than helping the police solve a crime? She had really screwed everything up. If she went to them now she'd have to explain to everyone how self-centred she was. They would have perhaps lost valuable evidence that might have helped to catch him.

Then, Amy had another thought. Ruth went to the crime scene of Sinéad Daly's murder. According to the manuscript the garda who spoke to Ruth took down her details. Would they not have thought it a coincidence that Ruth's name appeared in such a strange way in another case? But knowing what she knew from the manuscript, it was a coincidence, a macabre connection between a victim and her murderer. He committed the crime but he couldn't have known that the object of his affection would jump on a bus to Dublin and check out the crime scene. Ruth could never have thought, as she took the bus to Dublin, that the scene she was going to could be the precursor to her own. Perhaps the note in the police notebook of Ruth Devine's trip to the crime scene just got lost. Such things do happen. You read about them all the time. Connections that should have been made but never were.

Straight after lunch Amy excused herself and went for a walk, taking her folder with her. She couldn't spend all day in her room or Nuala would really get annoyed with her. She had a couple of choices in finding a place to continue reading. There was the coffee shop but she risked Moira asking her too many questions. She decided she'd go to Molloys' pub. It had three rooms and a snug so there was bound to be a little corner somewhere where she could spread out her papers and read in peace. The day was bright and cold, the perfect afternoon for a walk. The village was quiet as she walked through.

Inside Molloys' there were a couple of old regulars sitting at the bar and the rest of the place was empty. Amy ordered a glass of Heineken and, finding the snug completely empty, decided to slip in there. Being a sucker for order she separated the pages, placing the half she had read neatly to her left hand with the ones she hadn't read yet at her right hand. The page she was reading was held in her right hand leaving her left hand free to pick up her beer. When she was satisfied that she was prepared for reading, she took a moment to look around her and let the silence of the bar calm her down. After a few minutes of this ritual she turned her eyes to the page still held in her hand and started to read.

On the first word she was interrupted. Initially her thoughts turned to anger so she turned irritated eyes on the newcomer.

Brian stood there in uniform.

She bundled the papers together and stuffed them into her folder.

"Did I disturb you?"

"No." She was an unconvincing liar.

"I saw you walk by so I took a look out to see where you went to. I had a break coming up."

"Great." There was hint of sarcasm in her tone despite her attempt to be normal.

"I did disturb you," he said. "I'll keep going."

Amy felt terrible. She really didn't want the police anywhere near her but as a man he was very nice and she didn't want to be rude.

"No! Really. Stay." She stood up as she spoke to get the barman's attention. "I'll get you a pint to say sorry."

"No. It's tempting but I'm on duty."

She started to laugh. "We wouldn't want to see the local constabulary intoxicated in the early afternoon!"

"I'll just blame the blow-in from Dublin. I've had a spotless reputation up to now."

Amy ordered him a mug of coffee and a Kit Kat as a peace offering and sat back down.

"You made me look into some old files yesterday," he said.

"Did I?" Amy was cautious.

"Yes, your cousin's case. I wanted to familiarise myself with the details. I'm the sergeant here now and I don't like having unsolveds on my books."

"I'm sure." Despite her questions yesterday, today she couldn't be any more non-committal.

He turned towards her with a definite look of

suspicion on his face. "I've never heard anyone take that reserved attitude to a family member's disappearance before. We have your aunt and uncle checking in a couple times a year trying to get a fresh look at the case. Each time there's a television mention of cold cases they're in here telling me I'm not doing enough and the police just don't care."

"So why wait until now to start doing something? I hope you're not doing *me* any outrageous favours." Amy could feel her hackles rising.

He stared at her in bewilderment and stood up. "No. I just think it's about time we did something more for Nuala and Maurice. Well, Amy, I just wanted to talk to you. If I am going back to this case any personal relationship between me and you would be a conflict of interest."

"It certainly would be a conflict of interest – that is, if there were any possibility of a *'relationship'*." She found herself using air quotes, something she never did and hated with a passion. "So obviously we won't be having dinner either." Amy felt like crying, completely thrown by how angry she was feeling for no good reason that she could see.

"Right then. I'll see you around." His eyes hardened and he turned as the barman arrived with the coffee. Brian took the Kit Kat and a large gulp out of the black coffee, then walked off without looking back.

"He was in a hurry!" The barman left again with the coffee, smirking to himself, while Amy glared across the room after him.

Why had she been so angry with Brian? It was panic. If he was revisiting the case then she was obligated to hand over her manuscript to him. She was withholding valuable information, not only on Ruth's case but also on that poor man held for Sinéad Daly's murder.

But Amy felt that the man feeding her this information was the only link between her and what her parents were really like. Also she wanted to know what Ruth really felt about her. Even that was strange. Why on earth should it matter to her now, what Ruth came to think about her in her adult life? Amy had suffered a much deeper scar at the banishment from her childhood home and the cruelty of her cousin than she'd ever realised. With the same reverence as before she took out the manuscript, smoothed out the pages and rearranged them in the same way. She ordered another glass of beer because she'd gulped down the last one in temper. When she'd calmed down once more, she went back to her reading.

As you can see, at this time Ruth was an open wound. She was terrified and depressed and in this volatile state I pushed too far. I watched her too closely. Every place she went I was there so it was bound to happen that she would finally recognise me. It wasn't until back in Ballyreid but it was still a little ahead of my schedule.

Ruth went into Powers' pub for a drink and sat at

the fireplace. I came in behind her, confident that she wouldn't have a clue I was there. She stayed for about an hour just gazing into the fireplace, complete in her own world, not interested in talking to any one. I couldn't take my eyes off her but I did have to be discreet so I chatted away to the guys at the bar. Sometimes I was just watching her reflection in the mirror behind the register. Do you remember that mirror? The old girls used it to keep a discreet eye on their customers.

Finally, Ruth got up to leave and brought her glass to the counter, placing it just beside me. I didn't look at her but she saw me. Back in my original environment the penny dropped and straight away recognition lit her face. I nearly fell off the stool in my excitement but I had to maintain my composure and act as calmly as I could. I sensed immediately that she would latch onto anyone then who could be her friend. I offered to buy her a drink for old time's sake. Not that we were drinking beer at ten and fourteen but you know what I mean. She quickly agreed to drink with me.

We took our drinks and sat back at the fireplace, reminiscing about the good old days. Then she told me about college and her house. She never mentioned any of her fears or anything of the goings-on in her life over the previous months. I wished she would. It would have been lovely to be her confidant.

God. I throbbed with excitement sitting there in the pub, holding her hand when she flirtatiously reached out as we talked. It hurt when she pulled it back but I knew it was fear. She wasn't an expert at flirting. If we could only have time to get to know each other, she'd hold my hand and never take it away. She didn't know me well enough yet to trust me. She would realise in time that I was her saviour. I would protect her from harm.

I never wanted to hurt Ruth. I never wanted to hurt anyone. The situation with Sinéad caught me by surprise. I thought she was just a silly little twit with a crush on me. At the time I thought there was no harm in indulging that a little. I certainly wasn't expecting the nasty streak she had. One day on the train to Dublin I thought it would be safe to casually ask her if she knew Ruth Devine. I wasn't prepared for all that woman-scorned business. She latched onto my thoughts like lockjaw. She laughed at me having a crush on the geek. That's what they called Ruth in the class because she always sat at the front and kept to herself. I just saw red.

With her spiteful little face all screwed up she mocked me and made fun of Ruth. Then she threatened to tell Ruth that I had a crush on her.

I couldn't have that. I couldn't let her ruin everything by running with tales to Ruth at this stage. God knows what she would have said.

"Ruth has her head in those stupid crime books all day – she's such a freak," her voice droned on in the background.

I let her talk herself out but I had a plan to ensure

my future with Ruth. Sinéad wasn't going to stand in my way.

I couldn't get this incident out of my head. It was just a matter of time before she spoke to Ruth or told one of her friends. Either way it was inevitable that it would get back to Ruth eventually and she would start to join the dots. So I arranged to meet her in Bushy Park and talk to her. She thought it was a date. From the first moment she had flirted with me and used all her little-girl charms to reel me in. We walked and she talked until we got to the waterfall. By now she was totally comfortable with me and convinced I was under her spell. We stopped by the waterfall and she leaned forward to kiss me. I kissed her, holding her tightly against me and then looked down into her face. Her expression went from flirtation to surprise and then to pain in three distinct steps. The thrust of the knife in her flesh was firmer than I thought it would be. It had bothered me when I thought about it. Would this be easy? Now I knew. It was firm, a little push, but easy as I'd missed the bones. I thought I would have panicked and ruined everything if I'd hit bone. I wanted it to be one neat stab and then leave. The idea of metal on bone made my teeth clench. I've always been a bit squeamish. But I had to do it right. That was important.

For a moment I held the knife but she was sort of suspended on it so I let it go. She was small, but heavy as a dead weight. Her body fell in slow motion. There was still sufficient life in her legs to allow her to sink gracefully to the gravel path, onto her knees and then face down in the small stones with a soft crunch. Her hair, the colour of corn, fell to one side and her left cheek was exposed to the rain.

It made me sad. I brushed my fingers over her cold skin. Her cheek curved like a small child and her blue eye stared without sight into the wet path. I took the sight from that blue eye, an eye that saw everything.

Roughly I rubbed the lipstick off her pouting lips. Her face had a clown-like look to it now with a red smear like a gash cutting to her ear. I rearranged her clothes and her hair. I didn't want to degrade her.

I stood back and imagined what it would look like tomorrow when they found her. It would have been wonderful to be there when they did. I walked away, looking over my shoulder until she was out of sight. It was almost fully dark now. I looked at my watch. Damn it! I'd missed the bus and I was going into town. I turned my collar up against the driving rain and hurried out of the park. Now I was going to have to walk.

Chapter 16

Amy's heart was thumping. This was a confession. But of course all this information was probably in the papers. Would the gardaí just think that he was a fantasist? Every case had its own share of those.

Powers' was the pub just down the road from the Devines' house. In fact the yard in the back of the pub bordered their yard. It was always Amy's favourite the odd time she did make it down to Ballyreid. The present structure was over a hundred years old and built around an older tavern. One side of the room had chairs surrounding an open fireplace while the other side housed the bar. At one stage of its evolution it seemed to have been a sitting-room and many of the residential features were still visible.

Over the fireplace hung an old crane. Like an arm it rested across the fireplace with cooking pots suspended from it, reminiscent of the olden days when the maid would have bent over the fire tending to the pots, ladling soups and stews for hungry passers-by.

Two women ran the pub, Elsie and Mary Power. Elsie was the mother. Amy supposed her to be around ninety. She didn't work much in the pub those days unless it was very quiet. She sat at the window in a wicker chair and kept an eye on things, more for entertainment than for surveillance purposes. Little happened there that passed her by. Even when she slept she had the uncanny ability to open her eyes at just the right moment.

Powers' was possibly the least intimate pub in Ireland. You couldn't find a quiet corner there for a chat. It was a square space with chairs positioned around the sides of the room facing into the bar so it was impossible to cut yourself off from the rest of the customers. Anyone who drank in Powers' at the bar, conversing with the regulars, had to be very well known in there indeed.

So Ruth trusted him and started a conversation with him when she was returning her glass. In the environment of Powers' she recognised him.

Amy was convinced that he would have come up on the radar screen after Ruth's disappearance and must have been questioned. There was no way that the Powers wouldn't have come forward with that information in an investigation.

She was elated. She was possibly moments from finding out who he was, without having to go to the police. She would go straight to Powers' immediately and ask the two women about that conversation. They were bound to remember it.

She gathered her belongings again and rushed out the door of Molloys'. The rain had started to fall heavily and a wind was whipping up so she walked quickly. It only took her a few minutes to get to Powers'. As she approached it she looked with dismay at the sign over the entrance. A brand new sign said *Devereaux*. Nobody had told her the pub had changed hands. When she walked down to the village she just took it for granted that nothing had changed and didn't even look up at the sign. With a sinking feeling she walked through the pub doors into the bar. Immediately she knew she was wasting her time.

The pub was about twice the size it had been the last time she saw it. Knocking the wall behind, which had separated the pub from the storeroom, had extended the bar. There was a television silently displaying football in the far corner and a loud stereo playing from behind the new bar. Amy didn't like their taste.

A man in or around thirty stood at the till, counting the day's takings. Amy was devastated. Not only was a huge chunk of her childhood memories torn out and replaced with this modern monstrosity but it looked like she might have to suck lemons and speak to Brian after all.

She looked to where the old fireplace had been. It was built over now and a padded booth was against that wall. You would never even guess that a fireplace had once stood there and always with a fire roaring up the wide stone chimney. Elsie had always sat at the window. She was small and thin yet you would never see her near the fire. Perhaps she could keep a better eye on everything from her window. Maybe the older generation just had warmer blood.

Warmer blood or not, she'd looked as if they drained the blood from her body years ago. Her skin was a pale yellow colour and thin as parchment. The blue veins in her temples were visible. Her eyes were like black beads piercing through the lenses of her wire-rimmed glasses. There was no television in the pub no matter what the occasion.

There was no music either. Elsie always said the thing about music was everyone had different tastes and some had no taste at all. So the only time the old radio played was in the early morning when Mary and Eileen Bowe cleaned the bar. For many years they religiously tuned into the *Gay Byrne Hour*. Eileen's mother had written to his show a few times about various disputes she had in the town and just the mention of Gay sorted it out. But this was a different generation, they always lamented sadly.

The only sound above the talkers in the pub was the ticking of the old pendulum clock and the crackling timber in the fireplace. It certainly wasn't the place for a quiet gossip unless you whispered. You could hear every last word anybody uttered. Sometimes people would just sit and stare into the flames, their thoughts running through their heads, oblivious to the other conversation in the background. It was the most peaceful place on earth.

"Can I help you?" The man behind the bar had

become aware of the woman standing by the door staring at the chair by the wall.

"Hi. I was just surprised. I haven't been in here in about fifteen years."

"Oh. You remember when the place was called Powers'. We have a lot of people coming in here looking for the old pub."

"How long has it been Devereaux'?"

"About seven years now, I would say. I bought it off Mary Power's nephew."

"Her nephew?" Amy had never heard of a nephew.

"Yes. The old woman Elsie died and it was a bit much for Mary. She took in some help for a couple of years but then she passed on and the nephew inherited it."

"Where did this nephew come from?" Amy was still shocked at losing the chance of getting the information she'd been hoping for.

"I don't know. He was from away some place. I'm sure you remember the women weren't much for talking about their personal lives. I think he sold it almost as soon as he got it. Do you want a drink?"

Amy had turned and left the pub while he was getting the question out. Could this mystery man be the nephew? That would explain how he could sit by the bar and not cause any raised eyebrows. The manuscript didn't say whether Elsie was alive at that time. Maybe Elsie and Mary hadn't said anything about Ruth's friendship with him if he was their nephew. But how could Ruth have recognised him?

Amy knew she would have to go to the police soon.

Chapter 17

That night after they'd had their tea, Amy on impulse went to close the curtains.

"Have you gone mad, Amy?" said Nuala. "Why are you closing the curtains? You know I like those open."

"Why?" Amy asked.

"Amy! I just do, leave them. Where did all this paranoia come from? Last night you didn't want to let the dog out alone and now you're afraid to leave the curtains open."

"Okay. Leave them open. I forgot where I was. I always close mine in Dublin."

"Well, you're not in Dublin now. A stray cow is about all you'll find looking in windows around here."

Amy knew differently. She knew he could be outside right now watching their every move. For the tenth time that day she told herself she had no right to keep her secret from them.

"When did Powers' become Devereaux'?" she asked, trying to sound conversational.

"About seven years ago, I would think." Nuala was about to go back to her book.

"Who bought it?" Amy looked at her with wide-eyed innocence.

"Luke Devereaux. He's from Dungarvan."

"I met him today – at least I assume it was him – he seems nice enough." Amy was still fishing as inconspicuously as she could.

"He's an insolent little pup. He's ruined that pub. It's got very loud on a Friday night. It keeps Maurice awake if we leave the window open. You know we're only a few hundred yards from it but there's no talking to him."

"Yes. It's very different all right. You'd only barely recognise it. Why did he buy it?"

"I suppose he just saw it up for sale." Nuala was getting bored with the conversation.

"Sure he knew the bar well," said Maurice from his corner.

"You're right." Nuala looked at him.

Amy waited patiently for them to tell her why he was right. Conversation with them was like pulling teeth.

Maurice continued. "He worked there after Elsie died. He helped Mary with the bar on weekends when he was in college. I think he studied hospitality. Liam Grady that owns the supermarket is his uncle so he used to stay out with them. Ruth and himself were friends at one time too, I think."

Nuala suddenly looked interested. "That's right, they were, weren't they?

"A little," said Maurice. "I think she was in secondary school with his sister."

"That's right," Nuala said again.

Amy was about to let the subject drop there when she remembered Mary Power's nephew.

"Did Mary Power have a nephew?"

Nuala and Maurice looked at each other.

"What?" Amy noted the conspiratorial look on their faces.

"You know him."

Amy twisted on the spot, her eyes on stalks. "I do?"

"Yes."

"Brian Poole," said Maurice.

"Brian?" This was a name she hadn't expected to pop up in this line of questioning.

"Yes. He was her husband's nephew but Mary stayed very close to him despite her marriage ending."

"I hear you had a coffee with our good sergeant." Nuala smiled at her.

"Moira didn't waste any time spreading it around, did she?" Amy sounded cranky and she couldn't pinpoint why.

Brian was a guard so he couldn't have been a student when Ruth disappeared. Or was he lying about the timeframes? But why didn't Mr Devereaux just tell her the nephew was the local guard? Typical country place, keeping secrets that weren't even necessary to keep.

"So what's the harm in that?" said Nuala with a frown.

"I'm not used to people sticking their beaks in my business," Amy retorted.

"Sticking their beaks!" Nuala's voice rose in temper and Amy had seldom seen her so angry. "This is a small community, Miss, and if you spend time here you can respect that people are just showing a well-intentioned interest."

"I'm sorry." Amy suddenly wanted to get away from them and think. "I'm going to bed."

"Fine."

Nuala was upset with her and Amy didn't blame her. She came to visit and Nuala was under the impression it was to improve family relations but instead Amy came and floated around the house, full of woes and mystery, in Nuala's view looking down her nose at their community.

Maurice looked up again. "There was post for you today. A big envelope."

Amy's heart leapt. She had to stifle her sense of annoyance. "Oh. Where is it?"

"In your room."

"When did that arrive?"

"This afternoon. It must have been hand-delivered while we were out." Maurice went back to his newspaper.

"What time was that?" Amy wanted to shake him.

"Why are you here?"

Nuala's question threw her. "What?"

"Why are you here? It's obviously not to spend time with us. I'm not stupid." Her voice broke as her eyes locked into Amy's. "You're so like your mother. When she stopped confiding in me she became very like you are now – secretive."

Amy remembered back to the manuscript and what it said about her parents' fights.

"She stopped confiding in you? What do you mean? You were both so close."

Nuala swallowed. She'd opened the door. Now she was sorry. There was a long pause while she collected her thoughts.

"Your parents were having problems."

Maurice spoke up. "There's no need to dredge up the past."

Nuala turned flashing eyes on him. "No need when it's your family I'm exposing!"

"Nuala. Please. I have to know what happened." Amy was afraid Nuala would stop talking but Nuala seemed to have been waiting a long time to get this off her chest.

As she started speaking Maurice got up and left the room.

"James was jealous of anyone who spent time with Kitty. He gradually started cutting her off from everyone. For months before she died he'd stopped her going to Molloys' with us. Any time I rang or went up to the house Kitty wouldn't come out. He'd give me a message from her. Your grandmother covered it up. She'd never admit that anything was going on in that house. She hoped if she ignored it perhaps it would all go away. But I saw the bruises. Kitty had bruises on her wrists one day when I picked her up from work. Another time I met her walking on the road and I saw a nasty bruise on her neck. It looked like a handprint. I begged her to tell me what was going on but she used to laugh and say everything was fine."

Amy was shaking. She remembered her daddy. This wasn't the man she knew at all. When she read Ruth's words in the manuscript she hoped it was a mistake or a lie or a misinterpretation of Ruth's words, by him.

"Nuala. I remember my father. He wasn't like that."

"Honey, you were only four years old. Kitty kept it all away from you. Your grandmother, in fairness to her, adored you. She would have died before she ever let you know your daddy was a cruel bastard."

Tears started streaming down Amy's face and she had to walk to Maurice's chair and sit down. She couldn't look at Nuala as she talked by the fire. Instead she just let her words drift through the air behind her like the narrator of a play.

"As you got older and were taking up more of Kitty's time, James deeply resented you and spent less time with you. That was why they were going to Clare that weekend. Kitty loved children and wanted lots. Ruth and herself were very close. James could make adults stay away because Kitty complied with him – but not Ruth. She could be very devious and she made it her business to see Kitty every day whether he said she could or not. She'd sneak up through the fields and wait until he left the house and then she'd go into the house and talk to Kitty. I encouraged it because Kitty needed someone to care for her and a little girl was better than nobody. That weekend was Ruth's birthday and she wanted Kitty to be her guest of honour. Ruth had totally wound you up so that you were as excited as she was. James took Kitty away to punish Ruth and Kitty for sneaking around behind his back."

"Did Ruth know at six about all of this?" Amy needed to be careful how she worded her questions.

"Not the details. Not the bruises or the controlling. I just know she was aware that the atmosphere was different when James was there. She was too little to know anything else."

"I don't remember any of it. I thought my father loved me." Amy was trembling.

"I know, darling. I'm sorry to tell you all this. Maybe I shouldn't have."

"Did he love me at all, do you think?" Amy couldn't resist asking the question though inside her heart yearned for a lie.

"Not then. I think you were just the competition. But I think if they had survived that weekend there would have come a time when he would have realised what he threw away. I think he didn't understand children and he was very insecure about himself. I don't think he could believe his luck to have found a wife like Kitty and it was all my fault, all my fault they ever got together."

For a moment Nuala was too full of emotion to go on. Amy waited as she composed herself.

"When I fell in love with Maurice I encouraged Kitty to go out with James. She wasn't sure about him. I thought the idea of two brothers and two sisters was wonderful. I was the elder sister, wanting to see my little sister taken care of. They split a couple of times before the wedding. Kitty was too young and had way more in her future than James had. He knew that if she waited a couple of years they would never have got married because Kitty could have done so much better. But I pushed her. I saw to it that she got a good education and walked into a decent job and this was my final task in looking after her. As soon as they were married he was on a mission to get her pregnant and talked about nothing but babies and then when you were born he said he never wanted children. He said she'd manipulated him. He played mind games with her. He knew that in the seventies a woman with a small child in rural Ireland was trapped. He'd never lose her then."

"They were only in their twenties, weren't they?" Amy spoke softly, picturing them in her mind.

"Yes. Kitty was just twenty when they got married and twenty-two when she had you. It took quite a while for Kitty to get pregnant and this also upset James. Kitty told me before James separated us that he was worried about what the lads were saying. You know. James Devine not being able to get his wife pregnant. He heaved a sigh of relief when you appeared. You were evidence of his abilities in the bedroom."

At this point Amy started sobbing loudly and the spell they had been under broke and suddenly they were back in the kitchen with the clock ticking away in the background. Nuala saw how visibly upset her niece was and she knew the only reason she told her all this was selfishness. She wanted everyone to know that James Devine robbed her of her little sister. But she shouldn't have told his daughter, the woman who carried half his DNA and cherished memories of a man they all helped invent for her. Nuala found herself feeling disgust at her own selfishness.

"I'm sorry, Amy. Maybe I shouldn't have told you any of this."

"No. I don't think you should have. I'm going to bed, Nuala. I'll talk to you in the morning."

Amy turned and walked from the room, leaving a silent Nuala sitting alone by the fire.

Chapter 18

Amy felt her heart breaking into little pieces. Could it all have been a lie? Her beautiful mother was a dominated and abused wife. Her father was a controlling man who beat her and wished his daughter was never born. Her grandmother was complicit in the whole thing, enabling her son to carry on beating his wife. Ruth turned it all on Amy. She blamed her for the demise of her relationship with Kitty and then of trying to steal her mother. Now Nuala, one of the only blood relatives she had left, had ripped her heart out by destroying all she held sacred about her parents. Was a lie such a bad thing if it was the only thing left in your life which provided you with any comfort?

She sat on the bed and looked at the threads in her carpet. She felt very alone. There was nobody who she could talk to about any of this. When it came to the personal stuff there was nobody in her life who she was that comfortable with. Then she remembered her hand-delivered envelope.

Nuala had propped it on her dressing-table by the clock. The envelope was the same as all the others with the same writing on the front. There wasn't anything he could tell her tonight that could beat what she'd heard from Nuala. She carefully slit open the envelope, avoiding the gummed flap. This might provide the police with DNA evidence once she handed it all over. She held the envelope upside down and shook its contents onto the bed. There was the usual sheaf of papers and some more photographs. The photographs were dated in the same way as the others had been. The first was a photograph of Amy standing on the street just this morning, looking at the sign over Devereaux'. The second was Amy leaving the pub. The third one was Ruth looking directly into the camera. The look in her eyes shocked Amy. Amy didn't have many photos of her and none from this period in her life. It was obvious she was looking at him, directly into his face and she knew who he was. The fear was palpable even after more than a decade. She was sitting in an armchair in somebody's sitting-room, but not at home. The last photograph was one of Amy's parents. Amy had never seen it before. Where could he possibly have got that? She heard a knock on the door as she was looking at it. She shuffled the papers and photos under the pillow.

"Come in!" she called out.

Nuala opened the door and stood in the doorway. "I'm going to bed too, Amy. I just wanted to say goodnight."

"We said goodnight." Amy had a note of petulance in her voice.

"Amy. Please. I'm very sorry."

"Nuala, I could let it go if I thought you did it for my sake but you didn't. You were mad at me for not taking enough notice of you since I came down and you've been mad at my father for over thirty years. You didn't tell me because I needed to know – you were just lashing out, lashing out at a dead man. My good opinion of him was the last thing of his left to destroy. You didn't give a toss that you could destroy me with it."

"You're right. I am so angry with him but there's nothing I can do to him now. He's dead. I hated that you adored him so much when he wasn't the man you thought he was."

"Well, now I know. Do you feel better? I don't."

"No."

As they talked Nuala had walked into the room and stood closer to the bed. Amy noticed her eyes riveted to something on the floor. Amy looked down to see what it was. It was the photo of her parents. Nuala bent down and picked it up.

"Where did you get this?" Her voice was hard and cold.

Amy had never heard her speak like this before.

"I've had it for ages," she lied.

Nuala knew she was lying. She could see it instantly on her face. "No. No, you didn't. I had the only copy of that photograph and I gave it to Ruth. That photo was framed and in her room until she disappeared." Nuala's face was set in a hard mask.

"You must be mixing it up with another photograph."

"*I am not!*" She screamed the words, causing Amy to jump.

At once Maurice came running from his room to see what was happening.

"Nuala! Please leave her alone!"

Nuala turned to him. "Look at this photograph!"

Maurice walked across the room and reached for the photograph. Instantly he raised his eyes and looked into Amy's, a look of bewilderment evident there.

"Amy. This is Ruth's. It was listed as missing from her house after she disappeared."

"You're wrong. Ruth gave it to me. I visited her before she came home for Christmas that year. She gave it to me."

"You're lying!" Nuala's voice was rising again.

Maurice was still looking suspiciously at Amy. But he knew he wouldn't get anything out of her tonight.

"Nuala, let's go to bed. We can talk about it in the morning."

Nuala's face was wild with fear and shock. "You know something, don't you? You know something about her disappearance."

"No. I don't." Amy couldn't believe this had happened. "Nuala, how can you think that?"

"Amy, tomorrow we're going to the guards. I've been asking them for years to look into this case again and now I have a reason to do that."

"What reason?" Maurice hadn't kept up with Nuala's rapid thoughts.

But Amy had.

"We have a new suspect. She hated my Ruth. Why else did we have to send her away? Even as a child she hated her."

"Are you mad?" Maurice couldn't believe what he was hearing. "You know she had nothing to do with this. There's a simple explanation for this, isn't there, Amy?"

"Yes. Ruth gave it to me."

"That's a lie." Nuala spoke softly now, deflated after this shock.

"We'll talk in the morning," Maurice said. He led his wife from the room.

Amy was shell-shocked. How could she have been so stupid? She should have been more careful but even still she couldn't possibly have known the significance of the photograph. It was obviously very special to Nuala or she wouldn't have been so adamant after fifteen years that it was the same one. Amy understood why she was so upset but there was nothing she could do to help her. It was a lie she'd fallen into with no way of undoing it. Nuala was close to breaking and Amy was pushing her that little bit nearer.

How on earth did it come around to this? Her aunt suspected her of being involved in Ruth's disappearance. It was the craziest thing she'd ever heard. But would anyone believe it? Tomorrow morning Nuala would haul her before Brian and tell him she suspected Amy stole her daughter. Would he see how ridiculous it was? She lay back on the bed and pulled the pages back out from under the pillow. She knew these held the answer to everything.

But she couldn't stay here. She knew she couldn't spend another night in this house. Ever since the first day she set foot inside this door it had brought her misery and heartache and this trip had caused all the old feelings to come pouring out once again. She waited until all the sounds in the house had died down and then got up and packed her belongings. She put the entire manuscript into her document case and then took one last look around her old room. No matter what he asked her to do from now on, she could never come back here.

She opened the back window, stepped out into the orchard and made her way to the road. Despite the fact that the Devines were in bed, the rest of the village was still up and about. Devereaux' was pumping rock music onto the street and Amy saw a cab pull up outside, leaving a bunch of guys in their late teens outside the door. As they paid their fare Amy stepped up to the driver's door and knocked on the window.

"Yes." He spoke with his head down as he counted the notes they had handed him.

"Can I go into Dungarvan?"

"Sure." He looked at Amy, taking her in from tip to toe.

Amy sat in the back, aware that his eyes never left her face. She was in no mood for confrontation so the only way she had of maintaining any control was to turn her face towards the dark window. As they left the village lights, the car became a cocoon of darkness relieved only by the dashboard lights in the front. Amy could feel the stirrings of a panic attack building up inside. She hadn't had one of those since she was a child. The driver certainly wouldn't break any speed limits. Slowly the car melted the distance between the village and the bigger town.

Then his oddly light voice broke the silence. "Where do you want me to drop you?"

"Em . . ." Amy hadn't a clue.

"Clock's ticking."

"Give me a minute."

"Usually my fares have a destination," his voice sneered at her.

Amy felt tears pricking her eyelids but as she looked around her trying to gather some composure she saw a sign for a bed and breakfast with a *"Vacancies"* sign hanging below it.

"Here. Drop me here. How much do I owe you?"

"Twenty-five euro."

Amy knew she was being ripped off and normally she would have argued but tonight she wasn't in the mood. Her aunt hated her and assumed she was a murderer and she'd found out her parents' wonderful marriage was all a lie. A few euros this way or that hardly made much of a difference.

As she got out of the car she looked at her watch and realised the time was coming up to midnight. There was a light on in a window to the right of the front door. Amy felt ashamed coming to a door this time of the night looking for shelter. She was running and she knew that they would see this immediately – but could they possibly think worse than the real thing? They would just assume she'd had a fight with her boyfriend.

With beating heart she knocked on the door. It took a moment for anyone to answer. Finally a woman opened the door and stood there with an instant smile of welcome, which froze the argument Amy was preparing.

"Come in." The smile widened and she stepped back to let Amy in.

Amy decided to work with her so she smiled back and stepped inside.

"Do you have a single room?"

"I do. For one night?"

"I might need to stay a few days if that's all right."

"I just need to check the book. Follow me."

Amy did as instructed and stood behind her at the hall desk and watched as she skimmed pages and checked dates.

"I have a room for three days but then it's booked – you'd need to move to another room if you want to stay longer."

"That's great." Relief rushed over Amy. The excitement of the night had finally worn her down and all she wanted to do was sleep. There was no way she could wade through that manuscript tonight. She took the keys from the woman and walked to her room, her footsteps becoming heavier with each movement. At last she could lock a door and the watchful eyes of Nuala Devine were off her.

Chapter 19

The next morning Amy woke confused and disorientated and with a taste of shame in her mouth that at first she couldn't place. Then it all came rushing back. She'd hidden the manuscript from Ruth's mother. Her aunt suspected her of murder and her father; her handsome father, resented the fact that she was ever born. Amy felt like she'd found herself in an alternate universe. As she dressed after her shower she realised how hungry she was. Last night she'd forgotten about food. She really hoped this place gave a good breakfast. She needn't have worried. One full Irish and two slices of fresh soda bread and marmalade later and Amy was ready to face whatever the writer had in store for her.

Amy was just about to spread the pages on the bed when there was a knock on the door. Amy answered to a Polish girl in her early twenties, holding a box of cleaning supplies.

"Will I come back later?"

Amy was about to say yes when she suddenly thought she'd like some fresh air. She'd seen a small coffee shop on the quay the day she went to the library. That would be the perfect place to finish her reading. She grabbed her document case and her bag and left the house.

It was only a few minutes to the harbour. The tide was out today and the boats were stranded on mounds of sludge. Seagulls stepped daintily on their spindly legs, searching for treasures buried in the mud. Amy wished life was that simple. In this world she'd suddenly found herself in, she was finding mud amongst her treasures.

Inside, the coffee shop was quiet. It was too late for breakfast and not time yet for lunch. She chose a table just inside the door and ordered a large black coffee.

The minutes ticked by as she sat there. Nuala wasn't here, she'd found a place to stay, she'd had her breakfast, the cleaners couldn't disturb her and she had a cup of very good coffee. Amy was out of excuses and there was nothing but fear of what else she was going to find out about her family stopping her from diving into these pages and finally getting to the end of the mystery. Amy had to arm herself with more information before Nuala sent the police after her so she finally gathered her courage and opened the manuscript.

So Ruth and I had finally made contact and you can see why I had to get rid of Sinéad. So much depended on Ruth never hearing Sinéad's venom.

After eight years we sat in Powers' talking and laughing together like we were kids again. I had the sound of her laugh in my ears and the image of her face burned in my brain. I watched that face for months from a distance but that night I looked at it up close. I'd seen the little frown lines knit her brow when an unbidden thought entered her head and the look of relief when a light comment from me made her laugh and chase it away. I wanted to walk her home but I didn't want anyone in the pub thinking we were anything more than two people who met casually in the local to discuss some childhood memories.

That night after she left the pub, Ruth walked home and stood outside looking at the light in the kitchen window. She wanted to collect her thoughts before she went inside. She had received ten calls from me earlier that night. So you can imagine my shock when we met in the pub. I thought everyone must be able to read my mind. That was why I suggested we sit by the fire. I didn't want too much notice from Elsie and Mary. They couldn't tell how I felt from the back of my head.

I hadn't thought I could talk to her yet so I just called her mobile and listened to her voice on the other end. Even though I never spoke she knew the calls had to have been from me. Wherever I was when I made the calls, Ruth knew it was totally silent. There couldn't be many places like that, places with absolutely no background noise. At first she hung up in fear, but then she found herself listening to the silence on the other end. She thought there would be sounds, any sounds that might indicate where I might be.

After a while she started to wonder what I was thinking there in the silence as she stood at the other end listening. This went on for a long time and then she started to shout, "Talk to me!" into the silence, but of course nothing happened. I couldn't talk to her when she was so upset.

After several of these calls she started to feel stupid. It was too silent. She started to think perhaps it was somebody genuinely trying to get through to her. Maybe their phone was broken. Perhaps when they tried to call they couldn't make a proper connection. To test if this were the case she started to tap out a series of Morse code on the back of the phone. I knew what she was doing so at first the silence continued until she was about to hang up. But this was turning into a funny little game. I decided to repeat the exact pattern of taps back to her from my side. At first she got such a shock she dropped the phone. I could hear it hit the ground. Then it disconnected. It was the first genuine proof for her that there was someone silently there on the other end. Almost straight away the phone rang again and she picked it up instantly. Once more she listened to the silence and then she tapped once. I tapped once. She tapped two together and then one alone and I did the same. This sounds crazy. Ruth thought I could be crazy. She didn't know who I was, didn't know what I was capable of and here she was conversing with me by a series of taps. It was debatable which of us was the most out there.

All along I'd exploited her vulnerable spot, which was her isolation. Her fear made her accessible to me. Ruth's life had been a mess since she started back in college. Gradually, she deteriorated psychologically. During that autumn there were nights when she didn't sleep at all and days when she couldn't eat yet she feverishly ploughed her way through her college work and kept her house antiseptically clean. Ruth thought I'd read her words, been in her space and was possibly stalking her, yet here she was going along with me now as I made contact on the phone. Of course, I was starting to wonder if she enjoyed this in a perverse kind of way? Maybe she was just curious? Maybe anything was better than being totally alone.

Ruth opened the door of the house and went inside. Her parents were sitting there reading and watching television. Ruth stood for a moment and watched them. Would she ever find that? Find the peace they had in their lives? Ruth's parents didn't know that over the past couple of months at college she'd started attending a student counsellor. She was too ashamed to tell them. She didn't know anyone else who suffered from depression. Ruth had been brought up to believe that you just pulled yourself together. She had worried the first night I entered her room that I might have been part of her imagination.

For months her sleep disturbance had caused her high levels of anxiety until there were times when she didn't trust anyone around her. It was the stress of the college, she supposed. Her doctor gave her an appointment to visit a psychologist. During the appointment she told him that she hadn't slept in three days. She wanted pills but he said he'd prefer to get to the bottom of her anxieties. "Anxieties" was the word he used. She knew the cause of her main anxiety. It was that awful struggle during the moment when her body craved sleep and was shutting down, slipping into a sleep state. Immediately her mind manically sought college, cleaning, reading: anything to keep from the world of sleep. That moment when sleep finally caught her in its grasp was the worst. In that moment realisation of what was happening would hit her and she'd be propelled from her slumber like a shot from a gun. Ruth feared that place of darkness beyond the wall of sleep.

At home in Ballyreid Ruth went to bed early. It was the only place where sleep came fairly quickly. Her eyelids would get heavy and the sounds of the kitchen would slip farther and farther away. That night she kissed her parents on the forehead and said goodnight and made her way to her room. But old habits don't die out completely. Despite many times being on the verge of sleep she found herself losing her grip on repose each time.

Finally she was almost there when her sharp ears heard soft footsteps on the hall floor. She heard them stop outside her door. She was close to panic. Tears welled up in her eyes and her heart felt ready to explode.

Then a familiar voice whispered, "Ruth! Are you awake?"

Ruth silently sank back onto her pillow in relief. It was her mother. She must have stayed up late. The door opened, her mother's small feet padded across the room and she leaned down and kissed her daughter's forehead.

"Good night, darling."

Ruth groaned as though in her sleep and Nuala left the room. This was Ruth at that time. She was soaked in paranoia and under the care of a psychologist. Her family nor the police never found the diaries. I kept them to protect her. Some of her fears and worries were quite bizarre and it was obvious that she was heading in the direction of a breakdown.

Amy sat back on her chair and looked out the window at the marooned boats. The tide had turned since she'd come in and soon they would be bobbing again, straining for freedom on the water. The coffee shop was empty now and Amy was alone with her thoughts of Ruth.

Ruth had been seeing a psychologist. Why did he need to tell Amy that? What was his narrative building towards? He wouldn't take the trouble to compose and distribute this rhetoric to her if he didn't have a master plan in his mind. She sensed that she was being sucked into something that she might soon find to be beyond her control. This person was probably the reason that Ruth vanished and now he'd turned his attentions to her. The time was fast approaching when she would have to get help. She raised her head and gestured to the waiter to get her another coffee and while she waited she returned to the manuscript.

Chapter 20

The next morning, after another night's disturbed sleep, Ruth was feeling very low. She wanted to go for a walk but she knew her mother was on a mission after she presented her with a huge breakfast the moment she sat down.

"I'm not hungry." Ruth spoke as calmly as she could, hoping the normally bustling Nuala would go about her morning business and leave her alone.

But Nuala began a lecture on "the importance of a good breakfast".

Ruth could never handle interference and, when Nuala left the room for a moment, she grabbed her bag and Nuala's car keys and left, leaping into the Ford Fiesta and raising a bank of gravel as she accelerated out of the yard.

Ruth's instincts were like a homing pigeon's. When things got rough, she retreated to the sanctuary of Number 10, Convent Street. The number wasn't written on the door and the postman kept inadvertently leaving her post next door. Nobody visited her there and there was nothing on the door saying *Home of Ruth Devine*. It wasn't quite Number 10 Downing Street but she went back there every time she felt threatened, like a rabbit to a hole in the ground.

She turned the key in her lock and went inside. It was cold and a little musty after her trip home. The house missed her. Already there was an air of neglect. She walked around the house, opening windows, then grabbed a duster and dusted off ornaments and furniture. She pulled out her vacuum and within an hour it felt as though the house had straightened itself up and was looking the street in the eye again.

Um, I could murder a cup of tea, she thought, proudly looking around her. Tea: the Devine elixir of life. When she'd lit the fire she relaxed. She was so annoyed at her mother she momentarily forgot that here she had an intruder. She opened the biscuit barrel but there was nothing inside except a wrapper. She grabbed her purse and keys and ran around the corner to the shop. Mrs Dee was chatting to a customer so Ruth grabbed the biscuits and laid the money on the counter. She walked out of the shop and looked up and down the road but there was no one in sight. Her confidence was waning. She was a sitting duck here and she knew it. She hurried as fast as she could, without running. She let herself in and shut the door quickly behind her. Her heart pounded. She reassured herself that she was being silly. She boiled the kettle again and made herself another cup of tea. The first one lay cold and untouched on the counter. Taking her biscuits she went and sat on the couch and switched on the television. It was no use; her hands were shaking and she felt cold. She had the electric radiator on and she'd pulled her blankets closer around her but she still found herself shivering. The shivers came from the centre of her bones.

According to habit she flicked from one channel to another and then, when she got to the last one, she started the routine again. She settled on the news but it was all the same old bad news. She decided to lie down for a few minutes and listen to some music.

Ruth climbed the stairs but when she was halfway up she thought she would have to do something in case I came into the house when she was asleep. What could she do? Grabbing some thumbtacks she pinned two small wind-chimes over the front door and the back door. Then she placed two chairs under the handles. She was feeling silly but she thought better safe than sorry. Though she had been drawn into a form of communication through the phone calls, that was where she was drawing the line. Ruth couldn't explain it to herself but there was something seductive about a hidden force in her life but only as long as it stayed hidden. When she talked to herself in her head her internal dialogue told her that by acknowledging my presence and facing me head on she was minimising my power.

But alone like this she felt very exposed.

Her room was exactly as it had been before she went home. She scouted around but nothing looked even slightly out of place. She shut the curtains and crept into bed. She'd filled herself two hot water bottles for comfort and she was glad of them now. It was so cold. She held one in her arms and placed one at her feet. Gradually she calmed down. Warmth spread through her body.

Lying there, she worried. That morning she felt that Nuala was intimating that there was something wrong with her. If she'd known about the psychologist and the panic attacks she would be forcing her to come home. Nuala and Maurice owned fifty percent of her house. They had even started paying the mortgage full time to encourage her to go back to college. When she left school she had started to work in a local factory but Nuala and Maurice were both avid believers in further education. She wondered if they could force her to put her house on the market. Ruth's paranoia was escalating daily.

Ruth had never had a relationship. I don't think she had ever been sexually active. No one ever knew the circumstances surrounding her one and only sexual encounter. She still carried too much shame to talk about it. Ruth met him again once after she moved to Waterford. It was coming up to Christmas. She was shopping and he walked past with his wife and two small children. Gill Brown was the wife's name. Her father owned a small haulage firm. Her family had money and when Ruth knew her just a few years before she had been beautiful. Ruth had spent many years fixated on her. Now she hated him, but for some reason she hated his wife even more. The beautiful Gill was at least two stone overweight that day and her gorgeous smile had vanished. A mask of frown lines replaced the laughter. Perversely this gave Ruth some relief.

That day she watched them walk into Super Mac's. She would normally avoid fast food like the plague but she found herself following them at a discreet distance. They ordered and sat down at the front near the window. Ruth ordered coffee and sat as far away as she could and still see them. Gill spoke to the children. They screamed and complained continuously. He sat and looked out the window, ignoring his family. The only time he turned to them was when the little boy got up to run around. He grabbed him roughly and pushed him back onto the seat.

Ruth stood up and walked out the door. She felt dirty. He'd soiled her body and her life.

Ruth embraced order and rejected the arbitrary. She was rigid and stalwart in all areas of her life. I knew once I got closer to her that she was in the grips of an eating disorder. That was what grabbed her mother's attention when she came home that Christmas. Once she got a chance to spend time alone with her she could see that the baggy clothes hid the fragile body underneath. Since I'd started watching her she'd lost a lot of weight. Then there were the haunted eyes and the edgy body language. Yes. Nuala saw that there was a lot wrong in the world of her daughter. In only a few months, things had escalated considerably.

Ruth's attempts at control only got her deeper and deeper into a mire of loneliness. She couldn't go on like this. She slept. Sleep was her only real refuge these days since her doctor had finally relented and given her some sleeping tablets. It had become the safest place she had left.

At five o'clock the phone ringing downstairs wakened her. She was really tempted to ignore it but she knew it was her mother. Sleep was a wonder drug sometimes, a natural form of Prozac. During her nap all her anger had evaporated but she hated facing the groggy heaviness afterwards.

She picked up the phone and said a sleepy hello.

"Hi!" Nuala's voice answered. She sounded wary. "Are you okay?"

"Yes, I suppose I am. I'm sorry, Mum. I overreacted a bit."

"Just a bit!" Nuala laughed just to lighten the moment because Nuala wasn't amused. "You sound tired." She was trying to be concerned without getting her daughter's back up once more. She badly wanted to get her home again but she'd have to tread carefully.

"I was asleep."

"It's after getting dark."

"I'm sorry. I should have come back earlier with the car."

"Don't worry about the car. Come back now. But be careful – there's a black ice warning."

"Okay," Ruth concurred for once. Right now she didn't like the idea of being alone in the house. Ballyreid seemed like the safer option despite her mother's fussing. She suspected I did most of my wanderings under the cover of darkness. She wrote in her diary. *"Rats and monsters usually do."* I found this offensive but I knew she was under a lot of strain.

Before she left she did a final inventory of her house, putting everything in order and making sure it was all securely locked up. There were window locks on all the windows, installed by the previous occupants. Up until this Christmas she'd never actually used them. Waterford seemed like a safe town to her. Now she locked each one and put the safety lock on the front and back door. I would have to break in now and end the guessing game. She'd know for sure that she wasn't going mad.

She stood outside while she locked the front door. As she turned the key she got a creepy feeling between her shoulder blades. The hair on her neck stood up. She didn't need to turn around because she knew I was there. She tried in vain to maintain some composure. The last thing she wanted was a panic attack on her doorstep. Panting quietly, she slowly turned around.

Of course there was nobody in sight. The street was empty and very dark. Too dark. She knew something wasn't right. Then she realised the street light by her house was out. She looked up at the shattered glass. The fingers of panic were starting to massage her gut. The car was right under the light. I could be hiding under the car or worse still in the back. She was too scared to walk to the car so she just stood there like a stork on one leg trying to figure out what to do next. The last movie she'd seen was *Cape Fear* and at that time in her imagination my face was Robert De Niro's hiding under the car.

Then she heard footsteps approaching from her right. I watched her as she whirled sharply around. It was Mrs Dee and her husband. He always came to help her carry the takings from the shop. They tried to be discreet but everyone knew her large leather shoulder bag carried hundreds of pounds. They would walk the short distance to their car and drive to the AIB bank on the quay and deposit the money in the night safe. Miraculously, to that day not a penny had ever been taken from them. That was the kind of odds Ruth needed then.

Focusing her brightest smile on them, she greeted them cheerfully and they walked with her to the car. Babbling away, she inserted her key in the lock. They stood there, delighted at the friendly banter from the normally serious Ruth. They assumed an excellent Christmas must have been had in the Devine household that year. As they talked Ruth carefully examined the car. There was nobody inside. She turned quickly to her neighbours and reiterated how lovely it was to see them. Before they went out of range she hopped into the car. As soon as the door closed she snapped the button engaging the central locking. Only then did she heave a huge sigh of relief.

Ruth sat for a moment in the car, taking deep breaths to get herself calm enough to drive. Right now she thought she was in danger of a serious heart attack. She switched the engine on, put the car into gear and took another frightened look in the rear-view mirror to make sure I hadn't morphed myself in through the door or something equally daft. Finally relaxing enough to smile at herself, she turned to pull out from the kerb and there I was.

I was standing directly across the street from her, in the phone box once more with the lights out. For a heart-stopping moment we held each other's gaze though in the dark and in her tablet-induced daze she couldn't tell who I was. Then she accelerated out onto the street and drove as quickly as she could out of town. With her hands trembling, she had to slow a bit or she was in danger of crashing the car.

Amy took a break from her reading. Ruth had psychological problems, an eating disorder, and Nuala had been worried about her anxiety levels before she went missing. No wonder her aunt was so upset and so quick to blame anyone. Just like she did when Kitty died, Nuala probably blamed herself for not doing more to protect the people she loved. Did she really think that Amy could have caused all of this? No, Nuala was just lashing out and projecting her anger. Like she did when she told her niece about her parents' troubles, she was hurting so someone else had to be the cause.

Amy would have to find out something definitive soon to put an end to Nuala's torment. The Devines deserved to find a little peace.

Amy thought over what she'd just read. It scared her to see how close you could be to peril in your own space and be so unaware. Evil had walked in step with Ruth.

I watched her tail-lights turn towards the main road at the top of her street. At that speed she'd be home in about thirty minutes. Though terrified and aware of the black-ice warning she was driving way above the speed limit. She slowed down slightly as she left the town and entered the dark roads beyond its glow. The last thing she wanted was to crash.

As soon as Ruth left the street, I jumped in my car and followed. Knowing the road she'd take helped. I drove a little behind her so she wouldn't get spooked. Just as we were leaving Kilmeaden a Honda Civic pulled out in front of me and slowed to a crawl before gradually building up some speed again. The road was going into a bend so I couldn't overtake. I was going to lose her.

Suddenly and without warning the Civic passed her out on the bend. Another car was approaching from the other direction and the Civic had to pull back in quickly between Ruth and a car in front of her. She hit her brakes and her car spun around but unbelievably she did manage to keep it on the road. Honestly, Amy, I thought I'd lost her right there. It was a wide stretch of road with a good hard shoulder so she was able to pull right in and stop with her hazard lights on.

The Civic drove on so I stopped in a gateway and turned off my lights. We sat like this for an eternity. Then an idea came to me. I backed into the gateway in the dark in case she was watching me. Then, after a few minutes, I pulled out onto the road and drove back towards Kilmeaden. I would then drive back towards her. I wanted her to see my headlights coming from the village. If she saw a car turn on its lights on the hard shoulder and drive towards her it would just frighten her away.

In the village I pulled into the yard of the supermarket and turned before heading back out into traffic and driving back towards her. My heart was pounding because I didn't know if she'd still be there.

She was. I stopped in front of her and stepped out of my car. Her car door flew open and she jumped out.

She rushed to me. "God, I'm so glad to see you!"

Can you imagine how this felt? She was so glad to

see me. Ruth Devine was coming to me. She trusted me. I asked her what had happened as I checked out her car to make sure it was undamaged. It was fine, not a dent in it. I then turned my attention to her. Scraping the hair back off her forehead, I asked her if she was all right.

She was snow white. "I don't think I can drive home."

"I'll take you home." I couldn't believe my luck. Was this the triumphant feeling a spider felt when he welcomed a fly into his web?

"No," she said then. "I'm being silly."

"Not at all. You've had a fright."

She smiled widely at me. "I'm okay. No. Honestly, I'm fine." She seemed to be struggling with herself to maintain confidence.

"Of course you are."

It was like she became six inches taller the way she straightened up. It made me feel like a king to have been able to do that for her, to be needed by somebody. To be needed by Ruth.

"If you're sure." I smiled into her upturned face.

"Yes. I am." She smiled at me as she got back into her car.

"Hey, Ruth!"

"Yes." She pulled down her window.

"I'll drive behind you. I'd like to make sure you're okay."

"That would be great. Thanks." She wound up her window again against the biting frosty air and

201

turned her car back onto the road. Sitting there with her emergency lights still on, she waited for me to get into my car and signal to her that I was ready. Can you believe it? Less than an hour ago she was running from me terrified and now she was relieved that I was escorting her home. I felt so happy. I had the radio up full blast and I was singing along to something. I can't even tell you what the hell it was. I stayed with her as far as Ballyreid. I stopped in the main street of the village. Ruth stopped just up the road, got out and walked back. I wound down my window, shy now to be in her company. I couldn't meet her gaze. She didn't say much. She just touched my arm and said "Thank you." Then she turned and walked back to her car. I'm telling you, Amy, her walk was different, more confident. I felt good.

Amy was perplexed. At this point, despite their crazy beginning, this could have turned into a love story. No one need ever have known about the murder of Sinéad Daly. The State had provided him with the perfect scapegoat. He could have hidden all this from her. People's lives are full of secrets. Did Ruth find out about his past? Did he make a mistake? She was nearing the end of this section of the manuscript and he seemed to be skirting around what happened to Ruth.

Chapter 21

Amy, you must be wondering what I'm doing bringing you into this story. There are probably questions you're dying to ask. I'll help you with some information but obviously I'll need to keep some things to myself.

I've tried to give you a broader picture of what your cousin was like as an adult. Adulthood wasn't going to work out well for Ruth Devine. She was quite disturbed. She got it from both sides of her family, your family.

You know some of it now from reading my manuscript but your father was another prime candidate for psychiatric help. Maybe you've spoken to Nuala by now but I know she won't have told you the whole story. It's hard to completely shatter somebody's image of another, especially someone they love.

I think Nuala told Ruth a lot until she realised her

daughter might also be suffering from the family curse.

I got some of the story from Ruth's diary but most of it I gleaned from talking to people who knew your family, and you know Irish people – a hint of a scandal and they all want to jump in and tell you their own experience.

Nuala's mother was a local legend. You know she died when your mother was sixteen. The years prior to this were hell for the two girls. Nobody knew what was wrong with their mother and what to expect next from her. She was only in her forties when she developed symptoms. It was assumed it was early onset Alzheimer's disease though her memory wasn't seriously impaired. The progress was rapid until it became impossible for the two girls to take care of her. She needed to be watched around the clock.

Ruth asked her mother a lot of questions about the disease and spent a lot of time researching it when her own state of mind was deteriorating. She thought, and later her doctor agreed with her, that it was probably Pick's disease, a rare disease with many symptoms similar to Alzheimer's. He tried to reassure her that it wasn't hereditary.

Mrs Donnelly's daughters tried everything they could to hide it from the village but these things always get out. The two girls were very popular so out of respect for them people pretended not to notice.

One story told to me was this. About a year before your grandmother's death, the parish priest knocked at the Donnellys' door at three o'clock in the morning around Christmas to inform Nuala that her mother was trimming hedges in the church graveyard wearing a long white dress. A group of men leaving the pub had seen her and informed the priest. By the time they got to her she'd removed the dress and folded it on top of the trimmings. As they helped her back to the house she could be heard screeching in a coarse and harsh voice all over the village.

Nuala was devastated when her mother's behaviour got so extreme and eventually, for the sake of Kitty, she had to beg the local doctor to help her to get her mother into residential care. That was where your maternal grandmother died, in a residential home. Nuala started to panic when she saw Ruth's personality changing in front of her eyes. But it wasn't the same thing. Ruth was just depressed and trying to come to terms with life. Being starved of nutrients and sleep wasn't helping either. But Nuala didn't understand the whole situation, of course, and started fussing around her daughter.

Let's not forget the Devines. Your father's behaviour had been getting more paranoid and controlling almost daily in the year leading up to his death. His own brother Maurice had tried to get him help but he wouldn't have it. James knew about Mrs Donnelly's mental illness so he told everyone that

Kitty was the problem and she was driving him insane. I don't know how much of his problems Nuala has told you but other people have spoken to me of Kitty's secret trips to the accident and emergency, once with a cracked rib and once with a broken arm and cheekbone where he slammed her into a wall.

As Amy read this section she started to hyperventilate. She didn't know if it was the power of suggestion or a real memory but suddenly an image of her mother's beautiful face black and swollen appeared in her memory. A smell came with it. She tried to search her memory for the source of that smell but she couldn't find it. She closed her eyes and tried to force the memory. Her stomach knotted and she felt her panic attack deepening. She was only four when her parents died so this memory was obviously prior to that. Can you trust any memories that you have from that period in your life? It was no use. She couldn't capture the memory so she let it go and started back into his narration.

Ruth was terrified of not being able to control her world. A couple of days after the night I escorted her home, she moved back to Waterford. She promised her mother she'd eat more and take sufficient time from study. The second part of the

206

promise she kept. She took a complete break from study. I didn't see sight or sound of her for a couple of weeks at college so I started to get worried about her. I went to her garden and sat there all day watching for her but her house stood quietly mocking my vigil. I knew she hadn't left. I can't explain why but I knew she was at home. I thought if I went up to her door I could say I asked in Ballyreid where she lived as I wanted to see how she was. The first day I made that decision my courage ran out but the second day I knew I had no choice. There was still no sign of her.

I dressed carefully. I wore a nice jumper and jacket with blue jeans. I wanted to look like I made an effort but I also wanted to look casual. You might wonder why I cared about my clothes but these things do matter. In your job you must think likewise.

I approached the door and knocked loudly. There was no response. I stood back and looked up, knowing her fondness for checking out her visitors. Immediately I saw her pale thin face looking down at me. I smiled and waved as though unaware of how she looked. She waved back and gave a wan smile, then stepped back into the room. At first I thought she had just acknowledged a friendly face and gone straight back to bed.

I stood there in the cold, unsure of my next move. Then the door creaked open in front of me and her tiny form appeared in the opening. Honestly, Amy, I don't think she had eaten since she left Ballyreid. Her heavy black cardigan swung off her thin shoulders with a pair of baggy black leggings flapping underneath. I was shocked.

"Ruth!"

"Hi." She looked vacantly at me and smiled.

I knew instantly she was medicated. I don't know where she got her tablets from or what kind of irresponsible doctor would prescribe them.

"Hey, Ruthie." I spoke gently to her and followed her as she walked back into her house. "Are you all right?"

"Of course." She tried to laugh and make light of it but she was so edgy her face grimaced instead of smiling.

I led her to her couch and walked to the kitchen to make tea. The milk was sour and she was out of tea bags. I opened all her cupboards. They were stacked with tinned foods. She'd obviously been building up quite a collection over the previous months. There was no fresh food, no fruit and vegetables or any kind of meat. Her house was bitterly cold and mustiness had invaded it since the last time I'd been there.

I turned to her. "Ruth, are you hungry?"

She looked at me smiling. After a moment she remembered my question and shook her head. "I'm tired. I need some more sleep."

I was at a loss here. I didn't know what to do. I had never been in the company of someone in this state before.

"Don't go to bed, Ruth. Stay up with me."

She smiled at me again but shook her head. "Come back later when I wake up." She stood up to leave the room.

"Can I come too?"

She didn't answer, just walked up the stairs. I followed her. By the time I got to her room she was back in bed. Her curtains were pulled together and the room was shaded. Her bed was crumpled and unmade with clothes strewn all over the floor. The first time I'd been there just a few weeks ago that room was immaculate. I could tell her windows hadn't been opened in days. The air was stale. I couldn't let her stay there and die. I have no idea where she got them but she had two different types of sleeping tablet by her bed, on her locker, and a quantity of hash. Ruth had decided she was going to sleep for the winter but at her body weight this amount of narcotic could be disastrous. I made a quick decision.

"Ruth." I swung her legs off the bed and pulled her into a standing position. She resisted all the way but she hadn't the strength to stop me. "Come on, honey. You're coming home with me."

"No!" She started laughing.

"Yes, you are."

I let her sit on the edge of the bed while I packed a bag with enough clothes for a couple of days. As I'd waited on her doorstep I'd kept a sharp eye on the street to see if anyone saw me there but nobody had as far as I could see. Now I peeped between the curtains as Ruth had done and looked up and down the street but once again it was empty. Convent Road wasn't a main road so sometimes there wasn't a soul to be seen.

Placing my arm around her waist, I propped her up and walked her towards the stairs. I had to practically carry her down to the sitting-room. I let her sink onto the couch then I checked all the windows and doors to make sure they were locked. I used her keys to open the front door and take her out to my car. I'd parked it down the street a bit under an overhanging tree. The swaying branches concealed the muddy number plate and hopefully would make the colour of the car more difficult to remember as the evening shadows fell. I put her in the passenger seat, then locked the door and got into the car. She had already fallen back to sleep. Leaning her head against my shoulder, I buckled her safety belt.

That was the night she was reported missing. Nobody bothered to check on her when she was getting into this state but suddenly they were all over her house. According to the papers, about an hour after I left, her parents arrived and let themselves in. When they saw the state of the place they immediately got concerned. Nuala would have seen the drugs by her bed and the sour milk in the fridge.

Nuala and Maurice went to the police station in Ballybricken and made a missing person's report.

When I packed her bag I'd taken her diaries from

her wardrobe and that photo of your parents from her dressing-table. In case you were wondering where that came from.

I had to take her home with me. None of them had been much use to her. She would be safe with me on the farm.

Chapter 22

Amy's heart had started to race as she read through the last few pages. Now she was getting to what happened to her cousin. It all seemed so far-fetched. Amy had never heard about the drugs by her bedside. She wondered if Nuala and Maurice tampered with the evidence. Would they have discarded the drugs to protect the family image? To Amy it was inconceivable but who knew what way a parent's mind would have worked fifteen years in rural Ireland? In fact, thinking over how it would have looked to a casual observer, it was very possible that people would have seen Ruth's disappearance as a possible suicide. Drugs by the bed, house in disarray, spoiled food in the fridge and a recent history of psychological problems; it would certainly look as though self-harm or running away would have been the most likely scenarios. Maybe Nuala was just being smart. By removing the drugs she gave the police reason to treat it as a kidnapping or murder and not to write her daughter off as a runaway or suicide. This way they kept an open mind.

As she sat there the smell she'd thought of earlier popped into her head. Germolene. Her mother always used the pink ointment for cuts and scrapes. The haunting scent wafted through her memory. She pushed it and its unwelcome images of her mother's swollen face into the back of her mind.

She thought back over the manuscript. He brought her to a farm. Every farm in the county must have been searched thoroughly. Did he hide her or take her far away? Now, there was the outlandish possibility that she might still be alive. That had never seriously entered Amy's head before but now she was consumed by it and she dived feverishly back into the pages.

*O*nce *the effects* of the drugs wore off I'd expected Ruth to come around and thought we could talk and make plans but that didn't happen. The withdrawal symptoms were awful. Many times I panicked, thinking that perhaps I was slowly killing her. I had to lock her into my bedroom and cover the window with wood in case she hurt herself with the glass. I removed anything from the room which she could use to harm herself.

Finally she seemed to give up fighting me and sank into a deep depression.

At times she appeared to be almost catatonic and

would sit in my armchair looking at the wall. It was futile to try to break into her thoughts. During those times she was lost on another plane. Maybe I caused the problem because I had to make her go cold turkey on the drugs. Over time this state seemed to weaken and she was obviously taking notice of all around her though she still hadn't resumed talking. Sometimes I would be walking about the room and turn around to find her beautiful eyes burning into me but if I tried to hold her gaze her eyes would flicker away back to the yard. It had actually become quite disconcerting for me to never know when she would awaken and fix her gaze on me. I'd smile and try to engage her but to no avail. Her face remained static and impossible to read.

I was young too and didn't know what was happening to her. Now I know she was in a major depression. I'm sure the pressure of trying to grow up and become the person she was meant to be was too much for her. Look at you. Athletics provided the launching pad for you. It gave you something to concentrate on, a sense of achievement, gave you recognition abroad for your achievements and anchored you while you learned who you were. You knew you were strong, determined, healthy and respected.

Ruth had none of that. She was a bully as a child – not through an evil heart but through fear and a lack of understanding. That carried through her teens as a sense of shame and guilt. I told you earlier about her first sexual encounter. This incident only intensified the shame she already felt. Ruth put everything she had into trying to reinvent herself and make herself perfect. Ruth became obsessed with perfection. Her little body was fading away in front of the world as she fought for control. Her house was scoured every day from top to bottom. I didn't have a clue how bad it was (and I watched her more closely than anyone) until I read her diary. When I picked her up that night to put her in my car I looked at her hands and saw her cuticles scarred and criss-crossed with healing wounds. When I read her diaries I saw why. She scrubbed her hands dozens of times a day with a nylon brush. I think what finally broke her was when she went back to college. The extra pressure on top of all she'd already been putting herself through was too much for her.

I had no television on the farm so I wasn't worried about her seeing the news but I kept the radio outside in the barn. Every day I tuned in to check on the progress of her investigation. They were searching for her everywhere.

She'd been with me a month when she really started to get healthy. I would sit in the room with her and talk for hours. We were like children again. There was no place for adult conversation. Who cared about a college degree, a mortgage or the future? We lived in a Bohemian world of now. I hadn't planned on taking her when I did but I had planned on having her with me at some stage so I'd prepared well. We had enough food and supplies to last for months yet.

The farm was far away from Waterford and very isolated. I inherited it from my grandfather and I renovated it with money I got from another source. I knew how much the world had hurt her so I created another world for her. My world had peace and tranquillity, which was something she hadn't had in a long time. Now I was there to take care of her.

Amy was sick inside. Whatever she thought of Ruth in the past she hated to think of the suffering she'd gone through as an adult. She couldn't imagine what it must have been like to allow yourself to get so low that you just wanted to sink into oblivious darkness. If what he said were true, Ruth would have been dead anyway if he hadn't intervened, another tragic drug statistic. Whatever was going to come next for Ruth, at that point he probably saved her life. But then Nuala and Maurice did finally arrive to sort something out. Amy knew them and knew the Ballyreid community. They would have placed her under a doctor's care, possibly institutional care, and that would have been with her for the rest of her life, defining her in her own harsh opinion. Ruth was destroying herself and that type of treatment would only have given her ammunition in the war against herself.

The lunch-hour traffic was now entering the coffee shop and Amy really didn't want to be confined in a crowd today. She decided to go for a walk and keep her eyes open for Nuala or Maurice. She swung her document case onto her shoulder and walked down the length of the quay until she got to the place known locally as the Lookout. She then walked up into the small town park with the beautiful view of Dungarvan Bay and sat on the bandstand. She had forgotten how lovely it was here. In front of her, out in the bay, a long sand bar jutted from the mainland and stretched its length towards Dungarvan town where she sat on the other side of the bay. This sandbar was known as the Cunnigar. It was grassy and barren, but provided valuable protection for the town of Dungarvan from the onslaught of the sea. Beyond the rim of this narrow strip of land the waves broke and tumbled, stealing bits of the Cunnigar away and sneaking ever closer to the bay beyond. Today the tide was going out, making the jutting piece of land stand out like a large rib, long and thin amidst the tossing waves. A narrow but deep channel of water separated the tip of the sandbar from the town providing access to the sea for the boats sitting in the harbour. Straight ahead of her, the shape of Abbeyside church sat on the headland of Abbeyside, an area almost like another town separated from Dungarvan by the Colligan River and the harbour.

Amy remembered, when she was a little girl, coming down here to the park with her grandmother, Nuala, Maurice and Ruth for picnics. It was a major treat on a Friday after the main weekly grocery shopping was done. Nuala would buy a couple of packets of biscuits and a large bottle of lemonade and they would drink the sweet liquid out of plastic cups. At that time the girls got on well enough but in only a few years Granny was dead and Amy was sent away. Life for her had never been the same again.

But despite all of that, life had been kind to her. She was respected in her job and in firm control of her life. Amy had never felt the despair that had led Ruth to such a low ebb. Even with her parents' death and her banishment from Ballyreid, Amy was always able to channel her emotions into something positive. She was able to use it to motivate herself to change her circumstances and build on whatever positive experience she could muster.

The shadows were lengthening as Amy sat in the park and the water was starting to whip against the sea wall. Behind her the trees in the Church of Ireland graveyard swayed as the first fat drops of rain fell. It was time for her to run. Damn, she thought. That guesthouse was further away than she thought. Her case flapped against her hip and a young guy in a jazzed-up BMW beeped at her fleeing form. Her retort was lost in the driving rain. At last she managed to get her key out of her rainsoaked case and stumble through the guesthouse door.

The house was empty. Amy was glad of the peace. She needed it after the excitement of the last few days. She let herself into her room and stripped off her clothes to take a long, hot shower. When she got out, her bed looked soft and inviting so she decided a little rest couldn't hurt. A ten-minute power-nap would rejuvenate her enough to deal with the rest of the manuscript.

Despite her plans to just have a nap, Amy's sleep was deep and punctuated by nightmares of Ruth's slight form fading away in the bed beside her. Then she saw him, shrouded in shadows, come though the bedroom door and reach over her, to take Ruth's lifeless body into the darkness. She tried to reach up and stop him but her hands were rigid by her side. Her mouth wouldn't open and no words could squeeze out. She awoke in a sweat with her heart pounding.

Amy heard the clock in the kitchen strike four o'clock. She had been asleep for hours. She wondered as she lay there if Nuala had been serious about dragging her along to the police station that morning. Even if she hadn't carried out her threat she would have made life impossible for Amy by going over and over the question of how she got that photo. Things were easier this way. Amy could read the manuscript in peace and come to her own conclusions about what she was going to do with it. The guilt she'd felt about keeping the manuscript secret when under Nuala's roof eased once she was away from there. Here it was back to being a story helping her to come to terms with her own past.

Amy had a bit more time now to find out but as she moved to get her case she realised how hungry she was. A quick look out the window showed a dry evening already slipping into darkness. She decided to pack the manuscript up and take it with her. She'd try and get a corner table where nobody would notice what she was reading.

Chapter 23

By the time she'd gathered her bag and case it was completely dark outside. A deep fog was encircling the cars on the street in its ghostly grip. Occasionally a person shimmered into view as the bank of mist closed the path they had just walked down. Its icy fingers caressed Amy's face as she walked. Her heart beat faster. On a night like this anything could happen.

In relief she got to the restaurant and pushed open the door. Immediately on entering she spotted the table she wanted. It was in the far corner, with a chair she could use and keep her back to the wall. Nobody could glimpse what she was reading as they walked by. Right now she needed to finish the manuscript and get some more information to arm herself with before she made a decision on what to do. Common sense told her that it was unlikely someone who managed to kidnap a woman and keep her hidden for fifteen years would now allow himself to get caught. What was it he said about Ruth? Guilt and shame caused her to break down. He played a huge part in the acceleration of her depression. So was that his motivation now? Reveal what happened to Ruth so he could clear his conscience? Or was he trying to break Amy into little pieces too? Was the destruction of Amy his end game? As her mind refocused on her surroundings she took the menu from the waiter's outstretched hand and tried to concentrate as he called out the specials. After he left her to consider her options she'd forgotten everything he'd said. The first one was fish but she couldn't remember what type. Luckily she liked all fish except for anchovies so when he returned she made her order. It turned out to be monkfish and it arrived very promptly.

Careful not to spill sauce on the manuscript, she went back to reading.

Time goes by too quickly when your life is as ideal as ours was during that time. I'd hidden her diaries while she was with me to keep her mind from wandering back to those dark times. Honestly, during those months with me it was like she was a different person. She seemed calm and content. Her old world was lost to her and I intended to keep it that way. I was willing to do anything for her, anything to keep her safe and happy. The most perfect moments of my childhood had been in her company and when I found her so low in her adult life I wanted to bring that back for her. Have you ever thought back to a wonderful childhood moment and wish you could reconnect with that and maintain it into adulthood? Well, that's what I did for her. She told me every day that she'd never been so happy and fulfilled in her life.

I was the happiest man in the world until the day she found the radio. I had become so comfortable with our routine that I let her have complete run of the house while I was at home. I kept the keys to the car and Land Rover with me at all times and I knew she wasn't going to walk anywhere. Ruth had lost all confidence in the outside world so she didn't want to see anyone. I have to admit, in the interest of the fullest disclosure possible, that I did try my best to nurture her mistrust of the outside world. You might think that this was selfish on my part but it was mostly for her. Ruth wasn't strong enough for the outside world.

But that day she was walking about and she decided to go and hang out in the barn. The first thing she did was to climb the bales of hay. I'd cultivated too much of the child in her. As she sat on the top looking down, the radio above the door caught her eye. I'd nailed a wooden box on top of the doorframe and the little transistor radio fitted neatly into it. Excited, she climbed down and pulled a bale over to stand on so she could get it down. Immediately she turned it on she found the RTÉ One news just starting.

Nuala Devine makes another appeal to her

daughter's kidnapper to let her go as the three-month anniversary of her daughter's disappearance approaches.

Ruth stood in shock. The outside world came rushing back in. As the headlines went on she looked up and there I stood in the doorway looking at her, trying to draw her back to me. But it was too late. The tentative hold I'd had on her was severed and I knew our time was over. Ruth would go back to the outside world, back to drugs, depression and the rest I couldn't even formulate into words. I couldn't let that happen.

She didn't speak at first, she just stood there watching me but I knew the look in her eyes. Finally her voice split the silence.

"It was *you*. It was *you* who was frightening me."

"Ruth, that's not true. You know that."

"You led me to believe it was the drugs and depression. You made me think I was losing my mind, but it was you!"

"Ruth. I love you. I did save you. The night I took you with me you were almost in a coma from drugs. I sat up all night with you, keeping you awake to stop you from dying in your sleep."

"You were stalking me. I was so scared. That's what made things so bad."

"And you thought you were safe in a barbiturate coma, did you?"

"No. But I wouldn't have taken those drugs if I wasn't so stressed."

"Chicken and egg, darling. You found out

224

someone was stalking you in December but you'd gone to a therapist in September."

"How do you know? I didn't tell you that."

"I had to arm myself with as much information as I could to take care of you."

I watched her eyes as they darted about the barn for a way out. I wasn't getting through to her at all. I couldn't let her go screaming out of here looking for help. As I talked to her, trying to calm her down, I walked towards her with my hand outstretched, soothing her with my tone of voice. She didn't believe me but I was confusing her sufficiently to keep her in one spot. When I was close enough I grabbed onto her wrist. She tried vainly to fight me off.

I picked her up with my hand over her mouth and carried her.

As I said before, I hadn't expected things to work out as they did. Originally I'd expected her to resist and I thought I would have to restrain her so now I had to return to Plan A.

I carried her to a wooden shack further behind the house. Inside I kicked back a sack on the ground and revealed a wooden door. Holding her tightly with one arm I pulled the rope I'd installed as a handle and dropped her down. It wasn't too deep. It was more of a pit I guess than a basement. My grandfather built it himself to store potato seed and other valuables. He was paranoid about thieves. Such suspicion was unusual for the time and he didn't have access to burglar alarms. My father told me that as a punishment he'd lock him in there as a child, until he'd come to his senses. He told me this before he put me down there. Maybe one day I'll tell you why. Now I'd have to lock my beloved Ruth down there.

For months she refused to co-operate. There were escape attempts and tantrums but, gradually, as time went on she calmed down and was once more becoming my Ruth. In case you are judging me for being a monster she did have sanitation there. I won't go into details but she was clean and comfortable and well fed as long as she chose to eat. I didn't force-feed her.

After a time her eyes no longer darted about looking for escape. Instead they focused on me and followed every flicker as I sat there with the door open talking to her. She looked so quiet and relaxed that I decided maybe it was time to bring her back to the house. I held out my hand and invited her with my eyes to come up to me. She smiled and stood up, her hands held over her head so I could help her up. When I had her standing beside me she leaned against me and I wrapped my arms around her, pulling her in to me. She didn't resist so I held her hand and walked her down the hill to the house.

I had to keep her on a much tighter leash after that but things did go back to normal for a time. Our room had an en suite bathroom so I didn't have to let her out of my sight for a moment. You're probably wondering what I really mean by "our room". Well relax, Amy. Our relationship was platonic. I wouldn't do that to her. Ruth couldn't make a decision like furthering our relationship until she was completely healed.

I couldn't take any chances like last time. All circumstances can't be accounted for and off the wall things will happen. The windows were nailed shut and any time I had to leave the house and go to town I locked the shutters which I fitted myself on the outside of the windows.

I think she was happy during that time. Her moods were balanced and though she didn't do a lot of laughing she smiled at me, long peaceful lazy smiles that went right to my heart every time I saw one. I loved her so much and that is probably why once more I let her catch me unaware but this time the consequences were greater.

As Amy hastily turned the page to find out what his mistake had been the waiter arrived to remove her plates. He hovered, trying to catch her attention.

She looked up into his face and smiled.

"I'm sorry, Miss, but this table was only available for two hours. It was booked for eight o'clock."

"I'm sorry. I'll be out in a moment."

"There's no need to rush, it's only seven thirty. Would you like a dessert?"

"No, thank you. Just coffee. And the bill, please."

She tidied her papers away while she waited for the waiter to return. She needed to be able to concentrate without interruption to face whatever terrible thing was now to come in the manuscript.

When he returned with the coffee and the bill, she paid and then drank the coffee off quickly.

Leaving the restaurant, she started to retrace her steps to the house. The fog had eased a bit but the streets were deserted and, without a visible moon, very gloomy. A deep sense of unease was starting to invade her being. The streets along this route were some of the quietest in the town and on a night like this and in her state of mind she wished herself anywhere else.

The area she was walking through now was entirely residential. Everybody was inside their homes. With relief she realised she had one more street and a roundabout to negotiate and she was there. The sense of trepidation she'd felt since leaving the restaurant was getting stronger. For a moment she stopped and listened. She heard an engine ticking over as though someone were sitting motionless in a running vehicle. As she thought this a car drove by and she laughed at herself – it was only that, just an innocent passer-by. The fog and the manuscript were consuming her with fear.

At last she passed into the road on which her guesthouse was located. The fog had lifted considerably now but this road was dark and in her present state of mind extremely lonely. Once more she heard a car coming from behind her but it was travelling at a reasonable speed and more than likely just more local traffic, just another individual coming in out of the cold.

Amy strode on without turning her head, picking up speed as she did, but just as the car was passing by it changed direction and screeched to a stop in front of her, its two front wheels on the footpath. It happened so suddenly Amy couldn't avoid it. She slammed into its side – it was a van – and was knocked off balance. She felt herself going down and landed heavily on her back. Everything seemed to be happening in slow motion. In terror and bewilderment she tried to struggle to her feet but then she felt a sharp knock on the back of her head, a bright flash of light suddenly lit the night and then there was total blackness.

Amy stood up without turning her head, putting both hands... she did, but this as the car was passing by it changed direction and struck it. It was not far from her in two front wheels over a bump... It seemed to go suddenly. Amy couldn't avoid it. She slammed into its side – it was a van – and was knocked off balance. She felt herself going down and landed heavily on her back. Everything seemed to be happening in slow motion. In terror and bewilderment she tried to struggle to her feet but then she felt a sharp knock on the back of her head, a bright flash of light suddenly in the machine and then there was only blackness.

PART THREE

Chapter 24

Amy lay on her back, looking at the skylight high above her head. She had tried to think of a way to get out through it but it was impossible. It was a Velux window high up at the top of a long funnel stretching upwards through the ceiling of the attic where she lay to the roof outside, which was at least twenty feet over her head. This was obviously an attic conversion. Once this room and the room next door were one – however, it was split at some point and the end with the window in it had been separated off to provide an en suite bathroom. That would have left this room windowless so the strange funnel-like window was built through the attic space above her head to compensate. The sides of the funnel were sheer slabs of wood impossible to get a foot or handhold on. Strangely, all she thought about was how anyone could possibly clean that window. It was obvious that cleaning hadn't been attempted recently because the window was layered in grime, dulling the weak rays of light shining down on her.

This house was a two-storey period house at the end of a long, steep driveway. Last night they'd passed an abandoned gate lodge on the way up. She could see it through the back window of the van. She couldn't see the driver. He had to stop to open the gate. She could hear him struggling to push it over the broken driveway – it must have sunk on its hinges. He got back in, drove through and then got out to close the gate. Amy had already tried to open the doors at the back of the van but they had held fast. She was a prisoner. The road up to the house was pitted with holes where the harsh winter rain had worn away chunks of the surface. It had obviously been a while since any repair work had been done on it. Large mature trees spread their branches over the road, giving it an eerie feeling. The sky was dark and the few stars that shone couldn't squeeze their light through the gloom. The road system leading up to the gate lodge was like a maze. From where Amy watched she couldn't see any other houses.

As the moon came out from behind the clouds they reached the end of the drive and entered a large clearing. The house stood in a vastly overgrown garden melting into the outlines of a dark expanse of trees and shrubbery in the distance.

When the van came to a halt outside the house the driver came around to the back doors. Amy waited with a knot of fear in her stomach as he stood for a moment outside and positioned herself just inside to kick him in the jaw and run. As the doors opened she aimed her foot and moved forward but she found herself flying through the air and onto her knees on the ground outside. All she saw in the darkness was a blur of black as she fell. While on the ground she tried to right herself and sit up but, before she could do this, once again the world slipped into the background.

It was still rather dark now but the dawn was breaking above her head – she could see its silvery fingers reaching weakly in through the skylight. She swung her legs over the side of the bed and sat there for a second while she started to process her situation. As she moved she felt the weight around her waist. She ran her hands along her waist and found a heavy steel chain wound around her and extending away from her.

She tugged at the chain but it held fast. She jumped up in a sudden blind panic and propelled her body to run but as she reached the door the chain snapped tightly knocking the wind out of her and causing her to fall on the wooden boards. She cried out in pain. Her head ached and she had to sit there for a moment to quell her rising panic.

Once she got her feelings under control, she got up and made her way back to the end of the chain. She found that it was attached to a ring buried deep in the wood of the floor. She tried to pull it out but it was firmly fixed.

She turned her attention to the rest of the room, which was emerging out of the night into the dim early morning light. She went into the tiny little en suite bathroom. She could just reach the toilet and sit. There was no way she could take a shower but she could reach the wash-hand basin. There was a small window in the wall beyond the toilet but she couldn't reach it.

She walked back out into the room and back to the bed. It was dressed in what felt like clean sheets. She lay down on her back. The sheets smelled clean and freshly laundered. She realised this was where he had always intended to take her. He'd organised it in anticipation of her arrival. Was this his home?

Her head hurt and she was coming down from the extreme high of her recent panic attack. So despite her surroundings, she slept.

Once again Amy woke up in the attic and straight away she knew she would have a problem marking time. If she were incarcerated as long as Ruth was, time would cease to exist for her and days and nights would blend together until life became a shapeless blur. She had to do something to fix this. She looked around the room. She could mark lines in the dust but then more dust would cover it and her sense of reality would be disappearing underneath. Then she saw the pristine white wall. Whoever locked her in here must have painted it recently. It certainly wasn't done when this house held servants. She would find something to mark the paint. She looked at her shoes. They had black soles. She took them off and using the sharp side of the sole she drew a small black line in the snow white. There she was. Every day another little one of these lines would prove she was still alive and that time was still there for her.

After two weeks Amy was glad she made her "calendar". She looked at her wall and saw fourteen one-inch black streaks in two neat blocks of seven. It was hard to believe. If she hadn't been smart enough to do this the first day she would be in a mass of time now with no beginning and no end. Darkness came every evening and she couldn't stop it. She would sit for hours under the skylight looking up, with fear causing her skin to prickle and her stomach to churn. The shadows spread further and she felt like she was at the end of a long tunnel, which was getting deeper and deeper. Once darkness had settled she ceased to fear it, but prior to that its onslaught filled her with dread. She feared that one day she wouldn't see the sun come back up and just as time was gone as she knew it, she too would cease to exist.

He always left food when it was dark. There were no bulbs in the sockets so once the sun went down the room was in darkness and stayed that way until the next day. He only fed her once a day. Every night at roughly the same time, a dark shape would stand silently in the doorway and leave the most delicious-smelling food for her on enamel plates with a large enamel mug of water. There was never a fork or knife, only a soup spoon. During the light of day she swore she'd throw the next offering in his face, but as soon as darkness started to close in she found herself looking forward to these visits.

Like Pavlov's dogs she would hear the key turn in the lock and liquid from her salivary glands would wash over her mouth and her stomach would ache for food. He never spoke though she tried in vain to draw some words from him. He just put the tray on the floor and picked up the other, ignoring her completely. The second night he had held the tray in one hand and with the other hand searched for the previous night's one. When he saw it wasn't there he disappeared silently with her dinner. It never happened again. Amy was a quick study. From then on she left her tray neatly by the door. She knew he was smiling at her obedience. This made her proud. She hated herself for this. The first night when he left the room and she heard the key scrape she ran to the door and listened. Perhaps there was a way of getting the key. But almost immediately she heard the sound of it being taken out of the lock and placed above the door. She thought of pounding against the frame of the door where she thought the key was, in the hope she could dislodge it and it would fall. But she was terrified that he would hear her if she did. Besides, it would probably fall out of her reach, and what good was it anyway when she was chained?

After he left, she would sit cross-legged in the dark and the hot savoury food would comfort her until shortly afterwards she would climb onto her bed and sleep a deep and satisfying sleep.

Today it had been seventeen days. She had two blocks of seven and one line of three. As she waited she heard footsteps and the key turn in the lock.

She was so hungry and unbearably lonely. She walked to the end of her chain and stood as he opened the door and placed the food on the floor. He picked up the other tray and placed it outside. Amy stood mesmerised because he didn't leave. He had a chair sitting in the hall opposite the door. He walked to it and sat down. It was dark but she felt as though he could see her every movement. She'd been alone for seventeen days with only light and darkness for company. She felt shy as she sat down on the floor to eat her food. She found herself looking at him as he sat there in silence. She assumed there were no windows in the hallway outside or else they were covered by heavy drapes because all she could see was his bulk outlined in the thick darkness. When she took a break from eating she listened intently to see if she could hear his breathing but all she heard was her own. By now she had given up trying to talk to him because he completely ignored all her attempts. As soon as she finished, she had no idea why but she tidied her tray and pushed it across the floor to him. Again she knew he was pleased with her. He walked over to pick up the tray and bent to pick it up. For a moment she stared at the top of his head as he crouched – it was covered by a dark wool cap. He never even tried to look at her. He picked up the tray as though she weren't sitting there and he was alone in the gloom of the attic. He placed the tray outside with the other one and then he locked the door, leaving Amy alone again in the dark. But she felt better. She'd had company for the first time in seventeen days. This time as she lay on her bed getting ready for sleep she found herself thinking thoughts like, "If I'm good, I'll get more from him." The few short moments of company had made her glow like a schoolgirl and all the next day she found herself looking forward to his visit.

The next night anticipation grew as the light faded until finally she heard his approaching feet. She thought he would sit with her again and maybe he would speak. Amy stood at the end of her tether, watching the dark shape stand there in the doorway. He didn't need to speak. They communicated without words. She instinctively knew how to please him. She stepped back a couple of steps and as she did he reached in and placed her tray on the floor. Immediately she knew something was different. The tray landed with a soft tap and she knew she heard the rustle of paper. He moved out of the room again and locked the door.

"Come back!" Amy shouted. "Don't leave me!"

But he was already gone and once more the house sat in heavy silence. She crouched down and reached towards the savoury smell of her food. He was a good cook whoever he was. Every night since she'd been here she'd had a lovely meal except for the night she didn't leave her tray for him to collect. He only fed her once a day and she knew her weight had dropped. She grabbed her food and devoured it in seconds. Manners hardly seemed important when she could barely see herself in this soupy darkness. When she finished she reached out again and found the papers on the floor. It was too dark to read them but she was happy to have something new in her world. She sat and smoothed the envelope and examined its thickness and shape.

Once she'd satisfied her immediate curiosity regarding the papers, she carried her dishes and mug to the bathroom and washed them. She then took them back out to the bedroom and lined them up, leaning them against the wall to drip-dry. She was so used to the darkness now that she could walk around the room as though it were daylight.

Amy dried her hands on her clothes and went back to the papers. She opened the envelope even though she couldn't see anything. It was a sheaf of papers like the manuscript. He'd brought her the manuscript to read. She held it in her hands, delighted to have something to do, but it would be many hours before she would be able to see the writing. She might as well sleep. But she feared he was playing with her and would just take them away again so she took them into bed with her and placed them under the blankets by her side.

Chapter 25

Amy had no concept of time any more so when she opened her eyes she just lay there looking at the dusty wooden floor until an urge to use the bathroom finally caused her to get out of bed. As she did this, the papers dislodged and fell onto the floor. She hurried to gather them up, desperate for a new activity to break up the monotony of life in the room. It was the manuscript as she'd expected. As soon as she was organised she sat in her favourite spot inside the room by the bathroom door where the rays of the sun shone directly down on her. Finally she could get back into the manuscript. On the night he kidnapped her she had just been about to find out the consequences of his trusting Ruth, when she had to leave the restaurant. The place where she was now, this house – was this where Ruth had been fifteen years ago? Only these pages could tell her that.

It was a Monday. I went to town and bought everything I needed for a special night. Before I let her out of our room I cooked a wonderful dinner. I knew she loved fish so I cooked salmon and served a medium white wine that I thought she'd like. I laid the table with care, using my best linen and crystal, smiling as I thought of her face when she would see it all.

When I opened the door and led her to it, her eyes sparkled in the flickering candlelight. She looked at me, smiled, and walked to the chair I indicated for her. The food was perfect and the evening was like a dream. I relaxed and totally let my guard down. As we ended dinner and were about to move to the sitting-room and talk, I leaned in to kiss her cheek. That was when she struck.

She grabbed the wine bottle that was still by her plate. With as much weight as she could manage she smashed the bottle across my face, sending me falling backwards until my head hit the floor. I immediately blacked out. When I came to she was gone and she'd taken the keys to my car. I ran outside and could hear the car disappearing down the drive so I knew I hadn't been out for long. I cursed my stupidity and kicked at the tree in the garden. I thought it was over. What could I do? She was gone and any moment the police would be driving up to my yard to take me away in handcuffs.

I was starting to sway from the blow to my head when I heard the crash. It was the loudest bang and in my mind's eye I could see the crumpled metal. I imagined her lying there dying.

I grabbed the flashlight in the hall cabinet and ran as fast as I could down the drive and onto the road. It had to be the next turn – it had nearly got me a few times and I knew this road like the back of my hand. I heard the door of the car creaking open as I descended the road so I knew she was still alive. I ran faster then, knowing I was just moments away from regaining control of the situation.

When I reached it, the car was buried in the wall on the left as I'd expected and the crumpled door on the driver's side was wide open but there was no sign of Ruth.

I presumed she drove looking in the rear-view mirror to see if I was following. The road curved around quite dramatically but she probably hadn't seen this until it was too late. I could imagine her fear. I had a broken headlamp and this would have impeded her progress. A stone had bounced off the road earlier that day and shattered the glass and the bulb.

Looking into the car I saw that the airbag had deployed on impact. For a moment the shock must have completely knocked the breath out of her.

She must have fallen from the car after she shoved the broken door open. I could see the smears of blood on the grass where she'd landed on the glass outside, on her hands and knees perhaps. Or perhaps she was bleeding from a more serious injury?

The lights of the car were still on and they highlighted the smears of blood on the stones in the whitewashed wall near the car. She must have climbed over the wall at that point.

I jumped the wall where the bloody stones were and examined the ground on the other side. I could picture her stumbling and running. About fifty yards along the wall she must have paused to adjust her eyes to the darkness or decide which way to run. I played the lamp along the ground and could see some extra drops of blood where I imagined she'd stood for a few moments.

I moved as fast as I could along the wall until I came to the end where another crossed at a right angle to it. I could see blood on the stones of the wall where she must have placed her hand to lean against it. Her long stay locked up in the room had played havoc with her muscle tone. She was very unfit.

At that moment she must have heard me following and seen the swaying beam of the lamp. She had jumped the second wall.

I leapt over it. I was on the edge of a large field. She must have already crossed it as there was no sight or sound of her. She would have known she couldn't go back onto the road because there I would catch up with her in a second.

Instinct told me she was not hiding nearby.

No, she had started to run again. Her lungs must have been burning and I could imagine the sharp pain in her side, the ache of her unfit muscles, hear her heart pounding in her ears. The safety belt must have bruised her chest on impact at that speed. I felt each symptom as though they were my own.

All her senses would be sharpening, her eyes completely adjusting to the night. I imagined the hair on the back of her neck starting to tingle and stand up. It was like I was tuned into her brain. Like I was following some electronic signal she was emitting.

I ran now trying to think of her next step and it seemed I had become Ruth as well as myself, the hunted and the hunter.

Later I pieced it all together.

Ruth had climbed over the second wall and swayed for a moment, trying to cope with the dizziness she now felt after her ordeal. She tried to get her bearings. She was afraid to go back out onto the road so she ran the length of the wall in the opposite direction until she reached the corner of the field and encountered another stone wall. She scrambled over it. She ran onwards in the darkness – perhaps there was another road over there or a farm. At the other side of the field she stood under a tree and scanned the darkness behind her. There was nothing to be seen – no torchlight, no pursuer.

Then as she turned her head she saw a steady light not too far away. It seemed to be the yard light of another farm. She broke into a run, trying to avoid turning an ankle. Coming to a barbed-wire fence she climbed it carefully – the last thing she wanted to do now was highlight her path. The farmyard was close. She had another small field, not much more than a garden to cross, and then safety. She ran on. She was sobbing and her breath was laboured but the light beckoned.

Ruth burst into the yard through an open gate and stopped.

She broke into panic-stricken sobs.

She was back where she started.

In the dark and dazed by panic she'd gone in a circle. The yard light was on but there was no sign of any other lights.

Perhaps there wasn't another house for miles. She screamed inside and then desperately forced herself to be calm and think.

She looked around her again. Maybe she could hotwire the tractor. No, she had only a vague idea how to do that and there was no time. To her left she saw the open door of the dairy. There was a hum starting in her brain. She was a farmer's daughter. She knew the run of a farm. And she had been all over this one. She had no idea what she was thinking but something was trying to work its way out of her head. She rushed to the dairy. It had a sliding door. She stepped inside and pulled it shut behind her.

All dairies had two doors, the outside one, which she'd just come through, and the inner one, which went into the milking parlour. As she shut the outer door she felt around the wall on both sides for the light switch. Precious seconds slipped by before she finally located it. She switched it on and had a good look around. There it was – what she'd been thinking of in the basement of her brain: a bucket of phosphoric acid detergent for washing the milking machine. Over the milk tank was a small plastic spray can and in front of her was a hose. She rushed over and filled the can with water. She put a good scoop of the acid into the container and screwed the nozzle back on. Now she had her own home-made mace.

She switched off the light and, carrying the spray can, walked through a door at the back. She was now in the tool shed, which had no windows. She adjusted again to the darkness and noticed a faint chink of light under a door to her left. She edged her way towards it. Opening it as quietly as she could, she stepped through. She was now in the milking shed. The bottom half of it was completely open to the air. She could see the night sky through the gap. The moon was fully visible now. The clouds had parted and the sky was a deep navy with little stabs of starlight.

She knew the shape and layout of the shed. If you'd seen one, you'd pretty much seen them all. Three years in Waterford and it felt like yesterday she'd sat on the wall stroking the cows' necks as her dad milked them. If you stroked them with little feather strokes all the loose skin quivered like it was trying to shake the cow out. Behind her, she heard a voice call out. She went through the milking pit and out the other end of the shed. She stood in a circular collecting yard. This was where the cows gathered prior to milking. She hugged the shadows by the wall tightly, listening for any sounds. None yet.

She looked to her right. This was where the winter cowshed was. In the moonlight she could see a line of munching faces looking at her expectantly. Probably hoping for a midnight feast. None of them had calved yet so they were all still confined there, where it was warmer for them to sleep and easier to feed them.

Her choices were limited so she decided to risk injury and walk through the cows.

She edged her way down the wall and through the gate towards the cows. If they were quiet maybe she could stand amongst them and be invisible. She still held her canister close to her. This was her version of chemical warfare. As she deliberated on what to do she heard the dairy door opening. It could have been the wind but instinct told her otherwise. Still hugging the wall she moved towards the gate.

Amy was terrified. A panic attack started deep inside her and she could feel it escalating until she could hardly breathe. This was the precursor to her story. That person chasing her cousin across country was now her jailor, the only person between her and a slow starvation in only God knew where. She stood up and paced the floor. Due to the lack of food the heavy chains around her waist caused her to wince as they banged against her now more prominent hipbones. She was totally at the mercy of a maniac. Amy knelt down and bent her body into the yogic child's pose and calmed her breathing. With tears streaming down her face she sat back in her sunbeam. He wanted her to crack. Well, she wouldn't. She had her calendar to keep track of time and she was strong. Somehow Amy was getting out of here. Maybe the answer was in the manuscript.

Chapter 26

There were only twenty-five cows, held back in their yard by a single strand of electric fencer wire. She knew there would be a plastic grip to open the wire at the side of the cow yard. She found it. Grabbing the grip tightly, she opened the wire enough to walk through. Then she closed it behind her and put the grip back.

Moving slowly, she manoeuvred her way amongst the cows. She didn't want them jumping about revealing her presence. She also didn't want one kicking out and breaking her knee. She edged her way back along the outside of the cow-house wall. So far the cows hadn't even moved. She was slipping through without making any visible difference to them.

Then a beam of light shot out.

I shone my lamp towards the other end of the yard,

away from her. Then I moved systematically in her direction.

"Ruth! I know you're there!"

She ducked down as low as she could behind the cows. She was praying the light wouldn't catch the top of her head but I'd already seen the movement.

"I'm coming in. I'm right behind you. I can't see you, baby, but I can feel you. You're close now, aren't you?"

I spoke quietly. My voice had a singsong quality.

She couldn't look up as she knew I would see her. All she could see from her vantage point were the backs of a Friesian cow's legs. If the cow spooked and kicked right now she would pulverise Ruth's jaw. That thought was enough to terrify her, never mind me behind the beam of light. I was still aiming the beam at the other end of the yard while I quietly walked towards her.

"Stupid bastard!" I shouted suddenly. I was concentrating so hard on edging up on her I'd sidled right into the electric fence. The shock was terrifying in the darkness of the yard. "Ruth, I'm losing my patience here. I don't want to hurt you. I love you. Don't treat me like this. I do things I regret when I'm upset."

Ruth was trying hard not to sob. She was so scared of me by then.

"Okay girls. Take a little walk."

Ruth couldn't believe what was happening. I'd opened the wire and was letting the cows out. In seconds she would be on view. The shadows would offer some protection but with that torch I had, the shadows wouldn't be dark for long.

The space around her was becoming greater as the cows surged forward. Any moment now she would be prime viewing. In desperation she shuffled backwards into the darkness. Her jeans and shoes were caked in muck. Feeling her way along the wall her hand found the doorway into the cow-house. As the last cows moved away from her spot she ducked around the corner out of the yard and into the inky darkness of the house.

Not a second too soon. Standing as far back as she could, she watched the beam of my torch form a pool on the ground outside the doorway.

"Ruth! I know you're in there!"

She realised I was getting closer. Her hands were wildly clawing the space around her for a weapon, anything to defend herself.

She reached above her head. This was a cow-house. Farmers often put things high up on the wall to stop the cows from injuring themselves. She was terrified of rats but she played her hands along the top of the shed wall through cobwebs and dust. Nothing. Then bingo! A pike. Too large iron clips held it. She stood up on her toes, trying to dislodge it.

"Ruth!" I shouted, playing with her. "It's rude not to answer."

At that moment the pike came away in her hands,

almost falling on her head. Gripping it with one hand and the canister with the other she stepped farther back into the inky blackness.

The torch beam was penetrating farther into the cow house. I was standing just outside the door. She jumped violently when my voice echoed out a few feet from where she stood.

"Why are you so scared of me, Ruth?"

Ruth shouted before she could stop herself. "You kept me locked up! My parents think I'm dead!"

"I love you," I said in a low and even voice.

"I don't believe you."

"I'm sorry about that." My voice had lowered to a whisper again. She could barely hear it and had to strain to catch my words.

Then I burst into the cow house. It happened so fast she didn't even know where or if she'd struck me. She just knew she was running and the pike wasn't in her hands any more.

She ran forward, back out into the cow yard, her first instinct to get away, but she ran blindly and then she was grabbing an iron post as the ground disappeared from under her. She'd run into the slurry tank. This was an old farm and the slurry tank was open-air and very dangerous. It was a large square tank made of concrete and filled with slurry cleaned out of the cowsheds and off the surface of the yard. If she sank here she would be drowned in a matter of seconds. Holding the post with a dead-man's grip she steadied herself again on solid ground and whirled around, searching for me. My torch lay on the ground in the shed and she could hear my groans and curses of pain from behind its glow. She would have to make another run for it.

Before she could gather herself for action I came out of the shed with the torch now trained on her face.

"Ruth, that hurt! Don't run! We're a team."

Her eyes darted wildly about for an avenue of escape. She could see none and she'd dropped her canister. I was moving towards her, trying to calm her down. I was about five stone heavier than she was and a foot taller. She knew sometimes small animals become mesmerised when faced with a predator and imminent death. That was how she felt now. Her legs were like lead, her eyes fixed on my advancing bulk.

Ruth made a desperate effort and rushed to the right away from me. I was slow following her because she'd pierced me in the side with the pike. I heard her thrashing across the yard. She was confused and disorientated.

I don't know why but she ran away from the road and out into the fields behind the house. I couldn't see her. I tried to follow her but I was losing a lot of blood from my side and I was dizzy from the bang to my head earlier. Back there I have forty acres of land and then hundreds of acres of mountain stretch into the distance. There was no hope of finding her at that time. It was too dark. I went inside, tended to my wound and tried to sleep for a few hours. I expected that any moment I would be hauled from my bed by the guards for kidnapping. I didn't care. I had lost her.

The following morning early, after a fitful sleep, I awoke and looked at my bedside clock. It was six thirty. Why weren't the guards at my door? A little part of me hoped that she had come to her senses and was even now coming back to me after calming down and realising that no one loved her like I did, but I knew that wasn't the case.

But I was puzzled. If Ruth had reached help the authorities would be there by now. I turned the news on but there were no breaking headlines.

I then realised the truth. The fact that I was here alone meant that something had happened to her. I knew it in my heart. I walked behind my house and up and down every field on my land for some sight of her but there was nothing.

Then I thought of the limekiln. It was beyond my land on the mountain where an old house used to stand before my grandfather's time. It was the only place out there where you could hide if you were hurt or exhausted or terrified. Standing almost twenty feet tall and built into the side of the hill it had a hole in the front of it like a fireplace. Structurally it was still in good shape. Very few stones had fallen out of it. There had been a gaping hole on the flat top surface of it called the pot where the lime was burned in the old days before being spread on the land as fertilizer.

I had filled this in, in case an animal fell into it, but otherwise it was intact. I walked towards it to see if she'd sheltered in the hollow at the base. My heart caught in my throat. At some stage during the night Ruth had run across the mountain and probably without seeing it she'd run across the top of the kiln and fallen to the ground beneath. I stood on top looking down at her body huddled and broken on the rocks below with a deep gash on her temple where a sharp rock had pierced her skin. Screaming, I climbed down and ran to her. I sat there in the early morning light, unashamed tears streaming down my face as I rocked her cold lifeless body. My tears mixed with the dew in her hair.

Amy sat and wept for a long while. Then fear displaced all other feelings. Trembling, she looked back over the pages she'd just read and tried to picture the setting. The house she was in now didn't sound like the same place that Ruth had been. Everything he said in the manuscript seemed to indicate a typical mountain dairy farm. He said there were forty acres of land, and mountain beyond that, and he had twenty-five head of cattle in the yard. This house had an old gate lodge and a long sweeping if neglected avenue up to the door. The little she'd seen of the house as they stopped seemed to indicate a large building in a wide-open but overgrown space. No, Amy was convinced that either he'd taken creative license with everything in the manuscript or else there were two locations: the one she was at now and the one from fifteen years ago. This place looked deserted and lost and didn't give Amy much hope of her being recovered. Once more a panic attack started to take control of her and the words on the pages swam out of focus, lost in the tears spilling from her eyes.

PART FOUR

PART FOUR

Chapter 27

The morning after Amy had been kidnapped, Nuala had woken at seven o'clock. She looked over to where Maurice lay. He was still asleep. Maurice would just stop her from having things out with Amy so she didn't disturb him. Quietly she slipped from the room and made her way to talk to her niece. Immediately she saw that the bed had not been slept in. She crossed the room and stood at the open window. So Amy had just taken off without explanation or goodbyes.

The day she got the call from Amy, to tell her she was coming to visit, Nuala knew that there was more to it than a simple visit to reconnect with her country relatives. Amy was the type of individual who had a purpose for everything she did. That girl had risen on the shoulders of them all. The death of her parents, being an only child, having to go and live with an elderly aunt – none of it had impacted negatively on Amy. She rose through the ranks quickly and effectively without any obvious impediment.

Yet her own daughter was taken from her. Ruth had everything. She had loving parents, she was intelligent, but none of it seemed to matter to her. Even if she hadn't disappeared when she did, Ruth was already on a fast track to self-destruction.

Nuala remembered how she felt when she entered Ruth's house after she had disappeared. She and Maurice had stood on the doorstep as the bell rang inside. Minutes ticked by and there was no response. Maurice crossed the street and went into the phone box. He rang Ruth's number. Nuala could hear that ringing inside but there was still no response. Really worried now, she took her own key out and entered the property. Normally she wouldn't invade her daughter's privacy like this but she had been trying to contact her for weeks to no avail.

As soon as she entered the house she knew that something was seriously wrong. The air was stale and all the curtains were open downstairs. A crumpled towel lay on the floor and teacups were piled in the sink. Nuala's worst fears were realised when she walked around downstairs and saw the lack of fresh food. Mouldy bread sat putrefying in the bread bin and all the cupboards were stocked high with tinned foods. Nuala looked at the utensils barrel on the worktop and she could see that an opportunistic spider had taken the lack of human activity as an opportunity to spin a web across the top of the barrel from the tin-opener to the large wooden spatula. Ruth was certainly not cooking in here lately.

"Nuala!"

Nuala would never forget the panic-stricken note in Maurice's voice when he shouted at her from upstairs. She ran to him, leaping up two steps at a time. He was standing in Ruth's room looking at her nightstand. Maurice was a simple man and very trusting. Nuala saw that die in him at that moment as he looked at the drugs lined up on the nightstand. Nuala knew hash smoking wasn't the big deal it was in their day and though she didn't approve it didn't cause the same hurt in her that it caused in Maurice. Maurice couldn't bear any reminder that his little girl wasn't perfect.

Nuala was a stronger character. She'd coped with her mother's illness and the loss of her little sister and always she had managed to carry on.

Now she laid a reassuring hand on Maurice's arm and tried to process what she was seeing. Along with the illegal drugs there were two pill bottles. She picked those up and looked at the labels. They were sleeping tablets, which were supplied by two separate doctors. She switched on the light and took a good look around the room. The curtains were partially open. The bed sheets were crumpled and stained. It was obvious they hadn't been changed in weeks. Alarm bells were going off loudly in Nuala's head. Her daughter was normally as organised as she was and kept a beautiful house. Nuala stood there in confusion, looking around her. The room was so musty. The windows hadn't been open in quite a while and the room smelt distinctly of sweat.

Hardly knowing what she was doing, Nuala smelt the bed sheets.

"Nuala!" Maurice was appalled. He still hadn't got beyond the shock of his little girl taking drugs. His brain hadn't turned yet to the possibility of something more sinister having occurred here.

"This bed smells of sweat. Ruth wasn't bathing, opening her windows or changing her bed sheets. This is not our Ruth."

"It's the drugs." Maurice looked hopeful that he could blame it all on the drugs.

"No, Maurice. She's had problems for a long time. I don't think drugs caused them. I think she was just trying to escape them."

"What problems?" The haunted look was back. How could his little girl have such problems and he didn't know about them?

"Didn't you see her weight loss?" Nuala's voice was sharp.

Maurice flinched from its implication. Nuala had always accused him of living in a parallel universe but he'd always thought it was their little joke. She took care of the details and he backed her up. That was what they did. But this time she hadn't confided her fears in him and he hadn't been able to see it for himself. Maybe she didn't want to shatter his opinion of his little girl. While she was worried about her daughter's health she was preserving her husband's delicate balance as well. Suddenly he felt very ashamed. He wasn't a real man. A real man would tackle problems before they became this awful hole that was opening up around them.

"I'm sorry, Nuala." He felt tears choking him and he didn't want to break down.

"Maurice, I haven't time to worry about you. This is about Ruth."

It was like a slap in the face and he crumpled in front of her. All these years later she could still see the expression on his face. They had never recovered from that moment. Neither of them had ever been good at exploring their feelings or expressing them and after that they completely suppressed them. Maurice tried harder to be a good husband but he was working blind because Nuala wasn't capable of telling him what she wanted.

Nuala's first thought that night was that maybe Ruth had hurt herself – but if she had, she would have used the sleeping tablets and just gone to sleep. No. The presence of the drugs only served to confirm in Nuala's mind that her daughter had met with foul play of some sort.

"Maurice, we have to get rid of these drugs."

Despite her fears, all Maurice could hear were the businesslike clipped tones of her voice.

"This is no time to worry about propriety, Nuala! Surely if something has happened to her the police will need to know all the details."

"You stupid man!" Nuala's voice was suddenly shrill in the quiet little house. "If they see these drugs they will just write her off as a suicide or a runaway."

"But maybe that's what it is." Maurice couldn't see why she was assuming foul play.

Nuala spoke slowly now with exaggerated patience. "If she wanted to kill herself she would have used these tablets." She let the words hang in the air for effect.

"I suppose," Maurice concurred though he was still unsure.

Nuala grabbed the bottles and put them in her handbag. Then she began to make the bed.

"Nuala, you can't do that!" Maurice was desperate.

Nuala ignored him and continued to straighten up the room. "I want them to investigate this properly and not tell us she was depressed and ran away or that she . . ." her voice trailed away for a second ". . . or that she hurt herself."

She moved on to the bathroom and quickly put things in order there, and finally dealt with the worst of the disorder in the kitchen, taking particular care to bin any stale food.

Then she went to the phone and called the police. They'd asked her how long Ruth had been missing and Nuala immediately said she'd been trying to contact her for days but to avail. When they started investigating they realised that she hadn't been in classes for weeks.

Because of Ruth's mental state at that time and her refusal to eat, nobody could give a clear timeframe as to when she was last seen. Her parents hadn't seen her for weeks, the local shop hadn't seen her for at least a week and she hadn't been at college.

Over the years both Maurice and Nuala had come to terms with the fact that their actions that night had greatly impeded the investigation and was probably the reason why Ruth was never found. Nuala knew there was probably trace evidence somewhere in the room which might have identified the kidnapper. At no time did she consider that perhaps Ruth had killed herself. That wasn't something her family did, because they were fighters. They never gave up.

Something changed in their marriage that night and they never got it back. They married in a time when divorce wasn't legal in Ireland and they both believed in the church and its teachings so for them it wouldn't have been an option anyway, but for the most part they lived separate lives, each trying to avoid the reproach in the other's eyes. Amy had picked up on that the night she came to stay.

Now Nuala sat on the edge of Amy's bed and looked around the room. There must have been a time in their lives, a single time when something happened that altered it all. Nuala had to be strong for so long. She lost her father, had to take care of her mother, then her sister, then her sister's child and all along a husband who seemed to have a world view unique to himself, but through it all there was nobody to take care of her. Without Moira she didn't think she could have survived. Moira had been with her since she was a little girl. They grew up together, played together and dated together. Moira was even pregnant at the same time as Nuala. But was there something along the way that she or someone else did that caused this tragic chain of events that became her life?

When herself and Kitty married the Devine boys she thought their lives had now begun and they could put the past behind them. It took many years to get over the effects of their mother's illness but on that beautiful day they thought it would all get better. But it didn't. Amy's arrival saw to that.

Chapter 28

Maurice had walked into the room and stood looking at his wife sitting on the bed. She wasn't aware that he was there. Her expression fascinated him. It was so filled with bitterness and hate.

Maurice too thought back to the night that they discovered Ruth had disappeared. Nuala had done a thorough clean-up in that room and he had watched as she did it. That photo wasn't there that night. The photo had to have gone with Ruth and the person who took her. How did it get back here now?

Maurice's mind worked by conjuring up feelings rather than pictures he would have to directly confront, so now he stood watching his wife as she sat there and he felt a gnawing ache in his gut. He couldn't put anything into words but something hurt when he pictured his wife that night rearranging the scene and the return of that photograph last night. There was no reason why Nuala would have kept that photograph and surely no reason why she would use it to torment Amy but he'd heard the way she destroyed his niece's memories of her parents earlier in the evening. Nuala threw all she had at Amy. He assumed it was her last chance to hurt James – but did she hate Amy that much?

Many times he'd remembered Nuala ranting about the success of her niece and the loss of her daughter. Nuala was a woman of faith and she couldn't see why none of her prayers were ever answered. She had suffered so many tragedies in her life and after each one she'd turned to God and her church to help her make sense of it all and each time He'd let her down. Amy was a self-professed atheist and her life flourished and prospered. Maurice wondered how far Nuala's resentment would take her. As he watched her, eyes scrunched up and her mouth pursed, he got that uneasy ache again in the pit of his stomach. He should be able to say he knew his wife and what she was capable of but ever since that night he realised he knew nothing about the secrets she held in her heart. The woman who found such damning evidence of her daughter's despair and then took the time to clean up before calling the police was a person he knew little about. That night he realised she was capable of anything.

At that moment Nuala looked up. Immediately she saw the doubts on his face. A rush of anger built up inside her. No wonder she valued her best friend so much. Her husband had been no good to her or Ruth. He was weak and couldn't be trusted when things got tough. The Maurices of the world looked about for comfort when tragedy struck while people like Nuala had to soldier on.

Maurice's heart jumped when he saw those bitter eyes turned on him. "Nuala! Where is Amy?"

"She ran away in the night. Does that sound like a girl with a clear conscience?"

Maurice was afraid to say what he really felt, that those were the actions of a girl who was terrified of spending another night at home with her aunt.

"I've got to go out and see to the cattle." Maurice was already turning in the doorway.

Nuala stood up. "I'll get the breakfast started."

"I'll be back in fifteen minutes," his voice carried from down the hall.

Maurice loved farming. He was never meant to be a farmer. The farm was going to go to James while he was set to work in the local co-op. But after James died he'd had to step in and take over, but he found he loved it. Maurice was no longer the son without a goal, the ex-biker who was in a fight every night in the village. Once he took over the farm and the care of his mother he felt a pride in himself he'd never experienced before that. Anyone who knew him now wouldn't be able to reconcile the image with the young Maurice Devine. Time really does alter lives. Like Amy, Maurice found in tragedy a quiet strength and the ability to dig about and form a plan. It was such a simple philosophy that he couldn't understand why his wife didn't feel it too. If you stopped fighting and trying to control life things just gradually got better. Maurice wasn't a man of words so he found it hard to tell her this. Instead he stood by and watched her get more angry and disillusioned every day.

Maurice fed the cattle with hay and walked through them, checking to see if any of them were ready yet to calf. All of them seemed healthy and fit. He walked back up to the dairy and put on the boiler to clean the milk tank. It hadn't been used in so long he didn't want any bacterial build-up in the pipes. To be truthful, he didn't want to face his wife yet. Breakfast could wait. He was hoping she would leave the food in the grill and go down to Moira. He wanted a quiet morning to process all the happenings since yesterday.

Nuala sat at the table. Her plate was empty and she'd drained her second cup of tea and still Maurice hadn't come back. He was outside, sulking like a child, leaving her to figure out what to do next. Her temper ready to explode, she walked outside to the cow house to see what he was doing. There was no sign of him there but she heard him rattling about in the dairy. She went back out into the yard and walked around to the dairy door. Maurice had his back turned to her. She couldn't believe her eyes. His breakfast was on the table and their lives were in a mess and he decided to spring-clean the dairy! Cleaning the tank was a chore that didn't need doing right now. Why was he always hiding in the pretence of a normal life? They didn't have a normal life and hadn't had for many years.

Nuala was choked with her anger. She stood and watched him for a moment longer then decided she'd had enough, enough of this sham of a marriage.

There was no sound from the house as Maurice finished the cleaning. She was inside brooding. The rest of the day was going to be tough. As he was about to bring the boiler back down to the shed he heard Peter barking, followed by a painful howl, then silence.

Maurice ran towards the sound of the howl, his heart racing. He stood in the shed, unable to comprehend what he was seeing. Peter, his old friend, was lying in the straw in the last twitches of life, a pike piercing his body, pinning him down.

"Peter, Peter, what happened?"

He crouched by the dog and went to pull the pike from his body but the image was too much for him. He fell to his knees crying with an abandon he hadn't experienced since he was a child. Even losing his daughter hadn't evoked such a response but the image of his old friend who'd followed him since he was a bandy-legged little pup lying dead in the straw unleashed all his pent-up pain from the last fifteen years. Maurice felt more alone than he ever thought it was possible to feel. Nuala was the only family he had and he saw the boiling hatred in her eyes this morning. As he sobbed he heard a sound high above his head in the rafters of the barn. He looked up and saw the bank of huge round bales come rolling down on him. The first bale struck his neck and the pain stopped.

Chapter 29

That day Maurice was expecting a delivery of heating oil. Hours later the lorry drove into the farmyard from the entrance off the main road. The driver drove passed the front of the shed and across the yard to the tank. He jumped from the cab and ran around to the hosepipe. Pressing the switch, he released the fuel and stood there looking around the yard as the tank filled, but keeping an eye on the gauge to make sure he didn't go above the order. He started to whistle and leaned back against the tank. There was no sign of the dog. He was fond of dogs and Peter was a particular favourite of his. He'd known the old dog since he was a pup. When the oil was off-loaded he closed the tank and replaced the hose on the lorry. He went to the cab and took out the order book and filled out the docket. It was strange that Maurice wasn't here. He'd never arrange a delivery and not be there to pay him. Maurice was always very reliable.

He shut the door of the cab and went over to the dwelling house through the other gate. The house was as silent as the farmyard had been. He rang the bell a few times but there was no answer. Nuala must be out somewhere. He turned and walked back to the farmyard, closing the garden gate behind him. Releasing a spit into the flowerbed by the dairy door he had a quick look inside to see if Maurice was working in there. The boiler was still out with the tools Maurice had been using earlier to check the pipes. Well! He thought Maurice couldn't be too far away. He called out his name as he walked through the farm buildings but there was no response. The old dog never left the yard and though he was a friendly old guy he always barked loudly to alert Maurice that they had company. His legs might not be operating too well but his ears were fine. So were his vocal cords. He was never locked in even when they were away because he was too old to wander past the yard. He should have come to him as soon as he drove up.

He walked through the animal sheds. The cows were all inside happy and contented, chewing the cud and watching him with their big beautiful eyes.

He walked to the open doorway of the cowsheds and spat again onto the ground. The collecting yard where the cows exercised had a few more cows standing in a row, pulling chunks of silage out of the pit. They stood contentedly swishing their tails as they tugged, mashed and swallowed their food. They would in turn go in and lie down soon to chew. He turned back into the cowshed again and made his way to the hay barn. There was a big window-like opening between the shed and the barn. This made it easy to toss bales of hay into the shed for the hay bins. He looked through the window. The barn was a mess, unlike every other area he'd just passed through. A bank of round bales had fallen down cluttering up the front section which usually stood bare, ready to board sick cows where it was warmer. It was always clear and ready just in case one fell ill suddenly.

The driver vaulted through the opening and stood in the shed. At first he could see nothing out of the ordinary but he had an uneasy feeling. He walked around the large bales and an arm was immediately visible from under the bales, twisted in a grotesque manner. He ran over and put his back against the bale and pushed it off Maurice but he knew instantly that he was dead. His body was still warm but his head lay 'at an odd angle. It was obvious that his neck was broken. Dark blood oozed from his nose and ear.

The driver rushed backwards with shock and fell on his back on the ground. Though a grown man he found himself sobbing. The poor old dog was there too, pinned to the ground by a pike. He took a minute to compose himself, turning his back on the spectacle he'd just witnessed. Sniffing loudly he prepared himself to speak to the police. He walked from the shed back out into the fresh air and pressed the emergency numbers on his phone, then he walked back to the cab to wait. As he crossed the yard his legs nearly collapsed under him.

Sergeant Brian Poole was at his desk when he got the call. He was only down the road so it just took him less than five minutes to get to the farm. It took the rest of the emergency services a little longer but while he waited for them Brian had a good look around. There was no evidence anywhere in the shed that it was anything more than a tragic accident, though it was odd how the dog had died.

He took his notebook and walked over to the driver to get his statement. This man delivered heating oil to Brian also so he'd known him for a long time and he'd never seen him look so shaken up. His face was snow-white and his hands shook as he chain-smoked. When Brian tried to get his statement the poor man's voice stammered and the tears began to flow.

Brian walked back to the uniformed guard who'd come up with him.

"He won't be able to drive anywhere, the state he's in. We'll need to get a doctor to have a look at him."

As they spoke the ambulance and the local doctor arrived. Maurice was pronounced dead at the scene and loaded into the ambulance.

Brian knew he'd have to go looking for Nuala. If she wasn't here he guessed she would be with Moira or at the very least Moira would know where to find her. This was the part of the job he hated. The tears and the emotion wasn't something that Brian ever wanted to see.

He dialled the number of the coffee shop and asked for Moira. Minutes ticked by as he waited for the girl to go and get her. He kicked a stone around the yard as he waited.

"Brian. What can I do for you?" Moira's cheerful voice seemed macabre in the current situation.

"Moira, is Nuala Devine with you?"

"Yes. She is."

"Can I speak to her? Please."

Moira's voice lost its sparkle. "What's wrong?"

"There's been an accident. It's Maurice."

"Oh God." There was silence for a moment. "Is he hurt badly?"

Brian's uncomfortable silence said it all as he tried to find the correct words.

"Oh. He's gone then." Moira's voice shook as the realisation hit her.

"Yes."

"Don't say anything to her now, Brian. I'll bring her up to the farm. I'll look after her."

"Thank you, Moira. I'll be here when you come up. Doctor Lawlor is here as well."

"That's good. We'll be there as soon as we can."

Brian hung up and went back to speak to the doctor and the lorry driver.

Moira walked out from behind the counter and returned to her friend. They had been talking for the last few hours. She didn't know what to say to her now. Nuala had spent the morning telling Moira that this was it. She was leaving Maurice Devine and there was nothing Moira or anyone else could do to stop her. Moira knew you didn't tell Nuala what to do so instead she tried to gently remind her of the good times but it hadn't been her best idea. Nuala was still adamant that it was over. Absolutely finished this time.

Moira sat by her side and held Nuala's hand in her own.

"What?" Nuala frowned slightly and turned her intense gaze on her friend.

"Nuala . . ." Moira couldn't finish the sentence.

"Spit it out!" Nuala had little patience at the best of times.

"Honey. It's Maurice. There's been a terrible accident." Moira was trying to hold back her tears to be strong for her friend.

But Nuala's reaction scared her.

"Is he dead?" Nuala's voice was void of any emotion.

Moira put it down to shock. "Yes, pet. He is. We have to go up to the farm. The guards are there."

Nuala stood up. "Okay. I want to talk to Brian about something anyway."

When she heard the coldness from her friend, Moira frowned. That kind, gentle if a little eccentric man, who was lying alone at the farm deserved a little more than this. This was a Nuala she didn't know and for the first time in her life didn't like. But she pulled herself together. Once again she told herself it must be shock. They had been married for nearly forty years.

Nuala had to care a little for the man who'd shared those years with her. Moira followed her friend out the door and walked with her to her car. In a few moments they were at the farm.

Maurice was already covered and in the ambulance when they got there. Moira held Nuala's hand and gently guided her towards the door but as she got there she turned.

"No. I don't need to see him."

Then she walked back to the house through the garden, leaving Brian and Moira staring after her in amazement.

Chapter 30

Nuala entered the house and went down to her room. It was exactly as it was this morning when she left it. She'd been too angry then with Maurice to tidy up so she left and went straight to Moira's. Moira didn't believe her when she said it was over for good. Nuala could see that on her face. But Nuala never changed her mind when it was made up. That morning when she left the house and saw Maurice hiding in the dairy Nuala knew she could never look at him as her husband ever again. He had let her down once too often.

Now she sat on the bed, confused and bewildered. She didn't miss him. She should be sobbing her heart out because she'd lost her husband, but she couldn't raise a tear. Maybe she was just used to death and loss now. Maybe it had lost its ability to shock her. The only feeling she had right now was a little twinge of anger at Moira for judging her.

Nuala never judged Moira. Moira was her family.

Suddenly an unbidden memory that she'd spent years suppressing came rushing back and she was swamped by it. She tried to think back to the exact time it happened. It was in the late eighties. Ruth had gone out. No. It was a couple of years before Ruth disappeared. It was the end of the holidays and she would be going back to school shortly. Nuala remembered Ruth moaning about how fast the summer had gone. It was the year before she left school. That was it.

Nuala always stayed up and waited for her to come back and they would have a chat before Ruth went to sleep. The moment Ruth walked through the door Nuala knew something was wrong. The bright smile and the confident step she had developed since she'd started going out was gone and her eyes couldn't meet her mother's worried gaze.

"I'm tired, Mum I'm going to bed." She moved to walk past Nuala.

"What's wrong? How did the night go?"

Ruth blushed. "It was fine, I'm fine but I'm really tired. I want to go to bed."

Nuala grabbed her hand, yanking her arm a lot more roughly than she'd intended but she was so worried. The first thing she thought of was that her little girl had slept with someone and didn't want to talk to her about it.

"What did you do?" Nuala's voice was rising despite telling herself that an angry response wasn't a good response.

Ruth's anger eclipsed her own. "What did I do? How dare you immediately accuse me of something when you don't know the story!"

"Well, how can I know when you won't tell me?"

"I was assaulted tonight." Ruth pulled back her fringe and showed her mother the big blue bruise.

Nuala started opening the buttons on Ruth's trench coat, which was closed tightly despite the warm night.

"Mum!" Ruth screamed the word.

Nuala pulled open the coat and looked at the short skirt and tight top underneath. "Look at what you're wearing! I told you you couldn't go out like that! What did you do? Did you get changed at that girl's house?"

"Mum!"

"Could you be pregnant?"

Ruth looked at her mother like she'd never seen her before. "Is that all you're worried about? You still haven't asked me if I'm all right, or if you can do something for your daughter."

Nuala slapped her daughter sharply on the face. "Don't you answer back! Could you be pregnant?"

"No, Mother, I couldn't be. He didn't quite make it in there before I head-butted his nasty little face. I got away."

Nuala breathed a sigh of relief. "I'm so glad."

"You stupid woman! I was terrified. He had his hands all over me."

"Where were you?"

"I don't understand what you mean."

"Where were you?"

"I was at The Copper Pot."

"I know that. It didn't happen inside, did it? You went outside with somebody."

"Yes." The anger dissolved from Ruth and she sat at the table. "I didn't see the harm in it."

Nuala came and knelt by her side. "I know, darling. I'm sorry. I was just so worried in case any permanent damage was done. Do you know him? Maybe we should get the police to talk to him?"

Ruth blushed again and Nuala knew by her face that it was someone they all knew.

"Who was it?"

"Philip."

"Philip?"

"Yes. Moira's Philip."

"You went outside with a man who's eight years older than you and has a wife? Ruth, what were you thinking?"

"She's not my wife. She's his, so why should I be loyal to her. I've known him all my life and his mother is your best friend. I thought it would be fine."

Nuala stood up and walked to the range. She turned and looked at her daughter. "I don't know you. You're a different person to me after this."

Just then both women heard a sound. They turned and saw Maurice standing in the doorway. They had no idea how long he'd been standing there. Ruth was mesmerised by the look of sadness and disappointment she saw there. She opened her mouth to speak but before she got a chance he grabbed his cap and rushed across the kitchen and out the back door. The door slammed and for a few minutes the kitchen remained in complete silence. Maurice had never interfered in Ruth's life even when she was a little girl. He didn't tell her what to do or give her advice because he thought she was perfect. Nuala knew Maurice gave Ruth an unconditional A-Plus the day she was born and in his mind he'd never have to downgrade her. His little girl could do nothing wrong. The adoration was mutual. Nothing meant more to Ruth than her father's opinion of her. But that night as Maurice stood in the doorway he knew his little girl had lost her grade. Maurice felt like the world had shifted on its access and he'd lost his anchor.

Ruth saw her father's heart break in front of her eyes. Without another word to her mother she started sobbing and left the room. Nuala heard the bedroom door click shut and she didn't follow her. She was so angry with her. Moira loved Philip and was very fond of his wife. If they pursued this, Moira would be devastated and it could ruin Nuala's friendship with her. How could her daughter be so stupid? Nuala started to rationalise the situation. The clothes Ruth wore gave off a clear signal. If she thought that, the guards certainly would too. Plus she'd gone outside with him. Nuala decided that she was only protecting her daughter's reputation. It was better to let it settle. She wasn't raped. No harm was done. She couldn't be pregnant.

They never mentioned the subject again. Maurice

buried it in that place he put everything else he couldn't understand. Once he'd safely compartmentalised, he could carry on as though nothing had ever happened. Nuala didn't forget but she decided it was one of those things that sometimes you were better off just learning from.

But Ruth never forgave her. Nuala never mentioned that night again and neither did Ruth but it hung between them like veils of reproach. In time Ruth pulled further and further away from her. That's the pain that really burned in Nuala; the guilt of knowing that the drugs lying on her daughter's nightstand could have been there because of her. If Maurice was a man she could have confided in she could have shared that burden but her husband wasn't a communicator.

Now, Maurice was gone and she was alone. Just one more layer of pain for Nuala Devine.

Chapter 31

Moira gave Nuala a few hours to rest and get her head around what had happened. About seven o'clock she knocked on the door and went in with a cup of hot tea. Nuala was still asleep. Moira put the tea on the nightstand and called Nuala's name. Her friend murmured in her sleep and then opened her eyes.

"Hi." Moira leaned down and kissed her forehead. "Are you all right?"

"I'm feeling a bit better. Thanks for the tea. I'll get up in a minute."

"Okay. I'll be in the kitchen. Take your time."

Moira had cleaned the kitchen and lit the fire so when Nuala arrived the room was warm and a plate of dinner sat on the table.

"Thank you, Moira. I'm starving." She sat down and reached for her food.

Moira was worried. She expected Nuala to show some emotion. Her husband had just died.

Nuala ate her dinner in silence and then the two women took their tea to the sofa by the stove. For a while neither woman spoke as Moira was finding it difficult to break into Nuala's thoughts.

"Do you want me to contact Amy and tell her?" Moira was searching for something to get Nuala talking. She'd picked the wrong topic.

"No." Nuala didn't want that girl involved in Maurice's funeral. She knew where to find her when she needed her.

"He was her uncle."

"Leave it, Moira." Nuala closed the subject. Once she buried Maurice she was going to the police. Right now she wanted to think. Amy took the photo. Nuala had searched for it but it wasn't anywhere in the room. She had no evidence and she knew they would think her crazy.

"Right," said Moira. "I'll help you with the funeral arrangements. You don't need to worry about anything."

Nuala smiled. "Thank you."

Silence returned to the room. Nuala wasn't the only one who'd suffered bereavement in her family but Nuala only saw how things affected her. Moira had lost her son Philip shortly after Ruth's disappearance. Like the disappearance of Ruth the case of Philip Lennon was still open. Philip married in his mid-twenties and gave Moira two beautiful grandchildren but his marriage was unhappy and by the time he reached thirty he was separated and his wife didn't want anything to do with him. After he disappeared Moira set about reconciling her family with her daughter-in-law and her grandchildren and now it was like Moira had been given a second chance. She adored the two children, a boy and a girl. It broke her heart when her son's drinking escalated and his marriage broke down. But now she was watching her grandchildren grow into wonderful people and she had developed the ability to only remember the good points of her son before the drinking got out of control. It was easier to bear if there was a substance to blame.

The following days were a blur of people, food, drink and arrangements, phone calls to the priest and blocking off the sitting-room so they could get everything ready there.

Nuala moved around with frightened eyes that reflected old ghosts. Every so often panic would grip her. I've lost everybody, she thought.

Maurice was brought from the hospital to the funeral home. Looking back she couldn't remember all of it. For most of it she'd blacked out and took a mental sabbatical. But she got through it. In the background Nuala's neighbours rallied around and with Moira they shouldered the heavier load for their friend Nuala. This just gave her a lot of time to brood.

She sat in front of the coffin, looking at the priest, trying to concentrate as the sermon and the church swam in and out of focus. She didn't look at Maurice once. During the wake she walked into the room with her head lowered and sat at the front of the coffin looking at the bump where his feet were. To save her life she couldn't look up. Memories of Kitty and James' burial were replaying in her head like old movies.

When she went to sleep just a few nights ago, she never expected any of this. Life kept throwing her curveballs.

Moira didn't understand the reasons behind Nuala's attitude towards Amy. She assumed that Nuala just didn't want to burden her, that Nuala was going to get herself back on her feet and then try and speak to her niece. It was the only way Moira could make sense of it all. Nuala had told her that Amy had gone back to Dublin but she never told her she'd left through the bedroom window in the middle of the night. Nuala hadn't confided anything to her about the photograph or how she saw Amy as the catalyst that destroyed her family, the family she fought so hard to build.

But Moira couldn't let it lie. Amy had a right to know that her uncle had died and if Nuala wouldn't tell her then maybe somebody should do it for her. Moira thought that once Nuala calmed down she would regret her decision to exclude her niece.

So she picked up the phone and rang Helfers. She told a little white lie and said she was Nuala Devine and she was looking for her niece Amy. Moira explained about Maurice's death.

"I'm sorry," Amy's assistant said. "Amy is away on holidays. Em . . ." He paused for a moment. "Is she not in Waterford with you?"

"She went back to Dublin and I just thought she might have called into work."

"No. She's still away. We haven't heard from her here."

Moira hung up and sat down by the window. The coffee shop was almost empty so she had a few minutes to think. Nuala wouldn't talk about Amy and insisted she had gone back to Dublin. It was almost a week now since she would have left but she never went back to work and they thought she was in Waterford. Moira knew something serious had happened between Amy and Nuala and she wanted to know what. But Nuala was so stubborn she would never tell her. Moira decided to find out for herself. She knew if she asked Nuala for Amy's numbers she'd be told to mind her own business but she had to try and contact the girl.

"Mind the fort, Louise!" Moira threw her tea towel behind the counter and went out to her car. Moira knew that Nuala was away this morning in Waterford.

She drove up to Nuala's house and put her hand behind the trellis and took out the spare key. She went inside and straight to the hall table where the phone books and Nuala's address book always sat. She picked up the book and flipped to the correct page and there they were – Amy's house and mobile numbers. She copied them down into her own address book and put everything back exactly as she'd found them. Then she left the house, locked the door and put the key back in its place. Just as she was heading back to the car, Nuala drove into the yard.

"What are you doing here?" she asked.

"I just came up to see if you were back yet. I thought we could have a cup of tea."

"Well, come inside then." Nuala unlocked the door and they went inside.

Moira really didn't want to be there. She was itching to get back to work and call Amy.

Nuala put the kettle on and took down the biscuit barrel.

"Did you buy anything nice in Waterford?" Moira asked.

"No. I had to register some paperwork for the new calves. It got delayed with the funeral and everything."

"You can do all that stuff on-line you know."

Nuala laughed. "I never used a computer in my life."

"Honey, that should be your next plan. Buy yourself a computer and maybe take some lessons."

"That's not a bad idea."

Finally, after a pot of tea, Moira excused herself and headed back to the coffee shop. It was still quiet so she gave Louise her break and she started calling Amy. The house phone rang out each time and then went into the answering machine. She turned her attention to her mobile and it too went straight to answering machine. She left a brief message on both machines and then waited. There was no reply all that evening. The next day she did the same and got no reply and finally on the third day it was obvious that something had happened to Amy Devine. It was Moira's guess that Amy hadn't been seen since the day that Maurice died.

Chapter 32

Brian looked up from his paperwork and saw the worried face of Moira Lennon looking around the door. He'd only barely heard the tentative knock that the normally boisterous Moira gave on his office door.

"Moira. Come in."

Moira walked in and popped a coffee and a muffin down on the desk in front of him.

"I need a favour."

He smiled at her. "Are you bribing a police officer, Mrs Lennon?"

"Just maintaining your strength."

"Sit down. What can I do for you?"

Moira sat. "I want you to contact someone for me. Someone I'm very worried about."

"Why can't you contact her?" he said through a mouthful of muffin.

"I've been ringing her house phone and mobile for

a few days. I haven't had any reply. As far as I know it's been a week since anyone has seen her."

"Is it someone I know?"

"Amy Devine."

Brian's face froze. "Amy Devine?"

"Yes. I think something has happened to her."

"Why are *you* searching for her? Why isn't Nuala looking for her?"

"I don't know. I think herself and Nuala have had a fight or something because Nuala won't talk about her and she wouldn't even allow me to tell her about Maurice. I let it go until the last couple of days when I started to get worried. I think something is wrong."

"What do you want me to do? It sounds like she might have gone away after a family argument."

"Something isn't right, Brian. I know it."

"I'll get someone in Dublin to go around to her house and have a look. She's probably there and doesn't want to talk to anyone. I'll go and talk to Nuala."

"I'm probably being silly but it's been a week. I'd hate to think she was missing and nobody even looked for her."

Brian didn't look convinced that there was anything to worry about.

Moira went home and now she waited by the phone for Brian to call.

A few days later Brian called in to Moira's in the afternoon. Amy's phone hadn't been used since the day Moira thought she'd disappeared. Her job hadn't heard from her since around the same time. He'd spoken to

Nuala but she just kept saying she had no idea where she was and frankly she didn't seem too worried.

"So we got a warrant to go to Amy's house and check it. Judging by the pile of mail inside the door she hadn't been back to her house at all."

Amy Devine was now officially a missing person.

He didn't tell Moira about the wild accusations from Nuala about the photograph.

For days afterwards every time Moira turned on the radio or the television all she saw was Amy's photograph and various pleas for her safe return. Nuala refused to co-operate. The police had asked her numerous times to make a personal plea to her kidnapper but she kept saying she'd "rather not".

The media loved it. It was just like Ruth all over again. They kept showing the old photographs of Ruth's case side by side with Amy's, exploring all possible reasons why two cousins might disappear fifteen years apart. They camped out in the village. Their vans lined the street and groups of reporters hung out in the pubs and Moira's coffee shop.

When Nuala learned of Moira's part in the investigation being opened she stopped calling her. Moira wouldn't have gone behind her back and done this if their friendship was still strong. Nuala wanted no part in the search for Amy and now she wanted no part of Moira either. Nuala was grieving for so many losses. It was a black kind of grief that was burying her and she couldn't get out.

After the first few days of the investigation, a clear

timeframe emerged as to when Amy went missing. A re-enactment was shown on the evening news, showing a girl with striking similarities to Amy leaving the guesthouse, going to dinner and leaving the restaurant afterwards. The car that had passed her on the road just before her approach to the guesthouse gave an almost-to-the-minute time for her disappearance. The whole country knew that she had left the restaurant and walked towards the house and within three hundred yards of the house disappeared, but nobody had a clue what might have happened to her.

PART FIVE

Chapter 33

On the twenty-first day Amy stood waiting for her food. Her senses were as fine-tuned as a cat's now and she heard his footsteps approaching her door. She stepped forward in anticipation but immediately she knew there was something wrong: there was no smell of hot food. She could hear him reach for the key above the door and the scratching sound as it entered the lock. He opened the door and stood there silently in the darkness but there was no tray. Amy could just see his outline.

Unexpectedly she found tears in her eyes.

"Where is my food?" And then the tears were spilling from her eyes. She roughly brushed them away, angry with her herself for having turned into this person.

He walked to her. She could feel the heat off his body in the cold room. He placed his hand on her arm, causing her to flinch. When she touched her she thought he was going to punish her for something.

Quickly, she ran through an inventory of all she had done this week to see if she'd done something wrong.

He leaned forward towards her and as he did she saw he had a silk scarf wound around his face. It covered the lower part, from his nose to the base of his neck. His eyes were covered in large dark shades, his head covered in a wool cap pulled low over his forehead. It was impossible to tell what kind of hair he had. She could smell his hair and feel the silk and wool brush her cheek. He'd used a sweet-smelling shampoo. Quietly, he unlocked the lock and unwound a few loops from her waist and then he locked it again. She felt lighter as some of the heavy coils fell to the ground. He'd given her a longer range.

He went back and brought a bundle of clothes from outside the door. He handed it to her. For a moment he stood beside her, his size and presence overbearing in the claustrophobic darkness. He was taller than she was but it was more than that. He stood too close. This was the closest she'd been to another human being in three weeks. Amy's personal space was something she always protected and usually she was the one getting too close to make a point. His chest was in front of her face and she could tell it was broad and muscular. A musky masculine smell emanated from his body in contrast to the smell from his hair. He stood like that for a moment, looking down on her head. Her eyes were lowered. She knew that behind those glasses his eyes bored through her. Slowly he raised his hand and pushed the hair gently back from her face. The heavy leather gloves he wore felt harsh against her skin. Then he turned and slowly and silently left the room, clicking the door shut behind him. As the door closed it felt as though it sucked the energy out of the room and left her behind in a vacuum.

Amy didn't know what to think.

Suddenly, she realised she could now reach the shower and was excited at the prospect. It was brighter in the bathroom as the rays from the half moon visible through the small window brightened the gloom. She turned the taps and quickly grasped the new cake of soap that up until now had been just out of her reach. As quickly as she could she tore off her clothes and stepped into the shower, aching to get the awful smell of her own unwashed body washed away. It was an electric shower so the water was hot. She could feel the small room filling with steam. She soaped herself, lifting the chains and washing underneath, flinching when she rubbed the spot where the extra loops of her chains had been. Her flesh was raw there and covered in bruises and scratches. She was worried in case the wounds would get infected.

The clothes he'd given her fit perfectly – white underwear, a fresh pair of jeans, a blue shirt and a warm grey cardigan – though the new jeans chafed her bruised and raw hips badly. Her hair was long and straight so she brushed it with a brush he'd placed in the bundle. When she finished she walked to the door and knocked. There wasn't a sound outside. For a few moments she stood waiting for something to happen, then she turned the handle and was scared and elated to see it open. Slowly she pulled it back and looked out. The hall was no longer in total darkness. She was able to move a couple of feet into the corridor beyond the door. A table was set there with a tablecloth, candles and flowers. A meal was laid for one. The plates and cutlery were plastic and laden with what looked like Indian food. He must have bought takeaway tonight. A paper cup of wine sat to her right and a plastic bowl of fruit was placed in the centre.

Amy remembered a similar scenario from the manuscript the night that Ruth died. Ruth brought that on herself, she thought. Ruth fought him without a plan. Amy wasn't going to fight, at least not until she had a plan and a strong opportunity.

The only light came from the little candles so she sat down in the flickering pool of its glow, which only spread a few feet beyond the table. The chain was just exactly the right distance for her to reach the chair, almost as though he had measured it.

"Hello!" she called out to the darkness as she ate.

She heard her voice echo back to her. This corridor was long. She tapped the ground under her feet. It was made of wooden boards. As her eyes became adjusted to the light she could see the outline of the corridor as it stretched away from her in both directions into pools of darkness at each end. The walls seemed to be covered in some type of wallpaper though she couldn't see what the pattern was from where she sat.

"Do you know how long you've been here?" a voice

called out of the darkness. The corridor must be quite long because the voice sounded distant and muffled.

"No," she lied.

Her voice broke. She'd barely used it in three weeks. Sometimes a little lie was the only way you could preserve some form of autonomy, a way to preserve a little piece of the world for yourself. She didn't want him to know about her wall. That was for her.

"It doesn't matter anyway," he said. "This was only the preparatory phase – from now on things will get better."

"What do you mean?"

"You'll see."

Amy smiled into the darkness. She knew he was watching her sitting there. He'd arranged her like a piece of performance art for his own amusement. Subtly lit and expertly arranged, she continued the rest of the meal on her plastic plates with her plastic cutlery. He wasn't taking any chances with her lashing out with a weapon.

"Why is it so dark here?" she asked.

"It's an old house so there are shutters on most of the windows. They keep out the light better than black-out blinds."

Like the night on the phone his voice was strange. It was definitely disguised and he wasn't going to speak too close to her. That confirmed for her that this was somebody she knew.

As she finished her food and pushed back her plate he spoke to her once more.

"Go back inside."

Amy was too scared to confront him. She knew exactly what he was capable of. She walked back inside and shut the door behind her. A couple of minutes later she heard his footsteps outside the door and the key turning in the lock.

Once he closed the door Amy went to the end of her chain to see how much further she could walk in the room. For a few moments she amused herself by running her hands along any areas of the wall she hadn't been able to touch before. Her body felt so much lighter without the extra coils looped around her waist. She did some squats to emphasise how much freedom she had. People can go crazy locked up like this, she thought.

Finally she lay down on her bed and tried to sleep. As she lay there she knew that there was a flaw in his plan. He was so arrogant that he thought with a bit of training women would do as he wanted. This was certainly true while he held the key to her chains but Amy had managed to keep alive, inside, an ability to function independently from him. That little spark of independence was still there and when a safe opportunity arose she would use it. Amy wasn't beaten yet.

The next morning she was wakened by a sound outside the door. He never came to her in the morning. No! Terror invaded her. If she saw his face she knew she was dead. She jumped off the bed, the sound of the chain reverberated around the room. Almost choking in her fear she ran into the bathroom and shut the door as best she could with the chain trailing behind her. Outside, the door opened. She could hear it sliding across the wooden floor. A heavy footstep landed on the doorjamb and then he stood still and silent. Amy's breath was coming in pants as she stood with her back pressed against the door. This stand-off continued for a few minutes and then she heard his laugh ring out in the bare room and a rustle of papers before the door closed. Amy waited there, unable to move. What if he was still in the room? His game-playing was escalating and Amy knew now that it would continue to, until he got bored and killed her.

Finally she calmed sufficiently to realise that she was alone again. She opened the door and stepped out into the room. Just inside the door lay a bundle of papers just like the rest of the manuscript that she had already read. What more could he have to tell her? She knew now that Ruth was dead.

So, Amy, how do you like my house? It's peaceful here, isn't it? You are probably wondering how you got here. I'm sure there are a lot of questions you would like answers to. I'll start at the beginning, work my way through and hopefully I will give you answers to all of them. As I'm sure you've figured out by now I'm close to Ballyreid and I know people there. Imagine my surprise when a friend of mine tells me about the strange fare he had one night from Ballyreid into

Dungarvan! He told me about this tall blonde girl with the posh Dublin accent who sat in his taxi for ten miles, looking out the window, without speaking a word. My friend is talkative and he was offended by the total lack of interest this girl showed in being friendly. I asked him where he dropped her and he laughed.

"She had no idea where she wanted to go. She sat there like a shop dummy while she made up her mind. I had to prompt her to hurry up. I dropped her at a B&B just outside the town."

As you can imagine I was fascinated to hear of your desertion of Ballyreid. That wasn't our deal, was it? I asked you to come down but I never told you when you could leave. Obviously I wanted you down here for a reason and there you were, running away in the night.

The next day I sat near that guesthouse waiting for you to come out. I watched you all day as you came and went, waiting for an opportunity to bring you here. Since you stopped co-operating I had to take matters into my own hands. I watched you leave the restaurant and I saw the direction you turned to, so I knew you were on your way home. The rest you know. I drove onto the footpath in front of you and you hit the van. You went down and I loaded you into the back. Then I drove you here. That was brave of you to try and fight me when we got here but I'm not stupid, Amy, and don't ever think that I am. You are helpless now. I am in charge and you will do as I dictate. I want you to think about this and absorb it.

Chapter 34

The residents of Ballyreid lowered their heads and increased their pace to avoid speaking to the buzzing hoards of photographers and journalists that had all but taken up residence in their village. Moira's coffee shop was doing a brisk trade on take-out coffees, something that generally wasn't needed in Ballyreid. The locals had stopped going in because they were accosted by questions the moment they sat down.

Moira loved the news and she'd always loved a sensation but now she saw in detail the destruction and heartache behind the headlines. She was exhausted. The police had spoken to her of course but she couldn't tell them anything. They all wanted to know why she felt that Amy was in trouble. Moira was careful how she answered. She didn't want in any way to implicate her friend. But she knew her silence was only making things look odder for both of them. Damn Nuala's stupidity! If she had only tried to contact Amy after Maurice's death,

Moira would have been kept out of the whole thing. Breaking into her best friend's house to steal two phone numbers was one of the details she kept to herself. The obvious first question would of course be why didn't she just ask her for them? If Moira said it was because Nuala wouldn't give them to her, they would certainly think Nuala was somehow involved in her niece's disappearance. Despite their recent problems Moira still had residual loyalty left.

Moira ran a cloth over a table by the window and stood looking out on to the street outside. As she stood there she realised that the car parked straight outside the coffee shop was Nuala's.

Her friend sat there staring right through her with a look that Moira couldn't comprehend. Moira raised her hand and waved but Nuala just held her gaze a moment longer and drove from her parking space and down the road.

Since the day she went to the police Nuala wouldn't return her calls and hadn't been into the shop. Moira was sure she sensed that in some way her best friend had betrayed her. Nuala had always protected herself by a thick shroud of mistrust. She'd always needed to keep people at arm's length. Moira wondered how deep Nuala's pain went and what it could lead her to do? People do very strange things when they are backed in to a corner and Nuala's life was after tumbling down around her and she no longer trusted anyone.

Moira turned as the door opened. Brian Poole walked into the shop.

"Brian. What can I do for you?"

"Five coffees to go."

"Have you got any news of Amy yet?" Moira knew it was a silly question. She'd know as soon as they had anything.

Brian just shook his head.

Moira turned her back on him for a few minutes while she fixed his coffees. When she turned around he was staring at her.

"We've spoken to Nuala and she seemed surprised to hear that 'she' called Helfers to tell her niece about Maurice's death."

Moira knew then why her friend was being so strange to her. Nuala knew that it was Moira who made that call, without running it by her first.

"She's under a lot of stress. Nuala just lost her husband. Maybe she forgot she made the call."

"I'm sure." Brian's eyebrows rose and his lips curled into an amused smile. "We checked Amy's phone messages. They are all from you. Not one from Nuala. Her aunt!"

"So?"

"Don't you think that's a bit strange?"

"Why?"

"You're not a relative, are you?" Brian still looked amused.

"No."

"I don't see Nuala coming in here much at the moment."

"Was that a question?" Moira was getting annoyed.

"No. As I was crossing the street there I saw her sitting outside."

Moira was sure he'd seen her wave and then Nuala driving away. They were making themselves look like suspects.

"Do you want anything else, Brian?"

"No, Moira. Thanks."

He turned and she watched him manoeuvre himself awkwardly through the door with his coffees and cross the street back to the station.

Brian walked into the station and sat in his office. What was the matter with those two? It was interesting to watch. Since the day he arrived in Ballyreid the two women were inseparable. When he'd left the station for his coffee he'd got delayed on the footpath talking to someone. What a surprise to see the intense emotions on the face of Moira Lennon as she looked into the face of Nuala Devine! He couldn't see Nuala's face but she deserved a ticket for the speed she used leaving that parking space.

He sipped his coffee and looked down at the files spread over his desk. Nuala's daughter disappeared. Now her niece was missing too. Moira's son also disappeared. A lot of mystery surrounded these two women. Brian had been here for ten years. This town was like one of those sleepy little backwaters where there was a veneer of normality with a boiling mess underneath. Brian started off in the force with the ideals of a boy scout and the profound wish to make things better, but over the years he'd got to see the underbelly of people and it wasn't pretty. He'd seen it all as a guard, even here in this supposedly quiet village. Scratch the surface on any of them, he thought, and there would be something rotten underneath. But that was true of people everywhere. Who knew that better than he?

Chapter 35

Nuala tossed and turned, unable to sleep. The music blaring from that pub was drilling through her brain. God, she missed the two Powers. The pub was wonderful when they were alive but once that Luke Devereaux took over, the place changed beyond recognition. She turned again and punched her pillow with her fists. It was karaoke so not only was the music loud, but it was totally off key. Eleven thirty and the music was only getting louder. Nuala's temper finally snapped.

She jumped up and got dressed. Without even stopping to think about what she was doing she marched down her drive, turned left and walked down the road to the pub. Taxis were stopping and leaving more people on the path outside so the ruckus was set to continue on for hours yet.

Nuala pushed her way through the crowd and up to the counter.

"Luke."

"Nuala. How are you?"

"I'm tired!" she shouted, but it was so loud in there that he didn't notice how angry she was.

"Would you like a Red Bull or something else to wake you up?"

"No. I want some *peace!*"

"What? This conversation is a strange one to be having with your neighbours at eleven o'clock at night. How can I help you with that?"

"You can do something about the noise in here."

"But Nuala this is a licensed premises. We have a late licence."

"Well, you shouldn't have and I'm going to see to it that you don't get it renewed."

"Nuala! Come in the back. This is not the place to have this discussion."

Luke turned and led the way around the bar and down a narrow corridor to the office in the back. Nuala followed him.

"Nuala. I'm running a business here. We all have to make a living." Luke didn't even offer her a seat.

"I have to get some sleep. My bedroom window is only a couple of hundred yards from this pub."

"And your farmyard is only a couple of hundred of yards from this pub. Last summer I tried to introduce a beer garden and the smell of cow shit drove my customers away."

"Don't be ridiculous!" Nuala had lost the ability to smell the cow yard over the years so she thought he was making fun of her.

"I'm not. I had daily complaints."

"Well, that's neither here not there." Nuala wasn't going to be sidetracked.

"It is. It's called live and let live. Did I go up and ask you to move your slurry tank somewhere else?"

"Don't be ridiculous. How could you? We were there first."

"Nuala, maybe you need some sleeping tablets." He spoke with an exaggerated calmness like he was soothing a small child who was having a tantrum.

His soft tones were having the opposite effect on Nuala. "Don't you placate me! I'm not a child."

"You're behaving like one."

He actually had the cheek to smile at her.

"How dare you!" She shrieked the words at him.

"Nuala. Go home. You're being unreasonable." He turned and walked out of the room and left her standing there.

Nuala angrily brushed a tear from her cheek. She couldn't believe he'd spoken to her like that, the jumped-up little worm!

Nuala was so angry she was shaking. He'd just dismissed her like her opinion didn't matter. She'd lived all her life in this village. Her in-laws had owned this farm for four generations. That little twerp had only lived in this village since he bought the pub. He was from Dungarvan. His uncle owned the local Spar, so he did have connections but he was a blow-in none the less.

Despite her assertion that he was a blow-in Nuala

had known him since he was a little boy. He went to school in Dungarvan and spent weekends here with his uncle. Nuala had always found him an arrogant child with no respect. She never liked him hanging out with Ruth. She was so angry she could spit.

Nuala slammed the office door behind her and marched through the pub. Luke was behind the bar talking to a customer. He waved to her as she passed through. She turned her little nose up in the air and left. Eventually, when the noise died down at about two thirty, she slept.

As she drifted off she decided. Tomorrow she would put the farm and dwelling house up for sale and she would get herself a house in the village. In the morning she would put everything in motion. Some fights weren't worth having. Nuala grew up in the village; maybe her future was there.

The market was good and it shouldn't take too long to sell. There were a few fields that she could sell as separate sites. The farm was big and the land was good. Nuala deserved a new direction. Her life had had many false starts over the years and she felt that it was time she started thinking about herself. She wasn't old. She could take a computer course and get herself a job. Just for company. With the proceeds of the sale she probably wouldn't have to. Her plans finally helped her to sleep.

The next morning she got up and made herself some breakfast. For the first time in weeks she felt energetic. She called the estate agent straight after breakfast and made an appointment for before lunch. It wasn't going to take long because she was only interested in houses in the village.

There was only one that caught her eye. It was a stone cottage with a neat front yard and a back garden. It had been recently renovated and the kitchen extended. A wooden deck with an outdoor dining area could be reached through a set of patio doors from the dining area in the kitchen.

Nuala left the estate agent's mulling it all over in her mind and bumped straight into Brian Poole.

His eyes immediately fell to the brochures in her hand. "Buying a house, Nuala?"

"I'm thinking about it." The barriers went up again and the frown that had been absent that morning returned to knit her brows.

"That one is near Moira Lennon's." His sharp eyes had pinpointed the location of her house.

"It's a small village, Brian. Everything is near Moira Lennon's."

Brian smiled. "It will be handy to have someone close by."

"I've got to go, Brian." She went to walk around him.

"You never ask me about Amy." Brian watched her face closely.

Nuala's eyes narrowed slightly and for a moment she hesitated but then she walked on, feeling his eyes bore into her back.

Nuala Devine wasn't letting the grass grow under

her feet. To be fair it would be difficult for her to take care of the farm by herself. Brian was beginning to see the real Nuala. That was the secret of her survival. She did what had to be done without self-pity. Nuala didn't dilute her control by asking for help. She took care of business herself.

Later that week Luke Devereaux drove his van into the yard behind the pub. He saw the *For Sale* board up outside the Devines'. That was interesting. Her husband was barely in the ground and her niece was missing yet Nuala had the energy to move house. She was a tough woman, a lot like her daughter.

Chapter 36

Nuala couldn't believe how fast life changes without giving you any chance to keep up. After just a few days on the market she was offered more money for the land than she ever thought she could dream of. It turned out that a developer had had his eye on their land for a long time and, with the death of Maurice and Nuala wanting a quick sale, he jumped at the opportunity. But before Nuala got a chance to decide what she wanted to do, a village contingent approached her demanding that she sell to a local farmer who needed grazing land and protect the integrity of the village. Nuala wasn't a stupid woman. She knew the farmer in question and she didn't doubt his honourable intentions but he was in poor health and had two children who never lifted a finger on the farm since they left school. Nuala knew they were encouraging him to buy. One of the children was a solicitor and the other an accountant. The solicitor's wife was on the village committee that approached Nuala.

Nuala knew that either she sold now and made enough money to live comfortably for the rest of her life or the Gleeson children would sell in ten years' time. She just had to decide if she could cope with the disapproval of the village. Nuala decided to hold the developer off for a few days. He'd waited for five years so he could wait a while longer.

During this time Nuala was alone in her house with the ghosts of family. She longed to reach out to Moira but she couldn't get past Moira's betrayal. She could see why Moira wanted to look for Amy. Nuala was behaving oddly, but a friend would have come to her and spoken to her face to face and made her take a look at her actions and then they could have gone together to the police. Nuala wasn't thinking straight at that time. Amy had churned up all her feelings of loss over Ruth and then she had lost Maurice. And where did that photograph come from? Nuala didn't know what to think. Amy had known something that she didn't want to talk about. Nuala could see it in her eyes when she mentioned the photograph. How could Amy know anything about Ruth's disappearance and where was she now?

Nuala sat alone and wondered.

The reporters were losing interest in Ballyreid. More current and more newsworthy events had taken over. The people of the village had stopped hiding from the news teams and now they were back in the pubs and Moira's and they were talking openly about the curse of the Devine-Donnelly union. The only one left was Nuala, a relic of a broken family line.

Eventually Nuala made her decision and accepted the offer from the developer, leaving him free to reshape the village. Nuala looked around her as she drove down the street. She'd lived here long enough. Each time her life fell apart she picked herself up and soldiered on but now she saw what they were really like. What she had seen as a community was a tight-knit group of interfering busybodies. Amy had been right about that. Nuala had made it her business all her life to ingratiate herself with the right people. Ever since she was a little girl she felt the need to be popular. It protected her from the bad things when they happened. Everybody rallied round the pretty popular girl. But now she was the middle-aged woman with the curse on her family, and life or the community weren't so forgiving.

She stopped at a crossroads and held up the old photograph of herself and Kitty with Moira and Gemma as tears streamed down her face. Kitty was dead. Gemma went to England shortly after the photo was taken and eventually moved back to Dublin where she died of breast cancer in 1990. Gemma was always laughing. She had a little elfin face that was always up for some form of mischief. Herself and Kitty were best friends and exact opposites. Kitty was tall and willowy with a classically beautiful face and Gemma was a little waif with a big smile. Together they were forever laughing. Maybe if Gemma had stayed around she might have been able to talk Kitty into leaving James when things got bad but she'd gone to England by that time. It was easy to hide the bruises in a friendship that spanned the Channel.

Nuala couldn't put her own legacy into words. The happy smiles and the bright shirts shone out of the frame, drawing her back to their summer of love. That life was gone a long time and she'd tried to keep it going long after it died. Then a thought struck her. Had it ever been like that or was it as carefully constructed in her memory as this photograph had been on the night? Her heart ached to believe once again in the illusion.

A car behind her beeped: so Nuala laid the photograph down on the seat and drove on. This morning she decided to do what she should have done in her teens. That was the time when she should have picked herself up and moved on with her life but she struggled on, trying to become somebody in the village. Nuala never had her own identity. She was Mrs Donnelly's daughter, a pedigree she carried around for many years crushing her soul, then she was the sister of that beautiful tragic Kitty that the whole village was in love with, then she was the grieving mother of Ruth Devine the girl who disappeared into thin air, and now if she stayed in that village she would end her days as the widow of Maurice Devine. From today onwards she was Nuala Donnelly again, out to build a new and wonderful life. Maybe there was virtue in being the last one standing. If you got to this point nothing could break you.

Nuala drove on to Dungarvan. She went straight to an estate agent and asked to view a listing they had on their books.

By that evening Nuala Devine was the proud owner of a small coffee shop with an excellent reputation in the town. The owners were retiring to the country. Nuala had run a house for many years and she had always been a good cook. She decided to put these skills to good use. She didn't need the money but she wanted to do something for herself. She sat in the square and looked at the façade of her coffee shop. She knew already what she would call it. *Nuala Donnelly's.* It would be shortened to Nuala's but she wanted everyone to finally know who she really was.

Chapter 37

As the news of Nuala Devine selling out to South East Development Group hit the local grapevine, every household in Ballyreid was talking about it.

Moira was just putting on another pot of coffee. They emptied as quickly as she got a chance to fill them. Because of her connections to Nuala everyone thought she would know what was going on but she was as much in the dark as anyone. Nuala Devine had shut them all out and retreated into her own world.

Moira never saw this coming. By getting involved she'd angered Nuala and set everything in motion. If Nuala had even had Moira to support her, she probably wouldn't have gone to these extremes. Now the whole village was going to suffer. Once SED Group got their hands on that land they would swallow the village in their corporate jaws. Nuala had taken the worst form of revenge on her village.

Moira knew how hard life had been for Nuala. She

bravely held her head high throughout her mother's illness and pretended she didn't hear the town laughing about Mrs Donnelly's *"latest episode"*. When Ruth disappeared she told Moira that she knew it was someone in the village who had taken her. Since then Nuala had watched everyone with a new sense of mistrust.

But what Moira didn't realise was that Nuala had watched nobody more closely than Moira's own son. But thinking back, Philip had seemed oblivious to Nuala's attention. He was oblivious to most things except his own selfish needs. Nuala's fears took root in her. If Philip could assault Ruth, could he kidnap her? Nuala had felt sick with the guilt of keeping all that from Moira but she couldn't shatter Moira's love for her only son. Yet she couldn't get the thought of it out of her head that Philip could steal her daughter. She went to the police and told them her suspicions and asked them to question him in private without letting Moira know, but these things always get out in a small place and before long the whole village was talking about Philip Lennon being called in for questioning about Ruth Devine's kidnapping.

Nuala blushed deeply one night during dinner as Moira begged her to tell the guards that Philip couldn't have done it.

"I can't do that, Moira. Everyone is a suspect to the police until she is found." They changed the subject but Nuala's veiled accusations hung between them at the table.

Moira left the restaurant and drove straight to Philip's house but his housemate told her he was in Molloys'. Moira left the curious man standing in the doorway and drove straight to the pub. Philip was sitting just inside at the end of the bar. The pub was quiet. Typical of Philip, he sat there, just him and his pint, the safest place for an alcoholic to hide – in the bottom of a bottle.

Moira sat on the stool beside him and dropped her keys onto the bar. He didn't even raise his head.

"Philip."

At the sound of her voice he turned to her. "What?"

"I just had dinner with Nuala Devine."

"So?"

"I think she suspects that you took Ruth."

"What about you, *Mother*?" He emphasised the word mother as thought he were spitting it out. And immediately the barriers went up and a hunted animal look came into his eyes.

For the first time ever Moira saw him clearly without a mother's eyes. She didn't like what she saw.

"Could you hurt that little girl?"

"It depends, Mother, on your definition of hurt." He started to laugh.

Moira raised her hand and slapped him sharply across the face. He ignored her as though she were swatting a fly and went back to his drink. She picked up her keys and left the bar. That was the last time she spoke to her son. For a couple of months she endured the sight of him drunk in the town when he should have been home with his wife and children and then one day he too disappeared and was never seen again.

From then on both women became bound together by a tight rope of suspicion. Moira suspected that perhaps the police were right and maybe her son took Ruth but then where did he go? Did he run away or was it something more permanent that she couldn't bear to put into words?

Once more the village was in turmoil as everyone looked to each other with suspicion. What kind of a village could lose two young people in the space of a year maybe at the hands of some of their own?

Nuala had closed on the purchase of her new business. She was planning to live upstairs over the café. It would be closed by five thirty so the apartment would be quiet but still she would be in the heart of the town. Her bedroom was to the back over the yard so it was away from the noise of the square at night. Nuala knew she was going to be very happy here.

After she moved the last of her belongings that she wanted to keep into her new flat, she sat at the front window looking over the square. Slowly she sipped her first cup of hot coffee in her new home.

Brian Poole had looked at her the last time they spoke as though she were a suspect of some kind. It wasn't helping that she'd picked up and moved her life so quickly. But Nuala's suffering had been festering for years and, after the pain she'd suffered, a husband she wanted to divorce and a niece she couldn't stand to be around didn't seem like such big losses. Nuala had really lost her daughter the night Ruth told her about the assault. She had never forgiven her mother for how badly she'd handled the whole thing. Nuala had never forgiven herself.

Nuala suspected that Moira knew that it was she who had put the police onto Philip. Was that why Moira went behind Nuala's back to make Amy's disappearance known? Was it some sort of payback? Was Moira waiting all this time for revenge?

Nuala remembered the day she arrived back from Waterford and found Moira in the garden. That must have been how she got Amy's numbers. Moira knew where she kept the spare key behind the trellis. She could have taken that and opened the door. Moira had seen Nuala often enough taking the address book off the table in the hall when she needed to phone someone.

Nuala was glad she'd moved into town. She needed this space away from Moira's prying eyes. Ballyreid was too small.

Brian Poole was surprised at the absolute way that Nuala Devine had disposed of the village that had been her home for her entire life. She couldn't have blasted a bigger hole in its heart if she'd taken a gun to it. Everywhere he looked people were reeling from what they saw as her betrayal.

The only one happy with the outcome was Luke

Devereaux. He had plans to buy the Devine house and yard and use it to turn his pub into a super pub for the new development. He'd need the new houses, Brian thought, because nobody in the existing village was talking to him because he had refused to sign the petition or make an approach to Nuala to get her to change her mind. He just laughed and told them you can't halt progress. Just like Amy the day she first stood in Deveraux' pub, Brian's mind wandered back to Powers' and the warm personality of his aunt and Elsie. Once Luke got his hands on Powers' and gutted it as he did, the writing was on the wall for Ballyreid. Progress had come to the village.

Brian remembered the day he turned on the television and saw Amy Devine open the Helfers extension in Mayo. At the time he didn't know who she was but he mentioned it to someone at the station the next day and they told him she was Nuala Devine's niece. She had proudly stood in the centre of a small town and talked of the development expected in the area. Amy said it would change everyone's lives. Progress does that all right, he thought. This town was never going to be the same again.

Luke Devereaux carried an empty keg out into the cramped yard behind the pub. You could barely walk around out here, he thought, with such a small space. He climbed up on a box by the wall and looked over it into the Devines' front yard. Soon this was going to be his. He already had visions of his empire floating deliciously through his head as he slept at night. That poky little bar he purchased in the nineties was going to be a super pub with a complex of shops and other retail units surrounding a central parking area. It would be a landmark complex, just perfect for the new housing development about to start once they all got the planning permissions they needed. They had toiled long and hard to get the Devines to finally give up that land but the wait was worth it. With the price of land and housing these days they were going to make a killing on this project. Luke didn't have the same capital as the other investors but he did have a brand-new sound system installed which blasted loud music out into the night and over the wall into Nuala's garden. And where would his pub be without a late licence, which prolonged the pleasure of his music deep into the night? Luke had friends in high places who were willing to grant him any planning permissions he wanted if he could get the Devines off that land. The new direction of the Devereaux pub had been pivotal in getting Nuala out of her house, though he hadn't expected her to give up so quickly. He'd had a few more projects in mind that he'd never had to employ. It was a pity in a way – the nightclub would have been more fun than the late bar and the karaoke.

Chapter 38

Amy was finding her confinement in the attic harder this week. It was six weeks now since she'd been locked up here and she had five groups of seven black lines marking her wall calander. She sat looking at them, picking lines at random and wondering what people did on those days. Somebody must have missed her by now. Thinking about the media reports amused her for a while. They had probably drawn comparisons between her disappearance and Ruth's. The village must be in an uproar. Then an odd thought entered her head, something that hadn't dawned on her before. Fifteen years ago both Ruth and Moira Lennon's son disappeared. Was that a coincidence? Was he the writer? Did he kill Ruth and then vanish? Had he returned now to play games with Amy Devine? Two sisters and their best friend all had a child that disappeared. How could that be a coincidence?

She wondered how long it had taken Maurice and

Nuala to call the police. Of course Nuala mightn't have reason to contact her for months unless she managed to get an investigation reopened into Ruth's death. Maybe Nuala still thought she knew something about Ruth's disappearance and just ran away.

The day wore on and the sun sank lower in the sky. Amy sat in her usual spot under the skylight watching the light diminish to be replaced by a square of navy. She was so hungry tonight she found herself pacing the floor in anticipation of his arrival. There was a very strict routine now. He unlocked the door each evening at the same time and let her out for her food. The table was always set with delicious food and decorated by a tablecloth, flowers and the same nightlight candles. As she ate, sometimes she wondered what he would do if she set fire to the house. But she didn't dare because she suspected he might let her burn.

Was that his plan? Was he trying to break her down slowly so that she would take her own life?

Amy looked down the corridor into the pool of darkness at the bottom and wondered if he was watching her. He hadn't spoken to her at all tonight. The house was silent but she suspected he was always there watching every movement and gesture she made.

After she finished her meal she sat for a long time, not wanting to go back into the musty room, until finally his voice rang out in the darkness, making her jump.

"Amy! Go back to your room."

Amy stood and reluctantly stepped inside the open door of the room. She wished she could fight him but with a chain around her waist and no weapon, she had few options. She stood there watching the door and listening to his footsteps descending the hallway. He appeared in the doorway. His face and head were still covered but Amy knew his shape and build now. He was tall and he had a cat-like agility when he moved. Amy suspected some martial arts training at some stage of his life. This made her even more wary of him. His clothes had once been expensive but they were well worn and getting a bit baggy in the wrong places.

Tonight almost as soon as he entered her line of vision he turned and placing his hands on the wick of the candles he extinguished them both. The hall was thrown into complete darkness. Amy could still see his shape in the doorway and knew he was standing there staring at her as she stood five feet away. Seconds stretched into minutes and then he turned and closed the door, locking it behind him.

Amy started to sob and for the first time since she got there she found herself punching the mattress and pillows in frustration. Finally, exhausted, she lay on the crumpled bed and slept.

The next morning Amy walked to the bathroom. As she washed her face and tried to tidy her hair at the sink a tiny little sliver of metal poking out under the skirting board caught her eye. It was almost beyond her reach but she managed to edge it out and grasp it in her hand. It was an old metal nail file. Immediately she was overcome with an idea. She rushed to her bed and tried to pick the lock on the chain around her waist but it was a futile effort. He had bought a very expensive lock of a type that Amy had never seen before and it seemed to be pick-proof.

She put her mark on the wall in case she forgot later and sat on the floor with her back to the bed, holding her nail file in her hand. It was rusted and old and gone past nail filing but Amy knew in her heart she could put it to some use. She turned her head sideways to look at the door. She could try and see if she could pick that lock but then she packed that away as a bad idea. She would still be chained up and the door would be unlocked when he came with her food tonight. His reaction to that was something she didn't wish to see.

The afternoon wore on and Amy still sat there rubbing her fingertips over the rough edge of the file. Then the penny dropped. She turned over onto her knees and crept across the floor to the ring of her chain embedded in the wooden floor. It was rock solid but Amy had an idea. Carefully she started to chip away the wood around the ring. It was working. A circle was widening around the metal and getting slowly deeper as she chipped on through the afternoon. The wood chips that she dug out she stuffed down through a knothole in the wooden floor just in case he entered the room and noticed them. Before she was anywhere near the depth that she needed the sun got too low for her to continue. By now she was starving, more so than usual because of the extra activity.

His arrival was the same as the night before. She walked out and had her meal in silence, looking at the wall opposite. As she ate his voice boomed out of the shadows.

"I heard you last night."

Amy turned and looked down into the shadows but she said nothing.

"I thought you were finally cracking."

"Is that what this is all about? Do you want me to break down?"

"It's interesting to see how long it will take."

Amy turned away from him and went back to staring at the wall. Silence returned to the hall for a while and then he broke the silence again.

"You've perked up today, I see."

Amy was frightened he'd figured out her secret. She didn't want him to steal her little sliver of hope. She didn't answer and they both sat in silence for a few minutes. Then he spoke.

"Amy! Go back to your room."

She stood up obediently and returned to her room. This time he just quickly put out the light and then she heard him slip something onto the floor of the room. It was an envelope. He locked the door, leaving her alone again. She knew by their conversation earlier that he was confused. He must have stood listening outside until she broke down and then tonight she felt sure he saw the renewed strength in her expression. She didn't want to arouse his suspicions. She crossed the room and picked up the envelope. She took it back to her bed and lay down where she slept almost immediately.

The next morning as soon as she woke and marked her wall Amy ripped open the envelope and removed just two sheets of paper. Not his usual missive. Hungrily she pored over it, desperate to see what he had to say.

*L*ife *must be* quite strange for you now, Amy, cut off from the rest of the world and you must be worried about what is going on in your absence outside. You will be surprised at the changes taking place in Ballyreid.

First there is some bad news and I'm sorry to be the one to break it to you.

Maurice!

Your uncle was killed in a farm accident over a month ago. A bank of bales fell on him in the shed. Peter died in the same accident.

Amy was overcome by grief. She cried until she was drained, then lay on the floor in a ball. There was no need to ask: Amy knew already he did it. He killed them both. He had held her here, torturing her, and he killed her uncle and his dog on the outside. It was her fault. If she had only gone to the guards at the start none of this would have happened. She deserved what she got for her stupidity – but Maurice – he was just an innocent bystander. He was dead over a month now. All that human drama going on outside of here and she was locked in this dark hell he'd made for her.

When she had at last composed herself she went back to the manuscript.

Do you know, Amy, during the funeral and the days that followed Nuala didn't even look for you and include you in the drama. People asked her where you were and she fobbed them off until finally Moira got suspicious about your midnight flit. Moira contacted your job and found out you hadn't returned since your break. Then she left messages on your phone and you didn't respond so she got really worried. She contacted the police in Dublin and they went to your house. Obviously the pile of mail behind the door and the dust looked suspicious. Couple that with a guesthouse owner in Dungarvan contacting the police about a missing guest and they put two and two together and came up with you.

You should have seen the village. It was buried under a blanket of media coverage that beamed into every residence in Ireland for the last four weeks. When they realised that you were a first cousin of *the* Ruth Devine they were ecstatic. You were juxtaposed in every broadcast. I finally managed to bring you two together after all these years.

Despite the media saturation Nuala has still

managed to cut you out of her life. She was like a bulldog when it came to Ruth's disappearance but she has gone out of her way to avoid the police in your case. I really set the cat amongst the pigeons, didn't I, in bringing you home?

Home! That's another story. You no longer have a home in Ballyreid, Amy. Today Nuala closed a deal with a developer and the Devine land will be no more unless the good people of Ballyreid can block his planning permission. I've heard his plans through the grapevine and he has some influential friends. By the time he is finished with your land he will have built a complex that will swallow your village. Your legacy, Amy, destroyed your family and finally set in motion a chain of events that will destroy Ballyreid as you've known it.

You were the one nobody wanted. Your father didn't want you and your mother would probably still be alive if she didn't have you. Nuala and Maurice wouldn't have lost their siblings and my Ruth would never have turned inwards as she did, destroying herself. Your birth, Amy Devine, was the catalyst that destroyed them all; yet you thrived on their misery. You lived in your multi-million-euro house on the LUAS. You were the figurehead of Helfers. You hired and fired, still dictating the direction of the lives of others. You've gone through life as the victim, Amy, the forgotten one. But remember your world of gourmet food and polished wood and think of the victims you've left behind. Now who's the victim, Amy?

Chapter 39

Amy was stunned. The venom emanating from those pages shocked her. Somehow she sensed that this was his final communication with her. Whatever he had in store for her would have to be permanent and was certainly imminent.

With a new feeling of urgency she went back to chipping away at the ring in the floor, more determined than ever to get out of this attic. She couldn't take another morning waking up in here. His wrath if she got caught was something she was willing to risk.

All day she chipped and lay on the bed for a few minutes to relieve the ache in her lower back and finally sometime in the later afternoon the ring came out of the floor in her hand.

Amy started to shake. She was going to have to be very careful. If she weren't here at dinnertime he would look for her and kill her. If he noticed she was free he would lock her up even tighter and punish her. She needed to be very smart. Quickly she walked around the room, keeping her ears sharp for any sound from outside. There was no way she could get up to the skylight.

The bathroom window was just big enough for her to get out of but it was painted shut, one more job for her nail file. Her heart hammering, she sliced through the paint all around the window frame. Then she tried the window and it opened. Amy was at bursting point with excitement. But she couldn't leave now or he would be just behind her. The room was almost dark now and he would be along any moment. She decided to do nothing until after he left. As she heard his footsteps descending the hall she pushed her chain back into the floor and stood in her usual spot, head down for effect, but every fibre of her being was on high alert.

Everything was the same as the night before although tonight he didn't speak to her at all. The food was delicious as always, though for once she found it hard to enjoy it despite having spent the whole day alone. Amy tried to be as desolate-looking as possible though her mind was racing through all her possible avenues of escape. The last thing she wanted was for him to recognise the new-found light in her eyes. Maybe it had worked. He didn't seem to notice that anything was amiss. Once the door closed she pressed her ear against it but she didn't hear a thing. Suddenly she knew he was still outside listening for movements from her. Time passed and she was thinking that maybe she should move when she heard the door handle rattle. She ran quickly, her chains rattling around her, towards the bathroom and she heard his laughter loud and raucous in the hallway. Then he turned, his footsteps walking away into the night. Amy ran back to the door and dropped to the floor with her ear to the keyhole. She could still hear his footsteps in the distance as though they were descending wooden steps. He was gone. Now she could try and get out of here.

Amy moved towards the bathroom realising her chain was going to be a problem as it trailed along the floor behind her. She opened the window and looked down. The moon was high and though this side of the house was shaded she could make out the ridge of a roof below her. She judged it to be about ten feet down. It was impossible to know what part of the house that roof was covering. If it was a part he was in now, he might hear her. It faced a walled garden so it could be a kitchen or scullery, she thought. Ten feet was too far for her to drop onto a ridged roof as she would be in danger of sliding off and landing in the yard. She looked up but the wall was sheer and there was no way she could climb up there.

Defeated, she went back inside and sat on the floor. She was on the verge of panic but she tried to remind herself that she'd been here six weeks and now was not the time to lose her head when she was so close to getting out of here. Amy focused on her breathing and looked around the room. The sheets! She ran to the bed and pulled off the top sheet. She tried to tear it but it was surprisingly good quality cotton. On bended knees she tried to find the nail file on the floor. It took her a minute or two as her nervous fingers kept sliding over it. Finally, she grasped it and dug it into the sheet. It worked. When she tried again to rip the material it tore, though not easily. It was reassuring that it was such strong material. It was slow work but eventually she had managed to tear the sheet into wide strips. She intended to tie them together using a knot she'd learned during survival courses she took in college. It was called a sheet bend. How apt, she thought now. It was fast to tie and useful when joining two ropes of different diameters or a rope to a sheet corner or in this case two pieces of sheet. Her survival partner in college had ultimate faith that this knot would not open.

Now she needed to attach a few lengths of sheet to reach her destination on the roof below. Time passed as she struggled to tie the first knot as, under stress, she found it difficult to remember the complex procedure. After the first one, the others were easier.

She prayed the sheet-rope would hold as she went back to the window. She took a deep breath, hoping she'd tied the knots correctly. It had been a long time since college.

What could she tie this to? She looked around her. The toilet wasn't the most secure anchor but it was all her rope could reach and still give her some decent length. She tied it around the toilet but found that used up quite a bit of the rope. Dangling the rope out the window, she estimated that the base of the rope was still at least four feet from the ridge of the roof. Once more panic gripped her.

She hesitated. Should she make more strips by tearing up the other sheet? No, the process was too slow and she had spent enough time on this already. She must get out of this room before something went wrong and she lost her only chance.

Shaking, she worked her way out the window and reached back inside to pull the chain out. The chain was going to make it very difficult – the extra weight on her weakened arms was going to hurt. She pulled the last of the chain through and dropped it down the side of the wall. But she hadn't prepared herself. When the heavy coils of the chain reached their full extension they dragged her off the ledge and she only just managed to grab the windowsill. Slowly she pulled herself back up into a sitting position with the chain dangling below her. It took her a few minutes to get her strength back.

Once everything stopped spinning Amy lowered herself gingerly off the ledge. She gripped the sheet tightly. She'd been good at climbing when she was in college and took rock-climbing trips to Colorado. She read once that muscles had a memory. Now Amy hoped that was true.

Slowly she edged her way down the rope. When she got to the base of it her toes were still dangling in air. She was going to have to drop but the roof sloped away sharply and she had no idea what lay below. Amy counted back from ten to one in her head and then she let go of the rope. Her feet slid straight down the roof until she was lying flat on her stomach with her hands gripping tightly to the ridge. Her elbows and wrists ached from the strain but she managed to drag herself back up and now she sat safely astride the ridge.

She didn't know what to do next. If she slid right down over the side of the roof, it could be another ten feet to the ground and there was no way of knowing what was below – she could land on rocks or a wall. She couldn't risk breaking an ankle. She hauled the chain up and curled it onto her lap. She got a sudden urge to laugh. She'd broken out of her room after six weeks and now she sat here on the roof almost as big a prisoner as she was upstairs. A cool breeze blew across the roof and chilled her cheeks. Amy could hear the trees swishing in its grasp. As her mind and vision cleared, she tried to get her bearings.

There was no moon and hardly any stars in the sky. The night was dark with no visible lighting anywhere. Amy looked off to the distance and could see that the house stood in a clearing surrounded by a thick bank of trees. There wasn't a sound except for the wind in the trees.

Suddenly, she realised that below her to her left a tree was scraping off the roof. It was a tall evergreen tree with a wide expanse of branches so they should be quite strong.

The only hope she had of getting safely off this roof was to get to that tree.

Amy wondered whether, if she let the chain dangle under her body, she could slide down the roof towards the tree using the links as traction. It was her only option.

She worked her way along the roof-ridge until she was directly over the place where the branches were in contact with the roof. Carefully she swung her right leg over the roof-ridge to join the other. Then she let the chain slide down the slates. God, she hoped the slates were secure! She wiggled slightly and could tell straight away that the ridge tiles at least were safe. Again she counted down and, taking a deep breath, slid down the slope of the roof, her rump bone painfully rubbing off the heavy metal. The chain links slowed her slightly but she still gathered pace as she approached the edge until she found herself flying off the roof into the tree. Instinctively she threw her arms out, flailing to try and grab a branch. Painfully she landed with one leg on either side of a thick branch and her head banging into the great trunk of the old tree. Sobbing, she grabbed the trunk tightly. Liquid trickled down from her forehead, which was probably blood. She was dizzy with the effects of the bang to her head. Too terrified to move, she clung to the tree until her head cleared.

At last she knew she had to move. The night was still quiet and here in her tree she felt very safe but she had to move. She reached behind her and felt the chain. It was tight. She pulled it but it was caught on something above her head. She tugged but it was no good, the chain held fast. There was another branch above her head and the one she sat on now was solid so she dragged herself to a standing position, leaning heavily on the branch above. Carefully she let go with one of her hands and followed the chain upwards into the tree to where it was snagged on a branch just within her grasp. Amy freed it and held it tightly as she sat back down.

Then she dropped the chain through the branches below her, this time taking care to brace herself so she wasn't dragged off her branch.

She heard the chain hit the ground almost immediately so she knew it wasn't too far below after all. She decided to risk it and drop to the ground. She turned herself around and grabbed the branch as tightly as she could, then lowered herself until her arms were straight and her body hung straight down. She couldn't find the ground but it had to be quite close. Amy took one last leap of faith and dropped to the ground safely.

Chapter 40

Standing in the walled garden beneath her attic room and looking up, Amy was glad she'd chosen the tree as her escape route. The roof she had straddled was at least twelve feet high. If she had risked sliding off it, she would have broken her legs for sure.

Looking around, she spotted a wooden door in the far wall so she crossed to it, stumbling over the uneven ground which was overgrown with briars which tugged at her jeans. She thought it might once have been a vegetable garden. The door was old and rotting so it creaked open slowly when she turned the handle. She stepped through cautiously but found herself now in a walled orchard which was even more overgrown. There was a path but high thick shrubbery had taken it over almost completely. She moved forward cautiously through the foliage, with leaves slapping at her face and branches tugging at her hair, her chain draped over her arm like a wedding train.

A weak glow from a window lit a patch of clear ground in front of her. She halted, then pushed her way deep into the shrubbery to her right. She cautiously began to move past the window, taking care to disturb the foliage as little as possible and to make no noise. She peered out at the window as she passed. It was a large room, obviously the manor kitchen. It was lit by a couple of lanterns sitting on a large wooden table running down the centre of the room. The room was empty. Her heart hammered. He must be there or why would there be lanterns lit?

Hardly daring to breathe she moved on slowly through the shrubbery. She saw that the path led to the kitchen door which was shut but to her relief another path branched off it and led onwards along the back of the house. Amy prayed that it led to another door, one that opened into the grounds outside.

Her prayer was answered. She reached another door which she pushed open. She stepped outside. A broad path led towards the front of the house but she was afraid to use it. Luckily it was bordered by thick rhododendron bushes. She made her way through them until she reached the big open area to the front of the house where his van had stopped the night they arrived. She could see the driveway exiting the clearing – the one they arrived by. She wasn't going to use that to get out of here. The last thing she wanted was to meet his car on the way. She skirted around the clearing keeping well into the bushes.

Sometimes these old estates were walled. She had

better stay parallel to the drive and make for the main gate, the one they had entered the first night. She began to move through the trees and bushes in the direction of the main entrance hoping the gate wasn't locked. It hadn't been the night they drove through. In any case maybe she could climb over it.

Among the trees the visibility was low and the going was rough, fallen logs and thick patches of brambles slowed her progress. She struggled on, expecting to encounter the estate wall or fence at any moment. But the trees went on and on. Surely the drive wasn't as long as that? She found it hard to remember how far they had driven that first night. She hadn't realised that such large tracts of natural woods even existed any more in Ireland. Her hips ached where the chain around her waist dug into them and her head throbbed with every step. After a time, she halted, sat down and closed her eyes to relieve the ache in her head. This was Ireland for God's sake! It wasn't like Yellowstone National Park! She was in a little private wood somewhere in the South East. Once her head stopped spinning she stood up and started walking again. The chain now felt like a great weight, which got heavier with each step. Finally after what seemed like an eternity she found herself exiting the trees into a vast open space. Fields spread in all directions but there didn't appear to be any road. One thing for certain, she was nowhere near the gateway of the manor – someplace along her route she had got confused and changed direction, wandering out into farmland. At least there were no estate walls to trap her inside.

Her feet were killing her. It felt like she'd been walking for days. Once more she sat down and tried to figure out where she was. As she sat there her ears picked up what sounded like the noise of traffic to the right. It was faint but she knew she was hearing traffic on a main road. She picked herself up and once more started walking. As the sky started to lighten to a dull grey the sound of traffic got louder.

Amy's lungs were ready to explode and her head ached when at last she clambered over a wall and landed on the side of the road. She lay down in the tall grass to get her bearings. It was a main road and much of the traffic she'd heard was delivery lorries going towards the nearest town. It would be safer to stop a lorry than a car. For a few minutes she couldn't lift herself off the ground. She was so dizzy she could barely see straight. She concentrated really hard and willed herself into an upright position. She sat back against the wall and waited for the next lorry. It was still dark but the sky was certainly getting brighter by the minute.

Amy heard a lorry approach. Then it came into view. It had some kind of logo on the side. She waited in the tall grass to make sure it wasn't him and then she stumbled out, almost in the path of the lorry. She heard it skid to a halt as she fell onto the hard shoulder.

Brian Poole was sitting at his desk when his phone rang. It was the station in Carlow. A hospital administrator had just called to let them know that a woman had been found and transferred to St James' hospital in Dublin with a serious concussion and some minor injuries and bruises. The woman answered the description of Amy Devine. She had no identification on her and she seemed to be in shock. They hadn't questioned her yet.

Brian slowly replaced the phone in its cradle and sat back at his desk. He certainly wasn't expecting this. She was in Carlow so she was in a different jurisdiction and she wasn't really his business any more. But Brian hated to let go of something he felt he had ownership over. The Devine mystery was his. He supposed he should go and tell Nuala and Moira and put the two women out of their misery, though it had certainly been entertaining watching them circle each other like hyenas.

Brian grabbed his hat and left the station, crossing the street to Moira's. She was just putting out the sign for the day.

"Moira."

"Brian." Moira had lost her friendly nature over the last few months. She turned to enter the shop. It wasn't due to open for another hour and she wasn't in the mood to invite the local copper in for an early coffee. She'd seen enough of him in the last few weeks.

Brian stepped closer behind her.

"I have some news."

"What?" She didn't bother to turn around.

"Amy Devine was found this morning."

Moira turned and her eyes blazed into his. "Alive?"

"Yes. She was picked up on a main road in Carlow this morning by a lorry driver and taken to hospital. No serious injuries but very distressed."

"Has she said where she was?"

"No. She's heavily sedated. I thought you'd like to know." He watched Moira's face.

"Well. Thank you for that, officer."

He stood on the street thoughtfully as Moira shut the coffee shop door in his face. Now he probably should tell the other one.

He found Nuala in the coffee shop, unpacking some kitchen equipment. He could see immediately that she had a good eye for space and colour. This was going to be a very nice café when she was finished with it.

"What can I do for you?" She turned and looked at him, a large pot still in her hand.

"It's about Amy."

"What about Amy?"

Brian wasn't sensing any aunt-like concern from this lady at the mention of her niece.

"We've found her."

"You have?" Nuala's face erupted with bitterness. Her Ruth disappeared without a trace and the other one was found inside of two months. She couldn't hide it.

Brian watched in amazement. He had noticed they weren't very close but this level of hatred towards her niece was unexpected.

"Is she dead?"

"No. She's alive. She was wandering around on a road in Carlow."

Nuala's expression melted at this point and he saw tears fill her eyes.

"Brian, I need to be alone now." She moved towards the door to lead him out.

"Don't you want to know where she is?" he asked.

Nuala stopped and looked at the floor. Brian took that as an affirmative answer.

"She's in hospital – St James' in Dublin. She's in shock at the moment so nobody has had a chance to question her yet."

Nuala resumed walking and opened the door, guiding Brian out on to the street. He turned to speak to her but like at Moira's shop earlier he found himself looking at a closed door.

Chapter 41

Amy lay back on her hospital bed, tired but in one piece. She'd been there for two days and she was expecting to be released tomorrow. Her collision with the tree had resulted in ten stitches but it was inside her hairline so she wouldn't have a visible scar. She was quite underweight after surviving on one meal a day for six weeks but other than that she was in good shape.

They had to cut the chains off when they brought her in. She yelped with pain when they were taking them off and she felt ridiculously light for a while afterwards. Without the chains she realised how much weight she had actually lost. Amy pulled up her nightgown and examined the marks. She had raised weals on both sides of her hips on the bony protrusions. They still hurt when she accidentally put pressure on them and she wouldn't be wearing tight jeans for a while.

They gave her a private room so she didn't have to put up with gawkers coming in and having a look at the girl who came back. The nurses were bad enough – when they checked her charts or gave her medication she found their eyes staring into hers looking for the internal scars, the interesting ones. Was she beaten, did he rape her, is she insane and prone to running away by herself? Amy could see these questions flick across their faces as they stood by her bedside. But they didn't want to ask her straight out. They seemed uncomfortable in her presence.

Nobody from Ballyreid had been to see her since she came in. She supposed they didn't want the publicity. She also suspected that they were so angry with Nuala for selling out to a developer that they didn't want to hear mention of the Devines ever again. For fifteen years that family had put the village on the map for all the wrong reasons and now they were turning it into a housing estate.

The press were practically camped in the lobby of the hospital, waiting for a story on why the second Devine girl was found wandering on the roadside in Carlow first thing in the morning. Many times she heard reporters being turned away at the door as they tried to enter her room.

The police had been here, going over and over in detail what had happened to her. When she told them her story they went to the house to check it out and found clear evidence to confirm her story but no proof of who had kept her there. Whoever it was must have travelled there every night to visit her but it didn't appear that he lived there. The house had been empty for a long time and was in a bad state of repair so they supposed the kidnapper thought it was big enough for her to be hidden safely without being found. He had been right.

She explained the manuscript to them and told them where to find the pieces that he had given her while she was in the room but they found that they were no longer there. Amy knew then that he had come to her room at some stage after she left and must know by now that she was gone. But why had he come to her room at that time of day? He never did that.

She thought of Ballyreid. At first she thought it had to be somebody there who had kidnapped her but now she didn't know who it could be. Carlow was a long way from the village.

After all she'd been through and having spent six weeks in that house she still knew nothing about the writer of the manuscript. She thought back over her time with him. What was he like? She took out a note-pad and made notes on him. He was tall, taller than she was. He was wiry in his build, muscular and athletic, He wore thick outdoor clothes every time she saw him so she couldn't really be sure of his exact shape. What was his voice like? It was strange. He didn't speak when he was close to her: he usually spoke to her from a distance like from down the corridor. He knew she'd recognise him if he spoke when he was close to her. He was somebody she knew. His voice was always disguised.

The next morning as expected Amy was released from the hospital. There was nobody there to meet her. It made her suddenly realise how truly alone she was. Her week in Ballyreid was the first time she'd been there in years. There was nobody there she could call a friend or request help from. There was nothing for her to do but to go back to her house and try to put this awful business out of her mind.

That was easier said than done. Amy planned to set the house to rights and be at work early the next day but once she got into her house she immediately set the alarm and went to her room, jamming a chair under the handle. All that evening she spotted journalists outside as she peeped through the cracks in her curtains and occasionally she heard the bolder ones come to the door and try to speak to her. Amy just shrank back against the wall. The energy she'd used in getting home was sapped now and she just wanted to hide like a small animal in the dark. It took her hours to sleep as her ears scanned the night for intruders despite her sophisticated alarm system but finally sometime after four thirty she succumbed.

Next morning she felt a bit better but she was still too unsettled to go to work. She called the office. Greg answered. It was funny hearing a familiar work voice after all this time. His happy, slightly camp voice bubbled out of the phone to her. They talked for a while, avoiding anything controversial, just small talk. When he asked her when she was coming back she explained that she still needed some medical leave, glad that the doctor had given her a cert for another month.

"Take care."

He hung up and Amy was back in silence except for the humming receiver in her hand.

She spent all day cleaning her house until it was gleaming and then she made a list of food she needed. She had fully intended on going to the supermarket to fill her cupboards but she got no further than the front door. When she placed her hand on the keypad for the burglar alarm she started shaking. She couldn't go out yet. Instead she went back to her office, logged on, went to the supermarket website and ordered her groceries on-line. There was just enough time to deliver them before dinner.

Amy sat on the end of the stairs waiting for the delivery. It took nearly forty minutes. When the man rang the bell, she jumped. Cautiously she went to the door put the chain on and opened the door just a crack.

"Delivery for A Devine." They were using the name on her credit card.

"Leave it on the doorstep, please." She kept watching until he left the yard. Once he was gone she opened the door and picked up the box. Quickly she went back inside and locked the door.

That evening Amy cooked herself dinner, lit a fire,

opened a bottle of wine and tried hard to fool herself into thinking she was a lucky woman and this was a wonderful life.

The next morning Dermot Chase, the director, contacted her to see how she was. Once more she explained about her medical needs and said she was sorry she couldn't get back to work. But she needed something to do. He had the perfect compromise. He suggested that Greg email her daily with work that needed doing and if anything needed her signature he would drop them by her house.

Amy was thrilled. She couldn't face the Helfers family yet but she needed something to stimulate her brain. She knew the novelty would wear off soon enough and the company would forget about her adventure but right now she needed to hide out here where it was peaceful.

The next morning at ten o'clock Greg arrived at the door with a large folder of work that had built up since she left and a stack of mail.

"How are you?" Greg always showed an interest bordering on impertinence.

But Amy liked plain speakers.

"I'm fine. I just need to be alone for a bit."

"Didn't you get enough of that?"

"What do you mean?" Amy asked.

"It was in the papers that you were kept in isolation. Sorry, it's none of my business."

"It's all right. I'll need to start opening up eventually. I just don't like to talk about it yet."

"That's understandable." He looked down into her face with obvious concern.

"Thanks for these." Amy was friendly but she'd had enough talking. She just couldn't get used to company at the moment. Politely but firmly she guided her assistant out the door, shut it behind him and settled down to work.

This went on for a week and she found she was getting as much work done here as she would in the office. She didn't attend meetings but she spoke daily to the various departments on the phone.

On Friday morning Greg arrived with her mail and the usual folder of work and for the first time he suggested she go outside for a while.

"It will do you good."

"I don't think so. Maybe I'll go out later."

"I know you're not going out at all." He reached his hand out and touched her elbow. "I'm worried about you."

"There's no need. I'll be fine." But she couldn't keep her voice steady and she found her eyes filling up with tears.

"Are you fine?"

"Yes."

"Just come out with me for one coffee."

"Who's the boss here?" Amy tried to make light of it.

"Sir, yes, sir!" He kicked his heels together and flicked his hand out from his forehead.

"Stop. I'll go for one coffee."

"We'll go on the LUAS."

Amy's heart lurched. It was nearly three months now since she was last on that train or out walking on the streets. She felt palpitations starting.

"Come on. I'll stay with you."

This was like a role reversal and it made Amy slightly uncomfortable. She'd always been so super-confident at work, the ice queen on the top floor. In the past she was always friendly but brisk and professional with her assistant and now here he was taking care of her like this and the strangest thing was she was letting him. And for the first time since she left the hospital the idea of getting professional help seemed like a good idea. The doctors had suggested it as soon as she was ready for discharging but she had said no. It didn't do Ruth any good, she thought. But she couldn't go on like this. She had to do something. She'd think about it later.

They turned out of her street and walked to the LUAS. They got on at Beechwood and took it as far as Harcourt Street. Amy hesitated as he stepped off, then she joined him and they walked towards Starbucks. It was full and a line snaked out the door but in true assembly-line fashion the coffees were steamed, filled and distributed in record time and before Amy had time to get too uneasy they were paying and taking a seat by the window.

"How do you feel now?"

Amy smiled. "I feel all right but I don't want to stay out too long. I have a lot of work to do. I get tired easily."

"I think you're making the most of that."

If he'd spoken to her like that in the past she would have shot him down in a second but once more she felt tears pricking her eyelids. There was an element of truth in what he said. She didn't get tired, she just got scared.

Amy watched the street outside. For a while they sat in silence.

"They miss you at the office."

Amy started laughing. "What a load of rubbish! I'm the boss – nobody misses the boss." She guessed he brought her to this coffee shop because it was close to work and he thought he was breaking her in gradually.

"All right, I was being nice."

"Be honest – I prefer it."

"All right."

The door opened and another onslaught of coffee drinkers burst through.

Amy started to shake. "I've got to go. I'll talk to you tomorrow."

Without looking back she ran out of the shop and turned right down the street where she jumped onto the LUAS. All the way home she fought back tears and the urge to run up and down the carriage. As soon as the doors opened at her stop she jumped off and ran as quickly as she could until she got to her front door.

Once she closed it behind her the panic attack subsided and her breathing normalised.

Once she felt like herself again, she walked to the kitchen and made herself a cup of camomile tea.

For the rest of the afternoon she was blissfully lost in work. Just as she finished up to make dinner the phone rang.

"Hello?" She expected Greg to have another message for her.

"Amy."

"Nuala! How are you?"

Amy had put her on speakerphone.

"I'm fine. How are you?" Nuala's voice filled the quiet room.

"I'm getting better."

"I wanted you to know I've sold the house and land."

Amy wasn't sure what to say to this.

"Some of that inheritance is by right yours. We got the farm after your father died so I'm giving you fifty thousand euro." The room went silent again.

"Nuala! You know there is no need for that."

"I wouldn't have it on my conscience." Again there was another long pause.

"Nuala! Listen to me. I did nothing wrong." She was talking to an empty room. Nuala had hung up. Amy could certainly do with the money if she lost her job but she felt uncomfortable taking it. It was as though Nuala was washing her hands of her.

Chapter 42

The next day Nuala opened the front door to her new coffee shop for the first time. It was going to take a while to get it up and running successfully. She placed her menu board outside but after an hour the dining-room was still empty.

Nuala crossed to the window and sat there, crumbling for the first time since Maurice's death. It was like her heart was breaking into dust. Why couldn't she put the pieces in the right places? Here she was again and the last piece just couldn't be found.

Suddenly the door opened. Nuala looked up, a smile pasted on for her first customer but it slipped off instantly.

"Nuala." Moira stepped into the café.

Nuala stared, her expression frozen.

"Nuala, we have to talk."

Nuala still sat, unable to reach out or open her mouth. Moira walked towards her and sat opposite her.

"I'm sorry I went behind your back." Moira watched her friend struggle with her pain. "I really was just worried about Amy. It was odd the way she just left like that and you didn't contact her about the funeral. I really only wanted to talk to her first and see if I could help you two but then I knew she was missing. Now I'm worried about you." Moira reached across the table and held her friend's cold limp hand in hers. She could see the muscles in her cheeks flexing.

"Why did she come back, Moira, and Ruth didn't? I never got a chance to say sorry to my daughter." Even now she couldn't tell Moira about the assault.

Moira squeezed her friend's hand. "You were a good mother." Moira went quiet for a moment. "I lost Philip too."

Nuala reached out and held her hand, her head down so Moira couldn't see the hatred in her eyes at the mention of Philip's name.

"I know he wasn't a good man but he was my little boy."

Suddenly Nuala squeezed Moira's hand tightly. "I know he was, I'm sorry."

Moira had a thought. "Three children disappeared from our village and the three mothers were best friends. Nuala, don't you think it strange that our three children disappeared?"

Nuala nodded slowly, thinking. A fluttering had begun in her heart. It was unusual. She got up to make a pot of coffee.

Moira wondered should she speak to the guards

again. It seemed very far-fetched that there was any connection between the three disappearances. Maybe their friendship was just cursed.

Moira walked over to the counter and the two women brought their coffees back to the window. They both sat in silence, looking out on the street.

"I'm so lonely, Moira."

"I know, pet. Things have never worked out for you, have they?"

Nuala sniffed. "No."

"You're lucky you moved in here or the village was going to lynch you."

"I just wanted something for me."

"I know. They'll be fine. The businesses are already coming around to the idea of making more money. They just want to be martyrs. Luke Devereaux is already drawing up the plans for his super pub. He's a sly one."

"Little worm!"

Nuala spoke with such venom that Moira burst out laughing and for the first time in weeks Nuala laughed too.

"You don't like him?" she asked.

"Can't stand him."

Suddenly, Nuala felt she had to unload on Moira. That night was still playing on her conscience and the guilt was eating her up.

"Moira, I have to tell you about Philip."

"No, you don't. I know already."

"You do!"

"Yes. If you hadn't done it I might have." For a moment Moira lost her composure. "I suspected him too. I was considering speaking to the guards myself. But obviously we were wrong about him."

Nuala wasn't so sure about that.

As they were talking the café door opened once more and a group of about ten men entered.

"Do you want me to stay and help? Show you how to run a café?"

Nuala linked her friend's arm as they walked behind the counter. Maybe she'd find her missing pieces.

Later that day Sergeant Brian Poole was in Dungarvan and decided to have a quick look into Nuala's new café. He opened the door and walked in, sitting in the same seat Moira had sat in that morning.

"You seem to be having a good start," he said to Nuala when she reached the table.

"I'm happy with it," she said.

"Do you miss the village?"

"Do you want to order food?" Nuala ignored the question.

"A muffin and coffee would be lovely. The place looks good." As he spoke the door to the storeroom opened and Moira walked out with a large tub of mayonnaise. She was wearing an apron.

"So the friendship is back on," said Brian.

Nuala turned and walked away.

Brian watched their body language. They were

back to the old days, bonded and totally in sync. He could never understand women. Their ability to regroup and carry on regardless of their personal tragedies left him in awe. These two were realigned against the world.

Amy dragged herself through each day, taking care of as much business as she could from inside her house. She was getting the work load done but part of the boss's job was being there on the ground for so many different immediate issues that weren't worth crossing town for but were necessary in the moment. She was fostering their self-reliance, she kept telling herself. All of the petty little grievances that would have been brought to her were now taken care of by themselves but she knew it was only a matter of time before the director came to her and asked her to step aside. Amy wasn't going to fight him. There would be a severance package and it would be neat, civilised, but it would be final.

She still hadn't called a counsellor. Amy was never one for opening up to strangers and though she knew it might be a good idea she couldn't quite get up the courage to make the call.

Once a week Greg tried to get her out of the house. They didn't tackle the train or a busy coffee shop after the first outing and he no longer fought her when she said she was tired. He just let her go. There was always a limit. Once she reached that, she just stood up and ran back to her house. Because of this they chose restaurants in Ranelagh and always at an early hour when the dining-room wasn't too busy. Amy was really starting to look forward to these outings. Other than at those times she never left the house, not even to go into the garden. She ate well and exercised. She'd put back up the weight she lost during her confinement and on the surface she looked good, better than she had in years, but inside her emotions and sense of security were like shifting seismic plates. Once the pressure got to a certain level she just had to run. She only felt better once she was back in her home.

Today Greg was taking her to a new restaurant that had just opened down the road. Amy dressed with care and sat on the end of the stairs waiting for him to come for her. But he never showed up. She sat there letting the minutes tick by, unsure what time it was. She'd stopped wearing her watch and she didn't like to look at the clocks now that she was safe. Amy didn't want to see time slipping away. So tonight Greg was an hour late before she realised how time had moved on.

At last she knew he wasn't coming. She walked back to the kitchen and then remembered the phones. Always at five thirty she took the house phone off the hook and put her mobile on silent so work couldn't contact her. She'd given them her time by then.

Amy put the house phone back on the hook and grabbed her mobile off the desk in her office. There were three missed calls, all of them from Greg's mobile. She listened to the message.

"I'm sorry, Amy. Something's come up and I can't make it. We'll do it another night."

Amy texted him back: *That's fine don't worry about it.*

Taking a deep breath she walked to the front door and went out to the doorstep. It didn't feel too bad being out here alone. She went back inside and filled herself a glass of white wine and went back outside. This had been Amy's favourite place for most of her time here. As she sat there on the top step just outside the front door in the quietness of the deserted street she felt happier than she'd felt in a long time. Sitting here was better than a trip to a pretentious restaurant. After an hour a crowd leaving a bar walked down the street and started walking towards her. Amy decided to go back inside but a tiny spark of courage was returning and after that night she started regularly moving between the front doorstep and the back patio for her evening glass of wine.

But the past wasn't behind her as she hoped.

It worried her that she no longer had the manuscript. She'd lost all the earlier parts the night he kidnapped her – they'd been in her document case in her hand so presumably he'd kept them. The pieces he had given to her in the house had gone by the time the gardaí got to the house to investigate. Inside she still worried that they didn't really believe her story. After all, her proof was gone.

The writer, however, wasn't finished writing yet.

Chapter 43

Amy had just closed the front door and was washing her glass at the sink when she heard the fluttering of the letterbox. She waited silently in her kitchen. Whoever it was had gone so she walked into her hall. A large brown envelope lay on the mat with the writing face down. A ringing started in her ears and her heart started to palpitate. She knew he was still out there somewhere watching her.

Amy picked up the envelope and brought it back to the kitchen. She knew she shouldn't open it without the police being present. It was a good idea to be careful with it and preserve any possible evidence so she went upstairs and got the cotton gloves she used when she put on tights. Downstairs she picked the envelope up and carefully slit the top and pulled out two sheets of paper and a photograph. Amy looked at the photograph and once more panic gripped her. It was her sitting on the front step, drinking a glass of wine, and she was smiling. She must have been happy. He'd been watching her since she'd come back. No wonder she'd had those attacks. She'd known. Had he been close to her each time, watching her? The day she got a panic attack in the coffee shop, had he been watching her then? Maybe he travelled back with her on the LUAS. She put her head down and tried to control her panic. He could be anyone on the street. He was probably watching her all the time. This was her world now, the inside of this house, so he must have been out there on her street while she was trapped in here. She was still his prisoner as surely as she'd been in the house. Did he also appreciate the irony in this?

But shouldn't the police have guessed that too and been watching her – watching him watching her. She was so confused. Feeling sick to her stomach she reached for the sheets of paper, smoothed them out on the table and started reading.

Amy, I knew that night that something was wrong, something had been wrong for a few nights but I couldn't imagine what it could be. I was so confident that I had thought of everything and you were completely compliant to my wishes but that's what happens when you are overconfident.

I can only guess at how you got away. For the first time in this story you are the one who knows what happened and I am in the dark. That was a power shift and it came out of six weeks of isolation and sensory deprivation. I am in awe of you, Amy. In awe of how you struggled and maintained faith, broke yourself out and subsequently locked yourself up again. You are a mystery to me. There you are now like Rapunzel in your tower looking out at the world, a world you fought to get back to.

I was at work when I heard that the Devine girl was found wandering the roads in Carlow. Can you imagine my shock? You probably know now that I didn't live there or leave anything there which might identify me. I wore gloves at all times. So once I heard you had broken out I couldn't go back. They would have been watching for me night and day and I'm not that stupid. I didn't survive for fifteen years after the things I've done to get caught now. Someday soon, Amy, I will ask you to tell me all the details about how you got out. I know I should let it all go. At this stage I don't think I would get caught. Do you? Do you think the police will find me? You spent six weeks with me and you have no idea who I am. But I want to speak to you again. I'm always going to be with you, Amy. My plan had a very different ending and you stole that from me. You are a thief, Amy. You leech the goodness out of those around you. Don't you see the crumbling world you left behind? That's you; you stole the oxygen out of their air. Their lives are arid, blowing on the wind, because little Amy Devine came into their world and sucked out all the moisture. In fifteen years no one will even recognise that town. It will probably be thriving, a hub of commercial activity, a planned community of wealthy people able to shape the world they want. But the heart of your old world is broken, broken by Amy Devine.

How could someone hate another so much just for being born? Amy knew that he was right up to a point. Nuala and Maurice, Kitty and James, were two young couples starting out on their lives and they would have all got on with their lives if Kitty hadn't got pregnant with Amy. He was telling her she was the blast that blew them all apart. James obviously wasn't ready to be a dad. They had needed help to work out their marriage before bringing a child into the world.

But the cracks had been there before Amy. Looking at it logically, she knew this was the truth. It was because of themselves that the Devine house of cards came tumbling down. He wouldn't have got a foothold in their world if it weren't for the state of instability they found themselves in. Amy suddenly saw clearly that he was right. She was the catalyst that set it all in motion. But it wasn't her fault. If she hadn't been the one to do it something else would have. She wasn't going to feel guilty any more. Her life thrived, not because she was a thief, but because she worked hard and used her abilities. They made their own choices.

Amy picked up the phone and dialled the garda officer assigned to her case. She explained the letter.

The detective said she'd be with her as soon as she could. Amy went back to the end of the stairs and waited.

From then on she felt better. She had taken another proactive step by going to the police and every night afterwards she sat on her step in a defiant stance for anyone who might be watching.

Amy realised that sometimes your life had to reach rock bottom. It was in the rebuilding that you found your true strength.

After the letter, life during the day went back to normal. Greg brought her work in the morning or emailed her what needed to be done. Amy knew that in another week or two she would be able to go back to work. She was getting to the shops now and taking a walk in the park. One day she even managed to get the LUAS into town by herself. She thought she might bump into someone from work but the idea didn't fill her with dread. In fact she found herself almost looking forward to the idea. It was early days and she still got the occasional panic attack but she could see things were getting better.

Brian Poole had just heard from his Dublin counterparts about Amy Devine's letter. He'd really had nothing to do with this case. Amy was lost and found out of his jurisdiction but professional courtesy meant he was always kept informed. From the beginning in all of this, he was really just an observer.

Brian had good instincts and while he knew neither Nuala nor Moira were involved in Amy's disappearance he knew they had a secret and Amy's case had brought it to the fore. They were definitely protecting themselves from something but now that their friendship was back in one piece he knew they would never reveal what that was. They didn't want the guards involved.

Nuala opened the door each morning to a line waiting outside and her café was at least half full throughout the day. It had been like this since Moira had intervened and given her pointers on business. Originally she'd expected to have a greasy spoon café with hearty food and a wholesome atmosphere but instead she found herself with one of the trendiest establishments in town. One day she realised that most of the missing pieces of her life were now firmly in place. Ruth was no longer a pain she couldn't give words to; now the best of her was firmly placed in Nuala's memory. Nuala had taken out her most valued photographs and they were placed on the consul table in her hall so anyone entering or leaving could see them. It took fifteen years but she had finally come to terms with her losses. Nuala was no longer defined by her pain. She was a businesswoman and a person in her own right.

Moira was thrilled by her friend's success. She had taken her cue from Nuala and had looked around her.

If the village was in for a facelift, maybe it was time the café got one too. Every day it was full of a mix of builders, farmers, old villagers like herself and some of the new families who parked outside in their brand-new cars and jostled for the window seats. Moira wanted to be the business that blended the new village and integrated the people. So far it was working. A weight had been lifted from her shoulders when she and Nuala cleared the air.

Brian Poole entered the shop as she was clearing a table. He thought they had a secret. Well, he could stay hovering around waiting for the big story. Brian Poole was a village sergeant with nothing to do. Even Amy's case had been beyond his grasp. All he did was wander around beating bushes hoping something exciting would pop out. Really, they should pity him not fear him. She smiled at Brian in her new-found state of grace. Both of them turned as another local fixture walked in. Moira didn't see much of him usually, because he had his own coffee machine. Luke Devereaux nodded at Brian and took a stool at the counter. He had changed as much as any of them. He'd been an average guy with a small bar but suddenly he was driving a BMW and wearing a suit. He'd closed the deal on Nuala's farmyard and house and he was already in the process of demolishing everything that had been the Devines'. Moira wondered where that one got his backing. That's who Brian Poole should be watching, not herself and Nuala.

Chapter 44

Amy was planning to go back to work the following Monday morning so she had six more days to finish her recovery. At first she was going to do half days to see how things went. She could have extended her time off but she knew if she stayed here much longer she would reverse all the progress she'd made in recent weeks.

Amy looked in the mirror and put the finishing touches to her make-up. Greg was taking her out for dinner. She didn't know what this relationship was. Amy didn't feel anything for him and she didn't think he felt anything for her other than pity and perhaps a blossoming friendship. She had serious suspicions that he was gay but they never discussed personal issues. But this shift in their relationship could get awkward when she went back to work. However, if his conduct before she left was anything to go by, he was a model of propriety. He'd only been her assistant for six months prior to her trip south but he was a find. She'd never had an assistant who could do a better job and she didn't know what she would have done without him for the last few weeks.

At six thirty the doorbell rang. He was ten minutes early. Amy opened the door.

"You're early."

"Traffic wasn't as heavy as I thought it was going to be."

"I'll just be two minutes."

"I'll wait in the car."

"OK." Amy grabbed her bag and keys and set her alarm and then she followed him out the door.

She'd never seen his car before. Since she'd come back he'd come out on the LUAS to meet her and they only ate locally. For a moment she felt a twinge of unease. If the writer was following her could Greg protect her? He seemed too gentle.

"Are we going someplace different?"

"Yes. I thought we could drive out of the city a little bit. I know a lovely restaurant and it's very quiet. If you get tired we'll come straight back."

Amy couldn't ask for more than that. As they drove she was quiet. She couldn't help being a little uneasy. If she did have a turn, she couldn't run back to Ranelagh from way out in the country. But it was the next step in her recovery and she was willing to take it.

As they drove she saw they were going down to Wicklow. Greg chattered away as the car ploughed on, giving her all the gossip from work. At first she listened intently, enjoying all the gossip she'd been missing out on, but as the length of the journey increased she started to get nervous. This was a lot further than she felt comfortable travelling. She berated herself for being so childish – it really was time that she took herself in hand and got back to a normal life.

While they drove the gradient of the road got steeper, winding its way towards the mountains. Large architect-designed houses dotted the landscape, trying to blend in, but it was obvious they forgot what they were blending into. Perhaps the original plans were subtle but Amy suspected a few additions were paid for along the way: the odd portico here or extra storey there. They were beautiful houses but they shouted at the mountains, jockeying for attention, the occupants uncomfortable with the idea that anything could overshadow them. The longest any of these could have possibly been here was maybe ten years, symbols of the Celtic Tiger in all its glory.

They came to a small village. It was more of a settlement built up around a church with a shop in the front room of a bungalow. The original village probably had five houses. Small artisan cottages were still there now but interspersed amongst their majestic neighbours whose imposing lines dwarfed them.

"Those large house are lovely but they look a bit odd out here, don't they?"

"I agree," said Greg enthusiastically. "They don't

belong. Sites around here are being bought up by wealthy Dubliners and nobody here can afford them."

"That's the same everywhere, isn't it?"

Greg began to chat on about architecture and conservation but Amy lapsed back into silence.

They drove past a church and took a sharp right through the church parking area, then onto a narrow road almost hidden from view that stretched upwards steeply. Immediately Amy's heart gave a sharp lurch. This was too much. Even the country roads in Waterford weren't this remote and isolated. She could feel herself start to pant a little as her apprehension increased.

"Where are we?"

Greg turned and smiled. "It's okay. It's not far now. Don't worry, Amy, you'll be fine."

His voice was soft and reassuring and she calmed a little.

The road was narrow with encroaching bushes on both sides, making it seem like a tunnel. In the side mirror Amy saw a car appear, rapidly climbing the road behind them until it was just a few yards behind.

"What's he doing?" said Greg in exasperation. "He shouldn't be that close. If I have to brake he'll hit us."

With the rapidly fading sun and the high bushes the road was getting steadily darker. In her side mirror Amy saw the car behind switch on its full lights.

As the road climbed upwards, getting narrower and more remote, her heart beat rapidly in her chest. Was that the writer behind them? Should she say that to Greg? Would it be of any benefit to scare them both?

"There's not much room to pass here if we meet anyone," said Amy, trying to sound normal.

Greg smiled but said nothing as he concentrated on the road and the car behind.

They came to a severe bend in the road with the other car still keeping pace very close behind them. Greg slowed down cautiously and Amy kept her eyes sharply trained on both sides of the road. There was no way the car could pass them. Why was it keeping so close? What was going on?

And this place was so isolated! You couldn't even see another house up here, let alone a restaurant. Her breath was coming in regular light pants now. She was being silly – maybe this was one of those link roads, which would link up any minute now with the main road to Greystones or somewhere.

Amy stole a glance at Greg again, wondering should she tell him her worries. "It's a very quiet road," she said instead.

"Don't worry. It just seems that way after Dublin."

For another mile Amy's hands trembled and she never took her eyes off the mirror and the car behind stayed right on their bumper.

Greg slowed down and Amy saw a lane on her left. A pair of compact pillars bordered a neat iron gate, which was closed. High hedges rose on both sides of the lane behind the gate, which curved sharply concealing any house that might be up there.

Greg stopped the car. As he opened his door the car behind shot by, obviously relieved at the increase in pace.

"Where are we?" Amy couldn't keep the uneasiness out of her tone.

"It's a surprise." He got out. "A nice surprise." He leaned back in for a moment and smiled. Then he walked to the gate. The car lights were on now and he was standing in the pool of its lights as he opened the latch.

When Greg got back into the car Amy spoke again. "Really, where are we?"

"*Chez moi*. I'm cooking dinner for us tonight. I thought I'd surprise you."

"You live this far from Dublin!" Amy was shocked. "How do you ever get to work on time?" He'd never mentioned country living before, but then why should he?

Greg smiled at her. "It's difficult but you can do it if you get up at the crack of dawn. It's worth it at the weekends."

He drove through the gates, then got out and closed them again.

The drive wound between the hedges before coming to a stop in the yard of a neat farmhouse. It was L-shaped with a gravel yard in the front. It had a lovely aspect. As Amy got out of the car she looked around her. Her heart still fluttered with apprehension. She felt so far away from everything. The house looked down over a vast stretch of countryside with the lights of the village and another larger town visible in the far distance. It was so quiet. A barking fox in the distance was the only sound she could hear.

"You have a gorgeous home."

"Thanks."

Behind the house some tall trees stood starkly against the sky and behind the side wing of the house you could see a collection of old farm buildings. Unlike the dwelling house, they looked old and disused.

"Is this a working farm?" Amy asked.

"No. I'm no farmer. I inherited this place from my grandfather. I tried for a while to make it work but I'm a city boy. I do love it up here though – it's quiet and it's home now." He laid a hand on Amy's arm. "Come on or dinner will never be ready."

Amy followed him slowly into the house.

She was getting the familiar urge to run. Greg was her friend and she did feel safe in his company but the distance from town and the isolation of the farm was more than she could cope with right now. She was annoyed at Greg too for not understanding how vulnerable she felt. You shouldn't try to bully someone out of a depression. It would only have the opposite effect.

Still wrestling with her feelings she followed him through a large welcoming hall and into a warm sitting-room. The walls and furniture were cream and the floor was a pale wood. The only colour came from feminine accessories, pillows, throws and plants and a beautiful gold and black rug which lay before the fire. A gleaming glass coffee table stood in front of the cream couch. The brightness and cleanliness of it all surprised her. He must spend all his time cleaning and painting. It put Amy's house to shame and she was pretty neat. A strong smell of antiseptic assaulted her nostrils. That she didn't like. It reminded her of public rest rooms.

Greg poured her a glass of wine and led her to the kitchen. He pointed to a line of stools at the breakfast bar.

"Take a seat. I'll be back in a moment."

"Thanks." Amy sat down and looked around her. The counter was neatly laid out for cooking. Utensils and vegetables were lined up in the order they would be used. The smell of a roast wafted from the oven. She realised she was very hungry. The large gulp of wine she'd taken was starting to relax her. Maybe this might be fun. She hadn't been out to dinner in a long time and Greg was good company.

As she sat there Greg came back in.

"I'm going to finish dinner. Would you like some more wine?"

Amy smiled. "No. I'm fine."

"Go on!" He picked up the bottle.

"Okay. Just a little." She held her glass as he poured.

Greg went back to cooking. "I need some herbs. I'll be back in a moment. Help yourself to the wine." He picked up a pair of scissors and left the kitchen by the back door.

Amy looked around the kitchen. It was only her coming to dinner and he had gone to such effort. She could see him happily hosting dinner parties for twenty. It was the first time he had the boss as his dinner guest. Amy hadn't felt like the boss in a long time but she was, and she'd be back at the helm properly next week. Once more she hoped that this dinner wasn't blurring the boundaries a little too much.

Amy was ashamed to say that prior to her acquaintance with the writer she had milked being in control. The old Amy had been an expensive date with a love of fine wines and posh restaurants. She didn't feel like that person any more.

Greg came back in. "You've got to have fresh herbs."

"You shouldn't have gone to so much trouble for me."

"It's no trouble. It's an important meal."

"Important meal?"

"Of course. The first time you eat in somebody's house is an important event."

Amy smiled brightly at him. "That's a lovely thought."

"I'm glad you think so."

Time went on and Greg was at last ready to serve up the meal.

"I'll help you." Amy jumped and helped him to lay the plates on the table and bring the serving dishes. It all looked and smelled wonderful.

"You're a good cook." She smiled at him. "This smells delicious."

"Thank you, Miss Devine. I think you will enjoy it. Sit down now and eat."

He was no longer looking at her when he spoke to her and his voice no longer held the same bubbly tone it normally held. In fact, right now there wasn't even the slightest trace of his usual bubbly personality. As she watched him she couldn't explain it but he was changing.

Amy's panic attack started again and a horrible feeling she didn't want to acknowledge was covering her like a dark shadow.

Chapter 45

They ate in silence. The only sound was the humming of the fridge in the background. Since the day she hired Greg he had been a breath of fresh air and since her kidnap he had been her lifeline. He was a friend she could open up to, someone she could trust when she had no one else.

And then it hit her with full force. The image of Ruth, terrified after having a crash on the side of the road, jumping out to the writer in relief, thinking he would take care of her. Ruth who knew she was being stalked, talking to him like an old friend in her local pub. The writer was amicable and able to turn on the charm when it suited him. This man sitting in front of her wasn't her Greg. He was cold and had a hard glint in his eyes. He turned those eyes with full force on her now and she shrank. They had never seemed so sharp as they did now when they locked onto hers and bored through her. Suddenly, Amy knew those were the eyes that had been hidden from her behind a pair of dark shades and a silk scarf.

"More wine?" The eyes remained hard but his mouth teased itself into a hint of a smile, void of humour.

"No." Amy couldn't hold his gaze.

His smile found a little more purchase.

"Suit yourself." He went back to chewing his food and cutting the next piece of his steak.

The meal continued in silence, punctuated only by the clink of cutlery on china. Amy was finding it hard to swallow her food. She couldn't believe what a fool she was. After everything she'd gone through, the first thing she did when she got back was form a personal relationship with her torturer.

"What do you want?" Amy spoke softly, hoping it might keep him calm.

Underneath the mask that was once so familiar to her she could see another entity taking shape. A black and cruel thing hid there and Amy had walked right into his house. She'd come to his farm willingly.

"I'll tell you soon." Once more he forced that cruel smile on her.

Once they finished their food he got up and collected their dishes and brought them to the sink.

Quickly Amy cast her mind back to her jailor. The height was right, she thought. He was tall but he always wore outdoor clothes, a heavy jacket with a jumper underneath. Greg seemed to be a slimmer build but obviously that was a deliberate ploy to confuse her.

His hair was blond and his eyes were blue, but her jailor always covered his head and face and wore dark glasses so there was no way she would have known what colour his hair was. Then he started to lay a tray for coffee. Amy watched fascinated as he placed a snow-white cloth on the tray and took out a silver jug and sugar bowl and three cups. He didn't acknowledge the curiosity in her eyes at the sight of the third cup.

"Come with me." He stepped back and indicated for Amy to walk ahead of him into the sitting-room.

The cheerful room seemed to be struggling against the grim air that came with them from the kitchen.

"Sit there." He placed the tray on the glass coffee table and indicated for her to sit on the couch. Then he started pouring the coffee. She didn't bother telling him how she took it – no one knew better than Greg did.

He sat to her left on an armchair and alternated between watching her and watching the fire. She thought back over the manuscript and the writer's love of fire. She could see it now on his face. A glow lit his eyes and seemed to warm the icy blueness as he looked into the flames.

The fire crackled and the minutes ticked by.

Amy suddenly jumped. There was someone else in the house. She could hear the sound of footsteps coming down the hall.

Greg didn't even look up.

"Come in, darling. Amy, I'd like you to meet my wife."

Amy turned, her face etched in shock. He'd never mentioned a wife. She didn't know what to expect but nothing could have prepared her for who she saw standing in the doorway watching her. Amy found a strangled scream escape from her throat. She tore her eyes away from the woman standing before her and looked at Greg. As she looked at him, he got up and walked to the woman.

Why hadn't she seen it before? His walk was the one thing that should have given it away. He walked like a panther. But, no, her Greg never walked like that.

He turned and they both watched her, their eyes never leaving her face for a second. Nobody spoke. Amy knew they had watched her closely for the six weeks she had been confined. She had been an experiment. What did they have in mind for her now? Amy was under no illusions about their feelings towards her. The manuscript had detailed the depth of hatred the writer felt towards her but Amy had never even thought that there were two people writing it. Now it made more sense. The final pieces of the puzzle were falling into place.

Greg finally broke the silence.

"Amy Devine, I would like to introduce you to my wife, Julie Bannon, formerly Ruth Devine."

"Are you officially married?" They were the only coherent words she could get out of her mouth.

Again Greg answered. "Yes, we are." He smiled. "We weren't sure you would recognise her after all this time."

"She's so like Nuala." She turned to Ruth. "But you've changed."

"I've put on some weight. I was only seven and a half stone when Greg brought me here. Now I could do with losing some."

"You look good." Amy saw no point in antagonising her. On the surface, despite her initial shock, she tried to maintain as casual an air as possible.

She couldn't take her eyes off Ruth but Ruth barely seemed to register she was there now, as she sat down next to her on the couch and accepted coffee from her husband.

Amy suddenly got a flashback to the opening pages of the manuscript. Sinéad Daly, the girl who was murdered, died at the hands of this man sitting to the right of her. She watched his hands as he held his cup. He was more than capable of killing her right here in this room.

"Ruth. The manuscript said you were dead."

"No. It didn't." She smiled at Amy. "It said – I mean we said – her body was lying there huddled and broken. I exaggerated. She was badly bruised and she certainly had a concussion. But she was fine."

As if to emphasise the point, Ruth lifted the hair from the side of her face and showed Amy the scar just past her ear where she had fallen on the rocks.

"*I held her stiff cold body.*" Greg started to laugh. "Wouldn't you be stiff and cold if you had lain there for hours with a broken ankle unable to get up?"

"But you were running away from him! Why did you marry him? How did you marry him?"

"I was running that night but I didn't get very far, did I? I realised I'd been running for a long time. Why else was I starving myself to death and hiding in a haze of drugs? I wanted to disappear." She looked at Greg and Amy could see real love in her eyes. "Greg nursed me back to health and I realised I was in the safest place."

"But what about Nuala and Maurice? Why did you leave them?"

Ruth turned to Amy and for the first time Amy received the full heat of the wrath of Ruth, the adult version. Her eyes narrowed and glittered in the muted light of the room. "They left me long before that!"

The sudden angry outburst made Amy jump.

"Nuala loves you," she said softly.

Ruth's voice rose further. "I came to my mother after the assault and all she worried about was if I was pregnant and did I ask for it. Always very worried about the family name, was my mother. It was Greg who told me about our grandmother's mental illness. Nuala tried to bury her memory. When she thought I had problems she just worried in case I was going to turn into Granny Donnelly. I'm where I need to be." She went back to gazing at Greg.

Greg turned to Amy. "I put a postbox at the end of the lane and then even the postman didn't need to come up here. I owned the land and house free and clear. We were alone up here."

"But how are you married?"

"When Ruth was here a couple of years I found out

about a stillborn baby who was the same age as Ruth. It always seemed like a bit of a myth but it worked. It was before security in the country tightened up. I applied for a birth certificate in the name of Julie Creed. Then later after our wedding we got a passport as well. Though we only take the ferry. It's easier to hide. Ruth wears glasses with clear glass when we're out and nobody has ever recognised her. But we don't push our luck. She likes to stay here."

"Did you get married in Ireland?"

"Yes. It was a civil ceremony. She wore thick glasses and her hair was very long then. It was only five years ago so she was ten years older and two stone heavier than when she disappeared. With a birth cert and passport it was easy. Now her passport, driver's licence and credit cards all say Julie Bannon, my wife."

"Nobody has ever figured out who you are?" Amy was incredulous.

Ruth got up and left the room. She returned wearing a thick pair of glasses and a blonde wig. Amy was stunned. She looked like a completely different person.

"I have a number of wigs. It's easy."

Ruth pulled off the wig and glasses and sat down again.

"What do you want me for?" Amy asked abruptly.

Ruth laughed and went back to her coffee. "Drink up, Amy, your coffee is going cold."

Amy was mystified. They were living a happy life here by their own accounts *so* why did they do this to her? She drank, too scared to fight them. If anyone had the opportunity to observe them now, they would see three people having a civilised drink together without any hint of what they were capable of. Greg had murdered to get Ruth but was he still killing now? He hadn't killed Ruth. She couldn't believe any of this. Did he kill Maurice?

Again she turned to Ruth.

"Why did Maurice die?"

Ruth stiffened and then turned to her with hard and cruel eyes.

"I hated him the most."

"Why?"

"The night Mum turned on me, he just stood there saying nothing. I looked at him and I saw his face full of disappointment. He had tears in his eyes. I knew he couldn't love me any more after hearing what I did."

"But you didn't do anything." Amy tried to smile at her cousin.

Ruth screamed at her. "*I know I didn't!*"

Amy couldn't help herself – she jumped.

"He's gone now. Philip Lennon." Ruth smiled.

Amy turned to Greg.

He smiled too. But said nothing.

"My mother redeemed herself. That's why she's still alive. She was on every television show for two years trying to find me but I couldn't go back. That world is not for me anymore."

"But Maurice! Surely he didn't deserve to die – and Peter!"

"Ever since I disappeared my mum has been

everywhere trying to get me back and make up for what she did but him, he just sat around and did nothing, just like that night!"

Amy suddenly remembered how close Ruth and Maurice had been when she was a little girl. They adored each other. He must have really broken her heart the day she first saw disappointment in his face. Ruth always did take things very seriously.

They went back to looking at the fire and Amy quietly looked all around for any way to escape. Ruth and Greg had let her see their faces so she knew this was the end.

Ruth spoke again. "I always loved to sit in the top of the hay barn and watch the world go by. You must remember that?"

Amy did vaguely.

"I was sitting there that morning. I'd driven down. That's why the writer of the manuscript seemed to be all over the place. Greg could be here and I could be in Ballyreid. I was the one who photographed you outside Devereaux'. Greg didn't want me to risk being seen but I was always prepared. You passed me in the street once and didn't recognise me. I remember my heart nearly stopped, thinking any moment you'd see me, but the wigs are good, aren't they?"

"Yes. They are." Amy said.

Ruth laughed. "You watched me on closed circuit television dressed, as a boy delivering the manuscript to Helfers and you had no idea. You're not too bright." She continued on.

"I know every inch of our land and gardens in Ballyreid. It wasn't a problem for me to move around without been seen. I was sitting in the shed when that dog came in, the one who looked like Brandy, your stupid dog. It started barking at me. I would have been caught so I threw the pike at it. Then Dad came in and . . ." Her voice trailed away and for a moment Ruth looked as though she were in genuine pain. "He started wailing in grief over the dog. There was no wailing the night I came to them and told them about the assault nor did I see any public tears when Mum was making appeals for me but there he was crying over a stupid dog! I lashed out at the bale to shut him up. I couldn't listen to that sound, over a dog."

For a few moments silence returned. Amy broke it.

"Why me? Why now?" She wasn't sure she wanted them to answer.

Ruth spoke without looking at her. "I stayed in the old house where we had you in case anyone discovered you. You were meant to die there. We were hoping you'd do it yourself eventually. Not at once, of course – we wanted to enjoy experimenting with you first. But ultimately I wanted to destroy you, wanted you to end your misery. Starving you would have been too easy. I turned the radio on first thing the morning you disappeared and imagine how I felt when I heard "Breaking news. Amy Devine found on the roads in Carlow." I ran up the stairs to your room and found the rope and the open window. I gathered the manuscript papers together and got out of there as quickly as I could, taking any trace left of our presence."

"Why do you hate me so much?"

"Finish your coffee," said Greg.

Then they looked at each other and laughed.

Amy watched them both closely. She knew that Ruth was the weakest link. While her brain was capable and ready for violence, Amy was stronger and fitter than she was. Greg was the physical force she needed to fear but she was beginning to suspect that Ruth was the psychological force pulling the strings.

She repeated her question from earlier. "But why now?"

"We're leaving the country. We've put this farm up for sale and we have had a few offers. I thought I could go but I can't go while I have unfinished business here."

"But you could have gone and no one would ever know you were still alive. You could be happy."

Once more Ruth's face contorted with anger. "I wanted to sort out my family first." She stretched forward in her chair and grabbed her stomach, her features contorted for a moment in real pain.

Amy watched her, mesmerised.

"It hurt so much."

"What did?" Amy spoke softly. She didn't understand any of this.

"As long as I can remember, it hurt. Loss, death and pain, it just kept coming and nobody asked me how I was coping. Kitty died and everyone rallied around the sister and the baby but who gave a shit about me? Then my granny died and the baby came to live with us. Did anyone care that I lost my granny? No. How was Amy? Then she invades my home. I tried. I tortured her so they would see how much I hurt but did they? No. Evil Ruth was mean to the baby. Then he invaded my body and did anyone come to me and hold me? No. What did you do, Ruth? What did you make him do to you? What did the little girl do to the grown man to make him rape her? Yes, Amy. *Rape* her! I lied to my mother and I lied in the manuscript. I must have guessed her reaction because I couldn't tell her he raped me. It was bad enough to see the disappointment when I got away. Imagine if I didn't get away? Imagine if they knew how soiled I was?"

By now Ruth's face had a manic quality. Her eyes glittered and shone and seemed to be having trouble focusing. The hollows in her cheeks deepened as she sucked them in and clenched her teeth. Amy could see the boiling emotions underneath and then she turned to Greg. He was watching her with eyes of ice, cold and calculating. That was his strength. His emotions were in check at all times. Ruth was a mess of anger and fear and he kept her safe. He protected her. For the first time in her life Ruth found someone who lived for her, someone who took care of her, someone who would never let her down. Greg had seen the worst in the human heart and he would never condemn Ruth, never ask her what did she do to deserve the bad stuff, never look at her with eyes full of bewilderment and disappointment like her father had done.

Chapter 46

By now Amy was finding it more and more difficult to stop herself from panicking. Ruth was like a tinderbox ready to explode into flames and Amy knew that Greg would act in an instant if Ruth were threatened in any way. She settled back into the corner of the couch so she could watch them both. It seemed completely impossible but she suspected the only way she could ever survive this was to get Greg out of the picture and she would have to take him by surprise.

Ruth turned to Amy. "Isn't it funny?"

"What?"

"This. Us three spending the evening together."

Amy wasn't amused. "Greg's worked for me for the last six months. He was the perfect assistant. How long were you planning this?"

"Years. I think that with you gone my new life will be perfect." Ruth reached out and held Greg's hand. "It will be cathartic."

"What are you going to do with me?"

Greg smiled. "Most bodies are found because of shallow graves. I dug yours deep."

Amy's stomach flipped and she thought she was going to be sick.

"Would you like a brandy?" Greg got up and walked to a sideboard across the room.

With as much aplomb as he'd had with the coffee he took three snifters from the cupboard. He poured a generous measure for Amy, swirling it in the glass, warming it as he carried it back. Then he did the same for Ruth, stooping to kiss her forehead as he handed it to her. Then he got himself one and sat down.

"Drink up, Amy."

"I'm not going home tonight, am I?" Amy looked into her glass as she spoke.

"No."

"What are you going to do with me?"

"Nothing yet. Let's just enjoy the evening."

"The summer you two met, when you were children, how did that happen?"

Greg turned to her. "That summer my mother came down to Ballyreid to take care of my grandmother. My mother was a Ballyreid woman. Gemma Lynch."

Amy's head shot up as he spoke. But he continued, not inviting any interruption.

"We spent that month playing together. I was younger but Ruth was so small and lost. I made her feel better when I was with her. We never met again after that. Not until college. As I outlined in the manuscript."

Gemma Lynch. Amy couldn't believe it. The other one of Nuala's group, the one she'd never met. This was her son.

"Which of you actually wrote the manuscript?"

"Both of us. We did a good job, didn't we?"

Amy nodded. She bit her lip and tried once more to reason with them. "You don't have to do this. I'll never let on I saw you. You can just leave as Mr and Mrs Bannon and no one will ever know."

As she said this, a back draft blew down the chimney and sparks flew onto the beautiful rug. One was large and still burning. Immediately Greg jumped to his feet. As he bent to put it out, Amy leapt to her feet, drew back her leg and kicked as hard as she could into his kidney. She caught him off guard and off balance and he fell towards the fire, landing on the hearth and hitting his head against the marble surround of the fire with a resounding smack. As he lay there stunned Ruth started screaming and was about to rush to him when Amy grabbed her hair and dragged her back. Amy smashed her brandy glass off the table and held a large piece to Ruth's throat. In her fear she'd already cut her a little. A trickle of blood was running down Ruth's neck. Before the stunned Greg had a chance to react, Ruth was half pushed, half pulled by a panic-stricken Amy through the sitting-room door and into the kitchen. She remembered the ceramic bowl that Greg had placed the car keys in when they came in. Still grasping Ruth by the hair, she grabbed up the keys. Ruth was small and not a fighter. Amy was tall, strong and an athlete. With every ounce of strength that she'd ever had to muster to break through the runner's wall, she dragged Ruth through the back door.

Now she could hear Greg coming after her. Amy knew that as long as Ruth was under threat Greg would concentrate on her safety. As they went out the back door some instinct made Amy turn and smash Ruth's face roughly into the yard wall. Ruth went down instantly and lay stunned across the doorway while Amy ran for the car. She made the short distance in seconds but her trembling hands lost valuable time as they fumbled trying to get the keys into the lock. Finally she got the door open, threw herself in and thrust the keys in the ignition. In her peripheral vision she could see Ruth sitting against the wall and Greg sprinting towards the car. Amy drove straight for him. He jumped out of the way, landing on his side in the gravel.

Amy tore down the driveway. And then she remembered the gate. He'd closed it on the way in. She stopped the car and jumped out, leaving the door open and the engine running. She opened the gate, running with it back to the hedge. The gate struck her in the heel, causing her to yelp with pain. Hobbling painfully, she ran back to the car and climbed in. With the sound of footsteps running down the drive behind her, she drove through the gate with a sigh of relief. She didn't know where she was, but she was safe. The memory of the part of the manuscript when Ruth hit the wall came back to her. Amy had no idea whether that was a lie or not but she decided to slow down and be careful but still, just as she was rounding the bend, her car hit the grass verge and she almost lost control.

She drove recklessly down the narrow road. It seemed even longer than it did on the way up and she hadn't realised how steep it actually was.

Finally she reached the village. She tried to remember the way. She drove down past the church until she was about half a mile from the village and then she saw the signpost for Dublin and Bray. Bray was closest.

Finally calm, she drove to Bray and straight to the garda station to tell them what had happened.

Amy told her story to the detective on duty and explained where the farm was and then she sat back in the waiting-room, utterly exhausted, and waited.

A long time afterwards the detective entered the room, blasting her with cold air.

"Amy."

"Yes? Did you find them?"

"We found Ruth." There was a long silence.

"Have you arrested her? Is she in jail? What about Greg?" Amy couldn't ever go through this again.

"Ruth is dead. We didn't find Greg. We have an alert out to airports, ports and every garda station in the country. We will find him."

"I didn't kill her! I only injured her." Amy was starting to shake and the memory of Ruth's face hitting the wall came back to her.

"We know that. She was shot. We think Greg shot Ruth and then left the farm."

"She's dead! Why would he kill her?"

"We can't imagine what he was thinking. We need to contact Ruth's mother."

"I'm not in touch with her any more. I don't know her new number."

"That's fine, Miss Devine. We can handle that."

Chapter 47

Brian Poole and two officers arrived at Nuala's apartment to tell her the news. Moira was with her. When Moira saw the serious expressions on their faces she tactfully went to make tea but hovered in the background in case Nuala needed her.

"Nuala . . ." Brian cleared his throat. "There's no easy way to tell you this."

Nuala looked expectantly from one face to another.

"We found Ruth."

The look on Nuala's face shook them all. It was a combination of total joy at the news and absolute fear of what that news might be.

"She's dead, Nuala." Again Brian paused. "But she just died tonight."

Nuala made a gurgling noise in her throat and turned snow white. Moira rushed to her side and threw her arms around her.

"She was living with her kidnapper in an old farmhouse in Wicklow. It was they who kidnapped Amy and killed Maurice."

"Maurice? It wasn't an accident?" Moira's usually confident voice was soft like a child's.

"No. Amy said that Ruth confessed that she did it. We are looking into it."

"She was alive all this time!" Nuala started to sob. "The things we did for her and she was still alive! And the terrible thing I did!"

"What thing, honey?" Moira looked at her with concerned eyes.

Nuala seemed to be in shock but she kept speaking. "He assaulted our little girl. If he hadn't done that she would never have been taken from us. He assaulted her and we acted so badly. Nobody could fix the damage we did to her that night. The hurt in her eyes when we blamed her."

They all watched her with no idea what she was about to say.

"I killed him because he assaulted her and I couldn't make him say he took her!"

Moira turned to the gardaí. "She's in shock. She has no idea what she's talking about."

Brian called her name softly. "Nuala!"

She turned and looked at him.

"Who did you kill?"

"Philip. He assaulted my little girl and she never got over it and we thought he'd kidnapped her, Maurice and me. It made sense."

"My Philip." Moira was pulling away from her friend as she spoke.

"I thought he killed her. I asked him again and again where he'd put her and he thought it was funny. He laughed in my face and taunted me. He pretended sometimes that he had and that he'd never tell me. Other times he would just tell me I was mad."

"What did you do, Nuala?" Brian maintained his gentle approach and she was responding to it.

"I was driving home one night and I saw him on the road drunk. I had the jeep. I hit him. I accelerated and hit him. The impact threw him over the fence into our field."

Moira started to retch. She jumped up and ran to the bathroom.

"I was in such a state when I got home that it didn't take much for Maurice to get the details from me. We got a torch and walked through the fields to where the body lay to see if he were still alive but he wasn't. He was hanging upside down off the inside of the fence in the briars and you could see he was all broken. I'll never forget his face. It was covered in blood but his eyes stared at me in death. I didn't know what to do but that was the one time Maurice did. He didn't speak. He just went back to the house and got the tractor. He pulled the body down and put it in the trailer behind and drove it to the furthest corner of the land where he hid it. He'd been doing drain work there by himself for the last few weeks. He deepened one trench and buried him just like we assumed he did with Ruth."

Nuala looked up and saw Moira standing in the doorway.

"I'm sorry, Moira. I thought he'd killed my little girl!" Suddenly Nuala leaned over, grabbing her stomach like she was in pain and started to scream, a long and bloodcurdling scream that cut through them all. "I killed someone and she was alive all the time! She abandoned us!" Nuala started rocking herself forwards and backwards in her chair as the enormity of the events grasped her.

Brian walked towards her and held out his hand. "You have to come with us now, Nuala."

Like a child she stood up and followed him, taking a last look around at her new home.

Chapter 48

Amy dropped her eyes to the newspaper in her lap and read the article: *Sinéad Daly's murder is finally solved, while a miscarriage of justice in the Irish Judiciary system has been discovered and corrected*. The man who'd already spent nearly fifteen years in jail had been completely exonerated. But Greg Bannon had vanished. Every resource was exhausted trying to find him but so far to no avail. Amy knew she would spend the rest of her life looking over her shoulder. She would never feel safe again.

Amy raised her head and looked around her. Stephen's Green was alive this afternoon. The sun shone brightly down on where she sat. Local office workers walked by, enjoying a sandwich and a coffee to go. Students milled on the paths and congregated on the green, life as usual in Dublin. She folded her paper and sat back, taking a sip of her coffee. As soon as the hue and cry about Greg Bannon and Ruth

Devine had died down, Amy tried to re-enter her old life in Dublin but it wasn't the same. She walked back into work and stood for the Helfers' elevator but it was no longer a case of letting the proletariat glimpse the young boss first thing in the morning as she climbed to her corner office. Instead of the admiring glances of before, she now got stares and nudges, looks of speculation as to her state of mind rather than people jostling for her attention. Maybe it had never been the way her finely tuned ego had thought it was.

Amy had known for months about the proposed redundancies in the Dublin office and now she decided to be the first to put in her application. Considering her circumstances and her high salary, the powers that be gratefully accepted. Now she spent time working on her garden and taking the DART to Sandymount a couple of times a week to walk on the strand. Life had slowed down to a crawl and despite everything she loved it.

She'd also started a new career. As she sat sunning herself in the garden, every day she heard the whines of dogs locked in back gardens while their owners took two jobs to pay for this wonderful location. Amy placed a note in the corner shop at Beechwood, advertising herself as a dog walker and now she had five clients every morning. She walked them in the morning and read her paper in the park, weather permitting, in the afternoon. If it rained she went indoors to any one of a dozen of her favourite coffee shops. In the evening she cooked dinner and at night she sat in the dark listening to her favourite opera.

Brian and Amy had become very close friends and that morning she had got an email from him. He had put in for a transfer to Dublin and it had been granted. He'd outgrown Ballyreid. He was originally from Dublin anyway. Amy smiled. It would be nice to have him close by.

Amy had finally given in at Brian's insistence and gone for professional help, to come to terms with the legacy her family had left her. At first the fact that Greg was still out there somewhere sent her into a spin. She barely left her house and she had round-the-clock protection from the gardaí, but as the days turned into months she had to face the fact that she might never know where he went and she would have to learn to live with the shadow he'd left on her life. The therapy helped her to understand that none of it was her fault. She knew Ruth was broken for a very long time – maybe that's why Philip targeted her that night. He saw easy prey and in that awful act he unleashed a force none of them were prepared for.

Nuala had been found guilty of the murder of Philip Lennon. She was given fifteen years. One year for every year she'd been without her daughter. Despite what happened, when the full story of the rape and Ruth's state of mind came out in the court, Moira rallied round her friend and now once a month she travelled to visit her in prison. Nobody could ever understand the bond between those two women. Amy knew it had to do with a group of young women in the seventies with matching outfits and huge smiles, full of anticipation for their life to come. Kitty and Gemma were dead but Moira and Nuala still hadn't given up on the dream of that wonderful future they'd all smiled into that day.

Nuala never again spoke to Amy so the full story came to her through Brian's eyes and the court case. Nuala couldn't bear the mention of Amy's name. She was guilt-ridden over everything that her sister's daughter had had to go through by virtue of being born into their family.

The village was now a satellite town, which got closer and closer to Dungarvan with every new building permit. Amy's grandmother's house still stood at the end of Devine road, all the more notorious now because of the ever-growing legend of the people who'd once lived there. A group of local artists and craftspeople had turned the old farmyard into a craft village, aptly called Devine Artistry. The proud pillars still opened into the flagged yard and the stone buildings were now home to a cluster of artisan's workshops. The old village was all but gone, buried under the planned community that Luke Devereaux had envisioned for most of his adult life. Unfortunately when his bribes and dirty deals became public knowledge the new Ballyreid didn't look as great from a prison cell. The cartel that Luke was involved in had consisted of quite a few wealthy but unsavoury business people and politicians. Luke thought his contribution to the grand scheme was as important as money and he was right when they were looking for a scapegoat.

Amy was slowly coming to terms with the losses she'd suffered since she first read the manuscript. Before her life in Dublin she had been a child of the country and a part of her still needed to reconnect with that time. The manuscript had given her that. She'd lain to rest the ghost of Ruth Devine and made peace with the new image she had of her parents. They were flawed and tragic people but if anything she loved them even more.

The dog walking had been the start of a new business that she was very excited about. Now back at her house, she looked out the window and saw her mobile canine beauty parlour "Pretty Pups" standing at the kerb. Her emblem was a black and white collie she secretly named Peter. After just a few months she was getting more business than she could handle and she was already looking into taking on some help. The old Amy was rising to the surface and was already gaining in strength.

This home that Irene had given her was where her heart really was now. She looked at Irene's stern face in the photo over the hall table and she smiled. She raised a wine glass in salute. "Thanks, Irene!" The face seemed to frown at her. Irene never approved of alcohol.

Yesterday a package had arrived for Amy in the post. She opened it and found a copy of Nuala's photograph. The four young women flirted with the camera and you could almost hear the laughs and the orders from the photographer to get everything just right. They all looked young, confident and full of life. Amy guessed that Nuala had sent it to her so she could look at it and not blame four girls for the sins of their children. Amy put it away in a drawer. She needed to forget now. After months of fear she wanted to try and put it all behind her. She couldn't let anyone control her again.

Epilogue

And then, when she thought that the nightmare was finally over, the last piece of the manuscript was sent to her from Mexico. Its words imprinted themselves on her brain.

An international search was ongoing for Greg but Amy didn't believe they would ever find him. Not unless he chose to come back.

And, despite the foreign origin of the letter and the sentiments expressed in it, she could never shake the feeling that somewhere he was still watching her.

Ruth is gone. I'm holding her now as I write; her blood is smeared across the page blurring my words. I had to let her go but pulling the trigger broke my heart. I knew then that Ruth could never get the past out of her life and move on and she couldn't survive in a prison without me. I kept her pain in check and gave her some semblance of a normal life but our lives were intertwined and she couldn't go on independent of me. We had fifteen years together and I tried, I really did, to get her to leave with me and start a new life away from her memories but she couldn't let it go. The scars ran too deep even for me to ease them.

The first day I ever saw her she was sitting on the wall on Devine Road kicking her heels against the stones, her small face screwed up in a frown, but for some reason when she saw me she smiled. I went and sat beside her and we started to talk and we talked all day. We wandered through her father's land and played in the fields, two children with their whole lives ahead of them.

When I saw her again we were two young adults but both of us already had deep scars known only to us. My mother had recently died of cancer and my dad worked abroad. He couldn't bear to be near me. I looked very like her then except she was dark-haired. Did you know Gemma, your mother's best friend?

Together, Ruth and I made the pain bearable but apart we were lost. I didn't agree with her obsession with you because it put us in danger but I had to help her ease the pain and she thought that without you it would all go away. I knew it wouldn't but at least with you out of the picture she would see that and let me put her back together again.

But you were stronger than all of us. Amy Devine,

the little one nobody wanted. If Ruth had inherited the qualities you did, life would be so different now. We would have a wonderful future to look forward to.

Ruth is at rest now. I set her free. You were Ruth's obsession, Amy, not mine. So don't worry. *I will leave you in peace.*

Goodbye, Amy Devine.

If you enjoyed *Guilt Ridden* by Ellen McCarthy
why not try *Guarding Maggie* also
published by Poolbeg

Here's a sneak preview of Chapter one . . .

ellen mccarthy

Guarding Maggie

POOLBEG

Crimson

Reality surrounds us like a smoke screen. Sometimes, when the wind blows, you can see right through it.

Prologue

He closed his eyes and blew out his breath loudly. He'd always been cool and never lost his temper. But even in the darkness inside his head he could see the old man's retreating back. All he wanted was to talk to him. He needed to explain how he felt. Surely after all these years Pascal owed him that.

Tears threatened him. He couldn't reduce himself to a snivelling wreck in front of him. The wisest thing would be to go home but the pain was too much. He'd never felt such despair as he felt now. All his life it had been locked up inside, poisoning him. It had tainted everything. He needed to let it go.

God, he hated them so much! He realised he'd been moving after the old man despite his indifference. His stiff old back disappeared into the house and the door shut but then through the wood he could hear him shouting. He listened to the drama from where he stood and wished he could see what was happening.

Pascal must be taking his anger out on her. Finally the shouting stopped and the night dragged on.

He didn't know why he did it but at last he turned the handle of the door and pushed it open, then stood silently in the porch. They seemed to have gone to bed now. He opened the inside door quietly and stood looking into the kitchen which was void of life and stood in silence watching him back. He moved into the room, the inky blackness dissolving into a murky grey.

Then he heard something like a kick against wood to his left. The utility room. The door shook. Someone was locked in there. He heard her shout the old man's name. He must have locked her in. That was strange.

He knew where Pascal's room was. He moved forward.

He had no idea what he was doing now. He just wanted to talk it out with him.

As he approached the door he heard what sounded like drawers being dragged out and their contents dumped on the floor. Silently he entered the room.

At first he couldn't see him but he could hear his laboured breath. The room was in disarray. He certainly wasn't expecting that; Pascal was such a fastidious old goat. Then he saw him lying on the ground, still fully dressed. He hurried across the room and looked down at him.

Pascal was lying on the linoleum, gasping for air. Already his lips were turning blue and the panic in his eyes made them stand out, glassy and alive in his dead face. He was dragging his hand across the floor, his bony knuckles scratching on the floor's surface. The hand was gripped tightly around an inhaler.

Suddenly he felt cold determination. The old man made a more concentrated effort with the inhaler and without hesitation the man standing over him laid his foot on the back of the claw-like hand. He could feel it squirm slowly under his boot. It was like stepping on a mouse. The labouring breath was turning to choking rasps now and the eyes were slowing, letting go of life and moving on. He stared as hard as he could, trying to see the moment life abandoned him and left the shell lying there alone. He was disappointed. You couldn't see the exact time. One moment life struggled and some place along the way it gave up.

He sat back on the bed and looked at him. Gently the night faded and a brand-new day would soon be dawning outside. Pascal was gone. Gone from his life forever. Then he remembered her.

Part One

Chapter 1

Maggie sat with life pressing heavily on her shoulders.
There was no point in lighting the fire. She would be
going to bed soon. A roaring fire was a waste at this
hour. She gave a jump, splashing tea over her wrist as
a sound broke the stillness. Betty the tabby, attracted
by the movement, jumped onto her knee.

The sudden disturbance in the dead of the night
frightened Maggie. Her brain had slipped into a
trance. The sound she'd just heard must have been the
wind – it had whipped up to make quite a noise in the
last few hours. Up here by the mountains its howling
could be akin to shrieking voices as it beat against the
eaves and echoed down the chimney pipe.

Pascal hadn't come in yet.

For a moment a silent tear slid down her face but
she brushed it off. She had to be strong now. She
couldn't lose control.

Maggie pushed the chair back from the table,

clasping Betty to her heart. The cat stretched out, her soft feet briefly exposing her tiny claws to grasp the wool of Maggie's jumper in a loving grip. She started to purr and tenderly rubbed her cheek against Maggie's face. The loving gesture again brought a wave of emotion to the surface. For a moment the woman and the tabby cat held each other in an intimate gaze; two old friends sharing the night, their hearts filled with love.

Maggie held the cat close and rose painfully. Her bruised hip ached and she knew if there was ever a time to act it was now. Life could be different if she could spend it with Tommy. She eased her body into the rocking chair by the fire. Gently she guided the chair into a rolling motion and watched the slanted eyes of the cat get smaller and smaller until the purring turned to gentle snores and the gripping claws withdrew. She mustered all her courage. Invisible bands were constricting and gripping her, stopping her from lifting the phone. Pascal was due back soon. Would she have the strength to tell her news before then?

She glanced back at the clock. A quarter of an hour had passed since she'd spoken to Reeney and soon she would have to do it. She hoped she had the nerve. The rocking of the chair was getting more agitated as she wrestled with her courage. America was five hours behind so it was the perfect time. The rest of the family were together having dinner in New York and she was going to tell them about Tommy, tell them right now if she could get her fear under control. Some of them would understand, some would disapprove but, once they all knew, Pascal would no longer have a hold over her. She would be free to go and spend time with Tommy if he still wanted her.

Again a thump rocked her heart. It had been doing that a lot tonight. These palpitations were just a reminder to her that she was still alive. She needed those from time to time. She gently lifted the sleeping cat and placed her on the warm cushion of the chair.

Maggie moved her stiff bones towards her bag and pulled a little wallet out of the middle zipped pocket. Inside was a small book where she kept her phone numbers and her reading glasses. She held them in her slender fingers as she took them back to the chair. Betty saw her coming and bounced off. She knew from experience that Maggie was gentle getting out of the chair but had a habit of sitting on her when she came back, so she decided it wasn't worth the risk. She sat on the hearth with her slanted eyes looking through the stove door at the dying embers.

Maggie put on her glasses and opened the book. Flicking the pages she turned to Brian's number. Her own brother and she couldn't remember the last time she'd spoken to him. Pascal would call him from time to time but Maggie only ever answered the phone the odd time he called here. But tonight she had to make the move herself, for Tommy, her little Tommy. The best day of her life had been that first day when he stepped out of the car in the yard and introduced himself to her.

She'd been baking in the kitchen all morning when she heard the car pull up outside. She already had a tray of scones cooling and was about to take out the brown loaf, which was just nicely crisped on the outside. She had two rhubarb tarts to go in after the bread came out. Maggie always overdid the baking, giving some to her neighbours as gifts. She came from a large family and she'd never adjusted properly to it being just herself and Pascal. All that week her neighbour Dolores Blaney, who lived in the next farm over from theirs across the mountain, had men in helping out with some land reclamation. Five extra men, on top of the three she already had in the house, ate a lot of food so Maggie was glad to help out.

Sheila barked. That was nothing unusual. Sheila did a lot of that but this time she continued on unabated. Maggie marched to the door to order the old dog to the barn but stopped in her tracks. Sheila was walking circles around a strange man. He'd driven up in a big car – people-carriers she believed they were called. The back was full of cases. He was leaning against the opposite side of the car, gazing around him at the yard.

Maggie watched him for a few moments without speaking, thinking there was something familiar about him but she couldn't quite put her finger on it. He didn't look particularly aggressive. He looked a bit overwhelmed. Then he turned and looked into her eyes. Again she got a strong sense of the familiar as she looked back into his face.

He was very handsome. His skin was tanned and his eyes from where she stood looked like brown orbs. He smiled at her. It was a shy smile that lit up his face.

He had an intense gaze and Maggie found herself blushing. Being sixty years old, this wasn't something that she experienced often.

"Are you Maggie?"

She nodded.

"My name is Michael."

He walked towards her and extended his right hand. Maggie wiped her buttery hands in embarrassment on the front of her apron. Then she took his hand in her own trembling one. She had to pull her hand away as he held on, looking into her eyes. Now that she was close she could see that they weren't brown – they were hazel like her own and swimming in tears. She wanted to ask him why he was upset but she didn't know how to broach the subject without embarrassing them both. She felt no threat, even though she'd never laid eyes on him before – Pascal was around somewhere and there was always a neighbour passing by. Contrary to what the townspeople thought, there could be a lot of foot traffic in the country. Without hesitation she invited him in and offered him some tea. Like a little boy collecting for the local GAA draw he followed her meekly into the house.

"Sit down there." She gestured towards the two-seater couch by the fire.

She wet the tea and got a tray ready with a plate of scones, butter and jam and a piece of the tart she'd made yesterday. While she worked at the kitchen table she had her back turned to him but she could still feel his eyes on the back of her neck. As she turned around she was amused to see Eddie Molloy, her neighbour from down the road, taking sideways glances at the strange car as he crossed her yard to the upper gate. Eddie had land taken up there where he kept some cattle so he was a regular passer-by. He walked up every day to a hide he had there for hay. He fed them the hay and when the hide was empty he drove up on the tractor to replenish his supplies.

He had a smallholding that was doing okay but he didn't have enough grazing close by for his cattle. He needed that, especially in the winter, to feed them.

Maggie crossed the room and placed the tray on the low table by Michael's side. He drank some tea, then munched on his scone, never taking his eyes off her face. He seemed to be having a struggle with words. He appeared on the verge of speech more than once and then he went back to chewing and watching Maggie with the same unwavering gaze. Maggie used that opportunity to go back and put the finishing touches to her tart and place it in the oven. When that was done and the bread was on the wire tray she went and sat in the chair opposite him.

"It's about time you told me more than your Christian name, isn't it?"

He nodded. "My name is Michael Reynolds. I've come from Boston to see you."

"You have?" By now her curiosity was at boiling point but she didn't want to rush him. "How do you know me? Are you a relative?"

Like most Irish families the Breslins had a smattering

of American relatives and they often came knocking on the door looking for their roots. The old stone walls in Ireland were like a call from the mother ship for them. A pilgrimage they all had to make at least once.

As she sat now in the dead of the night, thinking back, the impact of his next words still hit her like a clenched fist.

"Maggie! I'm your son. I've wanted to meet you for such a long time."

Maggie was glad she was sitting. If not her legs would surely have given away. For a moment she looked around her, confused, trying to formulate her thoughts.

"Are you sure?" was all she could come up with.

"I wasn't! Not until I met you. But I am now. Instantly I felt like I recognised you. Didn't you feel it too?"

Maggie had. She knew now that was what she'd felt. He had her eyes and he had a look of Pascal when he was his age, the shape of the brow and the earnest expression. But the boyish smile and the easy charm, those belonged to someone else. Someone she wouldn't be able to give him much information about.

"Tommy!" she said almost to herself. "My little Tommy!"

"Tommy!" he repeated, looking puzzled.

With a break in her voice Maggie explained that Tommy was the name she'd chosen to call him the day he was born but she'd never been given the opportunity.

Like a stab wound, the pain of separation still burned in her. She'd felt stretched all these years as if the child she'd had to let go still had a grip of her and was tugging at her from a great distance. She hadn't realised that distance crossed the Atlantic.

The brown-haired man sitting in her kitchen suddenly stood up and reached out his arms awkwardly. She stood and stepped towards him. Shyly she returned his embrace and felt his hot tears wet on her cheek.

A sharp voice broke the moment. "What is this?"

Pascal her brother stood in the doorway, his dark shape blocking the light. His face was hardened into a frown and his eyes were like granite in his wrinkled face.

Pascal was the eldest son. He had inherited the farm when their father died. He'd been twenty years old at the time. Maggie was just a baby then and he'd been the only father figure she'd ever known. He was father, brother and provider all in one and he was the tie that bound her to pain all these years. His presence was like a band of iron constricting the house, even now at eighty years old.

Pascal had been the head of the household since the death of their father and neither Maggie nor her mother before her death had ever disputed this. Sometimes Maggie questioned it in her own mind but life hadn't produced many alternatives. A suitable husband hadn't come along since her return to Donegal and she hadn't wanted to settle for less; she'd known passion, brief as it was, and somehow she could never see that in the men around her.

Life just settled in, enclosing her. Gradually she succumbed to the weight left behind by the residue of her dreams and hopes. By the time the sixties came around for Maggie, her mother was in ill health and it was her place to take care of her. Pascal had the farm and the stock to look after. Áine Breslin's life ebbed and with it went Maggie's youth. For the last ten years it had just been her and Pascal.

She knew him and his ways. She knew how to get around him when he suffered the dark moods that sometimes rendered him almost motionless for days, days when the farthest he'd venture was the opposite side of the yard where he'd lean on the edge of the open gate and look down the lane ruminating on the past. Maggie knew him and never questioned their roles. It had always been so. Even in her own mind she didn't have a satisfactory answer as to why she put up with it. He was her brother, her family, beyond that she didn't explore it in any more depth. She learned to live within a confined space and the outside world fascinated but terrified her. Up until now there had been nothing abroad to tempt her out.

Michael was oblivious to the politics of the house but natural wariness made him leave the explanations to Maggie.

"It's Tommy, Pascal, he found me." She smiled hopefully at him. Hoping for some reprieve from her lot of the last forty-five years, hoping for some pity at this stage of her life. But none was forthcoming.

Pascal stood back stiffly and gestured to the open door. "Leave, please."

"Mr Breslin!" Michael pleaded.

But it was obvious pleadings would fall on deaf ears. Michael, being a diplomat, thought best to leave it for now. He thanked Maggie for the tea and walked slowly to the door. He turned back in the doorway, his hazel eyes fixed on her as if afraid he would never see her again.

Maggie wailed.

The sound surprised both of the men and they stood looking at her.

"Pascal, please!" she begged.

Pascal walked to the table and sat down. "Say your goodbyes. He's not welcome in this house."

Maggie clutched at the small concession her proud brother had granted her and ushered her son out the door.

They stood in the yard facing each other but Maggie couldn't look above his knees. The buildings and walls felt like they were gathering around, squeezing her in and keeping him out.

Michael's voice broke into her thoughts. "I'm going to write to you. He can't stop you reading a letter. I'll be in the town for another week. Meet me in Letterkenny. We can have dinner and I'll tell you about your grandchildren."

"My grandchildren!" Maggie's eyes finally rose to his and opened wide in her lined face.

"Yes, dear. You have two grandchildren: a boy Darren and my baby Trudy. Darren is twenty – he's in college and will be going to medical school soon – and

Trudy is seventeen – she wants to study law. I knew you were my mother when I saw you, you know. Trudy is very like you." He leant down and kissed her cheek. "I'm staying at the Beachwood Hotel. Call me when you're in town."

He climbed into his car and drove out of the yard. As he passed her she noticed again the luggage in the back. He must have come here to Cooleen to find her before he even went to the hotel to unpack. Her heart leapt. That made her feel very special. Slowly she turned back to the house, her movements robotic with her thoughts speeding down the road in a rented car.

She'd expected an argument when she went back inside but Pascal presumed the subject was closed.

"Is there any tea in the pot? I'm starving."

She bustled around cutting bread and getting his tea. Life was too short for complacency but Maggie's life got shorter every day. Inside, she knew silence was the reason she lost Michael. Silence allowed him to be taken from her, kept her locked up here all her life and took her life away from her. Pascal had to preserve the silence; inside silence you could hide so much. When everyone knew, Pascal couldn't keep them apart. She knew she had to act now and take back the years he'd stolen. Her first step would be to break the silence.

Interview questions

1) Have you always written or is it a new discovery?

I've always wanted to write and have always read a lot. I wrote a diary when I was a child and later that progressed to little pieces of prose just exploring the world around me. Initially I thought I might like a career in journalism but my imagination is too strong for me to stick to the factual. So I thought that my writing future lay with fiction and ultimately in writing novels.

2) Tell us about your writing process; where do you write? When? Are you a planner or "ride-the-wave" writer?

I have turned our dining-room into a writing corner. It's a great room because it has patio doors that lead out into the garden. It's a good place to daydream too. I love to write late in the evening and into the night but that's not always practical so I'm trying to discipline myself to write in the morning and into the afternoon. Where I live it's quiet by day so sometimes to break up my routine I will go to a local pub and write. It can get too quiet writing alone.

I don't like to plan my writing. Instead I prefer to let it develop from a single idea or an image of a character but now I find that planning a little saves time. I don't get sidetracked as much but I think it suits my style of writing better to just write and let things evolve. If I'm surprised I hope the reader will be too.

3) Since your first novel *Guarding Maggie* was published in May 2008 has your life changed much?

I'm a lot busier. I have to meet deadlines now and I have to publicise my books. Publicity is about as opposite as you can get to sitting alone in your room writing novels. So the real change for me has been taking my writing out into the real world. Allowing other people to read my work was very nerve-wrecking. But it's exciting. I love getting feedback from readers and the response to my writing has been very positive. Personally there has been no change at all. I still have the same day-to-day life. But I'm probably more confident. It's wonderful to have set a goal and to have achieved it.

4) Do you have a favourite character in *Guilt Ridden*?

I love them all. "The writer" was great fun to work on. "The writer" guides the book and controls Amy so there was so much scope to play with this storyline and the writer's psychology. I also loved Amy's aunt, Nuala. The poor woman goes through a lot and life never seems to get any better for her. But she has great spirit.

5) In *Guilt Ridden*, Amy gets a manuscript from what could be her cousin's murderer – what was it like getting inside the mind of what some would consider an "evil" character? Was writing about kidnapping difficult?

It took a long time. When I wasn't writing I was daydreaming about it. The writer is probably what used to be referred to as a psychopath with little remorse and moral boundaries so the scope to play with the character is greater. It would have been easier to just make the character pure evil but this character had to walk in society unnoticed for the most part. That makes the shock even greater when you realised the identity of the writer. Everybody fears kidnapping and being lost in the unknown. I tried to work with that.

I also wanted to show the void in the lives of the other victims of a kidnapping: the ones left behind, the family, friends and community. It was important to explore the sense of desolation they feel not knowing what happened. I think maybe that's the worst part, the "not knowing".

6) **What character and scene was most difficult for you to write in** *Guilt Ridden*?

I think perhaps "the writer" was the most difficult because the character was involved in so much. The manuscript told us what the writer wanted us to know. While most of that was untrustworthy I still couldn't lose the psychology built up in the manuscript. The unveiling had to be a surprise but yet at the end you had to understand why the character could be "the writer". It was a challenge to keep everything in order. The scene that was the most difficult was the revelation of who "the writer" was. I didn't want to let the reader down at that point.

7) **The setting in your novels seems very important. In** *Guarding Maggie*, **Maggie lives on a rural farm in the heart of Donegal. In** *Guilt Ridden*, **a small town in Waterford is the backdrop for a gripping drama. Why do you pick these places?**

For me when I think of the country I think of nature and the elements and these are unpredictable and outside our control. Also in the country you have to deal with isolation of a different type than in the town. You can isolate yourself in a town but you will still see people, hear traffic and be close to shops and services if you need them, but in the country you could potentially isolate yourself completely from society. The countryside lends itself well to atmosphere. Sometimes there is total silence and depending on your mood and frame of mind this can be terrifying. But also I grew up in the country and I love the shadows and the empty space. Small towns are wonderful because they are a complete view of society in miniature. Because they are small everything is on show so it's hard to hide your secrets.

8) You have an Honours degree in Literature and Sociology. Do you find that your academic background has influenced your writing?

It taught me how to think analytically and be a better researcher. Also I read more widely than I might have done otherwise. We all have our reading comfort zones and maybe stick to similar types of books so it's good when you have to read outside your normal range. That's why I like reading a book recommended by someone else. The quality of my writing would have improved also. I had to write a lot of essays and assignments and there was someone there with a red pen telling me where I could do better. It was good preparation for the editing process when writing novels.

9) Who are your favourite authors and favourite novels and why?

I love the classics and have a particular love for the old gothic-style romances like *Wuthering Heights, Jane Eyre* and *Rebecca*. I love the atmosphere and the brooding characters but I read mostly crime. My favourite Irish writers would include Tana French, Alex Barclay, John Connolly and Michael Collins, especially *The Keepers of Truth* – crumbling towns and institutions and how ordinary people living in these places can do bizarre things when their lives start falling apart fascinates me. Other books I've enjoyed would be Dennis Lehane's *Mystic River* and Robert Crais' *The Two Minute Rule*. I'm a fan of Stephen King, like *Dolores Claiborne, Misery,* and my favourite is *The Girl Who Loved Tom Gordon*. It's so simple – a little girl lost in the woods with only her overactive imagination for company.

10) Tell us a bit about your next book – have you started writing it yet?

I have started writing it. It's at an early stage and will go through many changes before I finish it so it would be pointless to say too much about it now. There is a grieving widow who finds out that the life she's built with her husband is not what it appears . . . and neither it seems was he!

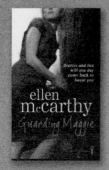